貿商英語溝通王

目錄 Contents

Chapter 4   貿易實務——談判桌上的較量

Chapter 5　貿易類型──貿易形式多種多樣

Chapter 6 商品報關——出入境的必要手續

Chapter 7 商貿辦公——日常這樣辦公

Chapter 1

商貿禮儀──
與新老客戶溝通

Unit 1 預約客戶

電話一直都是國際商務溝通的重要工具，許多商務磋商、買賣交易、口頭協議以及日常事務處理等往往是通過電話進行的。打電話在某種程度上能反映一個公司的管理水平和員工的業務素質，所以打電話的基本禮儀還是要學一學。

預約客戶必會詞

❶ appointment *n.* 預約，約會

商務交流活動中，時間至關重要。決定會面前，雙方提前預訂時間，並按時赴約是現代商務活動文明的體現。

❷ available *a.* 可得到的，空閒的

available 是電話找人時的高頻詞匯。

> **PS** He / She's not available. 他 / 她不在。

❸ schedule *n.* 日程安排

職場人士公務繁忙，安排會面前，都會先查看日程安排。

❹ cancel *v.* 取消

如遇突發事件無法赴約，要提前通知對方取消預約。

> **PS** cancel the appointment 取消約會

✎ 這些小詞你也要會哦：

secretary *n.* 秘書	arrange *v.* 安排	office *n.* 辦公室
out of the office 不在辦公室	leave a message 留言	urgent *a.* 緊急的
possible *a.* 可能的	postpone *v.* 推遲	put off 推遲
get back 回來	interest *v.* 對……感興趣	confirmation *n.* 確認

Scene 1

電話預約
Making Appointments through the Telephone

 場景對話

A: Hello, this is Tele System. Can I help you?	A：你好，這裡是 Tele 公司。有什麼需要幫助的嗎？
B: Yes, this is Andrea Smith from Kingsberg Corporation. May I speak to your CEO Edward Jones, please? I wrote to Mr. Jones last week, and he sent me a fax asking me to call and make an appointment with him. Would it be possible to see him sometime this week?	B：是的，我是金斯伯格公司的安德烈亞·史密斯。我能找你們的總裁愛德華·瓊斯先生通話嗎？我上週給瓊斯先生寫過信，他回了一封傳真讓我給他打電話確認見面的事情。我這週能和瓊斯先生見個面嗎？
A: Wait a moment, please. Let me check Mr. Jones' schedule.	A：請稍等。我得先看一下瓊斯先生的日程安排。
B: Thanks.	B：謝謝。
A: Ms. Smith, I'm afraid Mr. Jones is not available until this Friday.	A：史密斯女士，恐怕瓊斯先生要到本週五才有空。
B: Then can I go to the company to meet him at two o'clock on Friday afternoon?	B：那麼我週五下午兩點到你們公司見他可以嗎？
A: Yes, that will be fine.	A：可以，沒問題。
B: OK. Will you please tell Mr. Jones about the appointment when he is back?	B：好的。等瓊斯先生回來，你可以轉告他關於我跟他約見面的事情嗎？
A: Yes, of course.	A：當然可以。
B : Thanks a lot. Bye.	B：太感謝了。再見。

場景問答必會句

This is Andrea Smith from Kingsberg Corporation.
我是金斯伯格公司的安德烈亞·史密斯。

May I speak to your CEO Edward Jones, please?
我能找你們的總裁愛德華·瓊斯先生通話嗎？

還可以這樣說：

- This is Nick Jackson. Can I have extension 021?
  我是尼克・傑克遜，可以幫我轉接分機號 021 嗎？

對方可能這樣回答：

- Hello, general manager's office. What can I do for you?
  您好，總經理辦公室。我能為您做些什麼？
- Hello, this is Alisa from X Company. May I help you?
  您好，我是 X 公司的阿莉莎。有什麼能幫您的嗎？

extension *n.* 電話分機

this is... 表 示 " 我是……"

Will you please tell Mr. Jones about the appointment when he is back?
等瓊斯先生回來，你可以轉告他關於我跟他約見面的事情嗎？

還可以這樣說：

- Could you ask him to call me at 1234567?
  可以讓他往 1234567 這個號碼回電嗎？

對方可能這樣回答：

- Yes, of course.
  可以，沒問題。
- I'll make sure Tim gets this ASAP.
  我會儘快轉告蒂姆。

call me at... 表 示 "撥……號碼給我回電"

ASAP 是 as soon as possible 的縮寫形式，表示"儘快"。

Scene **2** 安排會面 Arrange an Appointment

 場景對話

A: Excuse me. Is this Tele System?	A：打擾了。請問這裡是 Tele 公司嗎？
B: Yes, that's right. What can I do for you?	B：是的，沒錯。有什麼需要幫助的嗎？
A: I'd like to see your CEO about the contract of cell phone. Here's my calling card.	A：我想見一下你們的總裁，談談手機合同一事。這是我的名片。
B: Thanks, Mr. Green. Take a seat, please. Do you have an appointment with Mr. Jones?	B：謝謝，格林先生。請坐。您和瓊斯先生有預約嗎？
A: No. But I need to have a talk with him. I've got some ideas about the contract.	A：沒有。但是我必須得和他談談。我對合同有些看法。

B: I see. I'll see if he is free now. Would you please wait a moment?	B：哦。我看一下總裁現在是否有空。請您稍等片刻，好嗎？
A: OK.	A：好的。
B: I'm sorry. Mr. Jones is talking with a client from Australia. Maybe he can meet you another time. Would you like to make an appointment for another time?	B：對不起，總裁正在和一位澳大利亞客戶談話。也許他可以在其他時間見您。能幫您預約到其他時間嗎？
A: OK.	A：可以。

🔠 場景問答必會句

> I'd like to see your CEO about the contract of cell phone.
> 我想見一下你們的總裁，談談手機合同一事。

還可以這樣說：

⊟ I'd like to see someone in charge of Marketing.
　我想見一下你們市場部的負責人。

對方可能這樣問：

⊟ How can I be of service?
　有什麼能為您效勞的嗎？

PS

in charge of 負責……

> No. But I need to have a talk with him.
> 沒有。但是我必須得和他談談。

還可以這樣說：

⊟ Yes, I had an appointment with Mr. Jones at three p.m.
　是的，我和瓊斯先生約在下午 3 點見面。

對方可能這樣問：

⊟ Does Mr. Jones know you will be here?
　瓊斯先生知道您要來嗎？

PS

have an appointment with sb. 與某人有約

Scene 3　變更時間 Change Schedule

 場景對話

A: Hi! My name is Zhang Lin. May I speak to Frank, please?	A：你好，我叫張林。我想找一下弗蘭克？
B: Speaking.	B：我就是。
A: Hi Frank, I'm calling to inform you that I can't keep our appointment tomorrow.	A：你好，弗蘭克，我打電話是想告訴你，明天我不能與你見面了。
B: I'm sorry to hear that. What happened?	B：很遺憾聽到這個消息，發生什麼事情了？
A: One of our clients will arrive early tomorrow morning and I have to meet him at the airport. Would it be possible to postpone our appointment?	A：我們的一位客戶明早到訪，我得到機場接他。可以推遲我們的約會嗎？
B: Sure. When is convenient for you?	B：當然。你什麼時候方便？
A: I wonder if we could put off our meeting until next Wednesday.	A：我想知道是否可以把我們的約會推遲到下週三。
B: Yes. It's okay by me.	B：好啊，我沒問題。
A: Great. Hope I haven't messed up your arrangements too much.	A：太好了，希望我沒有給您的日程安排帶來太大的麻煩。
B: Not at all.	B：沒關係。

場景問答必會句

> I'm calling to inform you that I can't keep our appointment tomorrow.
> 我打電話是想告訴你，明天我不能與你見面了。

還可以這樣說：

- I'm calling to know if it would be possible to cancel our meeting.
  我打電話是想知道是否有可能取消我們的預約。
- I wonder if we could make it some other time.
  我想知道我們是否可以安排別的時間。

> I wonder if we could put off our meeting until next Wednesday.
> 我想知道是否可以把我們的約會推遲到下週三。

還可以這樣說：
- Can we put it off ?
  我們推遲一下可以嗎？

對方可能這樣回答：
- Yes, it works for me.
  當然，我沒問題。
- Sorry. I won't be available at that time.
  對不起，我那時沒空。
- Could we meet on Friday instead?
  我們改在週五見可以嗎？

put ... off 推遲某事
instead ad. 代替

預約客戶 Tips

電話交流中常用句型

Answering the phone 接電話時	• Hello? 喂？ • Jody speaking. How can I help you? 我是喬迪，請問有什麼可以幫您的？
Introducing yourself 自我介紹	• Hello, this is Julie Clarkson calling. 你好，我是朱莉·克拉克森。 • This is she. 我就是。 • Speaking. 我就是。
Asking to speak with someone 想找某人接聽電話	• Is Susan in? 蘇珊在嗎？ • Is Jackson there? 傑克遜在嗎？ • May I speak with Mr. Green, please? 請問格林先生在嗎？
Connecting someone 我幫你轉給……	• Just a second. I'll get him. 稍等一下，我幫您轉接。 • Hang on one second. 請稍等。 • Please hold and I'll put you through to his office. 請稍等，我幫你轉接到他的辦公室。 • All of our operators are busy at this time. Please hold for the next available person. 我們的接線員都很忙，請耐心等待。

Unit 2 | 機場迎接

隨著外事交流的不斷深入，各國間的互訪也日漸頻繁，在機場迎接來訪客人時，周到、得體的禮儀一定會給遠道而來的訪客留下美好的第一印象。

機場迎接必會詞

① greetings *n.* 問候，打招呼

熱情、得體的招呼用語不僅會拉近與來訪者的距離，還會為一場成功的外事訪問打下基礎。機場常用打招呼用語有：

Did you have a good journey? 旅途愉快嗎？

How was your flight? 飛行順利嗎？

② schedule *n.* 時間表；計劃表

外事訪問時間短，日程複雜多樣，制訂清晰的計劃表尤為重要。

③ hotel reservation 酒店預訂

預訂酒店是外事接待的一個重要環節

④ arrange *v.* 安排

合理的日程安排，能使訪客順利完成工作的同時，還有時間飽覽異國風景。

這些小詞你也要會哦：

luggage *n.* 行李	flight *n.* 飛行	thoughtful *a.* 體貼的	check in 入住
check out 退房	business trip 商務旅行	confirm *v.* 確認	passport *n.* 護照

Scene 4 迎接客戶 Meet Clients

場景對話

A: Pardon me. Are you Tom Niven from A Company?

A：不好意思打擾。您是來自A公司的湯姆‧尼文嗎？

B: Yes, and you are?

B：是的，您是哪位？

A: My name is Zhang Hua. I'm here to meet you.	A：我叫張華。我是來這兒接您的。
B: Nice to meet you. Thank you for coming all the way here.	B：見到您很高興。謝謝您專程來接我。
A: No problem. Let me help you with your luggage. This way please. Our car is waiting in the parking lot.	A：不客氣。我來幫您提行李吧。請這邊走。我們的車在停車場。
B: Thank you. That's very thoughtful of you.	B：謝謝。您想得真周到。

場景問答必會句

> Are you Tom Niven from A Company?
> 您是來自 A 公司的湯姆‧尼文嗎？

還可以這樣說：

💬 Excuse me. Are you Susan Davis from Western Electronics? 對不起打擾一下，您是來自西方電子公司的蘇姍‧戴維斯嗎？

> My name is Zhang Hua. I'm here to meet you.
> 我是張華，我是來這兒接您的。

還可以這樣說：

💬 I'm Dennis of ABC Company. 我是來自 ABC 公司的丹尼斯。

💬 It's a pleasure to make your acquaintance. I'm Dennis, from ABC Company.
　　很高興認識你，我叫丹尼斯，來自 ABC 公司。

對方可能這樣回答：

💬 I have heard so much about you. Thank you for meeting me at the airport.
　　久仰大名，謝謝您來機場接我。

Scene 5　問候寒暄 Greetings

場景對話

| A: Hi! Mr. Hanson. It's great to finally meet you in person. | A：您好！漢森先生，很高興終於見到您本人了。 |

B: The pleasure is mine.	B：我也很高興。
A: How was your flight?	A：您的旅途怎麼樣？
B: It was a long trip but I was able to get some work done.	B：航程很長，但正好讓我完成了一些工作。
A: Is this your first time in China?	A：這是您第一次來中國嗎？
B: Yes. I'm very excited to be here.	B：是的。我很興奮。
A: I'd be happy to show you around and try some local food.	A：我很願意帶你四處逛逛，品嘗一些當地食物。
B: Thank you. That would be great.	B：謝謝。那就太好了。
A: You must be very tired after such a long trip. Let's get you to your hotel first.	A：經過這麼長時間的旅行，您一定很累了。我先送您回賓館吧。
B: Yes. I think I could have a little rest.	B：好的。我確實想休息一下。

場景問答必會句

> How was your flight?
> 您的旅途怎麼樣？

還可以這樣說：
- Did you enjoy your journey?
  旅途還順利嗎？
- Did you have a good trip?
  您的旅途還愉快嗎？

對方可能這樣回答：
- I had a long flight but I'm doing well.
  我坐了很久的飛機，但是還好。

PS

journey *n.* 旅途

> I'd be happy to show you around and try some local food.
> 我很願意帶你四處逛逛，品嘗一些當地食物。

還可以這樣說：
- Are there any places you want to visit?
  有沒有你想去參觀的地方？

對方可能這樣回答：
- I've always wanted to visit the Great Wall.
  我一直很想去爬長城

Scene 6 去往賓館 Go to the Hotel

 場景對話

A: Mr. Jackson, I've already made a hotel reservation for you. I'm here to drive you to your hotel.	A：傑克遜先生，我已經為您預訂了賓館房間，我來這兒開車帶您去賓館。
B: That's great. Thank you.	B：太好了。謝謝您。
A: Please take the back seat.	A：請坐在後座。
B: Okay.	B：好的。
(Ten minutes later.)	(10 分鐘後。)
A: This is the hotel where you're going to stay.	A：這是您要入住的賓館。
B: It looks fantastic.	B：看起來很棒。
A: Do you have your passport with you? We will need it when checking in.	A：您帶護照了嗎？一會兒我們入住時要使用。
B: Yes. It's right here.	B：是的。就在這兒。
A: We've booked a Western-style room for you. Shall we go to the reception desk and check in?	A：我們為您預訂了一間西式房間。我們到前枱辦理入住手續吧？
B: OK.	B：好的。

場景問答必會句

> I've already made a hotel reservation for you. I'm here to drive you to your hotel.
> 我已經為您預訂了賓館房間，我來這兒開車帶您去賓館。

還可以這樣說：

💬 We have reserved a room for you at Beijing Hotel. 我們已為您在北京飯店訂了一間房間。

對方可能這樣問：

💬 Are we going to the hotel? 我們是要去賓館嗎？

PS

reserve *v.* 預訂

> Shall we go to the reception desk and check in?
> 我們到前枱辦理入住手續吧？

還可以這樣說：

🗨 I'll show you to your hotel. 我帶您去賓館。

對方可能這樣回答：

🗨 Sure. 當然。

🗨 May I take a look at the room? 我可以看看房間嗎？

🗨 I have finished the check-in procedure. 我已經辦妥了住宿登記手續。

🗨 I think I've filled in everything correctly. 我覺得我已經準確無誤地填完了。

reception desk 前枱

procedure *n.* 手續，步驟

fill in 填寫

Scene 7 行程安排和確認 Arrange and Confirm Schedule

 場景對話

A: Mr. Jackson, I hope you enjoyed the hotel we booked for you.	A：傑克遜先生，希望您滿意我們為您預訂的賓館。
B: Yes. The hotel room is very good. I enjoyed the beautiful view and the big tub.	B：是的。賓館房間非常好。我很享受美景和大浴缸。
A: That's great. <u>Here's the schedule for tomorrow.</u>	A：太好了。<u>這是您明天的行程安排。</u>
B: Thank you.	B：謝謝。
A: Everyone here is looking forward to seeing you. Our CEO Mr. Zhang is on a business trip. <u>He will be in the office tomorrow around noon.</u>	A：大家都很期待見到您。我們的總裁張先生正在出差。<u>他將在中午時分到達公司。</u>
B: Okay.	B：好的。
A: Mr. Lee, our sales manager will meet you tomorrow morning and give you a little tour of our company. And Mr. Zhang is going to take you out for lunch.	A：我們的銷售經理李先生明天將接待您，帶您參觀一下公司。張先生將帶您去吃午飯。
B: Great.	B：太好了。

📱A 場景問答必會句

> Here's the schedule for tomorrow.
> 這是您明天的行程安排。

還可以這樣說：

💬 We are going to invite you to take part in a welcome party. 我們將邀請您參加一場歡迎會。

> He will be in the office tomorrow around noon.
> 他將在中午時分到達公司。

還可以這樣說：

💬 He won't be back until tomorrow. 他明天才能回來。

對方可能這樣問：

💬 Will I be able to meet him today? 我今天能見到他嗎？

PS

be able to do sth. 能夠做某事

┃機場迎接 Tips ┃

1. 機場迎接禮儀

- 備好外賓的照片及個人相關信息。
- 提前致電航空公司，確認外賓所乘航班是否準點到達。
- 計算好前往機場的時間，一定要提前到達，遲到在西方文化中會被認為是極不禮貌的行為。
- 提前準備好接機牌，以醒目的顏色、字體書寫好外賓的姓名。
- 與外賓見面時，舉止得體，坦然接受西方人在初次見面時的禮節，大方應對。

2. 機場英語標識

airport shuttle 機場班車	airport lounges 機場休息室
information center/desk 問詢處	check in area / zone 辦理登機區
international flights 國際航班	domestic flights 國內航班
emergency exit 安全出口	exit to all routes 各通道出口
flight connections 轉機處	customers lounges 旅客休息室
departure time on reverse 返航時間	destination airport 目的地機場
left baggage 行李寄存	lost property 失物招領

Unit 3 安排住宿

商務旅行 (Business Travel) 涉及的一個重要問題就是住宿。安排好住宿，可以讓商務旅行無後顧之憂。住宿包括預訂房間、登記入住、詢問客房服務和退房等事宜。

安排住宿必會詞

1 room service 客房服務

客房服務包括很多方面，有客房清理服務 (Room-cleaning Service)、鋪床服務 (Evening Turn-down Service)、喚醒服務 (Wake-up Call Service)、洗衣服務 (Laundry Service)、醫療服務 (Medical Service) 等。

2 check-in 辦理入住手續

辦理入住手續需要讓客人填寫入住表格，內容包括：姓名、性別、國籍、居住地、身份證 (外國人用護照) 號碼、聯絡電話、入住日期和天數，並支付押金，領取押金單以及酒店房間鑰匙。

3 standard room 標準房

酒店的標準房一般是指標準雙人房。酒店的房間類型還可以分為單人房 (single room)、雙人單床房 (double room)、雙人雙床房 (twin room)、三人房 (triple room) 和家庭房 (family room) 等。

這些小詞你也要會哦：

registration form 登記表	in cash 現金支付	make a payment 付款
reservation *n.* 預訂	lobby *n.* 酒店大廳	reception *n.* 接待處
porter *n.* 行李搬運工	bellboy *n.* 侍者	headwaiter *n.* 餐廳領班

Scene 8 預訂房間 Book a Room

 場景對話

A: Good morning, Crown Plaza Hotel. May I help you?

A：早上好，皇冠假日酒店，有什麼可以為您服務的？

B: Hi, good morning. I'd like to make a reservation for the night of March 10th. Do you have any vacancies?	B：嗨，早上好。我想要預訂 3 月 10 日晚上的房間。你們有空房嗎？
A: Yes, Sir. What kind of room would you like?	A：有，先生。您想要什麼房型？
B: Do you have any business suites available for that night?	B：那天的商務套房還有嗎？
A: Hold on, please… I'm afraid business suites are fully booked on that day. What about an executive suite instead?	A：請稍等⋯⋯恐怕我們已經沒有商務套間了，高級套房可以嗎？
B: OK, I will take that executive suite, thank you. By the way, what's the rate for the room?	B：好的，那我訂高級套房，謝謝。順便問一下，房費是多少？
A: One hundred and eighty dollars per night.	A：每晚 180 美元。
B: Fine.	B：好的。
A: How long will you be staying?	A：您要住多久呢？
B: One week.	B：一周。
A: May I have your name, please?	A：可以告訴我您的姓名嗎？
B: Bruce.	B：布魯斯。
A: What time will you arrive?	A：您什麼時候到呢？
B: Around seven p.m. on March 10th.	B：3 月 10 日晚上 7 點左右。
A: Thank you sir. We look forward to serving you.	A：謝謝您先生。很期待為您服務。
B: Thank you.	B：謝謝。

場景問答必會句

> I'd like to make a reservation for the night of March 10th.
> 我想要預訂 3 月 10 日晚上的房間。

還可以這樣說：

🗨 I would need a room from April 12th to April 15th.
我需要一間房間，從 4 月 12 日到 4 月 15 日。

🗨 I would like to book a standard room for three days, for the 21st to the 23rd of March.
我想預訂三天的標準間，3 月 21 日至 3 月 23 日。

PS standard room 標準間

> By the way, what's the rate for the room?
> 順便問一下，房費是多少？

還可以這樣說：

💬 Can you tell me the rate for a single room, please?
請告訴我一間單人房的費用，好嗎？

💬 Does the charge include everything?
這費用包括所有的服務嗎？

💬 Do you charge for phone calls? 電話收費嗎？

💬 Do I get a discount if I have a Golden Card?
我有酒店的金卡，能打折嗎？

對方可能這樣回答：

💬 It's $75 per night. 每晚 75 美元。

💬 It includes housekeeping and gym facilities.
費用包括房間整理和健身器械使用費。

PS

by the way 順便問一下

charge *n.* 費用

PS

housekeeping *n.* 客房服務

Gym *n.* 健身房

Scene 9　登記入住 Check in

 場景對話

A: Good morning, sir. Welcome to the Hilton Hotel. What can I do for you?	A：早上好，先生。歡迎來到希爾頓酒店。我能幫您什麼嗎？
B: My name is Ronald Dickson. I have a reservation. <u>Can I check in now?</u>	B：我叫羅納德・迪克森。我預訂了一間房，現在可以辦理入住登記嗎？
A: Certainly, sir. Let me see. Yes, Mr. Dickson, I have your booking record here. Your reservation is for a single room for three nights. Is that correct?	A：當然可以，先生。我看一下，是的，迪克森先生，有您的預訂記錄。您預訂了三晚的單人房，是嗎？
B: Yes.	B：是的。
A: Could you fill in the registration form, please?	A：請您先填這張表格。
B: Sure. (Fill out the form.) Here you are.	B：好的。(填表) 填好了。
A: May I confirm your departure date?	A：我能確認一下您的離開日期嗎？
B: Yes, <u>I should be leaving on the 8th.</u>	B：嗯，我應該在 8 日離開。
A: Do you have your passport with you? I need to take a look at it.	A：您帶護照了嗎？我需要看一下。

24

B: Sure. Here it is.	B：有，在這裡。
A: OK, Mr. Dickson, here is your passport... room key. Your room number is 1123, on the 11th Floor. Just a moment please. A bellman will show you to your room. I hope you will enjoy your stay here.	A：好的，迪克森先生，這是您的護照和客房鑰匙。您的房間號是 1123，在 11 樓。請稍等片刻。服務員會帶您去您的房間，希望您在這裡過得愉快。
B: Thank you very much.	B：非常感謝。

 場景問答必會句

> Can I check in now?
> 現在可以辦理入住登記嗎？

還可以這樣說：

🗨 I need to check in. 我想辦理入住手續。

🗨 I'd like to check in.I have a reservation under the name Gregory.
我要入住。我預訂時的名字是格雷戈里。

🗨 Am I all set? / Am I all checked in? 我可以入住了嗎？

對方可能這樣問：

🗨 What name is the reservation under? 您預訂時的名字是什麼？

🗨 Do you have a reservation? 您預訂了嗎？

> I should be leaving on the 8th.
> 我應該在 8 日離開。

對方可能這樣問：

🗨 What's your check-out time?
您何時辦理退房手續？

🗨 May I have your check out time, please?
請問您什麼時候退房？

PS

departure date 離開日期

Scene 10　詢問客房服務 About Room Service

 場景對話

A: I wonder if the hotel has a morning call service.	A：你們酒店是否有叫醒服務？
B: Yes, sir. Would you like a morning call?	B：是的。您需要我們早上叫醒您嗎？
A: Exactly. Would you call me up at six sharp tomorrow morning?	A：對，明天早上 6 點整叫醒我，好嗎？
B: Certainly, sir. Anything else I can do for you?	B：當然。您還需要其他服務嗎？
A: When will the bar open?	A：酒吧什麼時間開始營業？
B: It opens at ten o'clock p.m.	B：晚上 10 點。
A: And where can I have my laundry done?	A：那髒衣服送到哪裡洗呢？
B: An attendant will come to collect your laundry.	B：服務員會去您房間收。
A: Do you offer room service?	A：你們提供客房服務嗎？
B: Yes, we do.	B：是的，我們提供客房服務。
A: Thanks a lot.	A：非常感謝。
B: It is my pleasure.	B：這是我的榮幸。

場景問答必會句

> And where can I have my laundry done?
> 那髒衣服送到哪裡洗呢？

還可以這樣說：
- Can I get my suit ironed? 幫我把西裝熨平好嗎？
- How much does your laundry service cost?
  洗衣服怎麼收費？

對方可能這樣回答：
- I'll have someone take care of it. 我會讓人去處理的。
  Regular laundry is free of charge, with an extra charge for dry cleaning.
  普通洗衣免費，乾洗額外收費。

iron v. 熨

laundry n. 待洗的衣服

dry cleaning 乾洗

> Do you offer room service?
> 你們提供客房服務嗎？

還可以這樣說：

💬 Room service, please. 我需要客房服務。

💬 I need my sheets changed. 請把我的床單換掉。

💬 I wish you could do our room earlier in the morning. 我希望早上能早點打掃我們的房間。

對方可能這樣回答：

💬 Housekeeping will come by at about ten o'clock. 整理房間的時間是 10 點鐘左右。

room service 客房服務

Scene
11 退房 Check out

 場景對話

A: Good morning, ma'am. Can I help you?	A：早上好，女士。有什麼能為您效勞的？
B: Yes. I'd like to pay my bill now.	B：是的，我想現在結帳。
A: Would you please tell me your name and room number?	A：請問您的姓名和房間號碼？
B: Eileen Green, Room 1208.	B：艾琳·格林，我住 1208 號房。
A: How about the charge for the days you shared the room with your friend?	A：您與朋友合住那幾天的費用怎麼算呢？
B: Please add it to my account. Thank you.	B：請記在我的賬上。謝謝。
A: Please wait a moment. I need to check our records. Here is your bill. Five nights at one hundred and ninety-eight yuan each and here are the meals that you had at the hotel. That makes a total of 1,260 yuan. Could you please check it?	A：請稍候。我需要查一下我們的記錄。這是您的賬單。共 5 個晚上，每晚 198 元，加上您在酒店用餐的餐費，總共 1 260 元。請您核對一下吧。
B: Yes. Here you are.	B：好的，給你錢。
A: Here's your change and receipt. I'll send a bellman up to get your luggage.	A：這是您的零錢和收據。我馬上讓行李員去取您的行李。
B: Thank you.	B：謝謝。
A: You are welcome. Good-bye.	A：不客氣，再見。

場景問答必會句

> I'd like to pay my bill now.
> 我想現在結帳。

還可以這樣說：
- May I check out now? 現在能結帳嗎？
- Can I settle my account? 請給我結帳好嗎？
- What is the latest check-out time? 最遲幾點退房？

對方可能這樣回答：
- Sure, let me get your bill. 當然可以，我看看您的賬單。

settle an account 結帳

> Please add it to my account.
> 請記在我的賬上。

還可以這樣說：
- Can you give me an itemized bill? 能給我看看明細表嗎？

對方可能這樣回答：
- This charge was for your international calls.
  這是您打國際長途的費用。

itemize *v.* 逐條列記

- You used a bottle of water and two cans of Sprite in your room. That's what that charge is.
  您喝了房間裡的一瓶水和兩罐雪碧。就是這筆費用。
- That's for the extra bed, sir. 這是加床費，先生。

安排住宿 Tips

1. E-mail 預訂房間

To: Hilton Hotel

Subject: Reserve four single rooms from 20/12 to 30/12

To whom it may concern,

　　We are four Chinese businessmen who will take a business trip to England next month. I would like to reserve four single rooms at your hotel from 20/12 to 30/12. Do you have any vacancies?

　　Could you tell me your room rates and payment method? Do I need to pay a deposit? And also, any other information you could provide would be highly appreciated.

Thank you for your attention. I'm looking forward to hearing from you soon.

Yours Sincerely

Zhang Xiao

收件者：希爾頓酒店

主　旨：預訂 4 間 12.20-12.30 的單人房

敬啟者：

　　我們是四位將於下個月到英國出差的中國商人。我們想在貴酒店預訂 4 間 12 月 20 日到 12 月 30 日的單人房，不知道貴酒店是否還有空房？

　　煩請貴酒店告知房費和付款方式。是否需要預付定金呢？如果有其他相關信息也煩請提供，十分感謝。

　　謝謝貴酒店人員在百忙之中閱讀我的信件，希望很快能收到您的回信。

張曉

敬上

2. 退房小貼士

- **退房前一定要保管好自己的房卡**
  在退房時酒店會向入住的客人索要房卡，一旦房卡丟失可能會帶來很大麻煩。

- **工作人員打印出賬單之後，一定要仔細核對消費明細**
  酒店工作人員在結算過程中也許會出現小差錯，所以付款前一定要看清賬單中的消費項目是否正確。

Unit 4 參觀陪同

在外貿經濟日益發展的今天，參觀陪同成為外貿活動中重要的一環，可以為與客戶的進一步合作打下基礎，讓客戶瞭解公司、產品，還能增進與客戶的感情。

參觀陪同必會詞

❶ recommendation *n.* 引薦
引薦在此可以理解為介紹 (introduce)，即介紹客戶。一般介紹時應先介紹客戶方，再介紹我方；如有職位差距，應先將職位高的介紹給職位低的；若有女士，則應先介紹女士。

❷ product line 生產線
生產線就是產品生產過程所經過的路線，即從原料進入生產現場開始，經過加工、運輸、裝配、檢驗等一系列生產活動所構成的路線。

❸ performance *n.* 業績
業績在這裡指的是公司的業績，要想提升公司的業績須重視兩點，即提升產品的質量和提升服務的質量。

這些小詞你也要會哦：

equipment *n.* 設備	found *v.* 建立	showroom *n.* 陳列室
durable modeling 定型耐久	technique *n.* 技術	staff *n.* 員工
sharp *a.* 急劇的	sightsee *v.* 觀光	design *n.* 設計

Scene 12 客戶引薦 Clients Recommendation

場景對話

A: Mr. Bryant, I'd like to introduce you to Mr. Morgan. This is Mr. Morgan, our sales manager. And Mr. Morgan, this is Mr. Bryant.

A：布賴恩特先生，我來為您介紹摩根先生。這位就是我們的銷售經理，摩根先生。摩根先生，這位是布賴恩特先生。

B: Nice to meet you. Here is my business card.	B：很高興認識您。這是我的名片。
C: Nice to meet you, too, Mr. Bryant. <u>Thank you for coming today.</u> We have been expecting you all the time.	C：見到您很高興，布賴恩特先生。<u>謝謝您今天的蒞臨。</u>我們一直在盼著您來呢。
B: My pleasure. Let me say the most sincere "thank you" for your warm and gracious welcome. Your staff is friendly and the accommodations you have provided are very comfortable.	B：這真是我的榮幸。我想向你們表達最誠摯的謝意，感謝你們對我熱情而親切的歡迎。你們的員工很友善，你們提供的住處也非常舒適。
C: I'm glad you like it. We are close business partners. In spite of the worldwide economic recession in recent years, there has been a steady growth in our economic cooperation and trade volume. It is our sincere wish that we can continue to work together closely to enhance our friendship.	C：很高興您都滿意。我們是親密的生意夥伴，儘管近年來世界經濟不景氣，但我們之間的經濟合作和貿易額卻一直在穩步增長。我們真誠地希望彼此之間繼續密切合作，進一步穩固我們的友好關係。
B: We share the same desire. We should cooperate more closely, share new ideas and developments. If we work together, we can all move forward quickly.	B：我們也希望如此。我們應該加強密切合作，分享新觀念新發展。如果我們通力合作，我們彼此都能快速發展。

場景問答必會句

> Mr. Bryant, I'd like to introduce you to Mr. Morgan.
> 布賴恩特先生，我來為您介紹摩根先生。

還可以這樣說：
- This is Tim, my boss. 這是我的老闆蒂姆。
- This is Mr. Lee from Comptronics. 這是來自康普川尼斯的李先生。

對方可能這樣回答：
- It's a pleasure to meet you. 很高興見到你。
- I've heard a lot about you. 久仰大名。

> Thank you for coming today.
> 謝謝您今天的蒞臨。

還可以這樣說：

hospitality *n.* 款待

On behalf of Ribold Corporation, I would like to welcome you all to the Meadowbrook Manufacturing Plant.
謹代表賴博企業歡迎各位蒞臨梅德布魯克製造廠。

We're honored to have Delco Finance visiting us this afternoon.
很榮幸戴克金融公司今天下午的造訪。

對方可能這樣回答：

Thank you for your hospitality. 謝謝你們的熱情接待。

Scene
13 介紹公司 Introduce the Company

場景對話

A: Welcome to Tele System, Mr. Fraser, and thank you for sparing the time to visit us.

A：歡迎來到Tele公司，弗雷澤先生，非常感謝您抽空前來參觀。

B: It is my pleasure. I hope we could take this opportunity to look further into each other and set up a long-term partnership.

B：這是我的榮幸。我希望能借此機會增進彼此的瞭解，並建立起長期的合作關係。

A: That's also what we expect. We will do our best to make your visit worthwhile. I think you must have some ideas of our company. We are in the telecommunications industry and mainly make cell phones and software for the telecommunications.

A：這也正是我們所希望的。我們一定會令您不虛此行。我想您對我們公司應該有一定的瞭解。我們從事電信行業，主要生產手機和製作通信軟件。

B: How long have you engaged in the industry?

B：你們公司從事這個行業多久了？

A: Over thirty years. The company was started as an electronic products exporter at the beginning and then transferred into telecommunications. Now we have become a main manufacturer and exporter in the telecommunications and our products are gaining popularity in many countries.

A：30多年了。公司剛成立的時候主要從事電子產品的出口業務，後來才涉足電信行業。現在我們已經是電信領域中最主要的生產商和出口商了，我們的產品在多個國家都受到廣泛歡迎。

B: I see. I heard that your company has a really good reputation in the telecommunications industry.	B：我知道。我早就聽説你們公司在電信業的聲譽非常好。
A: Yes. You know, we've been in this line for many years, and our prices are competitive comparing with those of the same kind of products on the world market.	A：是啊。我們從事這一行很多年了，並且跟世界市場上的同類產品相比，我們的產品非常具有價格優勢。
B: I have a feeling that there are bright prospects for us to cooperate after hearing what you said. I hope we could make a very good start in our cooperation.	B：聽了這些，我覺得我們的合作前景非常樂觀。希望我們的合作有個良好的開始。
A: We share the same desire.	A：我們也希望如此。

場景問答必會句

> We are in the telecommunications industry and mainly make cell phones and software for the telecommunications.
> 我們從事電信行業，主要生產手機和製作通信軟件。

還可以這樣說：

🗨 Our company is renowned for its personal computers.
我們公司以生產個人電腦著稱。

🗨 We are a capable and experienced distributor.
我們是一家有能力並且經驗豐富的經銷商。

🗨 We have a market share of 25% here.
我們擁有 25% 的市場佔有率。

🗨 Our retail outlets can be found in fifteen provinces.
我公司的零售網點遍佈全國 15 個省。

PS

distributor *n.* 經銷商

outlet *n.* 批發商店

對方可能這樣問：

🗨 Are you a professional manufacturer?
你們是專業的生產商嗎？

🗨 Where do your customers come from?
你們的客戶來自哪裡？

🗨 What's your sales target this year?
你們今年的銷售目標是多少？

PS

manufacturer *n.* 生產商

Scene 14　參觀工廠 Visit the Plant

　場景對話

A: Welcome to our factory.	A：歡迎來到我們的工廠。
B: What makes your factory different from others?	B：你們工廠與別的工廠有什麼不同？
A: Our production speed is almost twice the industry-wide average.	A：我們的生產速度是其他工廠的兩倍。
B: That's great! What is this?	B：太棒了！這是什麼？
A: This is the most fully-automated machine in the factory. This machine is the most up-to-date in the industry.	A：這是工廠全自動化程度最高的機器。這款機器是目前行業裡最新型的機器。
B: What does this machine bring to you?	B：這台機器給你們帶來了哪些好處？
A: We've increased our efficiency by 25% through automation.	A：它讓我們的生產效率提高了25%。
B: Could you tell me the cost of the production?	B：你能告訴我你們的生產成本是多少嗎？
A: I'm afraid I don't know. Let me ask the supervisor in this section.	A：不好意思我不太瞭解。我問問這裡的管理人員吧。

場景問答必會句

> Welcome to our factory.
> 歡迎來到我們的工廠。

還可以這樣說：

- I hope this visit will help you get a better understanding of our products.
  希望這次參觀能讓您更好地瞭解我們的產品。
- Let me show you where everything is. 讓我來為您介紹一下工廠內部。
- Would you like to see our product line? 您要去看看我們的生產線嗎？
- Let's start with our design development department. 請先參觀一下我們的設計開發部。
- Please feel free to ask questions at any point during our visit. 參觀期間，歡迎隨時提問。

> This is the most fully-automated machine in the factory.
> 這是工廠全自動化程度最高的機器。

還可以這樣說：

💬 These drawings on the wall are process sheets. 牆上的圖表是工藝流程表。

💬 Our research and development section is at the end of the passage.
我們的研發部門在通道的盡頭。

💬 Here is the main plant where most of the action takes place.
這裡是主廠房，大部分生產在這裡完成。

💬 The tour should last about an hour and a half. 這次參觀大概需要一個半小時。

對方可能這樣問：

💬 What are those drawings for? 那些圖表有什麼用途？

Scene 15　介紹產品 Introduce Products

💬 場景對話

A: Welcome to our sample room, Mr. Fraser. We've got a large collection of sample cell phones here.	A：歡迎來到我們的工廠。 A：歡迎參觀我們的樣品展覽室，弗雷澤先生。這裡有大量的手機樣品。
B: Oh, you do have a great variety of products on display.	B：哦，你們展出的樣品種類真不少。
A: Yes, here's our showroom arranged with a full lineup of our products. First of all, I would like to give you a demonstration of our latest and best-selling product, Modern S-80.	A：是啊，這裡陳列了我們所有的產品。首先，我想給您演示一下我們最新生產的暢銷品，現代S-80。
B: Oh, that is the model I'm interested in. I heard that it has met with great favor at home and abroad.	B：哦，這正是我感興趣的一款手機。我聽說這款手機在國內外都很受歡迎。
A: Yes, it is a hit among the young because of its fashionable design and unique functions.	A：是的。因為這款手機外觀時尚、功能獨特，尤其受到年輕人的青睞。
B: What unique functions does it have?	B：那它有什麼獨特的功能呢？
A: Well, one of the special features is that it can be used as a walkman music player beyond sending text messages and making voice calls.	A：嗯，除了發短信和打電話之外，它還可以被當作隨身音樂播放器來使用，這是它的一大特色。

A 場景問答必會句

> It is a hit among the young because of its fashionable design and unique functions.
> 因為這款手機外觀時尚、功能獨特，尤其受到年輕人的青睞。

還可以這樣說：

🗨 This product is convenient to carry. 這款產品易於攜帶。

🗨 It's the most popular cell phone brand among the young people nowadays.
現在最受年輕人歡迎的就是這個品牌的手機。

🗨 This kind of machine is very economical.
這款機型非常經濟。

🗨 This model of typewriter is efficient and durable, economical and practical for businessmen.
這個型號的打字機對商務人士來說，高效、耐用、經濟、實惠。

economical *a.* 經濟的

durable *a.* 耐用的

> One of the special features is that it can be used as a walkman music player beyond sending text messages and making voice calls.
> 除了發短信和打電話之外，它還可以被當作隨身音樂播放器來使用，這是它的一大特色。

還可以這樣說：

🗨 Our computer is characterized by its high quality, compact size, and is also easy to learn and operate.
我們的電腦特點是質量好、體積小，而且易學好用。

🗨 It offers flexible adaptations to the requirements of the company operation.
該系統操作靈活，適應公司運營的各種要求。

adaptation *n.* 適應

對方可能這樣問：

🗨 How's the quality of your product?
你們的產品質量如何？

🗨 What kind of unique functions does it have?
那它有什麼獨特的功能呢？

Scene 16 談論業績 Talk about the Performance

 場景對話

A: Mr. Morgan, if you don' t mind, may I see any information and data concerning your company' s business record and ranking in the last few years, please?

A：摩根先生，如果您不介意的話，我能否看一下貴公司近幾年來的業績資料記錄以及排名？

B: Yes, Mr. Fraser, we have already prepared the relevant information for you. Now let me explain it by showing you some graphs. <u>As you can see, this chart offers a good look at the annual sales results of last few years.</u> We have maintained a steady growth since 2008, and we especially made a great success in 2014 with the total revenue over one billion yuan.

B：當然可以，弗雷澤先生，我們已經為您準備好了相關材料。現在，我給您看一些圖表吧。如您所見，這張圖表清楚地呈現出公司近幾年的銷售狀況。自 2008 年以來，我們一直保持了平穩的增長勢頭，2014 年我們的年收入總額取得重大突破，超過了 10 億元。

A: Pretty impressive! I know that you developed a new type of cell phone last year; how about the sales situation?

A：真是很了不起啊！聽說你們去年研發了一款新手機，銷量怎麼樣？

B: Well, our new products were a hit in the domestic market. <u>We started the year out strong.</u> According to the graph, you can see the future growth of the product is positive.

B：哦，我們的新產品在國內市場非常暢銷。新產品銷售一開始就勢如破竹，從圖表上您可以看到，該產品未來的發展也很樂觀。

A: I see. Since you have achieved a great success in the domestic market, do you have any plans to explore the overseas market for the product?

A：我瞭解。既然你們在國內市場已經獲得了極大的成功，有沒有什麼計劃進軍海外市場呢？

B: Yes, that' s what we are doing right now. We conducted a survey in the North American market; it shows that there is enough room for us to get in.

B：當然有，我們現在正著手準備呢。我們已經在北美市場做了一項調查，結果顯示，那兒的市場空間很大。

場景問答必會句

> As you can see, this chart offers a good look at the annual sales results of last few years.
> 如您所見，這張圖表清楚地呈現出公司近幾年的銷售狀況。

還可以這樣說：

💬 From the graph we could see a slightly decline from a six-month high.
從這張曲線圖中可見，在 6 個月的一路走高後出現了小小的下跌。

💬 Our sales went quite well last year.
我們去年銷售情況非常不錯。

PS

volume *n.* 量

> We started the year out strong.
> 新產品銷售一開始就勢如破竹。

還可以這樣說：

💬 Customer satisfaction index rises to 93%.
消費者滿意度指數提升至 93%。

💬 Last year there was a sharp increase in sales.
去年的銷售業績大幅提升。

💬 According to a recent survey, 35% people are able to recognize our brand.
根據最新的一項調查，我們品牌的公眾認知度達到了 35%。

PS

customer satisfaction
消費者滿意度

Scene 17 陪同觀光 Go Sightseeing Together

 場景對話

A: Would you like to go sightseeing tomorrow?	A：您明天想不想去觀光遊覽？
B: Yes. Could you please recommend some interesting places?	B：是的，你能介紹一些好玩的地方嗎？
A: Of course. What kind of places would you like to visit? Historical sites or natural landscapes?	A：當然可以。您喜歡什麼樣的地方，名勝古跡還是自然景觀？
B: I prefer the latter.	B：我比較喜歡後者。

A: How about an eco-tourism in Cornwall? There are historic sites and stunning valleys with lakes.	A：那康沃爾的生態遊如何？那裡有歷史遺跡，還有迷人的山谷和湖泊。
B: Sounds great. Let's visit there. Is it OK for us to take pictures there?	B：聽起來很棒。咱們就去那兒吧。那裡可以拍照嗎？
A: Of course. The background of your pictures will be really beautiful!	A：當然。那你的照片背景會很美！

場景問答必會句

> **Would you like to go sightseeing tomorrow?**
> 您明天想不想去觀光遊覽？

還可以這樣說：

- Is there any place in particular you would like to go?
  您有特別想去的地方嗎？
- Shall I help you in your sightseeing around the city?
  我陪您到市區遊覽觀光好嗎？
- Are you into any outdoor activities? I can help you arrange a few.
  您喜歡什麼戶外活動嗎？我可以幫您安排一些。

對方可能這樣回答：

- I've been looking forward to visiting Mt. Laoshan. 我一直盼望着去嶗山看看。
- I'd like to go downtown to do some shopping. 我想去市中心買些東西。

PS

in particular 特別

> **What kinds of places do you like to visit? Historical sites or natural landscapes?**
> 您喜歡什麼樣的地方，名勝古跡還是自然景觀？

還可以這樣說：

- Would you be interested in watching a baseball game?
  I can get tickets.
  您想看棒球比賽嗎？我可以買到票。
- Would you like to watch a musical? 想不想去看場音樂劇？

對方可能這樣回答：

- Let's go check out the castle. 我們去查看那座城堡吧。
- What teams are playing? 什麼隊在比賽？

PS

historical *a.* 歷史的

landscape *n.* 景色

參觀陪同 Tips

參觀工廠

- **帶領客戶參觀工廠前的準備**

    明確客戶到訪的時間、航班、隨訪人員名單、手機號碼、職位等。客戶參觀工廠的行程表要事先溝通好，確定了以後再與工廠聯繫，讓工廠做好接待客戶的準備。

- **安排酒店**

    安排酒店是非常重要的一項任務。在客戶來訪之前，要與對方確定酒店的星級、房間類型等，要記得詢問客戶有沒有特別的習慣和要求。

    在酒店選擇方面，最好就近安排，比如選擇離機場或者工廠較近的酒店。但如果客戶有其他要求，比如想要住在市中心，那麼一切以客戶的要求為主。

    安排好了之後，告知對方酒店的具體地址及聯繫方式。

- **其他事項**

    訪問行程表、介紹工廠的資料、產品樣品以及資料、客戶要求的資料等，這些都要事先整理並裝訂好。

    根據客戶的國籍以及宗教信仰，準備好茶水和點心，如果客戶所在的國家有送見面禮的習俗，一定要提前準備，避免出現差錯。

商務宴請

商務宴請是外貿活動中很重要的一環，既可以表達接待方熱情、積極的合作意圖，又可以在宴請中討論、商定某些合作細節。商務宴請大致包括商務着裝、邀請客戶、訂座、推薦菜品、點菜、詢問上菜、評價菜品和結帳等環節。

商務宴請必會詞

1 main course 主菜
在西餐中，肉、禽類菜肴是主菜，和配菜 (side dish) 相對應。

2 appetizer n. 開胃菜
開胃菜通常是在主菜前或連同主菜一起食用，通常為烘焙食品或其他酸性開胃小菜。

3 dessert n. 甜點
甜點是一個很廣的概念，一般指餐後食用的帶甜味的點心。

🖋 這些小詞你也要會哦：

black tea 紅茶	beverage *n.* 飲料	paper towel 紙巾
napkin *n.* 餐巾	table cloth 桌布	chopsticks *n.* 筷子
soup spoon 湯匙	toothpick *n.* 牙籤	fork *n.* 餐叉

Scene 18 商務着裝 Business Dress Code

 場景對話

A: Hello, Mrs. Jones. This is Brenda. I'm calling to remind you the banquet we are going to have in your honor this evening.	A：您好，瓊斯太太。我是布倫達。我打電話來是想提醒您今天晚上有一場我們特地為您舉辦的晚宴。
B: That's very kind of you. By the way, is it a formal one?	B：你太有心了。順便問一下，是正式晚宴嗎？
A: Yes, very formal. Some of the officials from the Ministry of Foreign Trade and Economic Cooperation will be there too.	A：是的，非常正式。對外貿易經濟合作部的某些官員也將出席。

B: I see. Thank you for telling me that. Since this is the first time for me to attend such a formal banquet in Canada, I feel a little bit confused about what to wear. Brenda, is there any particular requirement for dressing tonight?

B：明白了。謝謝你告訴我。這是我第一次參加加拿大的正式晚宴，我有點不知道穿什麼衣服。布倫達，這次晚宴對著裝是否有特殊要求？

A: They didn't mention that, but <u>since it is very formal, it is quite usual for ladies to wear evening dresses or banquet dresses.</u> I remembered asking you to prepare such dresses before our leaving, didn't I?

A：他們沒有提及，不過既然是場很正式的晚宴，女士通常要穿晚禮服或宴會禮服。我記得出發前叮囑過您準備這樣的禮服，是吧？

B: Yes, but you know cheongsam is my favorite and I brought two of them. I wonder if I can wear it to the banquet tonight.

B：是的，但你也知道我最喜歡旗袍，這次我帶了兩件。不知道今晚我能不能穿旗袍？

A: As the banquet tonight has no particular requirement for dressing, you can wear your favorite. <u>Men are usually required to wear suits instead.</u>

A：因為這次晚宴對服裝沒有特別的要求，你可以穿你心愛的旗袍。男士一般要求穿西服。

B: I see. Thank you so much.

B：明白了。謝謝你。

場景問答必會句

Since it is very formal, it is quite usual for ladies to wear evening dresses or banquet dresses.
既然是場很正式的晚宴，女士通常要穿晚禮服或宴會禮服。

還可以這樣說：
- You'd better dress formally.
  你最好著裝正式些。
- We must wear white shirts and dark blue suits.
  我們必須穿白襯衫和深藍色西服。

Men are usually required to wear suits instead.
男士一般要求穿西服。

對方可能這樣問：
- Are we allowed to wear casual clothes?
  我們可以穿休閒服嗎？

PS casual clothes 休閒服

Scene 19 邀請客戶 Invite Customers

 場景對話

A: Hello, Mr. Robert. <u>Do you have any plans for this evening?</u>	A：您好，羅伯特先生。<u>您今天晚上有安排嗎？</u>
B: Not yet for the moment.	B：暫時還沒有。
A: <u>May I invite you to a dinner at a Chinese restaurant?</u>	A：<u>我可以邀請您去一家中餐館吃晚飯嗎？</u>
B: Oh, thank you. I'm delighted to go with you. I have had Chinese food before in New York. It was very delicious. What kind of Chinese food does this restaurant serve?	B：哦，謝謝。我很樂意和您一起去。我以前在紐約吃過中餐，很好吃。這家餐館提供哪種菜系？
A: Sichuan Food. It is hot and delicious.	A：川菜，很辣、很美味。
B: Well, I have heard about it.	B：哦，我聽說過這種菜。
A: You can have a taste this time.	A：這次您可以嘗一嘗。
B: OK. I think I may like it.	B：好的，我想我也許會喜歡吃。
A: I'm sure you will like it.	A：我保證您會喜歡的。

場景問答必會句

> Do you have any plans for this evening?
> 您今天晚上有安排嗎？

還可以這樣說：

- I wonder if you have had any plans tonight. 不知道您今晚有沒有安排？
- Are you doing anything special tonight? 您今晚有沒有什麼特別的活動？

> May I invite you to a dinner at a Chinese restaurant?
> 我可以邀請您去一家中餐館吃晚飯嗎？

還可以這樣說：

- Shall we have dinner together? 我可以邀請您一起吃晚餐嗎？
- Would you like to have dinner with me? 您願意和我一起吃晚餐嗎？

對方可能這樣回答：

- I'm glad to come. 我很高興前往。

Scene 20　訂座 Book a Table

 場景對話

A: Good morning. Madera's Restaurant. May I help you?	A：早上好，馬德拉餐廳，有什麼可以為您效勞的嗎？
B: Yes, I'd like to book a table for two for tonight.	B：是的，我想預訂今晚的兩人桌。
A: What time would you like to make a reservation for?	A：您想預訂幾點的呢？
B: Let's say around eight p.m.	B：晚上 8 點左右。
A: OK, eight o'clock tonight for two people. Sir, may I have your name please?	A：好的，今晚 8 點兩人桌。先生，能告訴我您的名字嗎？
B: Yes, it's Johnson.	B：可以，我叫約翰遜。
A: Thank you, Mr. Johnson, your table has been booked.	A：謝謝您，約翰遜先生，已經為您預訂餐桌了。
B: Oh, one more question. Can we have a table by the window?	B：哦，還有一個問題。有沒有靠窗的位置？
A: I am sorry, but we are almost fully booked tonight. We can't guarantee a window table, but I'll note your preference.	A：很抱歉，我們今晚的預訂幾乎已經滿了，我不能向您保證能為您安排靠窗的位置，但是我們會記下您的喜好。
B: OK, that's fine. But I would appreciate it if you could arrange that.	B：好的，沒關係。但是如果你能夠為我安排的話，我會非常感激的。
A: I'll try my best.Thans for booking at Madera's. We're looking forward to waiting on you this evening. Goodbye.	A：我會盡力的。感謝您在馬德拉餐廳預訂。期待今晚為您服務。再見。
B: Goodbye.	B：再見。

場景問答必會句

> I'd like to book a table for two for tonight.
> 我想預訂今晚的兩人桌。

還可以這樣說：

💬 I'd like to make a reservation. 我想預訂餐位。

💬 I'd like to book a booth for five people.
我想預訂能坐 5 人的包間。

PS
booth *n.* 包間

> Can we have a table by the window?
> 有沒有靠窗戶的位置？

還可以這樣說：

💬 Could we have a table close to the band? 我們能不能要張離樂隊近一點兒的桌子？

💬 I want to reserve a table by the window. 我想訂窗邊的座位。

對方可能這樣回答：

💬 All right. 好的。

💬 Sorry, they're booked up. 對不起，它們都被訂完了。

Scene 21 推薦菜品 Recommend Dishes

 場景對話

A: Mr. Song, thank you very much for inviting me to dinner. I feel very much honored.	A：宋先生，謝謝你邀請我一起吃晚餐。我深感榮幸。
B: Ms. Ross, I'm very pleased to get this opportunity to meet you when you have come from afar to visit our company.	B：羅斯女士，感謝您不遠千里來拜訪我們公司，使得我們有幸見面。
A: Your company has good long-term cooperation with ours. Surely it is a pleasure for me to come to your 5th anniversary celebration.	A：貴公司是我們很好的長期合作夥伴，我當然很高興能來參加你們公司創立五週年的紀念大會了。
B: I'm glad to hear that, Ms. Ross. <u>Which do you prefer, western food or Chinese food?</u>	B：很高興你這麼說，羅斯女士。<u>你想吃西餐還是中餐呢？</u>
A: Chinese food, of course. Can you recommend some typical local dishes?	A：當然要吃中餐。你可以給我推薦一些地道的地方菜嗎？
B: Well, <u>I recommend the main dishes of prime Shanghai crab and cordon bleu chicken.</u>	B：好，<u>那我建議主菜要上好的上海螃蟹和奶酪火腿雞排。</u>
A: It sounds delicious. OK, I'll take that.	A：聽起來就很美味。行，就點這個了。

| B: Now, I'd like to start tonight's dinner with a toast. For our friendship, cheers! | B：我先敬你一杯，以此開始今天的晚餐。為了我們的友誼，乾杯！ |
| A: Cheers! | A：乾杯！ |

場景問答必會句

> Which do you prefer, western food or Chinese food?
> 你想吃西餐還是中餐呢？

還可以這樣說：

📧 What would you like for lunch? 午餐你想吃什麼？

📧 What would you like to drink? 你想喝點什麼？

對方可能這樣回答：

📧 I'll have a cup of coffee please. 我要一杯咖啡。

> I recommend the main dishes of prime Shanghai crab and cordon bleu chicken.
> 那我建議主菜要上好的上海螃蟹和奶酪火腿雞排。

還可以這樣說：

📧 I think the lamb chops are excellent.
我認為羊排很好吃。

📧 Why don't you try the escargot? It's pretty exotic.
你不嘗嘗食用蝸牛？很有特色。

📧 The Niagara region is famous for its ice-wine.
尼加拉瓜地區以冰酒而聞名。

對方可能這樣問：

📧 Well, what's your recommendation? 有什麼可以推薦的嗎？

PS

chop *n.* 排骨

exotic *a.* 異國情調的

be famous for 以……著名

Scene 22 點菜 Order Dishes

場景對話

A: Good evening. What can I get you to drink?	A：晚上好。你們想要點喝的嗎？
B: May I have your wine list?	B：可否讓我看看酒單？
A: Here you are.	A：給您。

B: I'd like a whisky and soda. Make it a double.	B：請給我一杯威士忌蘇打水。要雙份威士忌。
A: Okay. We've got two specials for today, charbroiled steaks and legs of lamb. What would you like today?	A：好的。今天有兩份特價菜，炭烤牛排和羊腿。您想要什麼呢？
B: The leg of lamb sounds good.	B：羊腿聽起來不錯。
A: Okay. Our vegetables are peas, carrots, broccoli, corns, and string beans. Please choose your vegetables.	A：好的。我們的蔬菜有豌豆、胡蘿蔔、西蘭花、玉米和豆角。您要什麼菜呢？
B: Peas and carrots.	B：要豌豆和胡蘿蔔。
A: Okay. Which dressing would you like? French, Italian, blue cheese, Russian?	A：好的，您要哪種調料呢？法式，意大利式，藍奶酪還是俄羅斯式的？
B: Italian.	B：來意大利式的。
A: Okay, fine. Thank you.	A：好的，謝謝。

場景問答必會句

May I have your wine list?
可否讓我看看酒單？

還可以這樣說：

🗨 Could I have a menu, please? 請給我菜單好嗎？

🗨 Is there a copy of your menu in Chinese? 你們有中文菜單嗎？

🗨 Can we order now? 我們現在可以點菜嗎？

I'd like a whisky and soda. Make it a double.
請給我一杯威士忌蘇打水。要雙份威士忌。

還可以這樣說：

🗨 I'll have a glass of red wine please.
我要一杯紅酒。

🗨 I haven't figured out what I want yet.
我還沒想好點什麼菜呢。

🗨 I'd like an eighteen ounce steak.
我要一份 18 盎司的牛排。

🗨 We'll have custard pie for dessert.
甜點是蛋奶派。

custard pie 蛋奶派

Scene 23 詢問上菜 Ask about Serving

 場景對話

A: Excuse me, Miss.	A：小姐，麻煩你一下。
B: Yes, sir. May I help you?	B：先生，需要什麼服務嗎？
A: I ordered my meal at least thirty minutes ago. Why is it taking such a long time?	A：我至少在 30 分鐘前點了菜，為什麼這麼長時間了還沒送來？
B: I'm very sorry, sir. I thought another server had already brought you your meal.	B：真對不起，先生。我以為另一位服務員已經為您上菜了。
A: A waiter did come, but it was not our order.	A：確實有一位服務員來過，但是上的不是我們點的菜。
B: I'm really sorry. I will check it out right away.	B：真的很抱歉，我現在就去查一下。
A: Thank you. But before that, could you do me a favor?	A：謝謝，不過在你查之前，請幫我一個忙好嗎？
B: Certainly. What is it?	B：好的，請說。
A: We are pretty hungry, so could you please bring us some bread? And also more butter and jam, please.	A：我們真的很餓，請給我們送一些麵包，多放點黃油和果醬吧。
B: No problem. What kind of bread do you prefer? Whole wheat or white?	B：沒問題，您要全麥麵包還是白麵包呢？
A: I like white but my friend likes whole wheat. So could you bring us both?	A：我要白麵包，我朋友要全麥麵包。可以兩種都給我們一些嗎？
B: Of course. Anything else?	B：好，還需要什麼嗎？
A: Oh, I think we need more water, too.	A：哦，我想我們需要加點水。
B: OK. I will check on your order immediately and be right back with your bread and water.	B：好的，我會立刻查清楚你們點的菜，並送來麵包和水。
A: Great. Thank you.	A：好。謝謝你。

場景問答必會句

> I ordered my meal at least thirty minutes ago. Why is it taking such a long time?
> 我至少在 30 分鐘前點了菜，為什麼這麼長時間了還沒送來？

還可以這樣說：

What's the holdup? It's been thirty minutes.
怎麼還不上菜？已經 30 分鐘了。

We're really hungry; could you hurry it up?
我們都要餓死了，能快點嗎？

I'm sorry, but I didn't order this.
抱歉，我沒有點這個。

This fish is undercooked and the sauce is wrong.
這魚還沒有熟呢，而且醬汁也不對。

The soup is too spicy, but I ordered "not spicy".
湯太辣了，我明明點的是不辣的。

PS

holdup *n.* 耽擱

> We are pretty hungry, so could you please bring us some bread?
> 我們真的很餓，請給我們送一些麵包。

還可以這樣說：

Please bring me more napkins.
請給我多拿些餐巾紙。

May I have some toothpicks?
能給我拿些牙籤嗎？

I dropped my fork. May I have a new one?
我的叉子掉了，能換一把嗎？

Can I have another bowl of soup?
能再給我盛一碗湯嗎？

The room is too cold; could you turn up the air-conditioner?
房間太涼了，可以把空調溫度調高一點嗎？

Scene 24 評價菜品 Food Evaluation

 場景對話

A: The steamed fish looks so delicious. It is the specialty of this restaurant. It is said that they serve nearly 1,000 fish every day. Let's order it.	A：哇，這條蒸魚看起來很美味。它是這家餐廳的特色菜。據說他們一天能賣出近 1000 條魚。我們點一份吧。
B: OK.	B：好的。
(A moment later.)	（過了一會兒。）

C: Your fish, sir.	C：先生，你們的魚。
A: Thanks. It smells great! Let's try it.	A：謝謝。這魚聞起來很不錯，我們嘗嘗吧。
B: All right. It's terrific! <u>How do you like this dish?</u>	B：好的。真的很美味！<u>你覺得這道菜怎麼樣？</u>
A: I love the taste. The meat is tender. It's very fresh and flavorful. <u>Is this flavor suitable for you?</u>	A：我喜歡這個味道，肉非常鮮嫩。這道菜很新鮮也很美味。<u>這道菜合你的胃口嗎？</u>
B: I love it, but I think the soup is a little greasy.	B：我很喜歡，但是我覺得這湯有點油膩。
A: Indeed. We'd better have more fish. I've never tasted anything as delicious as this.	A：確實有點兒，我們還是多吃些魚肉吧。我從來沒有吃過這麼美味的東西。
B: Me too.	B：我也是。

場景問答必會句

> How do you like this dish?
> 你覺得這道菜怎麼樣？

對方可能這樣回答：
- It smells good.
  聞着真香。
- That's a far superior taste.
  這個味道要好得多。
- It's excellent.
  好吃極了。
- It's so light and fresh. 它很清爽而且很新鮮。

superior *a.* 上好的

> Is this flavor suitable for you?
> 這道菜合你的胃口嗎？

對方可能這樣回答：
- It doesn't taste good. 不好吃。
- The crabs taste too hot for me.
  這個螃蟹對我來說太辣了。
- It's salty / sweet / spicy. 真鹹 / 甜 / 辣。

suitable *a.* 符合的

Scene 25 結帳 Pay the Bill

 場景對話

A: Would you give me my bill, please?	A：您好，麻煩您給我結帳，好嗎？
B: Of course, Madam. I have it right here.	B：好的，女士，這是您的賬單。
A: What's that?	A：那是什麼？
B: That is the roast beef with baked potato.	B：這是土豆烤牛肉。
A: We didn't order that. All we had was one roast chicken dinner and a T-bone steak.	A：我們沒有點這道菜。我們點的是烤雞套餐和丁骨牛排。
B: Oh, there must be some mistake. Sorry about that. I will deduct the roast beef from the total and be right back with you. Madam, here is your new bill.	B：哦，那一定是哪裡出錯了。很抱歉發生這樣的事，我會把烤牛肉的價格從總金額中扣除，請稍等，我馬上給您拿新的賬單過來。女士，這是您的新賬單。
A: Does the total include the service charge?	A：請問總價裡面包括服務費嗎？
B: Yes, it includes a 15% service charge.	B：是的，含 15% 的服務費。
A: OK. Here is my visa card.	A：好的，這是我的信用卡。
B: Do you need a receipt?	B：您要收據嗎？
A: Yes, please.	A：是的，請幫我開一張。
B: No problem. I will be right back.	B：好的，我馬上回來。

場景問答必會句

> Would you give me my bill, please?
> 您好，麻煩您給我結帳，好嗎？

還可以這樣說：

- Check, please. 結帳。
- No dessert, just the check, please.
  不要甜品了，請結帳。
- Do I pay you or the cashier?
  我把餐費付給您還是到櫃枱結帳？

PS

cashier *n.* 櫃枱

對方可能這樣回答：
- Yes, 230 dollars in all. 好的，一共 230 美元。
- Please pay the cashier on your way out. 請離開時到櫃枱付帳。

> **Does the total include the service charge?**
> 請問總價裡面包括服務費嗎？

還可以這樣說：
- Does this include a tip? 這賬單上包括小費嗎？
- Here is your tip, please. 這是給你的小費。

對方可能這樣回答：
- Yes. A 15% service charge is automatically added to the bill.
  是的，賬單自動包含 15% 的服務費。

automatically *ad.* 自動地

商務宴請 Tips

1. 西餐禮儀

　　洽談外貿生意與合作，就會和外國人接觸，商務宴請中也就會涉及吃西餐。那吃西餐要講究哪些禮儀呢？
- 使用餐具最基本的原則是由外至內。當你吃完一道菜之後餐廳服務人員會收走該份菜的餐具，然後按需要會補上另一套餐具，就餐時要注意餐具的使用和更換。
- 吃肉類時（如牛排）應從角落開始切，吃完一塊再切下一塊。遇到不吃的部分或配菜，將其移到盤子的一邊即可。
- 用餐後切忌用餐巾用力擦嘴，正確的做法是用餐巾的一角輕輕印去嘴上或手上的油漬。
- 就餐時，即使座位很舒適，也要保持正確的坐姿，儘量不要靠在椅背上，身體可略向前靠。

2. 小費細節

　　在商務宴請中有些場所是需要付小費的。作為外貿人員，關於小費的知識當然要有所瞭解。
- 若賬單上寫着"含服務費"，就不必再額外給小費 (gratuity 也表示"小費")。英語國家中，新西蘭、澳大利亞等地不用給小費。
- 在美國餐館吃飯的時候，只會有一位服務員為你服務，其他服務員會專門服務自己的客人，所以你只要把小費付給服務自己的服務員即可。一般來說，午餐需付消費額 10%~15% 的小費，晚餐需要支付 15%~20% 的小費。當然，如果你對餐館的服務很不滿意的話，也是可以拒絕付小費的。

Unit 6 機場送別

作為接待客戶的最後一個步驟，送別也是不可鬆懈的一步。所謂善始善終就是這個道理。讓客戶帶著滿意的笑容離開，可以算是下一次交易的基礎條件。

機場送別必會詞

① stay *n.* 逗留，暫住

stay 指 "短時間的停留"。

PS How long will you be staying in China? 您預計要在中國待多久？
Did you enjoy your stay here? 您在這裡過得愉快嗎？

② see off 送行

see sb. off 表示 "為某人送行，送別某人"。

PS We saw our clients off at the airport. 我們在機場送別了客戶。

③ on behalf of 代表

on behalf of 是 "代表" 的意思，代表某人就是 on behalf of sb.，也可以表示為 on sb.'s behalf。

PS At the airport he made an address of welcome on behalf of the association. 在機場上他代表該協會致了歡迎詞。

④ regards 問候，祝福

give my regards to sb. 指 "向某人送去我的祝福"。

PS Give my regards to your family. 代我問候你的家人。

這些小詞你也要會哦：

economy class 經濟艙	cancellation *n.* 取消	window seat 靠窗座位
terminal *n.* 航站樓	generous *a.* 慷慨的，大方的	customs formalities 海關手續
honor *n.* 榮譽	early flight 早班機	destination *n.* 目的地

Scene 26 預訂機票 Book the Tickets

 場景對話

A: Excuse me, what time does the last flight to Paris leave? I'd like to make a reservation for a flight to Paris this evening.

A：請問，去巴黎的最後一班飛機幾點起飛？我想預訂今晚飛往巴黎的機票。

B: OK! Two international flights are available. Flight E31 takes off at eighteen o'clock and the other, Flight E32, 19:28.

B：好的！有兩次國際航班。E31 航班 18 點起飛，另一次航班是 E32，19 點 28 分起飛。

A: What time does Flight E31 arrive in Paris?

A：E31 航班什麼時間抵達巴黎？

B: At 20:15 two days later. And for Flight E32, two o'clock the same day.

B：兩天後的 20 點 15 分到達。E32 航班將於同日凌晨 2 點到達。

A: What? Why the later one reaches the destination first?

A：什麼？為什麼後出發的反而提前到達呢？

B: Dear Miss, if you take Flight E31, you will have to transfer in Tokyo.

B：親愛的女士，如果您乘坐 E31 航班，中途將在東京轉機。

A: Better take a look at Tokyo! How much is the airfare of Flight E31?

A：順便在東京到處看看倒也不錯！ E31 航班的票價是多少？

B: As for economy class, a one-way ticket costs 8,000 yuan and a round-trip ticket costs 12,000 yuan. First class and business class have been booked up already.

B：經濟艙的單程票價是 8000 元，往返票價是 1.2 萬元。頭等艙和商務艙已經訂完了。

A: OK. One one-way economy class ticket to Paris please.

A：沒關係。請幫我訂一張去巴黎的經濟艙單程機票。

B: Would you like to reconfirm your plane reservation?

B：您願意再確認一下您的機票預訂嗎？

A: Sure. Thank you!

A：好的。謝謝！

B: Flight E31 to Paris on April 1st, one economy class ticket, one-way. Is that right?

B：4 月 1 日飛往巴黎的 E31 航班，一張單程經濟艙機票，對嗎？

A: Yes! You are so helpful!

A：是的！感謝您的幫助！

?A 場景問答必會句

I'd like to make a reservation for a flight to Paris this evening.
我想預訂今晚飛往巴黎的機票。

還可以這樣說：
- I'd like to book a ticket for July 3rd to New York.
  我想預訂一張 7 月 3 日去紐約的機票。

make a reservation 預訂
（房間、票）

What time does Flight E31 arrive in Paris?
E31 航班什麼時間抵達巴黎？

還可以這樣說：
- When will the Flight E31 take off?
  E31 航班何時起飛？
- When is the plane due?
  航班什麼時間到達？

due to 由於，應歸於

對方可能這樣回答：
- It'll be leaving at 3:00 p.m.
  下午 3 點起飛。
- The flight has been delayed due to some mechanical troubles.
  該航班因機械故障延誤。

Scene 27　送行 See Off

場景對話

A: Mr. Jackson, <u>did you enjoy your stay here?</u>	A：傑克遜先生，<u>您在這裡過得還愉快嗎？</u>
B: Yes, I did. Your company and your hospitality have left a very good impression on us.	B：是的。你們的公司以及你們的熱情款待都給我們留下了非常好的印象。

A: I'm so glad to hear that. Your visit means a great deal to us. What a pity you have to leave so soon!	A：很高興聽到您這樣說。你的訪問對我們來說意義重大。真可惜，您這麼快就要走了。
B: It's hard to believe that we're actually leaving. The past two weeks has been wonderful.	B：真不敢相信我們就要離開了。過去的兩週很美好。
A: Have you got everything you need?	A：您的行李都收拾好了嗎？
B: Yes. I think so.	B：是的。收拾好了。
A: Great. Your flight will be taking off in three hours. Let's get you to the airport. Shall we leave now?	A：好的，您的航班將在 3 小時後起飛。我們送您去機場吧。我們現在可以出發了嗎？
B: Sure. Let's go downstairs and check out.	B：當然，我們下樓退房吧。

場景問答必會句

> Did you enjoy your stay here?
> 您在這裡過得愉快嗎？

還可以這樣說：

💬 How was your visit?
　　您此次訪問感受如何？

對方可能這樣回答：

💬 I enjoyed it very much.
　　我非常享受這次旅行。

💬 It's been very productive.
　　此次訪問很有成效。

PS

productive *a.* 富有成效的

> Have you got everything you need?
> 您的行李都收拾好了嗎？

還可以這樣說：

💬 Are you ready to go?
　　您準備好出發了嗎？

對方可能這樣回答：

💬 Everything is packed and I'm ready to go.
　　所有的東西都打包好了，我準備出發了。

Scene 28 道別 Farewell

 場景對話

A: Mr. Jackson. It's a great honor to have you here.	A：傑克遜先生，您的到來是我們的榮幸。
B: I would like to thank you for your kind reception.	B：感謝你們的熱情款待。
A: I hope you enjoyed your stay here.	A：希望您在這裡過得愉快。
B: Yes, I did. Everything was great.	A：是的。一切都很好。
A: Please remember me to your family.	B：請代我向您的家人問好。
B: I will. Thank you. Oh, there's my flight. I'd better hurry up. I shall miss you very much and thank you for your company. Goodbye.	A：我會的，謝謝。哦，我的航班到點了。我得快點了。我會想念你們的，謝謝你們公司的招待。再見。
B: Goodbye. Have a good journey.	B：再見。旅途愉快。

場景問答必會句

> It's a great honor to have you here.
> 您的到來是我們的榮幸。

還可以這樣說：

- It's always good to see you.
  與您見面總是很愉快。

對方可能這樣回答：

- I would like to thank you for your kindly reception.
  感謝你們的熱情款待。
- It's been a wonderful experience for us.
  我們過得很愉快。

Please remember me to your family.
請代我向您的家人問好。

還可以這樣說：
🗨 Keep in touch.
保持聯繫。
🗨 I'm looking forward to seeing you soon.
期待不久後再次見到您。

PS

keep *sb.* posted 保持聯繫

對方可能這樣回答：
🗨 I will keep you posted.
我會與您保持聯繫。

機場送別 Tips

1. 常用告別語

We wish you a safe and pleasant journey home. 我們祝您歸途一路順風。
Have a nice journey. 一路順風。
I look forward to seeing you again soon. 我期待很快再次見到你。

2. 送別小禮儀

　　中國人表達情感的方式相對內斂。在送別的時候，往往隱藏情緒，吝於擁抱，種種"冷漠"表現讓外國賓客深感詫異。所以，送別外賓時，舉止不妨灑脫奔放些，讓賓客感受到你的熱情。

　　在禮物方面，可以選一些具有中國特色且方便攜帶的小禮物，如絲綢、茶葉、珍珠或紀念 T 恤等。贈送禮物時可以說：

Please keep it for a souvenir. 請留下作個紀念。
Here is a little souvenir from Beijing. 這是在北京買的小紀念品。

Chapter 2

商務出差——
開發潛在客戶

Unit 1 乘坐飛機

乘坐飛機是商務出差的較好選擇，可以有效節省時間，提高辦事效率。在飛機上可能面臨各種情況，比如：座位問題、機上服務問題、飲食問題和暈機問題等。對於職場菜鳥來說，面對問題時不要慌張，有事可以找空姐幫忙。

▌乘坐飛機必會詞 ▌

❶ window seat 靠窗座位
靠窗座位，即靠近窗戶的座位，還有兩種座位是 middle seat（中間座位）和 aisle seat（靠走道的座位）。

❷ flight service 機上服務
機上服務有頭等艙和經濟艙之分，主要的區別體現在硬件設施和軟件質量上。

❸ airsickness n. 暈機
暈機時可能會有噁心、面色蒼白、出冷汗、眩暈等症狀。一般建議容易暈機的人在登機前 1~2 小時先服用暈機藥，可減輕症狀或避免暈機。

✎ 這些小詞你也要會哦：

board v. 上（飛機、車、船等）	baggage n. 行李	belt n. 安全帶
urgent a. 緊急的	overhead a. 在頭頂上的	press v. 按壓
air-conditioner n. 空調	volume control 音量調節	ashtray n. 煙灰缸

Scene 29 登機入座 Boarding and Seating

 場景對話

A: Excuse me, I think there's a problem with my seat. Can you help me?	A：不好意思，我想我的座位有問題，可以請您幫忙嗎？
B: Yes, of course. What's the problem?	B：當然可以，有什麼問題嗎？

A: Well, my boarding pass says Seat 13L, but there is somebody sitting in the seat. <u>Could you check it for me?</u>	A：我登機牌上的座位寫的是 13L，但那裡已經有人坐了。<u>您可以幫我確認一下嗎？</u>
B: No problem. Excuse me, sir. May I see your boarding pass please?	B：沒問題。先生，不好意思，我可以看一下您的登機牌嗎？
C: Is anything wrong?	C：哪裡不對嗎？
B: This is 13L. I think it belongs to this lady.	B：這個座位是 13L。我想這是這位小姐的座位。
C: Let me see. Oh, I'm sorry. My mistake. My seat is 30L. I'll move now.	C：我看看。哦，不好意思。我看錯了。我的座位應該是 30L。我現在馬上就換。
A: Thank you for your help. <u>By the way, could you help me with my carry-on luggage?</u> All the overhead compartments seem to be full. Is there anywhere else I can put it?	A：謝謝您的幫忙。順便問一下，您能幫我放一下行李嗎？行李架上似乎已經滿了。還有別的地方可以放嗎？
B: I'm really sorry about this. I will check to see if there are empty overhead compartments anywhere. If you'd like, you can also place your bag under the seat in front of you.	B：真的很抱歉，我會查看一下還有沒有地方可以放。如果您願意的話，也可以把您的行李放在您前面座椅的下方。

場景問答必會句

> **Could you check it for me?**
> 您可以幫我確認一下嗎？

還可以這樣說：

- Excuse me. Where is 13L located? 請問 13L 在哪裡呢？
- Is this seat 40A? 這是 40A 座位嗎？
- I guess my seat is taken. 我想我的座位被人坐了。

對方可能這樣回答：

- Let me see. It's in the third row near the window. 我看看，它在第三排靠窗戶的位置。

> **By the way, could you help me with my carry-on luggage?**
> 順便問一下，您能幫我放一下行李嗎？

還可以這樣說：

- Can I put my baggage here?
  我可以把我的行李放在這裡嗎？

PS

carry-on *a.* 可隨身攜帶的

Scene 30　機上服務 Flight Service

 場景對話

A: May I have a pack of cards?

A：能給我拿副紙牌嗎？

B: Sorry, we don't have any cards available right now.

B：對不起，我們現在沒有紙牌。

A: Never mind. I would like to listen to some music. But it seems my headphones are not working.

A：沒關係。我想聽聽音樂。但我的耳機好像壞了。

B: Let me get you another pair.

B：我再為您拿一副耳機。

A: Thank you. By the way, can I use the lavatories in first-class?

A：謝謝你。順便問一下，我能用頭等艙的洗手間嗎？

B: I'm sorry but those lavatories are for first-class passengers only.

B：很抱歉，但頭等艙的洗手間僅限頭等艙客人使用。

A: I see. Oh, can you show me how to use this remote control?

A：明白了。哦，你能不能演示一下怎麼使用這個遙控器？

B: Sure. Push the "up" and "down" buttons on your remote control, so you can change channels and adjust volume.

B：當然可以。按遙控器上的"上"和"下"按鍵，您就可以切換頻道和調節音量。

A: Thank you very much.

A：非常感謝。

場景問答必會句

> Let me get you another pair.
> 我再為您拿一副耳機。

還可以這樣說：

- Please enjoy this magazine while you are waiting.
  請在等待的時候，翻看一下這本雜誌吧。
- I will bring you a new pair immediately.
  我立即為您拿一副新的來。

> Oh, can you show me how to use this remote control?
> 哦，你能不能演示一下怎麼使用這個遙控器？

還可以這樣說：
- Please tell me how to fasten the seat belt?
  您可以告訴我怎麼繫安全帶嗎？
- Excuse me, how do I recline my seat?
  請問椅背要怎麼放下來？

對方可能這樣回答：
- Sure, let me help you.
  當然可以，我來幫你。
- Look, all you need to do is to press that button.
  看，只要按一下那個按鈕就可以了。

PS

remote control 遙控器

recline v. 使傾斜

Scene 31　機內飲食 Have Meals on the Plane

 場景對話

A: Excuse me, Madam. What would you like to eat?	A：打擾一下，女士，您要吃些什麼？
B: I'd like a beefsteak and a cup of coffee.	B：我要一份牛排和一杯咖啡。
A: Please put down the table in front of you. You can put your meal on it. Here you are. Enjoy your meal.	A：請放下您前面的小桌板，您可以把餐點放在上面。您的餐點。請慢用。
B: Thanks a lot. May I have some more bread, please? I'm a little hungry.	B：非常感謝。請問可以再給我一些麵包嗎？我有點餓了。
A: OK. Here you are.	A：好的，給您。
B: Thank you very much.	B：太謝謝你了。
A: You are welcome. Please press that button if you need any help.	A：不客氣。如果需要任何服務請按那個按鈕。
B: OK.	B：好的。

場景問答必會句

I'd like a beef steak and a cup of coffee.
我要一份牛排和一杯咖啡。

還可以這樣說：

💬 May I have a vegetarian meal instead?
我可以換份素餐嗎？

💬 I've finished. Please take the tray away.
我吃完了，請把餐盤拿走吧。

💬 Can I have lunch later? I don't feel well right now.
可以過會兒再吃午餐嗎？我現在有點不舒服。

對方可能這樣問：

💬 We have chicken with noodles and pork with rice. Which would you like?
我們有雞肉面和豬肉飯，您要哪個？

💬 Would you care for something to drink?
請問您想喝點什麼？

vegetarian *a.* 素食的

tray *n.* 餐盤

care for 喜歡

Scene **32** 感到不適 Feel Uncomfortable

 🗨️ 場景對話

A: Did you press the call button just now, sir?

A：先生，請問剛才是您按了呼叫鍵嗎？

B: Yes, I did. I feel like vomiting, and I'm dizzy.

B：是的。我有點想吐，感覺頭暈。

A: Sorry to hear that. I think you are suffering from airsickness.

A：很遺憾聽到您這樣說。我想您可能暈機了。

B: And I feel the pains in my head after take-off.

B：而且起飛後我還覺得頭痛。

A: That is caused by the change of air pressure.

A：這是氣壓改變導致的。

B: Yes, I know. Could you please get some airsickness medicine for me?

B：是的，我知道。請問可以給我一些暈機藥嗎？

A: OK. Please wait a minute. Here's the medicine and a glass of water. If you want to vomit, please use the airsick bag in the seat pocket in front of you.

A：可以，請您稍等一下。這是藥和水。如果您想嘔吐，請吐在位於您前方座椅靠背的清潔袋裡。

B: Thank you very much.

B：非常感謝。

A: You're welcome. By the way, you can relieve the earache by wearing the headphone. Thus you will feel better.

A：不客氣。順便告訴您，戴上耳機可以緩解耳朵疼，這樣您會感覺舒服一些。

| B: I hope so. It's my first time to take a plane. Thank you very much. | B：但願有效。這是我第一次坐飛機，真是非常感謝你。 |
| A: It's my pleasure. | A：樂意為您效勞。 |

場景問答必會句

> I feel like vomiting, and I'm dizzy.
> 我有點想吐，感覺頭暈。

還可以這樣說：

- After that turbulence, I feel like I might throw up.
  經過那樣氣流之後，我覺得我快吐了。
- I feel sick.
  我有點不舒服。
- My ears feel funny.
  我有點耳鳴。
- This is terrible. I have to go to the toilet.
  這太糟糕了，我必須去一趟廁所。

PS

vomit *v.* 嘔吐

dizzy *a.* 暈的

turbulence *n.* 亂流

> Could you please get some airsickness medicine for me?
> 請問可以給我一些暈機藥嗎？

還可以這樣說：

- May I have some medicine for airsickness?
  請給我一些暈機藥好嗎？
- May I have an airsick bag?
  請給我一隻嘔吐袋好嗎？
- Is there a doctor on board?
  飛機上有醫生嗎？

對方可能這樣回答：

- Sure, wait a minute. I'll be back soon.
  好的，請稍等。我馬上回來。
- Just a minute. Let me get the airsick bag ready. Here.
  等一下，讓我先把嘔吐袋準備好。給您。
- Here is an airsick bag.
  這裡有嘔吐袋。

PS

airsickness medicine 暈機藥

on board 在飛機上

在飛機上 Tips

1. 機上設施

• 機艙設施

fasten the seat belt 繫好安全帶	earphone jack 耳機插孔
attendant call button 空服人員的呼叫按鈕	rack 行李架
reading light 閱讀燈	reclining button 座椅調整按鈕
airsick bag 嘔吐袋	life jacket 救生衣

• 機上洗手間

OCCUPIED 使用中	VACANT 無人使用
RETURN TO THE SEAT 請回到座位	paper towel 紙巾
waste disposal 垃圾桶	toilet seat 馬桶座
emergency button 緊急按鈕	cosmetics 化妝品
faucet 水龍頭	

2. 飛機餐

• 飛機餐的種類

一趟航班上的飛機餐是根據你乘坐的艙位級別來定的：

a. 頭等艙及商務艙的飛機餐，進餐的順序以及食物都儘量模仿高級餐廳，不僅食物可口，餐具也是高級貨。除此之外還會提供鮮榨果汁。

b. 經濟艙的飛機餐，食物與快餐店類似。

c. 如果乘客有特殊需要，可以在訂票時或者出發前 24 小時通知航空公司準備特別飛機餐。特別飛機餐中包括兒童餐、供糖尿病等慢性病患者享用的低鹽或低糖餐、素食餐、特別宗教要求餐等。

Unit 2 行李事宜

商務出差或多或少都會帶些行李，出境時需要辦理行李託運，入境時要領取行李，如若不幸找不到行李了，還得去行李招領處報失。

行李事宜必會詞

➊ free allowance 免費額

這裡指的是行李免費額，即乘客可以免費攜帶的行李重量。各家航空公司免費行李的重量規定會有差異，在訂機票時記得詢問清楚。

➋ luggage tag 行李牌

指識別行李的標誌和旅客領取託運行李的憑證，是個帶有編號、名字、字母等信息的牌子。

➌ hand luggage 手提行李

和 hand luggage 相對應的則是 hold luggage，指託運的行李。hold 在此指的是船、飛機等的貨倉。

這些小詞你也要會哦：

scale *n.* 磅秤	allowance *n.* 限制重量	Luggage Depository 行李存放處
weigh *v.* 稱	check in 託運	kilo *n.* 千克
suitcase *n.* 行李箱	leather *n.* 皮質	medium size 中型

Scene 33 行李限重 The Allowance of Luggage

場景對話

A: Do you have baggage to check in?	A：請問您有行李需要託運嗎？
B: Yes, I have a suitcase and a briefcase.	B：有，我有一個行李箱和一個公文包。
A: All right. Please put the suitcase on the scale.	A：好的，請您把行李箱放在秤上。

B: OK. I think it weighs about twenty-five kilograms. Is it overweight?	B：好，我想行李箱大概重 25 千克。超重了嗎？
A: No. It weighs thirty kilograms and the allowance is fifty kilograms.	A：沒有超重，行李箱重 30 千克，而我們的限重是 50 千克。
B: OK. <u>Could I take this briefcase as my hand baggage?</u>	B：好的，<u>請問我可以把這個公文包作為隨身行李嗎？</u>
A: Sure.	A：可以。
B: Oh! By the way, I have already earned nearly 20,000 air miles. Can I upgrade to business class?	B：對了，我差不多已經累積了 2 萬英里的里程，可以給我升到商務艙嗎？
A: Sorry, there is no available business-class seat today. If you like, I can put you on the list for the return trip, though.	A：很抱歉。商務艙今天已經客滿了，如果您願意的話，我可以把您列到回程的升艙名單裡。
B: That will be great!	B：那太好了！

📖A 場景問答必會句

> I have a suitcase and a briefcase.
> 我有一個行李箱和一個公文包。

還可以這樣說：

🖮 I want to check these three pieces.
我想託運這三件行李。

🖮 Can I check in my cosmetics?
我可以託運我的化妝品嗎？

對方可能這樣問：

🖮 Do you need to check for any of your luggage?
您有行李需要託運嗎？

🖮 How many pieces of baggage do you want to check?
您有多少件託運行李？

cosmetic *n.* 化妝品

luggage *n.* 行李

> Could I take this briefcase as my hand baggage?
> 請問我可以把這個公文包作為隨身行李嗎？

還可以這樣說：

🖮 How many carry-on bags can I have?
我能隨身帶多少行李？

carry-on *a.* 可隨身攜帶的

Scene 34 提取行李 Claim the Luggage

 場景對話

A: May I help you, Madam?	A：女士，需要幫忙嗎？
B: Yes. Can you please tell me where the baggage claim area for Flight SU324 is?	B：是的，你能告訴我 SU324 航班的行李提取處在哪兒嗎？
A: It's right there, at carrousel No.5.	A：就在那裡。5 號傳送帶。
B: Thank you. But I haven't seen any luggage on the carrousel yet.	B：謝謝。但是我還沒在傳送帶上看見任何行李。
A: Don't worry. I'm sure it will come soon. And it is possible that the baggage which is checked in earlier would come out later.	A：別急，我肯定您的行李很快就會出來。有可能辦理託運時間較早的行李，出來的時間會晚一些。
B: You're right. Oh look, here is the baggage! The red one over there is mine. It is coming to us. Thanks a lot.	B：你是對的。哦，看，行李過來了！那個紅色的是我的。正朝着我們這邊來了。非常感謝。
A: You are welcome. Good-bye.	A：不客氣，再見。
B: Good-bye.	B：再見。

場景問答必會句

> Can you please tell me where the baggage claim area for Flight SU324 is?
> 你能告訴我 SU324 航班的行李提取處在哪兒嗎？

還可以這樣說：
- Which carrousel is for Flight TY836?
  請問 TY836 航班的行李在哪個轉盤？
- Where are the baggage carts?
  請問哪裡有行李手推車？

PS

carrousel *n.* 行李轉盤

baggage cart 行李手推車

> Oh look, here is the baggage! The red one over there is mine. It is coming to us.
> 哦，看，行李過來了！那個紅色的是我的。正朝着我們這邊來了。

還可以這樣說：
- This looks like one of my suitcases. 這看起來像我的一件行李。
- This one is definitely mine because it has my name tag on it.
  這一定是我的，因為上面有我的姓名牌。

Scene 35　行李報失 Report the Missing Luggage

 場景對話

A: What's the matter with you, Madam? You look pale and anxious.

A：女士，發生了什麼事情？您的臉色蒼白而且看起來很焦慮。

B: Jesus, I lost my baggage just now.

B：天啊，我剛剛把我的行李弄丟了。

A: Take it easy. Would you please tell me more details? I will try to help you.

A：別緊張，你能告訴我更多具體的細節嗎？我會盡力幫助你的。

B: Thank you. I just went to the cafe and left my luggage under the table. When I finished my coffee, I found my suitcase had gone.

B：謝謝，我剛才去了咖啡廳，並且把行李放在了桌子下面。當我喝完咖啡之後，我發現我的行李箱不見了。

A: What kind of suitcase is it?

A：您丟失的行李箱是什麼樣子的呢？

B: It is a large leather suitcase, with my name tag on the top and my personnel stuff inside.

B：是一個大皮箱，頂部有我的姓名牌，裡面是我的私人用品。

A: I feel sorry to hear that. Will you please leave your name and your address here? We will try to find the suitcase for you.

A：真的很遺憾聽到這個消息。您可以把您的姓名和地址留在這裡嗎？我們會盡力幫您找的。

B: How long will it take?

B：需要多長時間呢？

A: Sorry, I have no idea. Will you please wait here for a while? We are going to extend your ticket to the next plane, so you may have enough time to look for your luggage.

A：對不起，我也不知道。你在這裡等一下，好嗎？我們將幫你把機票改簽到下個航班，這樣您就會有充足的時間來找行李。

B: It seems that I have no other choice, doesn't it?

B：看起來我好像沒有其他的選擇了，不是嗎？

 場景問答必會句

I lost my baggage just now.
我剛剛把我的行李弄丟了。

還可以這樣說：

🗨 My luggage is missing.
我的行李丟了。

🗨 My baggage didn't come out of the baggage claim.
行李領取處沒有我的行李。

PS
missing *a.* 找不到的

It is a large leather suitcase, with my name tag on the top and my personnel stuff inside.
是一個大皮箱，頂部有我的姓名牌，裡面是我的私人用品。

還可以這樣說：

🗨 It's a red suitcase with wheels.
是一個有輪子的紅色行李箱。

對方可能這樣問：

🗨 What does your bag look like? 請問您的包是什麼樣子的？

🗨 Please describe your luggage. 請描述一下您的行李。

PS
tag *n.* 標簽

personnel stuff 私人用品

出入境流程 Tips

1. 出境流程圖

Step A	Check-in Counter 到機場航空公司的登機櫃枱辦理登機手續
↓	
Step B	Security Check 旅客及隨身行李檢查
↓	
Step C	Passport Inspection Area / Passport Counter 護照檢查
↓	
Step D	Boarding gate 進入登機口
↓	
Step E	Plane 登機

2. 入境流程

- **通關第一步：Immigration Counter 入境櫃枱**

  提醒大家一定要選擇正確的櫃枱辦理，專門給外國人辦理的櫃枱有：Foreigner（外國人櫃枱）、Non-Citizen（非公民櫃枱）、Non-Resident（非當地居民櫃枱）。事先準備好自己的護照、入境登記表和 return ticket（回程機票）。

- **通關第二步：Baggage Claim 提領行李**

  通關之後到指定的 baggage carousel（行李轉盤）尋找自己的行李，如果你的行李丟失或者破損，就要馬上找機場的工作人員處理。

- **通關第三步：Customs**

  如果你有東西要申報，則需要到 Declare 櫃枱出示你的海關申報表和護照。海關工作人員還會隨機抽查一部分旅客的行李。

Unit 3 兌換貨幣

兌換貨幣是商務出差前不可缺少的準備工作。兌換貨幣前，應先瞭解出差地貨幣的使用情況，事先兌換好當地貨幣，兌換時應儘量根據自己的使用需求，兌換合適的貨幣量。

兌換貨幣必會詞

1 currency exchange 貨幣兌換
指按照一定的匯率將外幣現鈔、旅行支票兌換成當地貨幣（簡稱"兌入"）或者將當地貨幣兌換成外幣現鈔（簡稱"兌回"）的一種交易行為。

2 rate of exchange 匯率
亦稱"外匯行市"或"匯價"，是一種貨幣兌換另一種貨幣的比率，是以一種貨幣表示另一種貨幣的價格。

3 credit card 信用卡
信用卡又叫貸記卡，是一種非現金交易付款的方式，是簡單的信貸服務。

這些小詞你也要會哦：

change n. 零錢	coin n. 硬幣	cheque n. 支票
receipt n. 收據	account n. 賬戶	deposit n. 存款
amount n. 金額	large bill 大面額鈔票	remittance n. 匯款

Scene 36 詢問匯率 Ask about Exchange Rates

 場景對話

A: Good morning, sir. What can I do for you?	A：早上好，先生，我能為您做點什麼呢？
B: Oh, I'd like to change some money. What's the exchange rate of U.S. dollar against British pound today?	B：哦，我要兌換些錢。今天美元兌英鎊的匯率是多少？
A: 1 : 0.62. Would you care to give me your passport?	A：1：0.62。可以把您的護照給我看一下嗎？

B: There you are. Can you exchange these U.S. dollars to British pounds, please?	B：給你，請問能把這些美元兌換成英鎊嗎？
A: Just fill out this form, please.	A：請填一下這個表格。
B: OK.	B：好的。

場景問答必會句

> I'd like to change some money.
> 我要兌換些錢。

還可以這樣說：

🗨 I'd like to change some foreign currency.
　我想兌換一些外幣。

🗨 I'd like to change two hundred US dollars to RMB.
　我想把這 200 美元兌換成人民幣。

PS currency *n.* 貨幣

> What's the exchange rate of U.S. dollar against British pound today?
> 今天美元兌英鎊的匯率是多少？

還可以這樣說：

🗨 What's the rate for the pound today? 今天的英鎊匯率是多少？

🗨 How much will that be in dollars? 換成美元是多少錢？

Scene 37 兌換零錢 Get Change

 場景對話

A: Would you please give me one hundred US dollar change?	A：請幫我換 100 美元零錢可以嗎？
B: How would you like it?	B：您想怎麼換呢？
A: Four tens, ten fives and the rest in ones, please.	A：4 張 10 元的，10 張 5 元的，其餘都要 1 元的。
A: Here you are. By the way, Ms. Zhang, I was wondering if you would ever think of conversing the unused British pounds back into U.S. dollars later.	B：給您。順便問一下，張小姐，不知道您是否考慮以後要把沒有用完的英鎊兌換成美元呢？

B: Yes, if I have British pounds left.	A：是的，如果有沒用完的英鎊，就換成美元。
A: Oh, if I may make a suggestion, please keep your exchange memo safe.	B：那麼，如果我還能提一個建議的話，請您保管好您的這張外幣兌換單。
B: Thank you indeed. I will.	A：我會保管好的。謝謝。
A: Not at all.	B：不用謝。

場景問答必會句

> Would you please give me one hundred US dollar change?
> 請幫我換 100 美元零錢可以嗎？

還可以這樣說：

🗨 Can I get coins for this bill?
我想把這張錢換成硬幣可以嗎？

對方可能這樣回答：

🗨 Sure, are quarters alright? 當然，25 美分的硬幣可以嗎？

quarter *n.* 25 美分

> Four tens, ten fives and the rest in ones, please.
> 4 張 10 元的，10 張 5 元的，其餘都要 1 元的。

還可以這樣說：

🗨 I need four twenties and twenty singles, please.
請給我 4 張 20 元和 20 張 1 元的。

對方可能這樣問：

🗨 How would you like the denomination? 您要什麼面額的？

denomination *n.* 面額

兌換貨幣 Tips

兌換貨幣小妙招

- **兌換貨幣找準時機**
  外幣的匯率每天都在發生變化，所以去境外出差前要根據自己所在地的外匯走勢情況兌換自己所需的外幣，儘量避免因匯率 (Exchange Rate) 轉換帶來的損失。
- **巧用銀聯卡**
  現在，境外很多國家都接受刷銀聯卡了，如韓、日、泰等。刷銀聯卡消費不但方便、快捷，而且在部分免稅店還能享受打折優惠，非常划算。

拜訪客戶

拜訪客戶是很多公司職員雖然頭疼卻不可避免的一項工作。通常，貿然闖進別人的辦公室是不禮貌的行為，所以拜訪客戶要事先預約，確認後才能去拜訪，以表示對別人的尊重。

▌拜訪客戶必會詞▌

① visit *v.* 拜訪
表示拜訪的常用短語還有 call at, drop in。

② spare *a.* 空閒的
拜訪前確認對方是否有時間見面。常用短語有：be available, have spare time, be free。

③ urgent *a.* 緊急的
表達有急事需要見面時就可以用這個詞，"急事"可以用 something urgent 或 to speak with someone urgently 來表示。

✎ 這些小詞你也要會哦：

greeting *n.* 問候	office hours 辦公時間	business card 名片
visiting hours 會客時間	letter of introduction 介紹函	doorbell *n.* 門鈴
reception room 接待室	attend to 照料	appointment 預約

Scene 38 預約拜訪 Make an Appointment

 場景對話

A: Mr. Robert, I'd like to talk with you about our new products. <u>Do you have any spare time today?</u>	A：羅伯特先生，我想跟您談談我們的新產品。<u>您今天有時間嗎？</u>
B: I'm sorry, but I'm all tied up today.	B：對不起，我今天很忙。
A: How about tomorrow?	A：明天怎麼樣？

B: I have a staff meeting at three p.m. I think we can meet before or after that.

B：明天下午 3 點，我有一個員工會議，我想我們可以在會議之前或之後見面。

A: Great. I will see you at two p.m. then. It won't take more than thirty minutes and I will bring some brochures with me.

A：太好了。那我明天下午 2 點去見您。不會佔用您超過 30 分鐘的時間，我會帶一些小冊子過去。

B: Sounds good. I'm looking forward to seeing you tomorrow.

B：很好。期待明天與你見面。

 場景問答必會句

Do you have any spare time today?
您今天有時間嗎？

還可以這樣說：
When is a good time for us to meet?
我們何時會面比較合適呢？

對方可能這樣回答：
Let me check my schedule first. 我先查查日程安排。

PS

spare *a.* 空閒的

I will see you at two p.m. then.
那我們明天下午 2 點去見您。

還可以這樣說：
I will see you this evening. 我們今天晚上見。

對方可能這樣回答：
That's fine with me. 我沒問題。
That's not a good time for me. 這個時間對我來說不太合適。

Scene 39 前往拜訪 Keep an Appointment

 場景對話

A: Hello! Is this the office of the General Manager?

A：您好！這是總經理辦公室嗎？

B: Yes. How can I help you?

B：是的。有什麼可以幫您？

A: My name is Jack, sales manager of the ABC Computer Company. I'm here to see Mr. Dorson.

A：我叫傑克，是 ABC 電腦公司的銷售經理。我來這兒見多爾松先生。

B: Do you have an appointment?	B：您跟他預約了嗎？
A: Yes. I have an appointment with Mr. Dorson at two o'clock.	A：是的，我和多爾松先生約在 2 點見面。
B: Please have a seat. I will let Mr. Dorson know you are here.	B：請坐。我去通知多爾松先生您來了。
A: Thank you.	A：謝謝。
B: Hi, Mr. Jack. Mr. Dorson is ready to see you. This way, please.	B：你好，傑克先生，多爾松先生已經準備好見您了。這邊請。
A: Thank you.	A：謝謝。

場景問答必會句

> **Is this the office of the General Manager?**
> **這是總經理辦公室嗎？**

還可以這樣說：

💬 Excuse me, could you tell me where the General Manager office is?
抱歉打擾，您可以告訴我總經理辦公室在哪兒嗎？

> **I have an appointment with Mr. Dorson at two o'clock.**
> **我和多爾松先生約在 2 點見面。**

還可以這樣說：

💬 Your sales manager told me to come by this morning.
貴公司的銷售經理讓我今早來找他。

💬 Your sales manager said I could come any time before noon.
貴公司的銷售經理說我可以中午以前任何時間過來。

PS

sales manager 銷售經理

對方可能這樣回答：

💬 Mr. Dorson will be right with you. 多爾松先生馬上就來。

💬 Mr. Dorson is a little behind schedule today. 多爾松先生今天的行程有些拖延。

拜訪客戶 Tips

常用打招呼、攀談用語

Nice to meet you. 很高興認識你。	You look great / nice. 你氣色很好。
It's a nice weather, isn't it? 天氣不錯，對吧？	I've heard so much about you. 久仰久仰。

Unit 5 交通出行

外貿活動離不開交通出行，現在各國交通都很便捷，公交、地鐵、出租車等一應俱全，為外貿人員的商務出行提供了很多便利。

交通出行必會詞

1 fare n. 票價
依照規定購買各種票證 (如車票) 的價格。

2 subway n. 地鐵
英國人習慣用 underground 和 tube 表示地鐵，而美國人則習慣用 metro 和 subway。

3 surcharge n. 附加費
常見的附加費有：燃油附加費 (fuel surcharge)、週末附加費 (weekend surcharge)、夜間附加費 (night surcharge) 等。

這些小詞你也要會哦：

block n. 街區	sleeper n. 臥鋪	express n. 快車
fast train 快車	through train 直達列車	ticket machine 售票機
inbound n. 入站	outbound n. 出站	drop v. 讓 (人) 下車

Scene 40 問路 Ask for Direction

 場景對話

A: Excuse me, Madam. Do you speak English?	A：女士，打擾一下，請問您會說英語嗎？
B: Yes. Can I help you?	B：是的，您需要什麼幫助嗎？
A: Do you know where the nearest supermarket Carrefour is?	A：您知道最近的家樂福超市在哪兒嗎？

B: Yes. You go straight ahead through three blocks to Freedom Street, then turn left. It's on the corner, across from the National Theater.	B：是的。一直直走，穿過 3 個街區，到自由大街，然後左轉。家樂福就在拐角處，在國家劇院的對面。
A: OK. Can I repeat this to see if I've understood everything?	A：好的，我能不能重複一下，看看我是不是都明白了？
B: Certainly.	B：當然。
A: Go straight ahead to Freedom Street. Take a left turn, and Carrefour is across from the National Theater.	A：直走到自由大街。左轉，家樂福在國家劇院的對面。
B: Yes, that's right.	B：是的，沒錯。
A: Thank you very much. <u>How far is it from here?</u>	A：非常感謝。<u>離這兒有多遠？</u>
B: It's a fifteen-minute walk.	B：走路 15 分鐘。
A: Thanks again for your help.	A：再次感謝您的幫助。

場景問答必會句

> Do you know where the nearest supermarket Carrefour is?
> 您知道最近的家樂福超市在哪兒嗎？

還可以這樣說：

🗨 Excuse me, are there any banks around here?
請問，附近有銀行嗎？

對方可能這樣回答：

🗨 Go straight down the street. You will find it.
沿着這條街直走，就能看見。

🗨 Keep going until you come to a dead end.
順着這條路一直走到盡頭。

PS

Go straight down...
沿着……一直走

dead end 盡頭

> How far is it from here?
> 離這兒有多遠？

還可以這樣說：

🗨 Will it take me long to get there?
到那兒要花很長時間嗎？

🗨 Excuse me, do you know how far we are from the nearest subway station?
請問，你知道這兒離最近的地鐵站有多遠嗎？

🗨 Is the Red Tea House just around the corner?
紅茶館是不是就在附近啊？

對方可能這樣回答：
- It's about ten minutes away.
  大約 10 分鐘的路程。
- It's not within walking distance.
  那可不是走路可以到的。

Scene 41　打車 Take a Taxi

 場景對話

A: Hi, taxi!	A：嗨，出租車。
B: Yes, Madam. Can I help you?	B：你好，女士，請問您要去哪裡？
A: 789 Madison Street, please.	A：麻煩去麥迪遜大街 789 號。
B: OK.Which road do you want to take?	B：好的，您想走哪條路？
A: Please take the shortest way. How long will it take to get there?	A：請走最近的路。到那兒要多久？
B: If there are no hold-ups, it's only about twenty minutes' drive.	B：如果不堵車的話，只要大約20分鐘。
A: That's fine. Could you crank up the heat?	A：好的。你可以把暖氣開大一點嗎？
B: Sure, no problem.	B：當然可以，沒問題。
(A while later.)	（過了一會兒。）
B: Here you are, Madam.	B：到了，女士。
A: What's the fare?	A：車費是多少？
B: Eighteen dollars, please.	B：18 美元。
A: Thank you so much indeed. Please keep the change.	A：太感謝了，不用找零了。

場景問答必會句

> Could you crank up the heat?
> 你可以把暖氣開大一點嗎？

還可以這樣說：
- May I open the window? 我可以把窗戶打開嗎？

💬 Could you please slow down?
可以開慢一點兒嗎？

💬 I'm in a hurry. Can you go a little faster?
我趕時間，麻煩您開快一點兒，好嗎？

· 對方可能這樣回答：

💬 It's the middle of rush hour!
這可是高峰時段！

PS
rush hour 高峰時間

> **What's the fare?**
> 車費是多少？

還可以這樣說：

💬 How much will this cost?
這一趟多少錢？

💬 How do I tip?
我怎麼付小費？

對方可能這樣回答：

💬 The meter reads $20.
計價器上顯示 20 美元。

💬 You usually need to tip about 15% of the fare.
小費通常是車費的 15%。

Scene
42 自駕 Drive a Car

 🗨️ 場景對話

A: May I help you?	A：我能幫你什麼嗎？
B: Yes. <u>Fill it up with regular, please.</u>	B：是的。<u>請幫我加滿普通汽油。</u>
A: Sure.	A：好的。
(At the parking lot.)	(在停車場。)
B: <u>Excuse me, is there a parking place?</u>	B：<u>請問一下，還有空停車位嗎？</u>
C: Yes. We have plenty of parking places available now.	C：有的。我們現在還有很多空停車位。
B: All right.	B：好的。
C: Park as far as possible in the parking lot.	C：請盡可能往遠處停放。

B: What is the parking fee per hour here?	B：停車費每小時多少錢？
C: Three pounds an hour.	C：3 英鎊。
B: How much would it be if I park here for an hour and fifteen minutes?	B：那如果我要停 1 小時 15 分鐘，應該付多少錢？
C: Six pounds, because we charge by the number of hours.	C：6 英鎊。因為我們是按小時數收費的。
B: I see.	B：我懂了。
C: Here is the ticket.	C：給您停車票。
B: Thank you.	B：謝謝。

場景問答必會句

Fill it up with regular, please.
請幫我加滿普通汽油。

還可以這樣說：
- Fill it up with unleaded gas, please.
  請加滿無鉛汽油。
- Two gallons, please.
  請加兩加侖汽油。

fill up 裝滿

unleaded gas 無鉛汽油

Excuse me, is there a parking place?
請問一下，還有空停車位嗎？

還可以這樣說：
- Can I park the car here?
  我可以在這兒停車嗎？
- Is there any paid parking lot near the office building?
  寫字樓附近有收費停車場嗎？

對方可能這樣回答：
- The parking lot was jammed with cars.
  停車場滿了。
- You can park your car in front of the building.
  你可以把車停在大樓前面。

jam with 擠滿

in front of 在……前面

Scene 43　坐火車 Take the Train

 場景對話

A: Hello, I would like to buy a ticket to London.	A：你好，我想買一張去倫敦的車票。
B: Regular or express train?	B：普通車還是快車？
A: Is it going to make a big difference if I take the express?	A：如果我坐快車會有很大區別嗎？
B: Well, you can arrive in London two hours earlier. Meanwhile, it costs more. The next express train departs at 2:15 p.m.	B：坐快車可以提前 2 個小時到達倫敦，但同時，票價要高一些。下一班快車在 2 點 15 分發車。
A: Is there a student discount if I buy the express ticket?	A：購買快車票，有學生優惠價嗎？
B: Yes, there's a 20% discount if you have an international student card. First class costs seventy-five pounds, and second class sixty-two pounds.	B：是的，如果您有國際學生卡可以打 8 折。一等座 75 英鎊，二等座 62 英鎊。
A: OK. I will take one first-class ticket for the express.	A：好。那麼來一張快車的一等座票。
B: All right.	B：好的。

場景問答必會句

> I would like to buy a ticket to London.
> 我想買一張去倫敦的車票。

還可以這樣說：
- Two lower bunks in a soft sleeper, please.
  我要兩張軟臥下鋪車票。
- Is this a through train?
  這是直達車嗎？

對方可能這樣回答：
- One moment, please, I'll check it out. 等一下，我查查看。
- No. There are three stops. 不是直達。途中要停三站。

PS

lower bunk 下鋪

through train 直達快車

Is there a student discount if I buy the express ticket?
購買快車票，有學生優惠價嗎？

還可以這樣說：

Is there a discount for children?
兒童票打折嗎？

How much for a ticket to New York?
去紐約的票價是多少？

How much more do I have to pay for the express? 買快車票需要加付多少錢？

Scene
44 公交出行 Take the Bus

 場景對話

A: Move along, please. There are more people waiting to get on. Move to the rear.	A：請往後走。還有很多人等着上車，請往後面走一下。
B: How much is the fare, please?	B：票價是多少？
A: Fifty cents. Drop it in the box.	A：50 美分。請直接投到投幣箱。
B: Thank you. I'd like to transfer to the 55th Street crosstown bus.	B：謝謝。我想要換乘第 55 大街的穿城巴士。
A: Here you are. There's no charge for transfers.	A：給你轉車牌。換乘不收額外費用。
B: Is it good on any crosstown bus?	B：乘坐所有穿城巴士都可以嗎？
A: Yes.	A：是的。
B: I'm going to the Fifth Avenue. Is 55th Street my best way to get there?	B：我想去第五大道。是不是從第 55 大街出發是我的最佳路線？
A: No. Actually you should get bus No.9 across the street.	A：不。你應該到馬路對面坐 9 路公交車。
B: Oh, I see. Thank you very much.	B：哦，我知道了。非常感謝。

 場景問答必會句

How much is the fare, please?
票價是多少？

還可以這樣說：

💬 How much does it cost to get to the Fifth Avenue?
到第五大道多少錢？

💬 Can I use my commuter's pass?
可以用月票嗎？

Is 55th Street my best way to get there?
是不是從第 55 大街出發是我的最佳路線？

還可以這樣說：

💬 Which bus should I take?
我應該乘哪路車去呢？

💬 Will you tell me when I need to get off?
你能告訴我在哪兒下車嗎？

Scene 45 坐地鐵 Take the Subway

  場景對話

A: Excuse me, could you please lend me a hand?	A：勞駕一下，請問您能幫我一下嗎？
B: Yes?	B：怎麼了？
A: I'd like to go to Broadway by subway. Could you please help me?	A：我想坐地鐵去百老匯。您知道怎麼坐車嗎？
B: OK. Take this train and get off at the next station.	B：知道，坐這輛地鐵，然後下一站下車就行。
A: Do I need to transfer?	A：需要換乘嗎？
B: No, you don't.	B：不，不需要。
A: Where can I buy a ticket?	A：我在哪兒可以買到票呢？
B: Over there. At the token booth.	B：那邊。自動售票機那裡。
A: Okay, thanks. By the way, how can I get to the platform?	A：好的，謝謝您。順便問一句，我怎麼才能到站台上去呢？
B: Just go down those steps.	B：就從那邊台階下去。
A: Thank you.	A：謝謝。

場景問答必會句

> I'd like to go to Broadway by subway. Could you please help me?
> 我想坐地鐵去百老匯。您知道怎麼坐車嗎？

還可以這樣說：

- Which subway line should I take?
  我該坐哪趟地鐵呢？
- How often does the subway come?
  地鐵多長時間來一趟？

> Where can I buy a ticket?
> 我在哪兒可以買到票呢？

還可以這樣說：

- Do I have to pay an additional fare to change trains?
  換乘地鐵需要額外付費嗎？

對方可能這樣回答：

- Do you see that sign? It is just over there.
  看到那個標誌了嗎？就在那邊。

交通出行 Tips

1. 英國公交車票種類豐富，有一日之內有效的兩地往返票，有一日之內在一定區域內不限次數乘坐的日票等，各種票價位不同。
2. 英國火車非常發達，火車票分為單程和往返，且價格差異很小。
3. 在美國，市區的公交一般都是投幣式的，所以上車前一定要準備好零錢！如果需要轉乘的話，司機會給你一張 transfer card(轉乘卡)，這樣下一段公交車程就會比較便宜甚至免費！

Chapter 3

商貿營銷——
多方位多渠道的營銷

Unit 1　產品介紹

產品介紹是外貿營銷活動中的重要環節。在介紹產品時，應突出產品特色，措辭準確、客觀。

產品介紹必會詞

❶ feature *n.* 特點，功能
產品的特色是產品介紹的重點，具有鮮明特色的產品一定會給客戶留下深刻的印象。

❷ develop *v.* 開發，研發
介紹時，有必要描述產品的研發過程，包括研發週期、開發人員配備等情況來進一步強調產品品質。

❸ performance *n.* 性能
產品性能即產品的用途，是產品的價值所在，使用方便、價格合理，能提高人們的生活品質，或為人們的生活、工作帶來便利的產品，往往都是熱銷商品。

❹ updated *a.* 更新的
人們總是被新事物吸引，"新"也代表着更時尚、更高科技、更完善，強調所介紹的產品是更新換代的產品，也能為產品增色不少。

這些小詞你也要會哦：

high-tech *a.* 高科技的	selling point 賣點	suitable *a.* 適合的
unprecedented *a.* 前所未有的	profit *n.* 利潤	certified *a.* 有保證的
endorse *v.* 認可	version *n.* 版本	gratifying *a.* 令人滿意的

Scene 46　性能介紹 Performance Introduction

場景對話

A: Mr. McCain, you will find the new features of this digital camera very exciting.

A：麥凱恩先生，您會發現我們這款數碼相機的一些新特性非常精彩。

B: Tell me about it, please.	B：請跟我講講吧。
B: It has an auto-rotate feature; that is to say, it will automatically rotate pictures that you take.	A：它有自動旋轉功能，也就是說，它會自動旋轉你拍的照片。
B: How does it work?	B：具體怎麼實現？
A: Let me show you. You may just press this button to turn on the auto-rotate feature. Then the picture will automatically be oriented.	A：讓我給您展示一下。你只要按下這個按鈕就可以打開自動旋轉功能。照片就會自動定向。
B: I see. That's pretty cool.	B：我明白了。這非常酷。

場景問答必會句

> You will find the new features of this digital camera very exciting.
> 您會發現我們這款數碼相機的一些新特性非常精彩。

還可以這樣說：

🗨 You will be impressed by the new product we have developed.
我們開發的新產品一定會給您留下深刻的印象。

🗨 We present you with our newly developed digital camera.
讓我們向您展示我們最新研發的數碼相機。

PS
impress v. 給某人留下深刻的印象

digital camera 數碼相機

> It has an auto-rotate feature.
> 它有自動旋轉功能。

還可以這樣說：

🗨 The battery lasts longer.
電池的續航能力更強。

🗨 It's easy to carry around.
攜帶方便。

對方可能這樣回答：

🗨 Could you show me how it works?
你能演示給我看看這個功能是如何實現的嗎？

🗨 Would you demonstrate it, please?
能請你演示一下嗎？

PS
demonstrate v. 演示

Scene 47　產品定位 Product Positioning

 場景對話

A: Mr. Hanson, I'd like to emphasize that the softwares in this cell phone can be totally customized.

A：漢森先生，我想強調一下，這款手機的軟件可以完全定製。

B: Oh really?

B：哦，真的嗎？

A: Yes. This model is especially designed for business people. Once they submit their preference, it can be realized.

A：是的。這個型號是特別為商務人士設計的。當他們提交他們的偏好後，就可以實現定製。

B: Sounds pretty useful.

B：聽起來很有用。

A: Yeah. We also designed an email system which can receive emails for people who are away from their computers.

A：是的。我們還專門設計了一套電子郵件系統，可以幫不在電腦前的人接收電子郵件。

B: You mean the emails can be synchronized to their cell phones.

B：你的意思是郵件可以被同步到他們的手機上。

A: Exactly.

A：是的。

場景問答必會句

I'd like to emphasize that the softwares in this cell phone can be totally customized.
我想強調一下，這款手機的軟件可以完全定製。

還可以這樣說：
🖫 This device is waterproof. 這款設備防水。

對方可能這樣問：
🖫 What makes your smart phones stand out?
你們的智能手機為什麼可以脫穎而出？

PS

waterproof *a.* 防水的

This model is especially designed for business people.
這個型號是特別為商務人士設計的。

還可以這樣說：
🖫 This product is just what you need. 這款產品正符合您的需要。
🖫 We strongly recommend this for your company. 我們向你們公司大力推薦這款產品。
🖫 It is specially designed for housewives. 該產品是為家庭主婦量身定製的。

Scene 48 與競爭產品的比較 Compare with Competitors' Products

 場景對話

A: Mr. Lee, your presentation is very impressive. But how can you convince me that you are the best on the market?	A：李先生，你的演示令人印象深刻。但是你如何說服我讓我相信你的產品是市場上最好的？
B: First of all, <u>our design is more attractive.</u>	B：首先，<u>我們的設計更有吸引力。</u>
A: Yes. I can see that. The design of your product is very tasty.	A：是的。我看得出來。你的產品設計很有品位。
B: Second, <u>we adopted the most advanced technology.</u>	B：其次，<u>我們採用了最先進的技術。</u>
A: So far I have never seen any product that can do the same as yours.	A：到目前為止，我從來沒有見過任何其他的產品，可以做跟你的產品所能做的同樣的事情。
B: Right. And our product is more compact and easy to carry around.	B：沒錯，而且我們的產品更小巧，便於攜帶。
A: That's a big plus.	A：這是一個大優勢。

場景問答必會句

> Our design is more attractive.
> 我們的設計更有吸引力。

還可以這樣說：
- Our design is more pleasing to the eye.
  我們的設計看起來更賞心悅目。

對方可能這樣問：
- How do you compare this product to the others?
  這個產品與其他產品相比如何？
- What makes this model better than the others?
  這款模型跟其他相比，好在哪裡？

PS
attractive *a.* 吸引人的

> We adopted the most advanced technology.
> 我們採用了最先進的技術。

還可以這樣說：

💬 This product's selling point is its advanced technology.
這款產品的賣點是其先進的技術。

💬 Our price is very competitive.
我們的價格很具競爭力。

adopt *v.* 採用

advanced *a.* 先進的

Scene 49 商務諮詢 Business Consulting

💬 場景對話

A: Hello. My name is Jack. I'm working for Wanyuan Import and Export Company.

A：您好，我是傑克。我在萬源進出口公司工作。

B: Hello. How can I help you?

B：您好，有什麼可以幫您？

A: We are a manufacturer of bamboo products and your Chamber of Commerce recommended you as a possible agent for our products in your country. We wonder whether we could establish business relationships with each other.

A：我們是一家竹製品生產商。貴國商會向我推薦貴公司，說貴公司有可能在貴國代理我司產品。我們想知道，是否能與貴公司建立業務關係。

B: Would you care to send us some samples with the quotations?

B：您能發送一些樣品和報價給我們嗎？

A: No problem. Please send me your address in e-mail. My email address is jack@wanyuan.com.

A：沒問題。請用電子郵件發給我您的地址。我的電子郵箱是 jack@wanyuan.com。

B: Okay. I will send an email to you right away.

B：好。我會馬上給您發郵件。

🅰 場景問答必會句

Your Chamber of Commerce recommended you as a possible agent for our products in your country.
貴國商會向我推薦貴公司，說貴公司有可能在貴國代理我司產品。

還可以這樣說：

💬 I have got your company's information from the ABC website.
我從 ABC 網站得知了貴公司的信息。

💬 We found your contact information on line.
我們從網上得知了您的聯繫方式。

Chamber of Commerce
商會

We wonder whether we could establish business relationships with each other.
我們想知道，能否與貴公司建立業務關係。

還可以這樣說：
💬 We wish to trade with you in this line of business. 我希望在此行業與您進行貿易合作。

對方可能這樣回答：
💬 Could you tell me more about your company? 您能再多介紹一些你們公司的情況嗎？
💬 I would love the opportunity to work with you. 我很高興與貴方合作。

Scene 50　產品展示與體驗 Present and Experience Products

 場景對話

A: Hello, Miss Kim. It's a pleasure to meet you.	A: 你好，金小姐。很高興見到你。
B: Nice to meet you.	B: 我也很高興見到你。
A: Welcome to our trade show.	A: 歡迎您來到我們的展會。
B: I have been anxious to see your new product.	B: 我非常期待看到你們的新產品。
A: Thank you for your interest. Let me familiarize you with our newly designed foldable road bicycle. As you can see, it's compact and especially designed for the female customers.	A: 謝謝您對我們的產品感興趣。讓我為您介紹一下我們最新設計的可折疊公路自行車。您可以看到，車型很小巧，是專門為女性用戶設計的。
B: I like the color. Can I have a try?	B: 車身顏色我很喜歡。我能試騎一下嗎？
A: Sure.	A: 當然可以。
B: It's not hard to control.	B: 這車很好控制。
A: Yes. And it has multiple gears to make cycling much easier.	A: 是的，車有多種變速齒輪讓您的騎行更輕鬆。

場景問答必會句

Welcome to our trade show.
歡迎來到我們的展會。

還可以這樣說：

🗨 Welcome to our company.
   歡迎來到我們公司。

🗨 We want to extend our warmest welcome to all of you.
   熱烈歡迎大家的到來。

extend *v.* 給予

Let me familiarize you with our newly designed foldable road bicycle.
讓我為您介紹一下我們最新設計的可折疊公路自行車。

還可以這樣說：

🗨 You can download the catalogue on our website.
   您可以在我們的網站上下載產品目錄。

對方可能這樣回答：

🗨 I like the color of it. 我喜歡車身的顏色。

🗨 What's the selling point of it? 車的賣點是什麼？

foldable *a.* 可折疊的

catalogue *n.* 產品目錄

產品介紹 Tips

產品介紹常用句型

- **開場白：**

Thank you for taking the time to...
感謝你抽時間來……

I'd like to take this opportunity to present ... to you.
我想藉此機會向您展示……

- **介紹產品：**

The first thing I would like to talk about is...
首先，我想介紹的是……

Its ability to ... is particularly impressive.
它的……功能尤其令人印象深刻。

In comparison, our product is more...
相比之下，我們的產品更加……

- **結束句：**

Thank you for your attention. 感謝您的關注。

Now we will take the questions. 現在大家可以提問了。

Unit 2 參加商業展會

商業展會是指多家企業集中在一起，向參觀者展示自己的商品，從而把自己的商品銷售出去的一種促銷方式。

參加商業展會必會詞

1 exhibit *n.* 展品

exhibit directory 參觀指南 (主要列出參展商的名單和位置)。

> **PS** exhibit 還有 "展位" 的意思，此時可與 booth 互換。

2 Export License 出口許可證

在國際貿易中，根據一國出口商品管制相關法令規定，由有關當局簽發的准許出口的證件。

3 Import License 進口許可證

在國際貿易中，根據一國進口商品管制相關法令規定，由有關當局簽發的准許進口的證件。

4 move-out 撤展期

撤展期是指展覽閉幕的日期，要注意展品處理、展架拆除、道具退還等事項。

5 move-in 佈展期

展會開始之前佈置準備工作的期限。

這些小詞你也要會哦：

pamphlet *n.* 小冊子	patent *n.* 專利權	manual *n.* 手冊
attendee *n.* 出席者	venue *n.* 場所	plan *n.* 平面圖
installation *n.* 安裝	leaflet *n.* 傳單	sample *n.* 樣品

Scene 51 預訂展位 Booth Reservation

 場景對話

A: Hello! This is USA International Fashion Fabric Exhibition. What can I do for you?	A：您好，美國國際時裝面料展。有什麼可以幫您嗎？

B: Hi! I'd like to register for 2015 USA International Fashion Fabric Exhibition.	B：您好，我想報名參加 2015 年美國國際時裝面料展。
A: <u>Would you please tell me your name and your email address?</u>	A：能告訴我您的名字和郵箱地址嗎？
B: My name is Zhang Yan and my email address is zhangyan@gmail.com.	B：我叫張燕，我的郵箱是 zhangyan@gmail.com。
A: OK. Currently, there are only a few booths available. It is still possible for you to get one if you send us your registration form and registration fee within one week.	A：好的，目前只剩下幾個展位了，如果您能在一週之內將報名表及報名費提交完畢，還是能得到一個展位的。
B: Thank you. What is the charge for each?	B：謝謝。一個展位多少錢？
A: $4,000 for each corner booth and $4,020 for each center booth.	A：角落的展位是 4000 美元，中心位置的展位是 4020 美元。
B: I'll take a center booth.	B：我要一個中心位置的展位。
A: All right. I'll send you an email to confirm your reservation soon. Please don't forget to send us the registration form and reqistration fee. <u>Anything else I can do for you?</u>	A：好的。我會立刻給您發送一封郵件確認預訂事項。請勿忘記提交報名表和報名費。<u>還有什麼能為您效勞嗎？</u>
B: No, thank you very much. Goodbye!	B：沒有了，非常感謝。再見！
A: Thanks for calling. Goodbye!	A：感謝您的來電。再見！

🗨️ 場景問答必會句

> Would you please tell me your name and your email address?
> 能告訴我您的名字和郵箱地址嗎？

還可以這樣說：

🗨 Do you mind telling me your name and email address?
介意告訴我您的名字和郵箱地址嗎？

> Anything else I can do for you?
> 還有什麼能為您效勞的嗎？

還可以這樣說：

🗨 Is there anything else I can do for you?
還有什麼能為您效勞的嗎？

對方可能這樣回答：

🗨 No, thanks very much for your help.
沒了，非常感謝您的幫助。

Scene 52 展會準備 Preparation for Exhibition

 場景對話

A: Hi! I will participate in your 2015 USA International Fashion Fabric Exhibition. This is the first time for me to attend an exhibition. <u>Can you please tell me something about preparation for it?</u>

A：您好，我將參加 2015 年美國國際時裝面料展。這是我第一次參加展會。您能告訴我如何做準備工作嗎？

B: Of course. First of all, you should make a selection of exhibits. Second of all, prepare publicity materials and quotation.

B：當然。首先，您需要選擇展品。其次，準備宣傳資料和報價單。

A: <u>Do you have any advice about the selection of exhibits?</u>

A：關於選擇展品，您有什麼建議嗎？

B: You should select some new and typical products or samples. Make maximum use of the booth to show your products.

B：您應該選擇一些新的、典型的產品或者樣品。確保最大限度利用好展位來展示您的產品。

A: Got it. Can I distribute pamphlets involving local transportation and travel to attendees?

A：知道了。我可以將一些印有當地交通和旅遊信息的小冊子發給參展者嗎？

B: Sure. This is a good idea. You can also accept media interview.

B：當然可以。這是一個好主意。您也可以接受媒體採訪。

A: Great. How many business cards should I bring with me?

A：好。我應該帶多少張名片？

B: About ten thousand. Plenty is no plague.

B：大約 1 萬張吧。多多益善。

A: OK. Thank you for your advice.

A：好的，謝謝您的建議。

B: You are welcome. I hope you get many clients from this exhibition.

B：不客氣，希望您能在這次展會上收穫很多客戶。

A: Thank you.

A：謝謝您。

場景問答必會句

Can you please tell me something about preparation for it?
您能告訴我如何做準備工作嗎？

還可以這樣說：

🗨 Can you please tell me how to prepare for it? 可以告訴我如何準備嗎？

🗨 Can you please tell me how to make the preparation for it? 可以告訴我如何準備嗎？

對方可能這樣回答：

🗨 Without doubt. Select exhibits, and prepare publicity materials and quotation.
當然。選擇展品，準備宣傳資料和報價單。

> **Do you have any advice about the selection of exhibits?**
> 關於選擇展品，您有什麼建議嗎？

還可以這樣說：

🗨 Please tell me your advice about selecting exhibits. 關於選擇展品，請給點建議。

🗨 Would you like to advise me to select exhibits? 您願意在選擇展品方面給點建議嗎？

🗨 Do you have any suggestion about selecting exhibits? 關於選擇展品，您有什麼建議嗎？

Scene 53 展台搭建 Booth Construction

  場景對話

A: Hi! Does the organizer build the stands?	A：您好，展台是由組織者搭建嗎？
B: Usually, the organizer provides basic shells or modules, and the exhibitors prepare the stands themselves.	B：通常，組織者提供基本的框架和組件，參展商自己佈置展台。
A: Can the exhibitors design their own stands?	A：參展單位可以自己設計展台嗎？
B: Yes, we will do it this way. But, we still need a company that specializes in stand construction. I will discuss with a contractor about the design of our stand in detail this afternoon.	B：可以，我們會這麼做。但是我們仍然需要一個專業的展台搭建公司。今天下午我會與一家承包公司詳細討論展台的設計問題。
A: Yes, we cannot construct the stands ourselves. What things should be taken into consideration?	A：是的，我們不能親自動手搭建。還需要考慮哪些方面？
B: Range of products to be displayed, amenities to be provided, the number of staff on duty, etc.	B：參展的產品範圍，提供的服務設施以及當班人數等。
A: When will the contractor produce the design?	A：承包公司什麼時候設計呢？

B: After we offer some information, such as the space.	B：在我們給出面積等信息之後。
A: OK. Thank you for your help.	A：好的，謝謝您的幫助。
B: You are welcome.	B：不客氣。

 場景問答必會句

> Does the organizer build the stands?
> 展台是由組織者搭建嗎？

還可以這樣說：
- Do we build the stands by ourselves? 展台是由我們自己搭建嗎？

對方可能這樣回答：
- Generally, we use basic shells or modules provided by the organizer to build by ourselves.
  一般來說，我們用組織者提供的基本框架和組件來自己佈置。

> Can the exhibitors design their own stands?
> 參展單位可以自己設計展台嗎？

還可以這樣說：
- Can we design our own stands?
  我們可以自己設計展台嗎？
- Does the organizer allow us to design our own stands?
  組織者允許我們自己設計展台嗎？

對方可能這樣回答：
- Yes, I will design my stand. 是的，我將自行設計我的展台。
- No, the organizer will make that for us. 不，組織者將會為我們設計。

Scene 54 樣品展示 Sample Exhibition

 場景對話

A: Hi! Are these samples?	A：您好，這些是樣品嗎？
B: Yes, they are our new models.	B：是的，這些是新樣品。
A: Would it be possible for me to take some samples back to my company?	A：我可以將一些樣品帶回公司嗎？

B: Sure.It's going to be the pride of our company if you take our samples. We have a variety of styles.	B：當然，如果您帶走我們的樣品，這將會是我們公司的榮幸。我們有各種不同的款式。
A: Could I have these samples for free?	A：這些樣品是免費的嗎？
B: I'm sorry. Our samples are not free of charge, but we can offer you a 20% discount of each sample.	B：對不起，我們的樣品不是免費的，但是每款樣品我們可以為您提供 20% 的折扣。
A: How do you pack them?	A：你們將如何包裝？
B: We always pack it according to the specific request from our clients.	B：我們始終根據客戶的具體要求來包裝。
A: I will take your samples back and see whether our president like them.	A：我會將樣品帶回去，看看我們的董事長是否喜歡。
B: Our products have fine quality as well as low price.	B：我們的產品價廉物美。
A: I will contact you after I get the answer from my president.	A：董事長給出反饋之後，我會再聯繫您。

場景問答必會句

> Would it be possible for me to take some samples back to my company?
> 我可以將一些樣品帶回公司嗎？

還可以這樣說：

- May I take some samples back to my company?
  我可以將一些樣品帶回公司嗎？
- Is it possible for me to take some samples back to my company?
  我是否可以將一些樣品帶回公司呢？

對方可能這樣回答：

- Of course, we have various styles.
  當然，我們有各種不同的款式。
- Sorry, but you can take some brochures.
  不好意思，但是您可以帶走一些宣傳手冊。

> Could I have these samples for free?
> 這些樣品是免費的嗎？

還可以這樣說：

- Are the samples free? 樣品是免費的嗎？
- Could I have these samples free? 我可以免費拿走這些樣品嗎？

對方可能這樣回答：

💬 Sorry, but we can provide you with a 20% discount of each sample.
不好意思，但每款樣品我們可以為您提供 20% 的折扣。

Scene 55 展會中介紹產品 Introduce Products in an Exhibition

 場景對話

A: I'm sorry to interrupt you. I've found some of your exhibits very good in quality and beautiful in design. Would you like to show me the catalogue and the pamphlets?

A：抱歉打擾一下。我發現您的一些展品質量不錯，設計也漂亮。能把目錄和小冊子給我看看嗎？

B: Here you are. These are our silk blouses.

B：給您，這是我們的絲綢襯衫。

A: They are brightly colored and beautifully designed. I've heard that your company has high reputation in my country.

A：這些襯衫色彩鮮豔，設計精美。我聽說過您的公司，在我們國家享有盛譽。

B: Thank you. What about your company?

B：謝謝，您的公司是……？

A: Ours is a company specializing in importing clothes. Thus, I'm interested in your products.

A：我們是一家專門進口服裝的公司。所以，對貴公司的產品很感興趣。

B: Our products are known for good quality. They are very popular overseas and are always in great demand.

B：我們的產品質量優良。在海外很受歡迎，需求量一直很大。

A: Would you like to cooperate with me?

A：您願意跟我們合作嗎？

B: Sure, I wish to establish business relations with you. This is the pricelist, but it serves as a guideline only. I will offer you our best price.

B：當然，我希望能與貴公司建立業務聯繫。這是價格表，但僅供參考。我會給貴公司提供最優惠的價格。

A: Thank you.

A：謝謝您。

B: Do you have specific request for packing? Here are the samples of packing available now.

B：您對包裝有什麼特別要求嗎？這是目前我們使用的包裝樣品。

A: You are quite thoughtful. I think that your packing meets my requirement. Let's make a deal.

A：您想得真周到。我覺得這些包裝符合我的要求。我們做個交易吧。

場景問答必會句

> What about your company?
> 您的公司是……？

還可以這樣說：
- Could I know something about your company?
  我可以瞭解一下貴公司嗎？
- Please introduce your company.
  請介紹一下貴公司。

> Would you like to cooperate with me?
> 您願意跟我們合作嗎？

還可以這樣說：
- Would you like to become my partner?
  您願意成為我的合作夥伴嗎？
- Do you want to cooperate with me?
  您願意和我合作嗎？

對方可能這樣回答：
- Sure, I'd like to be your partner.
  當然，我想要成為您的合作夥伴。
- Of course. It is my honor to cooperate with you.
  當然，與您合作是我的榮幸。
- Yes, I'm very glad to cooperate with you.
  是的，我很高興與您合作。

Scene 56　產品推銷 Product Promotion

場景對話

A: Hello, James. How is the business?	A: 您好，詹姆斯。生意如何？
B: Pretty good. Would you like to have a look at some products which may be suitable for your company?	B: 不錯。您想看看一些產品嗎？這些產品很適合您的公司。
A: Of course. Show them to me, please.	A: 當然，請給我看看。

B: Here they are. What do you think of them?	B: 給您，您認為怎麼樣？
A: They are perfect. How much for each?	A: 非常好。一件多少錢？
B: Our prices are very reasonable. Here is the price list.	B: 我們的價格非常合理。這是價目表。
A: It seems a bit expensive. <u>Can you give me some discount on them?</u>	A: 這似乎有點貴。<u>能給我打折嗎？</u>
B: For friendship's sake, how about a 10% discount?	B: 看在朋友的份上，10% 的折扣怎麼樣？
A: OK. I'll take one hundred pieces. I will order more next time if it goes well.	A: 好的。我先訂 100 件。如果賣得好，下次再多訂些。
B: That's great. They haven't come into the market yet, but we are quite confident that they are going to be top-sellers.	B: 很好。這些產品還沒有上市，但是我堅信它們一定會很暢銷。
A: I hope so.	A: 希望如此。

場景問答必會句

> How is the business?
> 生意如何？

還可以這樣說：
- How is your business going?
  您的生意怎麼樣了？

> Can you give me some discount on them?
> 能給我打折嗎？

還可以這樣說：
- Can you offer me some discount?
  能給我打折嗎？
- Do you grant any discount for this order?
  您能給我這次的訂單打折嗎？

對方可能這樣回答：
- For the friendship's sake, how do you like a 10% discount?
  看在朋友的份上，您覺得 10% 的折扣怎麼樣？
- Sorry, this is the lowest price.
  不好意思，這已經是最低價了。

參加商業展會 Tips

參加商業展會函電

Dear Henry,

How are you doing?

We sincerely invite you and your company representatives to participate in the 2015 Shanghai Shoes Exhibition.

There were a lot of business dealings between us in 2014, but you have not ordered any products from us this year. I guess there is some misunderstanding. Thus, we invite you to this exhibition and we can communicate face to face.

It would be a great pleasure to meet you there. We expect to establish long-term business relations with your company in future.

Date: September 1 to September 9, 2015

Booth Number: 6688

Address: Shanghai Everbright Convention & Exhibition Center

Sincerely,

Zou Liang

親愛的亨利：

最近好嗎？

在此，我們誠摯地邀請您以及貴公司的代表參加 2015 年上海鞋展。

我們在 2014 年有很多的業務往來，但是今年貴公司還沒有在我司訂購任何產品。我猜這中間可能存在些誤會。所以，我們邀請貴公司來參加這次展會，我們也可以面對面地交流一下。

我們非常高興能在展會見到您。我們期待未來能和貴公司建立長期的業務關係。

日期：2015 年 9 月 1 日至 9 月 9 日

展位：6688

地址：上海光大會展中心

鄒亮

敬上

Unit 3 市場調研

市場調研，是指為了提高產品的銷量，解決存在於產品銷售中的問題或為開拓市場等進行的識別、收集、分析和傳播營銷信息的工作。

市場調研必會詞

1 questionnaire *n.* 問卷
市場調研是收集數據的一種方式，是一種通過將問題匯總，打印出來形成問卷，交給被調查者填寫從而獲得調查信息的方式。

2 evaluation *v.* 評估
指在市場調研活動中對調查數據的評價、判斷。

3 statistic *n.* 統計數據
通過多種形式的調研活動獲取的數據總稱。

4 strategy *n.* 戰略，策略
指為了實現經營目標而制訂的一定時期內的整體市場營銷規劃。

這些小詞你也要會哦：

conduct *v.* 進行	survey *n.* 調查	response *n.* 回應
customer loyalty 客戶忠誠度	identify *v.* 鑒別	business model *n.* 商業模式
competitor *n.* 競爭對手	insight *n.* 洞察力	determine *v.* 決定，判定

Scene 57 產品質量調查 Research on Product Quality

 場景對話

A: Hello. My name is Zhang Xiao. I'm working in the marketing department of ABC Company. Nice to meet you.	A：您好，我叫張笑。我在 ABC 公司的市場部工作。很高興見到您。
B: Hi. Nice to meet you.	B：你好。很高興見到你。

A: Thank you for taking the time to help us improve the quality of our product.

A：謝謝您能抽出時間來，幫助我們改進我們公司的產品質量。

B: My pleasure.

B：別客氣。

A: How long have you been using our laundry detergent?

A：您用我們公司生產的洗衣液多久了？

B: Well, about three years.

B：差不多 3 年了。

A: Have you ever used a different laundry detergent during this time?

A：在這期間您用過其他公司的洗衣液嗎？

B: Yes. I have.

B：是的。我用過。

A: Comparing to our competitors, is our product's quality better, worse or about the same?

A：與我們的競爭對手相比，我們產品的質量是更好、更差還是沒有差別？

B: Your product is better.

B：你們的產品更好。

A: So what about the price? Are our prices higher, lower or about the same?

A：那麼在價格方面呢？我們的價格是更高、更低還是沒有差別？

B: Your price is higher.

B：你們的價格更高。

A: How likely is it that you would recommend our product to a friend?

A：您會願意把我們的產品推薦給你的朋友嗎？

B: Well, I have already told some of my friends about your product and I would very much likely to tell other people as well.

B：我已經向我的一些朋友推薦了你們的 產品，我很有可能還會向別人推薦。

A: Is there anything that you don't like in our product?

A：關於我們的產品，你有什麼不喜歡的地方嗎？

B: I like the super cleaning power of your product and it cleans effectively in any water temperature, but I have to add an extra one-third dose compared to other brands.

B：對於你們產品的強大潔淨能力我很滿意，在任何水溫中都能將衣服洗得很乾淨，但是跟其他品牌相比，我必須要多加 1/3 的劑量才可以。

A: Thank you for your time.

A：謝謝您接受我們的訪問。

B: You are welcome.

B：不客氣。

 場景問答必會句

How long have you been using our laundry detergent?
您用我們公司生產的洗衣液多久了？

還可以這樣說：

🗨 Do you frequently use our laundry detergent?
您經常用我們的洗衣液嗎？

🗨 Have you ever used our laundry detergent before?
您用過我們的洗衣液嗎？

> **Is there anything that you don't like in our product?**
> 關於我們的產品，你有什麼不喜歡的地方嗎？

還可以這樣說：

🗨 What do you think has made us less competitive?
您認為哪些原因削弱了我們產品的競爭力？

對方可能這樣回答：

🗨 I think your price is too high.
我認為你們的價格太高了。

Scene 58　用戶偏好調查 Research on User Preference

 場景對話

A: Thank you for taking part in this research.	A：謝謝您參與此次調研。
B: No problem.	B：不客氣。
A: What's your occupation?	A：您是做什麼工作的？
B: I'm a housewife.	B：我是一名家庭主婦。
A: How often do you do online shopping?	A：您多久進行一次網上購物？
B: Twice a week.	B：一星期兩次。
A: How long does it take you to complete one shopping process?	A：您每次購物需要花多長時間？
B: Well, it depends. The more money I need to spend, the more time I will need to place an order.	B：這要看情況。所購買產品價格越高，下單所需要的時間越長。
A: How long have you been using our website?	A：您使用我們的網站多久了？
B: More than ten months.	B：超過 10 個月了。
A: Are you satisfied with the speed of our website?	A：你對我們網站的速度滿意嗎？

B: It usually takes longer on weekends to access your website.	B：通常在週末時打開網站所需要的時間比平時要長。
A: What do you think of the layout of our website?	A：您認為我們網站的佈局如何？
B: I think it is OK. But from time to time the advertisement pops out suddenly. It can be a little annoying.	B：還不錯。只是有時會突然彈出廣告，讓人有點心煩。
A: <u>Do you think we provide enough sorts of commodities?</u>	A：<u>您認為我們提供的商品種類足夠豐富嗎？</u>
B: Yes. I can almost find everything I need from your website.	B：是的，在你們的網站上，我幾乎可以找到任何想要的商品。

場景問答必會句

> How often do you do online shopping?
> 您多久進行一次網上購物？

還可以這樣說：

🗨 How frequently do you do online shopping?
　您網購的頻率如何？

對方可能這樣回答：

🗨 Four times a month.
　一個月四次。

PS

rarely *ad.* 很少地

physical store 實體店

🗨 I rarely do online shopping as I prefer to shop in physical stores.
　我很少在網上購物，因為我喜歡在實體店買東西。

> Do you think we provide enough sorts of commodities?
> 您認為我們提供的商品種類足夠豐富嗎？

還可以這樣說：

🗨 Are you satisfied with the items we offer?
　您對我們提供的商品滿意嗎？

對方可能這樣回答：

PS

authentic *a.* 正宗的

🗨 No. Some of the items I ordered from you did not seem to be authentic.
　不滿意。我從你們那兒訂購的一些商品看起來不是正品。

Scene 59 反饋意見和建議 Feedback

 場景對話

A: You are one of our most valued customers, Mr. Robert. Your feedback is most welcomed.	A：羅伯特先生，您是我們最重要的客戶之一。我們非常樂意聽到您的反饋。
B: Well, I do have a couple of suggestions for you. As you know, I have been very satisfied with your products and service. But recently, I notice that your service quality is going down.	B：我確實有一些建議。正如你所知，我一直對你們的產品和服務很滿意。但最近我發現你們的服務質量下降了。
A: Would you like to tell me more about it?	A：您願意跟我詳細地說說嗎？
B: Yes. The recent orders I placed have been delivered late. Last week, the packing case of the chocolate I ordered from you arrived damaged.	B：好。最近我下的訂單，送貨都不及時。上週，我訂購的巧克力到貨時包裝破損了。
A: This is unusual. We have our products checked very carefully before sending them out. Have you contacted our customer service department?	A：這有點反常。我們出貨前都會很仔細地檢查。您與我們的客服部門聯繫了嗎？
B: Yes. But one of your customer representatives was very rude to me.	B：聯繫了。但是你們有位客服人員態度很粗魯。
A: I'm so sorry to hear that. I wonder what I can do to compensate you for these unpleasant experiences.	A：聽到這個我很抱歉。我想知道，我能做點什麼來補償您這些不愉快的經歷。
B: Well, it's not necessary. I just don't want you to lose customers because of your poor customer service since your chocolate tastes so good.	B：沒關係。我只是不想你們因為差勁的服務而失去客戶，因為你們的巧克力味道很不錯。
A: I really appreciate your feedback. It's because of customers like you that we are able to correct our occasional problems.	A：非常感謝您的反饋。正是因為有您這樣的客戶，我們才能改正偶爾犯下的錯誤。

場景問答必會句

Would you like to tell me more about it?
您願意跟我詳細地說說嗎？

還可以這樣說：

💬 Would you like to discuss further details about it?
　　您想談談更多的細節嗎？

💬 Would you please be more specific?
　　您能說得更具體一點嗎？

PS

further *a.* 更多的

specific *a.* 詳細的

對方可能這樣回答：

💬 The computer I bought from you didn't make it through the first three months.
　　我從你們那兒買的電腦用了不到 3 個月就壞了。

> I wonder what I can do to compensate you for these unpleasant experiences.
> 我想知道，我能做些什麼來補償您這些不愉快的經歷。

還可以這樣說：

💬 How can I make it up for you?
　　我怎樣做才能補償您？

PS

compensate *v.* 補償，賠償

make sth. up 彌補

對方可能這樣回答：

💬 Please make sure this won't happen again.
　　請確保此事不再發生。

💬 I want to get my money back.
　　我想退款。

💬 I want to return these products.
　　我想退貨。

▌市場調研 Tips ▌

市場調研注意事項

> 1) 提前準備好相關問題，把需要問的問題列在一張表裡，防止遺漏。
> 2) 與受訪者打招呼時面帶微笑，詳細介紹調研活動。
> 3) 徵得同意後開始提問。先從簡單、輕鬆的問題入手，減輕受訪者的 心理壓力。
> 4) 做好記錄。簡明扼要地記下受訪者回答的重點內容。
> 5) 調研結束後向受訪者表達謝意。

Unit 4 | 售後服務

售後服務，是指在商品出售以後所提供的服務。在提供價廉物美產品的同時，向消費者提供完善的售後服務，已成為現代企業市場競爭的新焦點。

售後服務必會詞

① customer satisfaction 客戶滿意度
客戶滿意度指的是客戶期望值與客戶體驗的匹配程度。

② customer service hotline 客服熱線
客戶服務熱線通過人工、自動語音、短信、傳真、E-mail 等方式為顧客提供有關業務諮詢、業務受理和投訴建議等專業服務。

③ warranty period 保修期
保修期是指廠商向消費者出售商品時承諾的對該商品因質量問題出現故障時提供免費維修及保養的時間段。

④ after-sale service 售後服務
售後服務，是指廠商或經銷商把產品 (或服務) 銷售給消費者之後，為消費者提供的一系列服務，包括產品介紹、送貨、安裝、調試、維修、技術培訓和上門服務等。

這些小詞你也要會哦：

assemble v. 聚集；組裝	subscribe v. 訂購	deliver v. 送貨
manual n. 使用手冊	installation n. 安裝	membership n. 會員身份
refund v. 退還	guarantee n. 保證書	warranty n. 保修單

Scene 60　詢問產品銷售情況 Inquiry about Sales

 場景對話

A: Mr. Well, <u>how is the sale of our cameras?</u> Could you offer us some information?	A：韋爾先生，照相機的銷售情況如何？可以給我們提供一些信息嗎？
B: Oh, yes. The sales volume keeps rising this month. It's estimated that we'll have an increase of 5% compared with last month.	B：好的。這個月的銷售額持續攀升。預計這個月的銷售額會比上個月增加 5%。
A: That's not bad. <u>Have you conducted any surveys?</u>	A：很好。<u>你們有沒有做調查？</u>
B: Yes, we've just carried out a survey of both consumers and retailers.	B：有的。我們剛剛對客戶和零售商都進行了調查。
A: Did you get a response?	A：您得到反饋了嗎？
B: Well, it looks like our cameras are very popular.	B：看起來我們的照相機非常受歡迎。
A: Are people looking for cheaper ones?	A：人們在找尋更便宜的產品嗎？
B: Right. They want lower prices, but most important of all, the cameras must be reliable.	B：是的，他們希望價格便宜一些，但是最重要的是，照相機的質量必須可靠。
A: OK. Thank you very much, Mr. Well.	A：好的。非常感謝，韋爾先生。

 場景問答必會句

> How is the sale of our cameras?
> 照相機的銷售情況如何？

還可以這樣說：

🗨 What's the sales volume of our cameras?
　照相機的銷售情況如何？

對方可能這樣回答：

🗨 It's much better compared with that of last month.
　與上個月相比，這個月的情況好了很多。

🗨 Just so-so.
　馬馬虎虎吧。

> Have you conducted any surveys?
> 你們有沒有做調查？

還可以這樣說：

🗨 Have you done some researches?
你們有沒有做調查？

對方可能這樣回答：

🗨 We're ready to do that, but we haven't started yet.
我們已經準備好要進行調查了，但還沒有開始。

Scene 61 提供專業意見 Offer Professional Advice

 場景對話

A: Good morning, Mr. Bull!	A：早上好，布爾先生。
B: Good morning! I'd like to speak to the manager, please.	B：早上好。我想見你們經理。
A: I'm sorry, but our manager has been out. What can I do for you?	A：對不起，我們經理出去了。有什麼可以幫您嗎？
B: Are you good at computer? I bought two hundred computers from your company the day before yesterday, but 20% of them stopped working today.	B：你對電腦精通嗎？我前天從你們公司買了 200 台電腦，但是今天 20% 的電腦都不能用了。
A: What's the exact problem?	A：具體是什麼問題？
B: I turn on the computer and see nothing. Is there something wrong with the monitor?	B：開機後什麼都看不見。是顯示器有問題嗎？
A: From what you said, I guess it can be anything inside the computer.	A：從您說的情況看，我估計可能是電腦內部的故障。
B: No matter what the problem is, my staff need the computers to work.	B：不管是什麼原因，我的員工需要電腦工作。
A: I see. Could you bring them here? If not, our maintenance can go to your place.	A：我明白。您能將電腦送來這裡嗎？不行的話，我們的維修員可以去您的公司上門服務。
B: I would prefer if he can go to my place.	B：我更傾向於請維修員到我的公司。
A: No problem.	A：沒問題。

 場景問答必會句

> **What can I do for you?**
> 有什麼可以幫您嗎？

還可以這樣說：
- Is there anything I can do for you?
  有什麼可以幫您嗎？

對方可能這樣回答：
- Yes, can I have a refund?
  我能申請退款嗎？
- I think you've sent a wrong product to me.
  我想你們發錯貨了。

PS

refund *n.* 退款

> **What's the exact problem?**
> 具體是什麼問題？

還可以這樣說：
- Do you know what causes the malfunction?
  你知道引起故障的原因嗎？
- How do you know there is something wrong with it?
  你怎麼知道它有問題呢？

PS

malfunction *n.* 故障

Scene **62** 提供最新的產品信息 The Newest Product

 場景對話

A: Hi! My name is John Bird. Your bikes are very impressive.	A：嘿，我是約翰 伯德，你們的自行車讓人印象深刻。
B: Would you like to know more about our new bikes?	B：您想知道更多關於我們新款自行車的信息嗎？
A: Yes, I would. What does this button here do?	A：是的，我想知道。這裡這個按鈕的作用是什麼？
B: That button is for our call screening function. It allows you to identify the caller before you answer the call.	B：那個按鈕是來電顯示功能。它可以讓您在接電話之前先知道是誰的來電。

A: You mean the bike is with a phone on it?	A：你的意思是這款自行車上還有電話？
B: Yes, that's its new function.	B：是的，這是這款自行車的新功能。
A: What else can you tell me about the bike?	A：這款自行車還有什麼其他功能嗎？
B: This kind of bicycle can be folded in half and is handy to carry around, especially useful during traveling and traffic jams.	B：這款自行車可以對折，便於隨身攜帶，去旅遊或遇到交通堵塞時特別好用。
A: No kidding?What is the price of the bike?	A：真的嗎？這自行車多少錢？
B: The price is $110 per unit. We're offering a special discount of 10% off during the exhibition.	B：標價是每輛 110 美元。在展會期間我們提價 9 折的特價。
A: Well, I'll have to contact my office and get back to you. Thanks.	A：我得和公司聯絡之後再過來找你，謝謝。

場景問答必會句

> That button is for our call screening function.
> 那個按鈕是來電顯示功能。

還可以這樣說：

🗨 You can push it and you'll see what I mean.
　 你可以按下去試試，然後你就會知道我說的意思了。

> This kind of bicycle can be folded in half and is handy to carry around.
> 這款自行車可以對折，便於隨身攜帶。

還可以這樣說：

🗨 I can give you a brochure of the bike. You'll find a lot of details in it.
　 我可以給你一本這款自行車的宣傳手冊，裡面有很多詳細信息。

對方可能這樣問：

🗨 Could you give us some ideas about other functions of the bike?
　 你能介紹一下這款自行車的其他功能嗎？

🗨 Could you offer us more information of the bike?
　 你能多介紹一點這款自行車的相關信息嗎？

Scene 63 告知售後服務電話 After-sales Hotline

 場景對話

A: Mr. Sterling, I'm glad to do business with you. I think I've made a right choice to buy typewriters here.

A：斯特林先生，真高興和你做生意。我覺得來這裡買打字機真是個正確的選擇。

B: Thank you for your trust. Our products are surely of standard quality.

B：謝謝您的信任。我們的產品質量肯定達標。

A: What other services do you provide?

A：你們還提供其他服務嗎？

B: We provide delivery service for you if you need.

B：如果您需要的話，我們可以為您提供送貨服務。

A: Can you make sure that I can get it as soon as possible?

A：你能否確認我能儘快收到？

B: I'm sorry. We're in a busy period now, so it can't be delivered within three days.

B：對不起，我們這段時間正忙，所以 3 天內都不可能送貨。

A: Then, what is the earliest time it might come?

A：那最早能什麼時候送來？

B: Around 8:00 this Wednesday.

B：這週三 8 點左右。

A: All right. By the way, how long is the term of service?

A：好的。順便問一下，保修期是多長時間？

B: Within five years, any non-intentional damage will be repaired free of charge.

B：5 年之內，任何非故意的損壞我們都免費維修。

A: Do you have a hotline?

A：你們有售後電話嗎？

B: Yes, it's 400-820-8820. After receiving your call, we'll pay you a visit within twenty-four hours.

B：有的。電話號碼是 400-820-8820。在接到您的電話後，我們會在 24 小時內上門服務。

場景問答必會句

> We provide delivery service for you if you need.
> 如果您需要的話，我們可以為您提供送貨服務。

還可以這樣說：

🗨 You can also enjoy the home-delivery service.
您還可以享受送貨上門服務。

🗨 I'm sorry, sir. No more service in the limited-time discount zone.
不好意思，先生。限時折扣專區不享有其他服務。

PS
home-delivery 送貨上門

limited-time discount zone
限時打折專區

> Within five years, any non-intentional damage will be repaired free of charge.
> 5 年之內，任何非故意的損壞我們都免費維修。

還可以這樣說：

🗨 The goods are guaranteed for twelve months, from date of sale.
自銷售之日起，保修期為 12 個月。

🗨 The warranty will be extended for an additional two years from the day when they are brought in for repair.
保修期從產品送修之日起延長 2 年。

售後服務 Tips

售後服務常用句

損壞程度

How bad was the damage? 損壞情況如何？

Was the damage extensive? 損壞情況嚴重嗎？

Were all the materials in that case destroyed? 箱裡的東西都損毀了嗎？

解決問題

We'll check it right away. 我們會馬上開始調查。

Our shipping manager is looking into it. 我們的貨運經理正在調查這件事。

The person in charge is looking into it right now. 負責人正在調查此事。

We will find out whose fault this is. 我們會找到是誰犯的錯誤。

爭論

It was not damaged by us. 不是由我方損壞的。

We can't accept your damage claim. 我們無法接受你的索賠要求。

We are not responsible for this damage. 此次損壞我們沒有責任。

Your claim is unreasonable. 你們的索賠要求是不合理的。

致歉

We will compensate for your loss. 我們會補償您的損失。

We will offer you more favorable prices in the future. 我們將來會為您提供更優惠的價格。

Chapter 4

貿易實務——
談判桌上的較量

Unit 1 詢盤

詢盤在國際貿易中舉足輕重，買方有意進口某種產品之前，會向他比較感興趣的商家進行詢盤，詢問產品的相關信息。賣方在收到詢盤後會對產品進行報盤或報價。

詢盤必會詞

1 inquiry *n.* 詢盤
詢盤，又稱詢價，是指交易的一方為購買或出售某種商品，向對方口頭或書面發出的探詢交易條件的過程。

2 quotation *n.* 報價
指賣方向買方提供商品的銷售價格和銷售條件。

3 commission *n.* 佣金
佣金是指具有獨立地位和經營資格的中介在商業活動中為他人提供服務所得到的報酬。

4 FOB 離岸價格
Free on Board 又稱"船上交貨價格"，指在裝運港的指定船上交貨，風險由此從賣方轉移至買方。

這些小詞你也要會哦：

available *a.* 可獲得的	attractive *a.* 有吸引力的	enquiry *n.* 詢盤
indication *n.* 跡象	requirement *n.* 要求	confirmation *n.* 確認
acceptable *a.* 可接受的	assure *v.* 保證	open *a.* 有效的

Scene 64 索要目錄 Inquiry about Catalogue

 場景對話

A: Hello, sir. Is there anything I can help you?	A：您好，先生。有什麼可以幫您的嗎？
B: Well, I'm interested in your bed-covers.	B：哦，我對你們的床罩很感興趣。

A: We can supply bed-covers of all types and sizes.	A：我們可以供應各種款式和大小的床罩。
B: That's fantastic. Do you have any catalogue or brochure that I can take with me?	B：太棒了，你們有我可以帶走的目錄或宣傳冊嗎？
A: Of course. Here is a series of catalogue of our latest types, and here is a detailed list of our offer.	A：當然，這是我們最新的產品目錄系列，還有我們的報價清單。
B: Thank you. As soon as we have any further inquiries, I'll give you a call.	B：謝謝。如果我們想要進一步詢盤，我會給您打電話。
A: I hope we can do business together, and I look forward to hearing from you soon.	A：希望我們有機會合作，我靜候您的佳音。

場景問答必會句

> Here is a series of catalogue of our latest types, and here is a detailed list of our offer.
> 這是我們最新的產品目錄系列，還有我們的報價清單。

還可以這樣說：

💬 Here are our latest price sheets.
　　這是我們最新的報價單。

💬 We can send you our price list of quartz clocks.
　　我們可以給您寄我們的石英鐘價目單。

💬 I have here our price sheet on a FOB basis. The prices are
　　given without engagement.
　　這是我們離岸價的價目單，所報價格沒有約束力。

PS

price list 價目單

quartz clock 石英鐘

without engagement 指沒有約束力，價格還可以上下浮動。在外貿裡也稱虛盤。

> I hope we can do business together, and I look forward to hearing from you soon.
> 希望我們有機會合作，我靜候您的佳音。

還可以這樣說：

💬 We are looking forward to your reply to our inquiry.
　　期待你方對我們詢盤的回覆。

對方可能這樣回答：

💬 If your price is favorable, we can book an order right away.
　　如果貴方價格優惠，我們可以馬上訂貨。

Scene 65　詢問價格 Price Inquiry

 場景對話

A: Hi! My name is Blaine Fryer. I'm interested in your machinery tools. I've seen your exhibits and your catalogues. They are very impressive. Here is a list of my requirements. I'd like to have your lowest quotations, FOB Shanghai.

A：嘿，我是布萊恩 弗賴爾，我對你們的機械工具很感興趣。我看了你們的展品，也看了你們的目錄，給我的印象很深。這是我的需求清單，我想要你們上海離岸價的最低報價。

B: Thank you for your inquiry, sir. Could you also tell me the quantity you need?

B：謝謝您的詢價，先生。您能告訴我們您需要的數量嗎？

A: I will. But before that, could you give me an indication of the price?

A：可以。但是在此之前，您能給我一個估計價格嗎？

B: Yes, of course. Here you are, sir. All our FOB prices are listed here. But they are subject to our final confirmation.

B：當然可以。給您，先生。我們所有的離岸價都在這兒，但需要經過我們的最終確認。

A: In that case, may I ask how the final confirmation is decided?

A：要是那樣，我能問一下你們的最終確認價是怎麼決定的嗎？

B: Sure, you can. It's usually decided by the size of your order.

B：當然可以。通常是根據您的訂貨量而定。

A: Oh, I see. For how long will your quotation price remain open?

A：哦，我知道了。你的這份報價有效期是多少天？

B: It'll be open for three days. When can you decide the size of your order?

B：有效期 3 天。您什麼時候能確定您的訂單數量？

A: That will depend on your list price. If your price is acceptable, we can place an order immediately.

A：這取決於你們的標價，如果價格合適，我們可以立即下訂單。

B: I can assure you this is our best offer.

B：我保證這是我們最好的報價。

A: But compared with the same type of product elsewhere, the price is really too high. We need to consider it a bit more carefully. We'll get back to you tomorrow.

A：但與其他地方同類產品的價格比還是太高了。我們需要再仔細考慮一下，明天再來談。

?A 場景問答必會句

> Could you give me an indication of the price?
> 你能給我一個估計價格嗎？

還可以這樣說：

🗨 Can you give me a rough idea of the price?
可以給我大概的報價嗎？

🗨 Please let us know your lowest possible prices for the relevant goods.
請告知你們有關產品的最低報價。

對方可能這樣回答：

🗨 The price is dependent on the quantity.
價格取決於訂貨數量。

🗨 I'm sorry that we are unable to make you an offer at present.
很抱歉我們現在無法報盤。

> For how long will your quotation price remain open?
> 你的這份報價有效期是多少天？

還可以這樣說：

🗨 How long is the offer open?
報價的有效期多長？

對方可能這樣回答：

🗨 It's valid for three days.
有效期為 3 天。

🗨 Normally, for five days.
通常情況下，有效期為 5 天。

詢盤 Tips

10 種常用貿易術語

EXW (Ex Works) 工廠交貨	FCA (Free Carrier) 貨交承運人
FAS (Free alongside Ship) 船邊交貨	FOB (Free on Board) 離岸價格
CIF (Cost, Insurance and Freight) 到岸價格	CPT (Carriage Paid to) 運費付至……
CIP (Carriage and Insurance Paid to) 運費及保險付至……	DES (Delivered Ex Ship) 目的港船上交貨
DDU (Delivered Duty Unpaid) 未完稅交貨	DDP (Delivered Duty Paid) 完稅後交貨

發盤

在國際貿易實務中，發盤也稱報盤、發價、報價。發盤可以是應對方詢盤的要求發出，也可以是在沒有詢盤的情況下，直接向對方發出。

發盤必會詞

1 offer n. 發盤
通過傳真、電話、電子郵件、信函等方式向詢盤人提供產品的價格、規格、包裝和支付方式等相關信息。

2 quote v. 報價
告之用戶所詢問商品的價格。報價通常使用 FOB、CFR 和 CIF 三種價格。

3 quantity n. 數量
指訂購商品的總量。

4 delivery date 交貨日期
一般指拖櫃日期。工廠將貨物做好並驗貨後，委託拖車公司提櫃和裝櫃。

這些小詞你也要會哦：

specification *n.* 規格	reputation *n.* 名聲	workmanship *n.* 工藝
superior *a.* 質量上乘的	advance *n.* 預付款	confirmation *n.* 確認
validity *n.* 有效期	Import / Export License 進 / 出口許可證	

Scene 66 針對新客戶的詢盤 Answer a First Inquiry

場景對話

A: Hello, I'd like to get a quotation for the items listed in this catalogue.

A：您好，我想知道這份宣傳冊裡面產品的報價。

B: Thank you for your inquiry. Here are the quotations. Some of them are subject to final confirmation.

B：感謝您的詢價，這是報價單。裡面的一些價格以最終確認價為準。

A: I'm quite interested in your item No.5. Please quote me your lowest price, CIF Houston.	A：我對你們 5 號產品很感興趣。請報一下休斯敦到岸價的最低價。
B: What quantity would you like to take?	B：您的訂購量是多少？
A: I think I will take a hundred tons for starters.	A：我想先訂 100 噸。
B: Okay. We offer you firm a hundred tons of item No. 5 at 120 US dollars per metric ton CIF Houston.	B：好的，我們報實盤：5 號商品 100 噸，休斯敦到岸價是每公噸 120 美元。
A: I think the price is a little too high. Can you cut it down?	A：我覺得價格有點高，可以降一些嗎？
B: I'm afraid we can't.	B：恐怕降不了。
A: Your price is much higher than the quotations I've received from other sources.	A：你們的價格比我從其他渠道得到的報價要高出許多。
B: Well, you have to take the quality into consideration. Our products are renowned for the quality. I think that's why you come to us.	B：嗯，您應該考慮一下質量問題。我們的產品以優質出名。我想這也是您來我們這裡諮詢的原因。
A: You are right. But we can't order them at this price.	A：沒錯。但是我們沒法以這個價格下單。
B: Well, considering your quantity, we could reduce the price by 1%.	B：考慮到您的訂購量，我們願意將價格下調 1%。
A: Could you tell me the terms of payment?	A：你們的付款條件是怎樣的？
B: We only accept L/C.	B：我們只接受信用證。
A: I see. Could you make an exception and accept D/A?	A：我明白了。能不能破例接受承兌交單？
B: I'm afraid not. We insist on a letter of credit.	B：恐怕不行，我們堅持要求採用信用證付款。

場景問答必會句

> What quantity would you like to take?
> 您的訂購量是多少？

還可以這樣說：
- How much would you like to order?
  您要訂購多少？

💬 Would you let us know what quantity you need so as to enable us to work out the offers?
請問能否告知您所需訂購量，以便我方報價？

對方可能這樣回答：

💬 I'd like to place an order of 1,000 units.
我想訂 1000 件。

💬 We are in urgent need of two hundred tons of groundnuts.
我們急需 200 噸花生。

 so as to 以便，為了……

enable sb. to do sth. 使某人能夠做某事

work out 制訂出，計算出

place an order 訂購，下單

in need of sth. 需要某物

We offer you firm a hundred tons of item No.5 at 120 US dollars per metric ton CIF Houston.
我們報實盤：5 號商品 100 噸，休斯敦到岸價是每公噸 120 美元。

還可以這樣說：

💬 We offer you 1,000 sets of tablets model X1 at $225 per set CIF Huston.
我們的報價是：1000 台 X1 型號的平板電腦，每台休斯頓到岸價為 225 美元。

💬 The unit price is $14.
單價是 14 美元。

 tablet n. 平板電腦

Scene 67 針對老客戶的詢盤 Answer Inquiries from a Regular Customer

 🗨 場景對話

A: Good morning, Mr. Stewart.	A：早上好，斯圖爾特先生。
B: Hello, Mr. Zhang. How are you?	B：您好，張先生，您還好嗎？
A: I'm fine. Thank you. I understand you'd like to order more digital cameras from us, right?	A：我很好，謝謝。我瞭解到您想再從我們這裡訂購一些數碼相機，對嗎？
B: Yes, your products have enjoyed high popularity in our market.	B：是的。你們的產品在我們的市場很受歡迎。
A: I'm so glad to hear that. We always provide our clients with goods of superior quality and at a competitive price.	A：很高興聽到這個消息。我們一直以合理的價格為我們的客戶提供優質的產品。

B: Yes. Are the quotations you sent us yesterday on the basis of CIF terms?	B：是的。昨天您發給我的報價是到岸價嗎？
A: No. All the prices quoted are on the basis of FOB terms.	A：不是。所有的報價都是離岸價。
B: But I prefer to have your lowest quotation, CIF New York.	B：但是我希望你們給出到紐約港的到岸價最低報價。
A: Would you first please give us an approximate idea of the quantity you intend to order this time?	A：您是否能先告知我們這次大概的訂購量？
B: I think it would be better for us to know your quotation first. Then we will consider the amount we'd like to place.	B：我認為我們還是先瞭解一下你們的報價為好。然後我們再決定訂購多少。
A: All right. Here is our CIF New York quotation.	A：好吧。這是我們到紐約港的到岸報價。
B: Well, this price is a bit higher than it was last time.	B：這個價格相比上次有所上調。
A: Yes. The price of raw materials and labor has gone up. This is the best we can do.	A：是的。原材料價格和人工費都上漲了。這是我們能給出的最優惠價格。
B: I see. In that case, I will have to call my office first. Can I get back to you tomorrow?	B：我明白了。這樣的話，我需要先致電公司。明天再給您答覆，可以嗎？
A: Sure. Looking forward to hearing from you.	A：當然。期待您的回覆。

場景問答必會句

I understand you'd like to order more digital cameras from us right?
我瞭解到你想再從我們這裡訂購一些數碼相機，對嗎？

還可以這樣說：

- We are very pleased to learn that you would like to place another order.
  我們很高興地得知您想再次下單。
- So you are coming to us for a second contract?
  您是來再次簽訂合同的嗎？

對方可能這樣回答：

- Your products sell very well.
  你們的產品很暢銷。
- Your products are adored by our customers.
  我們的客戶很喜歡你們的產品。

🗨 Yes. But we'd like to talk about a different type of products with you this time.
是的，但是這次我們想跟你們商討的是另一款產品。

PS

adore *v.* 喜歡

All the prices quoted are on the basis of FOB terms.
所有的報價都是離岸價。

還可以這樣說：

🗨 All the quotations are on the basis of FOB terms.
是的，所有的報價都是離岸價。

Scene
68 給客戶推薦新產品 Introduce New Products

 場景對話

A: It's so nice to meet you again, Mr. McCain.	A：很高興再次見到您，麥凱恩先生。
B: Me too, Mr. Zhang. It's been a long time since we last met.	B：我也是，張先生。好久不見了。
A: Right, and you've come at an exciting time. We've come out with a new line of product. Would you like to have a look?	A：是啊。您來得正好，我們剛推出一條新的產品線。您想看看嗎？
B: Yes, I'd love to.	B：好的，我想看看。
A: Well, It's our new silk coaster. They can be used to hold cups, mugs and drinking glasses etc.	A：這是我們新出的絲綢杯墊。可以用作茶杯、馬克杯和玻璃杯的墊子。
B: Can I take a closer look at it?	B：我可以仔細看看你們的絲綢杯墊嗎？
A: Sure. Here you are.	A：當然可以，給您。
B: Thank you.	B：謝謝。
A: What do you think of it?	A：您覺得怎麼樣？
B: It feels very soft.	B：摸起來很柔軟。
A: Yes. It's of great quality. It can keep your table safe from stains and heat.	A：是的。這種杯墊質量很好。可以為您的桌子防髒、隔熱。
B: The pattern is unique too.	B：圖案也很特別。

A: Exactly. It's a specific designed pattern to show your great taste. Are you interested in it?	A：沒錯。圖案是專門設計的，彰顯顧客的高尚品位。您感興趣嗎？
B: I'm not sure what our end-users would think of it.	B：我不確定我們的終端用戶是否喜歡。
A: Well, they come in different sizes and colors and can widely be used at home, in coffee shops, pubs, hotels and restaurants.	A：我們的杯墊有不同的尺寸和顏色，可以廣泛用於家庭，也可以在咖啡廳、酒吧、賓館和飯店使用。
B: Sounds good.	B：聽起來不錯。
A: It is really good. I'm sure your customers will like it.	A：確實很好。我相信您的客戶會喜歡。

 場景問答必會句

> We've come out with a new line of product. Would you like to have a look?
> 我們剛推出一條新的產品線。您想看看嗎？

還可以這樣說：
🔲 You will be impressed by our improved products.
我們改良後的產品一定會令您印象深刻。

對方可能這樣回答：
🔲 It's very nice of you to do so.
感謝您為我們介紹。

PS

product line 產品線

impress *v.* 使某人印象深刻

> What do you think of it?
> 您覺得怎麼樣？

還可以這樣說：
🔲 Could we know your comments on our products?
您對我們的產品評價如何？

對方可能這樣回答：
🔲 It's the best I have seen so far.
這是目前我見過最好的。
🔲 The quality of the goods is not so good as the last shipment.
這批貨的質量沒有上一批貨好。

PS

comment *n.* 評價

not so good as…
不如……好

Scene 69　回答詢盤客戶的各種問題 Answer Inquiries

A: Can I help you?	A：有什麼可以幫您的嗎？
B: Yes. I'm interested in some of your stuffed animals such as pandas and giraffes. Would you please give us your lowest quotations CIF New York?	B：是的，我對你們的幾款填充動物玩具如熊貓、長頸鹿等很感興趣。能否請您給我們報一個紐約港到岸價的最低報價？
A: I'd be glad to. Here is our offer.	A：當然可以。這是我們的價格表。
B: The prices seem reasonable. What about the quality?	B：價格看起來很合理。質量如何？
A: I can assure you that our stuffed animals are made of environmentally-friendly material and are quite safe.	A：我可以向您保證我們所有的填充動物玩具都是採用環保材料製成的，非常安全。
B: That is what I have been worried about. Parents are very concerned about the safety of the toys.	B：我擔心的就是這點，家長們對玩具的安全非常注重。
A: No need to worry about that. Our toys will do no harm to children if they play with them properly.	A：這點您可以放心。只要孩子們正確使用，我們的玩具不會對他們造成任何傷害。
B: That's good. How long does it take you to make delivery?	B：太好了。你們什麼時候能交貨？
A: How about November?	A：11 月份可以嗎？
B: I'm afraid it's too late. I need the goods in October because there is great demand for toys before Christmas.	B：11 月份恐怕太晚了。我希望能在 10 月份交貨，因為聖誕節前夕對玩具的需求量很大。
A: I will manage to do that. Do you have any specific requirements for packing?	A：我會盡全力。您對包裝有什麼特殊要求嗎？
B: Please make sure they are tastefully packed as most of them will be presented as gifts.	B：因為這些玩具大多數將會被當作禮物送出，所以請確保包裝考究。
A: What about the packing materials?	A：包裝材料方面呢？
B: We want it to be packed in a plastic bag and then placed in a cardboard box with beautiful designs in bright colors.	B：我們希望每個玩具用塑料袋包裝好後放置在設計精美、色彩靚麗的紙盒中。
A: No problem.	A：沒問題。

場景問答必會句

> I can assure you that our stuffed animals are made of environmentally-friendly material and are quite safe.
> 我可以向您保證我們所有的填充動物玩具都是採用環保材料製成的，非常安全。

還可以這樣說：

- Our products are made of natural materials.
  我們的產品用天然材料製成。
- Our shoes are tasteful and give users a feeling of comfort.
  我們的鞋子式樣美觀，穿着舒適。
- We are responsible to replace the defective ones.
  我們保證換掉不合格的產品。

PS

environmentally-friendly *a.*
保護生態環境的，對環境無害的

> Do you have any specific requirements for packing?
> 您對包裝有什麼特殊要求嗎？

還可以這樣說：

- How would you like the goods to be packed?
  您希望如何包裝產品？

對方可能這樣回答：

- Culture must be considered when it comes to packing.
  在包裝問題上必須把文化考慮進去。
- The packing must be in line with the market preference.
  包裝必須符合消費者喜好。

PS

when it comes to 就……而論

in line with 與……一致

preference 喜好，偏愛

發盤 Tips

1. 發盤常用術語

關於包裝

carton 紙板箱	wooden case 木箱
container 集裝箱	box 盒子
iron drum 鐵桶	plastic bag 塑料袋
foam plastic bag 泡沫塑料袋	container 容器
outer packing 外包裝	inner packing 內包裝
foam 泡沫	

關於發盤

to make an offer 發盤	to make a firm offer 發實盤
to extend an offer 延長發盤有效期	

2. 發盤常用表達

- We are pleased to make you an offer for 5,000 pairs of women's gloves as follows.
  我們很高興為貴方做出 5000 副女士手套的報盤，具體如下。
- Thank you for your enquiry dated July 23rd and we offer as follows.
  謝謝貴方 7 月 23 日的詢價，我方報盤如下。
- The offer above is subject to your receipt of reply by us.
  上述報盤以收到我方回覆為有效。
- This offer is firm for three days.
  此報盤的有效期為 3 天。
- We believe you will find our offer satisfactory.
  我們相信貴方會對我們的報盤感到滿意。
- As the prices are likely to rise, we advise you to accept the offer without delay.
  價格有可能上漲，我方建議貴方立即接受此報盤。

Unit 3 還盤

還盤 (counter-offer) 是指一方在接到另一方報盤以後，要求更改報盤內容的函電。其中包括降低價格、更改支付方式或更改交貨期等，交易中可以多次還盤。

還盤必會詞

① uitable *a.* 適當的，合適的
還盤的主要目的之一是為了得到更合適的價格。"合適的報價"可以用 suitable offer 來表示。

② advise *v.* 建議
提出自己覺得合理的價位，或建議對方再報一個合理的價格。

③ possibility *n.* 可能性
詢問交易條件是否可以達成。

④ unable *a.* 不能的
對交易條件表示無法接受。"無法接受報價"可以用 unable to accept the offer 來表示。

這些小詞你也要會哦：

international market 國際市場	official offer 正式報盤	exporter *n.* 出口商
enter a contract 簽訂合同	stock *n.* 現貨	reject *v.* 拒絕
original offer 最初報價	packing condition 包裝情況	notice *n.* 通知

Scene **70** 關於價格與質量 Price and Quality

 場景對話

A: We are thinking about ordering 1,000 TV sets from you. But there's one problem.	A：我們正考慮從您這裡訂購 1000 台電視機。但有一個問題。
B: Oh. What's that?	B：哦，什麼問題？

A: Your price is too high. You left us with no profit margin.

A：你們的價格太高了。我們幾乎沒有什麼盈利空間了。

B: 210 USD is the best we can offer.

B：210 美元已經是我們所能給的最便宜的價格了。

A: I have got better quotation from other companies.

A：我從別的公司拿到了更優惠的報價。

B: You really have to take the quality into consideration. In other words, you get what you pay for.

B：您真的應該把質量問題考慮進去。換句話說，一分錢一分貨。

A: I agree with you on that. But if you could lower the price a little bit, we will place an order right now.

A：我同意您的觀點。但是要是價格能再降一點的話，我們現在就下訂單。

B: I need to talk to my supervisor before I can give you a definite answer.

B：我得先跟我的上級溝通一下，然後才能給您確切的答覆。

A: Okay. I will wait for your answer.

A：好的，我等您的答覆。

場景問答必會句

> 210 USD is the best we can offer.
> 210 美元已經是我們所能給的最便宜的價格了。

還可以這樣說：
- The price has been reduced to the limit.
  該報價已經降到最低了。
- This is the lowest price we can give you.
  這是我方所能提供的最低價格了。

對方可能這樣回答：
- Could you make a better offer?
  您能不能提供一個更優惠的價格？
- Your price is impracticable. 你方的價格有點不切實際。

limit *n*. 極限

impracticable *a*. 行不通的，不切實際的

> I need to talk to my supervisor before I can give you a definite answer.
> 我得先跟我的上級溝通一下，然後才能給您確切的答覆。

還可以這樣說：
- There is no room for any reduction in price.
  價格毫無再降的餘地了。

對方可能這樣回答：
- Assume I order fifty thousand outright?
  假設我總共要訂 5 萬台呢？

room *n*. 空間

assume *v*. 假設

Scene 71 關於折扣 Discount

 場景對話

A: Mr. Lemon, <u>we can offer you a 5% discount.</u>	A：萊蒙先生，<u>我們可以為您提供 5% 的折扣。</u>
B: Well, in that case, I won't be able to make a deal with you. We expect you to offer a much better price.	B：嗯，這樣的話，我們就做不成交易了。我們期待您能提供更優惠的價格。
A: What do you suggest then?	A：那您的建議是什麼？
B: You price is much higher than we are willing to pay. If you could not provide a discount of 18%, there is no point in further discussing.	B：你們的價格大大超出我們的預算。如果你們無法給我 18% 的折扣，那我們就沒有再談的必要了。
A: <u>You can't expect us to make such a large reduction.</u> Can we meet each other half way?	A：我們不可能提供這麼大的折扣。我們雙方能不能各讓一步？
B: What do you mean by that?	B：您是什麼意思呢？
A: How about I give you 12% discount?	A：我提供給你們 12% 的折扣怎麼樣？
B: Okay. Let's call it a deal!	B：好的。成交。

場景問答必會句

> We can offer you a 5% discount.
> 我們可以為您提供 5% 的折扣。

還可以這樣說：

🗨 We are prepared to give a 20% discount for an offer buying 100,000 pieces.
訂購 10 萬台才可享受 8 折的優惠。

🗨 If our order is more than 10,000 metric tons, will you give us an additional 5% commission?
如果我方訂購 1 萬噸以上的話，貴方能否額外給我們 5% 的佣金？

PS additional *a.* 附加的，額外的

> You can't expect us to make such a large reduction.
> 我們不可能提供這麼大的折扣。

還可以這樣說：

💬 What kind of reduction did you have in mind then? 那麼您認為減價多少合適呢？

對方可能這樣回答：

💬 The gap between us is too great. 我們之間的 (價格) 差距太大了。

Scene 72 關於付款方式 Payment

🗨 場景對話

A: Mr. Lee, what payment terms could you accept?	A：李先生，貴方能接受什麼樣的付款條件呢？
B: Is it possible for you to pay in Chinese currency? It's quite easy.	B：您能否採用人民幣支付？這很方便。
A: We've never done this before. It's convenient for us to make the payment in pounds sterling.	A：我們從來沒有用人民幣支付過。用英鎊付款對我們來說比較方便。
B: Payment by L/C is our method of trade in such commodities. Actually, many banks in Europe now are in a position to open letters of credit and effect payment in Renminbi.	B：用信用證支付是我們在此類商品中採用的交易方式。實際上許多歐洲銀行都可以開具信用證，並可以用人民幣支付。
A: Do you mean I can open a letter of credit in Renminbi in my country?	A：您的意思是說我可以在我的國家開立人民幣信用證？
B: Yes, and we would consider a longer credit period.	B：是的。我們還會考慮延長信用期。
A: Okay. I think we can accept this mode of payment.	A：好的。我想我們可以接受這種付款方式。

🗨 場景問答必會句

> Is it possible for you to pay in Chinese currency?
> 您能否採用人民幣支付？

還可以這樣說：

💬 How would you like to make the payment? 您想如何支付？
💬 What is the mode of payment you wish to employ?
您希望用什麼方式付款？

PS
employ v. 採用，使用

> Payment by L/C is our method of trade in such commodities.
> 用信用證支付是我們在此類商品中採用的交易方式。

還可以這樣說：

💬 We can do the business on sixty days D/P basis.
我們可以按 60 天付款交單的方式進行交易。

對方可能這樣回答：

💬 If you can't be more flexible, we won't accept your terms of payment.
如果你們不能變通一些，我們將不會接受貴方的支付條件。

PS
D/P (Document against Payment) 付款交單

Scene 73 關於交貨時間 Time of Delivery

 場景對話

A: Let's go into details of the time of delivery.	A：讓我們來談談具體交貨時間吧。
B: Okay.	B：好的。
A: I hope these goods can be delivered by the end of September. We'd like them to be ready in time for our Christmas sales.	A：我們希望貴方能在 9 月底前交這批貨。我們要為聖誕節銷售做好準備。
B: Unfortunately, it'll be difficult for us to make a delivery at that time. Our manufacturers are fully committed at the moment.	B：很遺憾，我們很難在這個時間交貨。我們的生產商已經在全負荷生產。
A: Do you think you can get them to step up the production?	A：您能讓他們加快生產速度嗎？
B: I'm afraid it would be hard to do that, since they are already working three shifts a day as new orders keep pouring in.	B：這恐怕有點難，由於不斷有新訂單進來，他們已經一天三班加速生產了。
A: I see. What's the best you can do then?	A：知道了，那你們最快什麼時候能交貨？
B: We can make the delivery by the middle of October.	B：我們能在 10 月中旬交貨。
A: We'll accept that.	A：我們接受這個時間。

場景問答必會句

> Unfortunately, it'll be difficult for us to make a delivery at that time.
> 很遺憾，我們很難在這個時間交貨。

還可以這樣說：

It's not possible for us to advance the time of shipment.
我們無法提前交貨。

對方可能這樣回答：

We have to modify the delivery date then.
那樣我們就不得不更改交貨日期了。

PS

advance *v.* 提前

modify *v.* 修改

> We can make the delivery by the middle of October.
> 我們能在 10 月中旬交貨。

還可以這樣說：

By the middle of July. This is the best we can do.
7 月中旬交貨。這是我們所能交貨的最快時間了。

對方可能這樣回答：

I'm afraid that'll be too late.
恐怕那個時間太晚了。

還盤 Tips

還盤小技巧

1) 在還盤中，我們要儘量獲取對方的需求，以瞭解對方。
2) 通過提問來獲得信息，驗證我們對對方需求的判斷是否準確。如：What do you think of our offer?
3) 用試探性的條件問句進一步瞭解對方的具體情況。如：What if we agree to a two-year contract? / Would you give us exclusive distribution rights in our territory?
4) 尋求共同點。如果對方拒絕我們的條件，我們可以另換其他條件。雙方繼續磋商，直至找到重要的共同點。

Unit 4 樣品細節

樣品細節是涉及樣品的各個方面，包括郵寄、運費、包裝、顏色和款式等。

樣品細節必會詞

1 sample *n.* 樣品

樣品是在大批量生產前根據商品設計而先行製作、加工的產品，作為交易中商品的交付標準。

> **PS** sample card 樣品卡
> sample book 樣品本
> sample number 樣品號碼
> sample-cutting 樣品切片

2 quantity *n.* 數量

商品的數量可以用 quantity 表示。

> **PS** in large quantities 大量

3 discount *n./v.* 折扣

買賣貨物時按原價的若干成計價，叫做幾折。

4 buyer *n.* 買家

買主，商品的購買者。

> **PS** purchaser 指已經訂貨的買主；buyer 指購買者但不一定買。

5 seller *n.* 賣家

賣主，商品的出售者。

這些小詞你也要會哦：

quality *n.* 質量	pattern *n.* 圖案	specimen *n.* 標本
model *n.* 模式	standard *n.* 標準	inspect *v.* 檢查
supply *v.* 供應	equal *a.* 相等的	shipment *n.* 裝運

Scene 74　準備樣品 Sample Preparation

 場景對話

A: I'm sorry for answering you late. <u>Do you feel like offering twenty pieces of samples for quality inspection?</u>

A：很抱歉沒有及時回覆您。<u>您能為我們提供 20 件樣品用來檢測質量嗎？</u>

B: We can, but they are not free of charge. You can enjoy about 50% off.

B：可以，但不是免費的。您可以享受 5 折優惠。

A: No problem. Can you send your full banking details to me?

A：沒問題。您能把銀行賬戶信息發給我嗎？

B: Yes, I can. <u>Do you need Proforma Invoice?</u>

B：好，沒問題。<u>您需要形式發票嗎？</u>

A: Yes, please also prepare Letter of Interest.

A：是的，請也準備一下意願書。

B: All right. Let me confirm that we should prepare twenty pieces of samples, Proforma Invoice, Letter of Interest and bank details. Yes?

B：好的，讓我確認一下，我們需要準備：20 件樣品、形式發票、意願書和銀行信息，對嗎？

A: Good. When can I get all these?

A：沒錯。我什麼時候能收到？

B: I guess we need about two days to prepare.

B：我想我們需要 2 天的時間準備。

A: I hardly forget to tell you the address. It is No. 6 Jiefang Road, Haidian District, Beijing, China.

A：差點忘記告訴您地址了，我的地址是中國北京海澱區解放路 6 號。

B: I will inform you when I get everything ready.

B：材料都準備好後我會通知您。

A: Thank you very much.

A：非常感謝。

場景問答必會句

> Do you feel like offering twenty pieces of samples for quality inspection?
> 您能為我們提供 20 件樣品用來檢測質量嗎？

還可以這樣說：

Would you like to send us twenty pieces of samples for inspecting quality?
您願意給我們發 20 件樣品用於質量檢查嗎？

對方可能這樣回答：

📖 Of course, our samples are free but you will have to pay the freight.
當然可以，我們的樣品是免費的，但是需要由您來支付運費。

📖 Sorry, our products are very good and we have not ever offered samples before.
對不起，我們的產品非常好，以前都沒有提供過樣品。

> Do you need Proforma Invoice?
> 您需要形式發票嗎？

還可以這樣說：

📖 Should I prepare Proforma Invoice?
我需要準備形式發票嗎？

對方可能這樣回答：

📖 Yes, please send to me for confirming.
是的，請發給我確認一下。

📖 No, that's enough. 不，已經足夠了。

Proforma Invoice 形式發票

Scene 75 樣品郵寄與相關費用 Sample Post and Related Expenses

💬 場景對話

A: Would you please send us samples before we make an order?	A：請問在我們下訂單之前，能給我們寄樣品嗎？
B: Sure, the samples will be prepared immediately. Do you have any requirements in mind?	B：當然可以，我們會立即準備樣品。您還有什麼要求嗎？
A: We always buy in large quantities, so do you mind if you are responsible for freight?	A：我們經常購買大量的產品，所以您介意由貴方承擔運費嗎？
B: It is a great discount that the samples are free.	B：樣品免費已經是很大的優惠了。
A: I know. I will buy three million once if your samples meet our requirement. For such a big sum, you should attach importance to it.	A：我知道。如果您的樣品滿足我們的要求，我們會一次性訂300萬件產品。對於數量那麼大的訂單，您應該給予重視。
B: We pay much more attention to our cooperation and the samples will include each type you probably buy.	B：我們很重視我們之間的合作，樣品將涵蓋您可能購買的所有品種。

A: That's perfect. This will be a big business for both of us.	A：那太好了。對於我們雙方來說，這都是一筆大生意。
B: OK. Free samples and freight will be paid by our company, and we will send the goods via Fedex. <u>Can you tell me the address where the samples should be sent to?</u>	B：好吧，樣品免費，運費由我方支付，我們會用聯邦快遞寄送。<u>能告訴我樣品寄送的地址嗎？</u>
A: Thanks. The address is No. 8 the Big World, Daowai District, Harbin, Heilongjiang, China.	A：謝謝。地址是中國黑龍江省哈爾濱市道外區大世界 8 號。
B: We should be greatly obliged if you inform us whether the samples are suitable for your requirement after receiving them.	B：如果您能在收到樣品後通知我方樣品是否合適，我們將不勝感激。
A: I will inform you as soon as possible.	A：我會儘快通知您的。

場景問答必會句

> Wound you please send us samples before we make an order?
> 請問在我們下訂單之前，能給我們寄樣品嗎？

還可以這樣說：

💬 Can we take a look at your samples before we decide to purchase your products?
在決定購買您的產品之前，我們能先看看樣品嗎？

💬 Whether we will cooperate or not depends on your products, so please send us some samples.
我們是否能合作取決於您的產品，所以請給我們寄些樣品吧。

make an order 下訂單

depend on 取決於

對方可能這樣回答：

💬 Sorry, with respect to samples, I have to report to my manager.
對不起，關於樣品的事，我得上報我的經理。

💬 No problem. We provide potential clients with samples.
沒有問題，我們會為潛在客戶提供樣品。

provide sb. with sth. 為某人提供某事物

> Can you tell me the address where the samples should be sent to?
> 能告訴我樣品寄送的地址嗎？

還可以這樣說：

💬 Please tell me the address to which the samples should be sent.
請告訴我樣品應該發送到的地址。

Scene 76 樣品反饋意見 Feedback on Samples

 場景對話

A: Hi, I'd like to speak to Lucy. Is she there?	A：您好，我想跟露西通話，請問她在嗎？
B: This is Lucy.	B：我就是露西。
A: This is Dong Yue form Beijing Beauty Co., Ltd. <u>Did you receive the samples sent by our company?</u>	A：我是北京美麗有限公司的董玥。<u>您收到我們公司發出的樣品了嗎？</u>
B: Yes, we got them yesterday.	B：是的，我們昨天收到了。
A: <u>Can you tell me your opinion about the samples?</u>	A：<u>能說說您對樣品的看法嗎？</u>
B: The quality is all right but the style of Type three is a bit outdated.	B：質量很不錯，但是<u>型號 3 的樣式有點過時了。</u>
A: I see. Actually we have other new styles with beautiful colors. Would you like to take a look at them?	A：知道了。實際上我們還有其他新款式的產品，顏色豔麗。您想要看看嗎？
B: Well, I think I'd better see them and then I will tell you the result.	B：好的，我想我需要先看一下再告訴您結果。
A: Thanks! I will send the new samples right now.	A：謝謝！我現在就給您發新樣品。

場景問答必會句

> Did you receive the samples sent by our company?
> 您收到我們公司發出的樣品了嗎？

還可以這樣說：
- Have you ever got our samples? 您收到我們的樣品了嗎？

對方可能這樣回答：
- Yes, they arrived yesterday. 是的，昨天到的。
- Not yet. 還沒有。

> Can you tell me your opinion about the samples?
> 能說說您對樣品的看法嗎？

還可以這樣說：

🗨 What do you think of our samples? 您覺得我們的樣品怎麼樣？

🗨 Do our samples meet your requirement?
我們的樣品符合您的要求嗎？

對方可能這樣回答：

🗨 Sorry, we have not tested them.
抱歉，我們還沒有測試。

🗨 Congratulations! The samples are very good.
恭喜你，樣品非常好。

🗨 Sorry to tell you that your samples are below standard.
很遺憾地告訴您，您的樣品不符合標準。

Scene 77　討論包裝和顏色 Discuss Packaging and Color

 場景對話

A: Can I bring up for discussing the packing?	A：我可以提議討論一下包裝問題嗎？
B: Yes, I also want to talk about it. I'd like to know your opinion concerning the matter of packing?	B：可以，我也正想要談談這個。我想知道您對包裝有什麼想法？
A: A packing that catches the eye will help us push the sales, so I hope the packing can be attractive.	A：吸引眼球的包裝有助於我們推銷產品，所以我希望包裝能設計得吸引人。
B: All right. Which color do you like for the products?	B：好的。產品包裝您想要什麼顏色？
A: Generally speaking, I think blue is good.	A：總體來説，我覺得藍色不錯。
B: OK. I will remind the designer about this.	B：好的，我會提醒設計師用藍色的。
A: Thanks.	A：謝謝。
B: Packing charge is about 4‰ of the total cost. Do you know that?	B：包裝費用占總成本的 4‰。您知道這個吧？
A: Yes, but we have agreed that the contract price includes the packing charge, haven't we?	A：知道。但是我們已經説好包裝費用包含在合同價內了，不是嗎？
B: Yes, just a mention.	B：沒錯，只是提一下。
A:Never mind.	A：沒關係。

？A 場景問答必會句

I'd like to know your opinion concerning the matter of packing?
我想知道您對包裝有什麼想法？

還可以這樣說：
Would you like to express your idea on the packing?
您想要說說您對包裝的想法嗎？

對方可能這樣回答：
I hope the packing can be attractive because a packing that catches the eye will help us push the sales.
我希望包裝能設計得吸引人，因為吸引眼球的包裝有助於我們推銷產品。

Sorry, nothing so far. 抱歉，到目前為止，還沒有什麼想法。

Which color do you like for the products?
產品包裝您想要什麼顏色？

對方可能這樣回答：
I think blue and green are good. What is your opinion?
我認為藍色和綠色不錯。您覺得呢？

Sorry, I can't decide it. 抱歉，我沒法做決定。

Scene
78 確認產品設計 Confirmation of Product Design

 場景對話

A: Hi, this is the shoes designed by our excellent designer. What do you think of them?	A：您好，這是我們的優秀設計師設計的鞋子。您認為怎麼樣？
B: Have you ever tried on the shoes?	B：您試穿過這款鞋子嗎？
A: Not yet.	A：還沒有。
B: I guess the heels are too high and the shoes will be uncomfortable to wear.	B：我覺得鞋跟太高了，鞋子穿著會不舒服。
A: I was also worried about that, but the designer's words make me rest assured.	A：我也擔心過這一點，但是設計師的解釋讓我放心了。
B: What is the designer's explanation?	B：設計師是怎麼解釋的？
A: He said he designed this pair of shoes according to the curvature of the human foot.	A：他說他是按照人體足部的弧度來設計的。

B: <u>Does that mean people wearing this pair of shoes will not feel uncomfortable and tired?</u>	B：<u>這是否就意味着穿這雙鞋的人不會有不舒服的感覺，也不會覺得累？</u>
A: Exactly.	A：沒錯。
B: Can I try them on now?	B：我可以試穿一下嗎？
A: Of course!	A：當然可以！
B: Well, the designer is right. They are very good.	B：嗯，設計師是對的。鞋子穿着感覺很好。
A: Wow, thank you for your confirmation.	A：哇，感謝您的肯定。

 場景問答必會句

> **What is the designer's explanation?**
> 設計師是怎麼解釋的？

還可以這樣說：

🗨 What did the designer say?
　設計師是怎麼説的？

🗨 Can you explain for me?
　您能為我解釋一下嗎？

對方可能這樣回答：

🗨 Let the designer explain.
　請設計師來解釋一下。

🗨 He said there was no need to worry about that.
　他説沒有必要擔心這一點。

> **Does that mean people wearing this pair of shoes will not feel uncomfortable and tired?**
> 這是否就意味着穿這雙鞋的人不會有不舒服的感覺，也不會覺得累？

還可以這樣說：

🗨 Can I understand people wearing this kind of shoes will be comfortable and without tired feeling?
　我可以理解成穿這雙鞋會讓人覺得很舒服，不會覺得累嗎？

🗨 Would you like to explain it in detail?
　您願意再詳細解釋一下嗎？

對方可能這樣回答：

🗨 You are right. 沒錯。

🗨 Sorry, I think you misunderstood. 抱歉，我想您誤會了。

樣品細節 Tips

1. 寄送樣品

> 對於有多年合作關係的老客戶，可考慮免去樣品費和運費。對於有誠意的新客戶，可告知雖然樣品免費提供，但需要請對方付運費。所以，寄送樣品是否免費，運費由誰來負責等問題要根據不同的客戶關係來決定。
>
> 另外，樣品寄送後的跟蹤也非常重要。樣品寄出後，一定要及時與客戶聯繫，聽取客戶的反饋，以爭取與客戶建立進一步合作關係的機會。

2. 樣品細節函電小模板

Dear Scoot,

I think you have received our samples, and I wonder if they meet your requirement.

I can guarantee that the quality of our products is the same as the samples you got. What's more, our prices are very competitive. You will get a 3% discount if you order more than Minimum Order Quantity.

Sincerely hope we can cooperate with each other!

Looking forward to your reply.

Best regards,

An Ran

親愛的斯庫特：

我想您應該已經收到了我們的樣品，我想知道我們的樣品是否符合您的要求。

我可以向您保證，我們產品的質量都會和您收到的樣品一模一樣。而且，我們的價格非常有競爭力。若您訂購的產品數量超過最低訂購量，我們會給您 3% 的折扣。

真誠地希望能與您合作。

期待您的回覆。

安然

致敬

Unit 5 訂貨

貿易雙方就報價達成意向後，買方正式訂貨並就一些相關事項與賣方進行協商，雙方認可後，需要簽訂購貨合同。

訂貨必會詞

1 order *n.* 訂單
訂單指訂購貨物的合同或單據。

2 delivery *n.* 交貨
交貨指根據買賣雙方的約定，一方把貨物交付給另一方。

3 freight *n.* 運費
運費指運載貨物時支付的費用。

4 make offers 報價
報價指賣方通過考慮自己產品的成本、利潤和市場競爭力等因素，公開報出的可行價格。

這些小詞你也要會哦：

official *a.* 正式的	place *v.* 寄予	change *n.* 變更
useless *a.* 無效的	increase *v.* 增加	confirmation *n.* 確認
previous *a.* 以前的	decrease *v.* 減少	trial *a.* 試驗的

Scene 79 確認訂單 Confirm the Order

場景對話

A: I would like to order your products. Are they in stock now?

B: Some of them are not. Which product would you like to book?

A：我想要訂購你們的產品。現在有庫存嗎？

B：有一些產品目前沒有庫存。您想要預訂哪一款產品？

A: The same as our last order, but I want five hundred sets this time.	A：與上一次的訂單一樣，但是這次我要訂購 500 台。
B: Let me check. We need to produce another fifty sets for your order.	B：讓我看看。我們需要再為您的訂單生產 50 台。
A: Can you guarantee the goods to be exactly the same quality as the previous order?	A：您能保證這次貨物的質量與上一次訂單的產品質量是一樣的嗎？
B: Of course. We need ten days to produce and fifteen days for delivery.	B：當然。我們需要 10 天的生產時間和 15 天的運送時間。
A: OK. I will send our official order to you today.	A：好的。我會在今天給您發送我們的正式訂單。
B: I can send Proforma Invoice to you tomorrow.	B：明天我能把形式發票發給您。
A: Sure, okay.	A：好的，沒問題。
B: We appreciate your order and look forward to cooperating with you again soon.	B：非常感謝您的訂購，期待很快能再次與您合作。

 場景問答必會句

> Are they in stock now?
> 現在有庫存嗎？

還可以這樣說：
💬 Do you keep a large stock of goods?
　　貨物的庫存充足嗎？

對方可能這樣回答：
💬 Sorry, our stock is nearly exhausted.
　　抱歉，幾乎沒有庫存了。
💬 Yes, we have enough goods now.
　　是的，我們現在有足夠多的貨物。

in stock 有存貨

> Can you guarantee the goods to be exactly the same quality as the previous order?
> 您能保證這次貨物的質量與上一次訂單的產品質量是一樣的嗎？

對方可能這樣回答：
💬 I think it will be better than the last order.
　　我想會比上一個訂單的質量要好。
💬 We are confident that you will be satisfied with our products.
　　我們相信我們的產品會讓您滿意。

be satisfied with 對……滿意

Scene 80 產品推薦 Recommend Products

 場景對話

A: Hi, I notice that you always order clothes with an ethnic style.

A：您好，我注意到您總是訂購有民族風情的服裝。

B: Yes, this is one of the main styles in our company.

B：是的，民族風的服裝是我們公司的主要款式之一。

A: We have many new designs of ethnic style this year. <u>Are you interested in them?</u>

A：今年我們有很多新款的民族風服裝。<u>您有興趣嗎？</u>

B: Great. Please send me the pictures. Would you mind stating the prices?

B：太好了，請將圖片發給我。您介意說明一下價格嗎？

A: Of course not. We have happily cooperated with each other over the past few years.

A：當然不介意。我們這些年合作得非常愉快。

B: Yes. <u>Can I have the same discount as before if I place an order for these new clothes?</u>

B：是的。<u>對於這些新款服裝，我可以享受和之前一樣的折扣嗎？</u>

A: I can't decide, but I will try to persuade our manager.

A：這個我不能做主，但是我會盡力說服我們經理。

B: Thanks a lot. I will tell you whether I will order them or not after taking a look at the pictures.

B：多謝。看過圖片之後，我會告訴您是否訂貨。

A: I will wait for your call.

A：我等您的電話。

場景問答必會句

Are you interested in them?
您有興趣嗎？

還可以這樣說：
- Would you like to have a look? 您想要看看嗎？
- They are supposed to be suitable for your company. 我猜它們適合您的公司。

對方可能這樣回答：
- Wow, this is what I'm looking for. 哇，這正是我在尋找的（款式）。

> Can I have the same discount as before if I place an order for these new clothes?
> 對於這些新款服裝，我可以享受和之前一樣的折扣嗎？

還可以這樣說：

🗨 Would you give me the same discount as before concerning this order?
  關於這份訂單，您能給我和之前一樣的折扣嗎？

對方可能這樣回答：

🗨 Yes, you can. 是的，您可以享受和之前一樣的折扣。

🗨 Sorry, these are new designs and we can't give you the discount.
  抱歉，這些是新款，我們無法給您打折。

Scene **81** 庫存無貨 Stock Unavailable

 場景對話

A: I'd like to place an additional order for the dresses. <u>Are they available now?</u>	A：我想要追加長裙的訂單。<u>現在有貨嗎？</u>
B: Which color would you like?	B：您想要什麼顏色？
A: I'd like forty blue dresses and twenty green dresses.	A：我想要 40 條藍色裙和 20 條綠色裙。
B: Sorry, we have no blue dresses and green dresses now. Both colors are very popular.	B：對不起，我們現在沒有藍色和綠色長裙了。這兩種顏色的長裙非常暢銷。
A: Wow, what should I do now?	A：那現在我該怎麼辦？
B: Our factories are stepping up production now. <u>Can we deliver the products two days later?</u>	B：我們的工廠現在正在加速生產。<u>我們可以在兩天後發貨嗎？</u>
A: They have almost sold out. Can you make it faster?	A：這兩種顏色的長裙幾乎要賣完了。能加快生產嗎？
B: Sorry, we are already working at the maximum speed. I hope you can understand that.	B：抱歉，我們已經在以最快的速度生產了。我希望您能理解。
A: Definitely. It is also OK that you deliver the products in two days.	A：當然。2 天後發貨也可以。
B: Thanks for the concession you made.	B：感謝您做出的讓步。
A: You are welcome.	A：不客氣。

場景問答必會句

> Are they available now?
> 現在有貨嗎？

還可以這樣說：
- Can I get them now? 我現在能拿貨嗎？

對方可能這樣回答：
- Yes, we have enough products in stock. 是的，我們有足夠多的庫存。
- Sorry, would you like to wait a moment and let me check?
  抱歉，您願意等一會兒嗎？我去查看一下。
- They are out of stock. 它們脫銷了。

> Can we deliver the products in two days?
> 我們可以在兩天後發貨嗎？

還可以這樣說：
- Do you agree that we will send the products in two days?
  我們在兩天後發貨，您同意嗎？
- What do you think of sending the products in two days?
  您認為兩天後發貨怎麼樣？

Scene 82　準備形式發票 Prepare Proforma Invoice

場景對話

A: Hi, I'm preparing Proforma Invoice now. Would you like to confirm some matters?	A：您好，我現在正在準備形式發票。您願意跟我確認一些事項嗎？
B: No problem. Please feel free to ask.	B：沒問題，請隨便問。
A: For No. 6659 of Women's Leather Shoes, a hundred pairs of the black shoes and fifty pairs of the yellow ones. Am I right?	A：6659 號女士皮鞋，黑色款 100 雙，黃色款 50 雙。對嗎？
B: Yes, that's correct.	B：是的，完全正確。
A: How many pairs of Women's Sports Shoes do you order?	A：您訂購了多少雙女士運動鞋？

B: Twenty pairs of No. S55, and fifteen pairs of No. S26, so the total amount is thirty-five pairs.	B：S55 號是 20 雙，S26 是 15 雙，所以總數是 35 雙。
A: Got you. I have no question now. <u>Do you have anything to add?</u>	A：知道了。現在我沒有問題了。<u>您有要補充的嗎？</u>
B: I will be on a business trip tomorrow and I will appreciate if you can send me the Proforma Invoice today.	B：我明天會出差，如果您能在今天把形式發票發給我，我會很感激的。
A: OK, I will try my best.	A：好，我會盡力安排。
B: Thank you very much.	B：非常感謝。
A: You are welcome.	A：不客氣。

場景問答必會句

> **Would you like to confirm some matters?**
> 您願意跟我確認一些事項嗎？

還可以這樣說：
- Please help me to confirm some things. 請幫助我確認一些事情。
- Can you confirm the order now? 您現在可以確認一下訂單嗎？

對方可能這樣回答：
- Yes, of course. 當然可以。
- Sorry, I have to go to a meeting right now. 對不起，我現在得去開會。
- Can you wait for me for half an hour? 您能等我半小時嗎？

> **Do you have anything to add?**
> 您有要補充的事情嗎？

還可以這樣說：
- Is there any change for the order?
  這次的訂單有什麼變更嗎？
- Is there anything you want me to confirm?
  有沒有您需要我確認的事情？

對方可能這樣回答：
- No, I have no question. 沒有，我沒什麼問題了。
- Yes, please pay attention to the quantity of the male shoes changed from sixty pairs to fifty pairs.
  是的，請注意，男士鞋由 60 雙變成 50 雙了。

Scene 83　訂單變動 Change Order

 場景對話

A: Can I speak to Daniel? This is Li Ming.	A：請問丹尼爾在嗎？我是李明。
B: Sorry, he is not here. Can I help you?	B：對不起，他不在。有什麼可以幫您嗎？
A: Yes, please tell him that my order has been changed.	A：請告訴他我的訂單有變動。
B: Can you please tell me which part has been changed?	B：請問您能告訴我變動的部分是什麼嗎？
A: Please replace green with yellow for No. 901.	A：請將 901 號的顏色用黃色替換綠色。
B: OK. Anything else?	B：好的。還有嗎？
A: The quantity of No. 806 is changed from thirty to fifty.	A：806 號的數量從 30 變成 50。
B: I've taken note of what you said.	B：我記下了您剛剛説的變動。
A: Then, the quantity of this order is twice the minimum order quantity. Do you agree to offer me 10% off based on our agreement?	A：那麼，這次訂單的數量就是最低訂貨量的兩倍。基於我們之間的協議，您同意為我提供 10% 的折扣嗎？
B: I'm sorry. For this question, Daniel will contact you.	B：抱歉。這個問題，丹尼爾會聯繫您的。
A: Thanks! Please contact me as soon as possible.	A：謝謝！請儘快答覆我。

場景問答必會句

> Can you please tell me which part has been changed?
> 請問您能告訴我變動的部分是什麼嗎？

還可以這樣說：
🗨 Can I know what has been changed? 我能知道變更的部分是什麼？

對方可能這樣回答：
🗨 I will send the new order to you later. 稍後我會將新訂單發給您。
🗨 Please check the attachment I sent and the changed parts have been highlighted with red.
請查看我發的附件，修改的部分已經用紅色標注了。

> Do you agree to offer me 10% off based on our agreement?
> 基於我們之間的協議，您同意為我提供 10% 的折扣嗎？

還可以這樣說：

💬 In accordance with our agreement, you should discount the price at 10%.
根據我們的協議，您應該給我打 10% 的折扣。

對方可能這樣回答：

💬 Sure, you can enjoy a 10% discount as long as the quantity meets the requirement.
當然，只要數量滿足 10% 打折的要求，您就能享受 10% 的折扣優惠。

💬 Sorry, I have to take advice from my manager. 抱歉，我得徵求一下經理的意見。

Scene 84 削減訂單 Reduce an Order

  場景對話

A: Please reduce the number of the order to five hundred pieces.	A：請將訂單的數量減少到 500 件。
B: It is a pity to hear that. <u>Could you please tell me the reason for this change?</u>	B：很遺憾聽到您要減少訂單數量。<u>可以請您告訴我變更數量的原因嗎？</u>
A: We've got a trial order from a new client. We will order more products from him if his products are OK, because his products are cheaper than yours.	A：我們從一位新客戶那裡得到了一份試用訂單。如果他的產品符合我們的要求，我們會從他那裡訂購更多的產品，因為他的產品比貴公司的產品便宜。
B: That's bad news. How cheaper they are?	B：這真是一個壞消息。便宜多少？
A: $10 less for each piece.	A：每件產品便宜 10 美元。
B: But our products are of high quality.	B：但是我們的產品質量很好。
A: I know it. But you know the price is important as well. Our boss is looking for producers who can supply products with better quality and lower price.	A：我知道。但是您知道，價格也很重要。我們的老闆一直在尋找能提供又好又便宜的產品的供應商。
B: Well, in that case, we have to quote again according to the new quantity. <u>Could you confirm this new quotation first?</u>	B：好吧。如果是這樣的話，現在根據您的新訂貨量，我們得重新報價。<u>您可以先確認一下新報價嗎？</u>
A: Yes. I'm sorry for this inconvenience.	A：可以。抱歉給您添麻煩了。

| B: You don't have to. Anyway, we respect your decision. | B：不必道歉。無論如何，我們都尊重您的決定。 |
| A: Thank you for your understanding. | A：謝謝您的理解。 |

場景問答必會句

> Could you please tell me the reason for this change?
> 可以請您告訴我變更數量的原因嗎？

還可以這樣說：

🗨 Would you like to inform me the reason for decreasing the quantity?
　您願意告訴我您減少訂購數量的原因嗎？

🗨 Please tell me why you change the quantity. 請告訴我您為什麼變更數量。

對方可能這樣回答：

🗨 Sorry, I really do not know and I only got the notice from my director.
　對不起，我真的不知道，我只是從我們主管那裡得到的消息。

🗨 We estimate that the market is not very good in the coming months.
　我們估計未來幾個月市場銷量不會很理想。

> Could you confirm this new quotation first?
> 您可以先確認一下新報價嗎？

還可以這樣說：

🗨 Please make a confirmation of this new quotation first.
　請先確認一下新報價。

對方可能這樣回答：

🗨 Sorry, I will be back in five minutes.
　對不起，5 分鐘後我再聯繫您。

Scene 85 取消訂單 Cancel an Order

場景對話

| A: This is urgent. I hope you have not started the production. | A：這很急。我希望您還沒有開始生產。 |
| B: What's wrong? | B：怎麼了？ |

A: Well, there is a serious quality problem with your products, so we have to stop the business between us right now.	A：你們的產品有一個很嚴重的質量問題，我們不得不立即叫停我們之間的業務。
B: I'm sorry to hear that. <u>Do you mean the order has to be canceled now?</u>	B：我很遺憾聽到這個消息。<u>您的意思是現在要取消訂單嗎？</u>
A: Unfortunately, yes.	A：很遺憾，是的。
B: <u>What will you do for the work we have done?</u>	B：<u>對於我們已經做了的工作部分，您會怎麼處理？</u>
A: We will handle it in accordance with our contract.	A：我們會按照合同來處理。
B: OK. Whenever you would like to cooperate with us again, we're glad to at your service.	B：好。無論何時您想再次跟我們合作，我們仍然很高興為您服務。

場景問答必會句

> **Do you mean the order has to be canceled now?**
> **您的意思是現在要取消訂單嗎？**

還可以這樣說：

🖱 So you want to cancel the order now?
所以您現在想取消訂單？

🖱 Can you further explain for stopping the business between us?
您能具體解釋一下為什麼停止我們之間的業務嗎？

🖱 Sorry, I'm not very clear about what you said.
對不起，我不是很清楚您的意思。

對方可能這樣回答：

🖱 No, please just suspend the production.
不，請只暫停生產。

🖱 Your product caused a huge problem.
您的產品引起了很大的問題。

> **What will you do for the work we have done?**
> **對於我們已經做了的工作部分，您會怎麼處理？**

還可以這樣說：

🖱 For the work we have finished, could you pay for it?
對於我們已經完成的工作，您能支付費用嗎？

🖱 What about the work we have done? 那我們已經完成的工作要怎麼辦？

對方可能這樣回答：

🗨 Yes, we will make the payment for it.
　是的，我們會支付的。

🗨 Sorry, we will talk about it later.
　抱歉，這個問題我們稍後再談。

▎訂貨 Tips ▎

訂貨函電小模板

Dear Cecil,

I'm very pleased to inform you that your order has been accepted. Thank you for your order.

Our products are always selling well with reasonable price and good service.

We appreciate our cooperation and we'd like to assure you that your order will be carefully processed.

Besides, we also have some new products. Please find the attachment for the current price list and the pictures.

Look forward to your feedback.

Best regards,

Liu Yuan

親愛的塞西爾：

很高興通知您，您的訂單已經被接受了。感謝您的訂購。

我們的產品價格合理，服務良好，一直賣得很好。

我們感激我們之間的業務往來，我們向您保證您的訂單會被妥善處理。

除此之外，我們也有些新產品。隨信附上了當前的價格表和圖片，請查閱。

期待您的反饋。

劉媛

致敬

Unit 6　簽訂合同

外貿合同即營業地處於不同國家或地區的當事人就商品買賣產生的權利和義務關係所達成的書面協議。外貿合同受國家法律保護和管轄，是對簽約各方都具有同等約束力的法律性文件，是解決貿易糾紛，進行調解、仲裁與訴訟的法律依據。

▌訂貨必會詞▌

1 contract of arbitration 仲裁合同
仲裁合同是指雙方當事人在自願、協商和平等互利的基礎上將他們之間已經發生或者可能發生的爭議提交仲裁解決的書面文件，是申請仲裁的必備材料。

2 payment terms 支付條款
支付條款是對貨款支付的貨幣、金額、方式和支付時間等的規定。按照合同規定支付貨款，是買方對賣方承擔的基本義務。

3 contractual-joint-venture 契約式合營
契約式合營是指來自兩個或兩個以上國家的企業，通過協商簽訂合同，規定各方的權利與義務，據以開展經營活動的一種直接投資方式，又稱合作經營。

4 contract price 合約價格
合約價格是雙方通過協商，以書面形式定下的價格，與市場價格之間可能存在一定差異。

✎ 這些小詞你也要會哦：

quantity *n.* 數量	packing *n.* 包裝	shipment *n.* 裝運
port *n.* 港口	document *n.* 單據	claim *n.* 索賠
arbitration *n.* 仲裁	signature *n.* 簽名	remark *n.* 備註

Scene 86　起草合同 Draft a Contract

 場景對話

A: Well, Mr. Watson, I think we had a good start of our cooperation yesterday. Let's go on with our business talk.

A：沃森先生，我想我們昨天已經有了一個良好的合作開端，現在讓我們繼續討論合作的問題吧。

B: Why not? I've reconsidered about your price. I have to say that your price is on the high side, which will put us in a tide corner. Is there any possibility to reduce the price?

B：好的。我重新考慮了你們的價格。我必須得說，你們的價格偏高，這會使我們陷入困境。有沒有可能請你們降低價格呢？

A: If you compare the quality of our goods with that of other companies, you will see our price is very reasonable. But we may consider making some concessions for the long-term friendship between us.

A：如果您比較一下我們和其他公司的產品質量，您會發現我們的價格非常合理。但為了我們之間長久的合作關係，我們可以考慮在價格方面做出讓步。

B: We really appreciate it. As to the payment, we would like to pay by confirmed and irrevocable L/C.

B：非常感謝。在付款方面，我們希望採用保兌的不可撤銷的信用證來支付。

A: OK. Then what about the method of delivery?

A：好的，那麼運送方式呢？

B: We'd like to have our goods sent by air.

B：我們希望用空運。

A: Any special requirements?

A：有什麼特殊要求嗎？

B: In order to avoid any possible damage in transit, we would like the goods to be packed in strong but small wooden cases.

B：為了避免運輸中可能造成的損壞，我們希望能用堅固的小型木箱來包裝貨物。

A: We'll do it on the condition that the extra freight has to be paid by you.

A：我們會照辦，但條件是額外運費由貴方支付。

B: That's all right. Will it also be written in the contract?

B：沒問題，這個要寫進合同嗎？

A: Yes, I'll make a note of that. I believe that we can proceed on those terms. Shall we draw up an agreement on a tentative basis?

A：是的，我會記下來。我相信我們雙方都會遵守這些條款。我們草擬一份初步協議好嗎？

B: That will be fine. Then we can confirm the terms at our meeting tomorrow.

B：好的，那麼我們就能在明天的會議上對條款作進一步確認了。

場景問答必會句

If you compare the quality of our goods with that of other companies, you will see our price is very reasonable.
如果您比較一下我們和其他公司的產品質量，您會發現我們的價格非常合理。

還可以這樣說：

💬 If the order is exceptional large, we will consider to increase the discount.
如果訂單特別大，我們會考慮增加折扣。

discount *n.* 折扣

💬 We are glad to provide a 5% discount for an order of 100 dozen or more.
對於訂購數量為 100 打或更多的訂單，我們樂意提供 5% 的折扣。

💬 The price we offer you is the lowest, we can't do any better.
我們給您報的是最低價，我們無法再讓步了。

> Shall we draw up an agreement on a tentative basis?
> 我們草擬一份初步協議好嗎？

對方可能這樣回答：

💬 OK. Anyway we've reached an agreement with each other.
好的。反正我們雙方已經達成了一致。

tentative *a.* 暫定的，初步的

💬 I think we can talk about the contract later, because we still have a lot of terms to discuss.
我覺得我們可以待會兒再談合同的事，因為還有很多條款有待商榷。

Scene 87　商定合同 Negotiate a Contract

 場景對話

A: Good morning, Mr. Green. I made a close study of the draft contract last night.	A：早上好，格林先生，昨晚我仔細審閱了合同草案。
B: Any questions?	B：有什麼問題嗎？
A: Yes. We were satisfied with the terms of this contract for the most part, but there is still a few points left over to clear up. First, we think that your terms of payment are too severe for us.	A：是的。我們對合同中的大部分條款都覺得滿意，但其中仍然存在一些需要弄清楚的問題。首先，我們覺得付款條款對我們來說太苛刻了。
B: Could you make it clearer?	B：您能仔細講講嗎？
A: Of course. You know, Mr. White, this is a really large purchase. I'm afraid we can't pay off at one time. We have to pay by installment.	A：當然。懷特先生，您知道，這確實是一筆大買賣，恐怕我們無法一次性將款項付清，只能分期付款。

B: <u>Do you mean you prefer a deferred payment?</u>	B：<u>您的意思是希望採取延期付款的方式？</u>
A: Yes, we can start our payment in half a year and the total amount will be paid off within two years by three installments.	A：是的。我們可以從半年後開始付款，所有的款項在 2 年內分 3 次付清。
B: That can be accepted on the condition that you begin your payment in four months and you have to pay the interest.	B：如果你們從 4 個月後開始付款並支付利息，我們可以接受這種付款方式。
A: That sounds reasonable.	A：聽起來很合理。
B: Good. Is there anything else?	B：很好。還有什麼問題嗎？
A: One more. We think it's necessary to include a force majeure clause in the contract.	A：還有一個問題。我們認為在合同中加入不可抗力條款很有必要。
B: I agree.	B：我同意。
A: That's all. Thank you very much.	A：就這些了。謝謝。
B: We'll revise the contract this evening, and have it ready to be signed tomorrow morning at ten. How about that?	B：今晚我們會修改一下合同，準備明天早上 10 點簽約，怎麼樣？
A: Perfect.	A：好極了。

 場景問答必會句

> **Could you make it clearer?**
> 您能仔細講講嗎？

還可以這樣說：

🗨 Could you talk about the terms in details?
可以詳細地說說嗎？

🗨 Please point out directly.
請您直接指出來吧。

對方可能這樣回答：

🗨 OK. I'd like to point out that your terms of payment are too severe for us.
好吧，我想指出，你們的支付條款對我們太嚴苛了。

> **Do you mean you prefer a deferred payment?**
> 您的意思是說希望採取延期付款的方式嗎？

還可以這樣說：
Do you mean you'll pay by installment?
您的意思是您將分期付款嗎？

對方可能這樣回答：
Yes, because it's difficult for us to get that large amount of money in a short time.
是的，短時間內要湊齊那麼多錢，對我們來說太難了。

Scene 88 審核合同 Review a Contract

 場景對話

A: Hello, Mr. Simpson. We've brought the draft of our contract. Please have a look.	A：您好，辛普森先生。我們把合同草案帶來了，請您過目。
B: OK. We don't have any questions about the terms, but I think we'd better make some changes in the wording of some sentences.	B：好的，我們對於合同條款沒有什麼問題，但我認為我們最好在這些句子的措辭上做些修改。
A: Would you mind pointing them out one by one?	A：您可以一一指出嗎？
B: That is exactly what I will do. Look at this phrase. I'd like to replace it with "after the date of delivery".	B：我正準備這樣做。我想用"自交付之日起"替換這個短語。
A: The two phrases just have the same meaning, don't they?	A：這兩個短語意思一樣，不是嗎？
B: Of course not. Although they look similar, there is a tiny difference between the two. We can't be too exact when preparing a contract.	B：當然不一樣。雖然它們意思相近，但也存在細微差別。我們在準備合同的時候一定要努力做到精確。
A: Yes, you're right. Do we have anything else to amend?	A：是的，您說得對。還有別的地方需要修改嗎？
B: Look here. The "port" should be the "port of destination" ; otherwise, it will be mistaken for the "port of loading".	B：看這裡。這裡的"口岸"應該改成"目的口岸"，否則會與"裝運口岸"弄混。
A: Got it.	A：我懂了。

B: Last, we have to make it clear in the contract that you are obliged to complete the delivery of the goods within the contractual time of shipment. "If the shipment can't be made within three month as stipulated, the contract will become void." Would you mind inserting such a clause in the contract?	B：最後，我們需要在合同裡確認貴方必須在合同裝運期內完成貨物裝運。"如果不能在規定的 3 個月內完成裝運的話，則合同視為無效。"你們介意在合同中加入這一條款嗎？
A: I won't object to reasonable requirements.	A：我不會反對如此合理的要求。
B: Perfect. There is nothing more. When shall we sign the contract? We're ready.	B：好極了。沒有別的了，我們什麼時候簽合同？我們已經準備好了。
A: How about tomorrow morning at ten o'clock?	A：明天早上 10 點怎麼樣？
B: Good. I'm looking forward to our cooperation in the future.	B：好的。我非常期待我們今後的合作。

場景問答必會句

> Would you mind pointing them out one by one?
> 您可以一一指出嗎？

還可以這樣說：

📨 Would you like to talk about them in a specific manner?
　　您可以仔細地說清楚嗎？

對方可能這樣回答：

📨 OK. Here, here and there. That's just my own opinion.
　　好的，這裡，這裡還有那裡。這些只是我的個人意見。

> I won't object to reasonable requirements.
> 我不會反對如此合理的要求。

還可以這樣說：

📨 That's fine. It will benefit both of us.
　　好的，這對我們雙方都有益。

📨 No, I don't think it's necessary to add the term.
　　不，我覺得這一條款沒必要加進合同。

Scene 89 修改合同 Amend a Contract

 場景對話

A: Good morning, Mr. Smith. Here is our contract. Please go over it and see if everything is in order.	A：早上好，史密斯先生。這是我們的合同，請您過目，看看是否一切妥當。
B: Let me have a look. Don't you think we're supposed to add a sentence here? "In case of breach of any of the provisions of this agreement by one party, the other party shall have the right to terminate this agreement by giving notice in written form to its opposite party."	B：我看看。您不認為這裡應該加上一句話嗎？"一旦一方違背了既定的協議，另一方有權終止該協議並書面通知對方。"
A: OK, I'll add it in the contract. <u>Do you have any comments on other terms?</u>	A：好的，我會把它加到合同裡。其他的條款呢？
B: Well, I think the contract needs some modifications. Our customer called us yesterday and told us they were in urgent need of the goods. They want to see the goods on display by the end of this month. Therefore, shall we adjust the delivery date, making it ten days or a week earlier?	B：我覺得合同需要做少許修改。客戶昨天致電我們，說急需這批商品，希望能在月底前看到商品展出，所以可以將交付日期提前 10 天或 1 週嗎？
A: <u>There is little possibility to meet your requirement unless the mode of transportation is changed.</u> As usual, it is much faster to have the goods sent by air than by railway, but in that way, you have to bear the extra freight.	A：除非改變運輸方式，否則很難達到您的要求。通常，空運要比鐵路運輸快得多，但那樣的話，貴方得承擔額外運費。
B: I see. Let's do as what you say. We transport the goods by plane and the delivery date should be 25th October. Is that OK for you?	B：我知道，就照您說的做吧。我們空運這批商品，交付日期定為 10 月 25 日，行嗎？
A: OK.	A：好的。
B: I'd like to emphasize once again how important your timely delivery is. If you fail to deliver the goods at the time stipulated in the contract, our clients may turn elsewhere. We just can't stand such kind of loss.	B：我想再次強調一下按時交貨的重要性。如果你們不能按照合同規定交貨，我們的客戶很可能會另尋合作夥伴，我們可承受不起這樣的損失。

A: Mr. Smith, it is our permanent principle that commercial integrity is maintained. So, anything else you want to bring up for discussion?

A：史密斯先生，守信是我們的一貫宗旨。您還有什麼問題要提出來討論嗎？

B: No, nothing more. The contract contains basically all we have agreed upon during our negotiations.

B：沒有了。合同基本上涵蓋了所有我們在協商中已經達成協議的內容。

A: Good. I'll have the contract amended tonight. Shall we sign the contract tomorrow morning?

A：好的。我今晚將合同內容修改一下，明天上午我們簽合同好嗎？

B: Oh yes. I'm glad that our negotiation has come to a successful conclusion.

B：好的。我很高興這次洽談圓滿成功。

場景問答必會句

> Do you have any comments on other terms?
> 其他的條款呢？

還可以這樣說：

What do you think about other terms?
其他的條款如何呢？

If you have any questions about other terms, please let us know.
如果您對其他條款有疑慮，請直說。

對方可能這樣回答：

Well, I think the contract needs some modifications.
合同需要做少許修改。

We are supposed to go over all the terms again before we sign the formal contract.
我們應該在簽訂正式合同之前再審視一下合同內容。

> There is little possibility to meet your requirement unless the mode of transportation is changed.
> 除非改變運輸方式，否則很難達到您的要求。

還可以這樣說：

Let me see. Oh, yes. We can do that.
讓我想想。哦，是的，我們可以做到提前交付。

對方可能這樣問：

So shall we shift the delivery to an earlier date?
所以我們能將交付日期稍稍提前嗎？

Based on that, shall we advance the delivery date?
基於此，我們可以將交付日期提前嗎？

Scene 90 簽訂合同 Sign a Contract

 場景對話

A: Mr. Holmes, the formal contract is ready, but I think we'd better go over a few details before signing the contract.	A：福爾摩斯先生，正式合同已經準備好了，但我覺得我們最好在簽訂合同之前重新檢查一些細節。
B: Shall we take up the matter point by point?	B：我們逐點研究一下好嗎？
A: That's fine.	A：好的。
B: How long will the contract last?	B：合同的有效期是多長？
A: This contract is valid for one year.	A：有效期為 1 年。
B: Isn't one year too short? This contract is supposed to be valid for at least three years.	B：1 年不會太短了嗎？這份合同的預計有效期至少得 3 年。
A: If everything's going smoothly, it could be extended for two years.	A：如果一切進行順利，可以再延續 2 年。
B: All right.	B：好的。
A: What do you think of the wordings?	A：您覺得合同的措辭怎樣？
B: The wordings are really idiomatical. I'm very satisfied with it.	B：用詞很地道，我很滿意。
A: Anything else you would like to discuss?	A：您還有別的問題嗎？
B: Finally we have reached a basic agreement on the problems that should be worked out.	B：對一些需要解決的問題我們終於基本上達成了一致。
A: Then it's the time for us to sign the contract.	A：那麼該是我們簽合同的時候了。
B: Done. Congratulations!	B：簽好了。祝賀！
A: I hope this will lead to our further business.	A：希望這次交易能促進我們之間的進一步合作。

場景問答必會句

> This contract is valid for one year.
> 有效期為一年。

還可以這樣說：
🗫 Two years, at maximum. 最多 2 年。

> What do you think of the wordings?
> 您覺得合同的措辭怎樣？

還可以這樣說：
🗫 Is there anything, as to the wordings, that requires amending in the contract?
　 您覺得這份合同在措辭方面有需要修改的地方嗎？
🗫 What's your opinion about the wordings? 您覺得合同的措辭如何？

對方可能這樣回答：
🗫 Frankly speaking, I think some words need to be changed.
　 坦白說，我認為有些地方需要換個詞來表達。
🗫 Not that idiomatical, but the expressions are clear.
　 不太地道，但表達清楚。

Scene 91　合同終止 Terminate a Contract

 場景對話

A: Mr. Black, nice to meet you. Sit down, please.	A：布萊克先生，很高興見到您，請坐。
B: Thank you.	B：謝謝。
A: Personally I should say friendly negotiation is the best way to settle the dispute between business partners. Therefore, I'm here, discussing about our problems with you.	A：個人而言，要想解決貿易夥伴之間的爭端，最好的方法就是友好的磋商。所以，我現在在這裡跟您討論一下我們之間的問題。
B: If you're talking about the goods delivered to Shanghai in October, could you give me five minutes first? I can explain the situation in details.	B：如果您說的是 10 月運往上海的那批貨，可不可以先給我 5 分鐘時間？我向您詳細解釋一下當時的情形。

A: It's not necessary to do that, Mr. Black. Both of us have seen the results. Actually I was wondering what we should do if either one of us would like to terminate the contract before its term's up?	A：布萊克先生，您沒必要那麼做。我們雙方都看到了結果。我想知道如果我們有一方想在期滿前終止合同，該怎麼操作？
B: You want to terminate the contract? But as the contract says, if we fail to make the delivery four weeks later than the time of shipment stipulated in the contract, you shall have the right to cancel the contract.	B：您想終止合同？但合同裡說，如果我們晚於合同規定日期 4 週交貨，貴方才有權取消合同。
A: Oh, I see.You are reminding me that you were just three weeks late? No, I won't terminate it now, but we aren't going to renew our contract next year.	A：我知道。您是在提醒我貴方只晚了 3 週？不，我不會現在終止合同，但明年我們不會續約了。
B: How come? I thought you were happy with our service.	B：為什麼？我以為你們一直以來都很滿意我們的服務。
A: I was until this year. In our line of work, we can't afford unreliable delivery.	A：今年之前都很滿意。但是我們這個行業承擔不起送貨不穩定的風險。
B: Don't you think it's unfair to deny us for just one mistake?	B：因為一次錯誤就全盤否定我們，您不覺得這不公平嗎？
A: We lost an important customer and paid fifty thousand dollars for your one mistake. Is that not enough?	A：因為貴方這一個錯誤，我們失去了一位重要客戶，還損失了 5 萬美元，這還不夠嗎？
B: We are very sorry. Please give us the opportunity to redeem ourselves.	B：很抱歉。請給我們彌補自己過失的機會。
A: That's all for our talk. I just want to inform you our decision.	A：我們的談話到此為止。我只是想告知您我們的決定。

🗨 場景問答必會句

> You want to terminate the contract?
> 您想終止合同？

還可以這樣說：

🗨 You'll have to pay a large amount of penalties to the other side.
您必須向另一方支付大量違約金。

🗨 Why don't you just wait for a period of time? If both parties do not agree to renew the contract at its expiration, it will automatically become void.
您何不多等一段時間？如果雙方在合同到期時不再續約，則合同自動失效。

If I were you, I would terminate the contract as soon as possible.
如果我是您的話，我肯定會儘快終止合同。

> Don't you think it's unfair to deny us for just one mistake?
> 因為一次錯誤就全盤否定我們，您不覺得不公平嗎？

還可以這樣說：

One mistake doesn't mean we're incapable of doing it.
區區一次錯誤不能說明我們沒有能力做這個。

對方可能這樣回答：

I know, but we can't stand the risk. 我知道，可是我們不能承擔這樣的風險。

Scene 92 　合同違約 Breach a Contract

　場景對話

A: Hello, Mr. Brown. It is nice to see you again.	A：您好，布朗先生，很高興再次見到您。
B: How are you, Miss Wang? It certainly is a pleasure to see you again here. I hope you had an enjoyable trip from Shanghai.	B：您好嗎，王小姐？很高興又在這裡見到您。希望您從上海來的一路旅途愉快。
A: Thank you, it couldn't be better. Mr. Brown, if you don't mind, I'll go straight to the point.	A：謝謝您，一切都很好。布朗先生，要是您不介意的話，我就開門見山直接談業務了。
B: You are concerned about the peaches if I'm not mistaken.	B：如果我沒理解錯的話，您想談桃子的事情，對吧？
A: Yes. Mr. Brown, I assumed that you have probably been informed of the serious damage done to the last consignment of fifty boxes. 40% of the peaches went bad.	A：是的。布朗先生，我想也許您已經知道最後 50 箱桃子損壞嚴重的事，40% 的桃子都爛了。
B: Have you discovered what the exact causes of the rot were? To be honest, we've never met such kind of situation.	B：你們找到導致桃子腐爛的原因了嗎？坦白講，我們從沒有遇到過這種情況。
A: This is due to the careless handling while the peaches were being loaded onto the ship.	A：這是由於桃子在裝船時搬運不當造成的。

B: We've never come across such a case of damage during loading.	B：我們在裝船時從未發生過這樣的損壞事件。
A: Maybe it's a singular case for you, but now the situation is not in conformity with those stipulated in the contract. Therefore, I have to file a claim on you.	A：對於你們來說可能是頭一次遇到這種情況，但現在的情況已經違反了我們的合同規定，所以我不得不向你們提出索賠。
B: It's reasonable for you to do that. We're very sorry for your loss, and we'd like to bear our responsibility.	B：你們這麼做很合理，非常抱歉讓貴方蒙受損失，我們願意承擔我們應負的責任。
A: Thanks so much for your cooperation.	A：非常感謝您的合作。

場景問答必會句

> You are concerned about the peaches if I'm not mistaken.
> 如果我沒理解錯的話，您想談桃子的事情，對吧？

還可以這樣說：

- Do you want to talk about the peaches?
  您想談談桃子的事嗎？
- Are we supposed to solve the problems of peaches?
  我們是不是應該解決一下桃子的問題？

對方可能這樣回答：

- Of course. That's why I'm here.
  當然，這是我來的原因。
- I think that problem is urgent to both of us.
  我想這個問題對我們雙方來說都急需處理。

> Have you discovered what the exact causes of the rot were?
> 你們找到導致桃子腐爛的原因了嗎？

還可以這樣說：

- Did you have the peaches checked?
  你們檢查桃子的情況了嗎？

對方可能這樣回答：

- Yes. We can show you the certification issued by a specialized agency.
  是的。我們可以出示由專業機構開具的證明。
- The inspection is under way.
  檢查正在進行中。

簽訂合同 Tips

外貿合同中的一些常見條款

1. The seller agrees to sell and the buyer agrees to buy the under mentioned goods on the terms and conditions stated below.

1. 買賣雙方同意按下列條款由賣方出售，由買方購入下列貨物。

2. Total Amount： With _____% more or less both in amount and quantity allowed at the seller's option.

2. 總值：數量及總值均有 _____% 的增減範圍，由賣方決定。

3. Force Majeure：

Either party shall not be responsible for failure or delay to perform all or any part of this agreement due to flood, fire, earthquake, draught, war or any other events which could not be predicted, controlled, avoided or overcome by the relative party. However, the party affected by the event of Force Majeure shall inform the other party of its occurrence in writing as soon as possible and thereafter send a certificate of the event issued by the relevant authorities to the other party within fifteen days after its occurrence.

3. 不可抗力：

由於水災、火災、地震、乾旱、戰爭或協議一方無法預見、控制、避免和克服的其他事件導致不能或暫時不能全部或部分履行本協議，該方不負責任。但是，受不可抗力事件影響的一方須儘快將發生的事件以書面形式通知另一方，並在不可抗力事件發生的 15 天內將有關機構出具的不可抗力事件的證明寄交對方。

Unit 7 貨物保險

對外運輸貨物保險是以對外貿易運輸過程中的各種貨物作為保險標的的保險。外貿貨物的運輸有海運、陸運、空運以及郵政投遞等多種途徑。

貨物保險必會詞

1 Free from Particular Average 平安險,簡稱 FPA
平安險指單獨海損不負責賠償。根據國際保險界對單獨海損的解釋,它是指保險標的物在海上運輸途中遭受保險範圍內的風險直接造成的船舶或貨物的滅失或損害。在三個基本險種中,承保責任範圍最狹窄。

2 with particular average 水漬險,簡稱 WPA
水漬險除了包括"平安險"的各項責任以外,還負責被保險貨物在運輸過程中由於惡劣氣候、雷電、海嘯、地震和洪水等自然災害所造成的部分損失。

3 all risks 一切險
一切險的責任範圍除包括水漬險的所有責任外,還包括貨物在運輸過程中,因一般外來風險所造成保險貨物的損失,如被竊、雨淋、滲漏、碰損、破碎、串味、受潮受熱和鉤損等。

4 insurance policy 保險單
保險單簡稱保單,是保險人與被保險人訂立保險合同的正式書面證明。

這些小詞你也要會哦:

theft n. 盜竊	damage n. 損害	shortage n. 缺乏
intermixture n. 混合物	leakage n. 洩露	clash v. 碰撞
contamination n. 污染物	odour n. 氣味	breakage n. 破損

Scene 93 保險險種 Types of Insurance

 場景對話

A: Hi, are you available now?　　　　　　A:您好,您現在有時間嗎?

B: Yes. What can I do for you?	B：有，我能幫您做些什麼？
A: I would like to discuss insurance with you, if you don't mind.	A：如果您不介意，我想和您討論一下保險的事情。
B: No, not at all. Have you bought insurance for the goods?	B：一點也不介意。您已經為貨物投保了嗎？
A: No, I will do it right after our discussion.	A：不，還沒有，我會在咱們討論結束之後着手辦理。
B: What risks do you expect to be covered?	B：您希望保哪些險？
A: Please insure FPA and against War Risk. What other insurances do you generally provide?	A：請幫我投保平安險和戰爭險。你們一般還提供哪些保險品種？
B: WPA or all risks.	B：水漬險和一切險。
A: How do you calculate the premium?	A：如何計算保費？
B: The premium is calculated according to the premium rates for risks to be covered.	B：保險費是根據投保險別的保險費率計算的。
A: Could you please give me an insurance rate?	A：您能給我一份保險費率表嗎？
B: Sure. Here it is.	B：好。給您。

場景問答必會句

> What risks do you expect to be covered?
> 您希望保哪些險？

還可以這樣說：

🗨 What kind of insurance should I provide for your goods?
　我應該為您的貨物提供哪些保險？

> Could you please give me an insurance rate?
> 您能給我一份保險費率表嗎？

還可以這樣說：

🗨 I'd like to see your insurance rate.
　我想要看看您的保險費率表。

對方可能這樣回答：

🗨 I don't have it right now and I will send to you via email after I get back to my office.
　我現在沒有，我會回辦公室之後用郵件發給您。

🗨 Here you are.
　給您。

Scene 94 投保 Effect Insurance

 場景對話

A: Hi! I'm very glad to inform you that we have insured your goods against all risks.	A：您好！很高興通知您我們已經為您的貨物投保了一切險。
B: Thank you for effecting the insurance on my behalf. Which company do you insure with?	B：謝謝您代我投保。投保的是哪一家公司？
A: I insure with PICC for your goods. You can submit an insurance claim if there is any damage to the goods within the scope of the coverage.	A：我為您的貨物投保的是中國人民財產保險股份有限公司。在保險覆蓋範圍內，若有任何損害，您可以提出索賠。
B: How long is the insurance valid?	B：保險的有效期是多久？
A: For thirty days after the arrival of the consignment at the port of destination.	A：貨物到達目的港的 30 天之內。
B: What should I provide the insurance company with in case of compensation?	B：為了獲得賠償，我應該提供些什麼材料給保險公司？
A: The survey report. Are the goods to be transported immediately to an inland city after arrival at the port of destination?	A：鑒定報告。在到達目的港後，貨物需要立即轉運至內陸城市嗎？
B: Yes, they will be transported to Harbin.	B：是的，貨物將被轉運至哈爾濱。
A: I can cover the inland insurance on your behalf and debit you with the additional premium.	A：我可以代您投保內陸險，額外費用將由您承擔。
B: Thank you very much.	B：非常感謝。

場景問答必會句

> How long is the insurance valid?
> 保險的有效期是多久？

還可以這樣說：

💬 What's the duration of the insurance?
　　保險的持續期限是多久？

💬 When will the insurance become invalid?
　　保險什麼時候失效？

對方可能這樣回答：

Less than thirty days (included) after the arrival of the consignment at the port of destination.
貨物到達目的港後的 30 天內 (包括第 30 天)。

> What should I provide the insurance company with in case of compensation?
> 為了獲得賠償，我應該提供些什麼材料給保險公司？

還可以這樣說：

What should I file to the insurance company for approval of compensation?
為了通過保險公司的賠償審核，我應該提供些什麼資料？

For approval of the insurance company, what should I prepare?
為了通過保險公司的審核，我應該準備些什麼文件？

對方可能這樣回答：

Any certificate from the third party.
來自第三方的任何證明。

In accordance with the requirement of insurance company.
按照保險公司的要求。

Scene 95　保險級別 Insurance Level

 場景對話

A: Is James there?	A：詹姆斯在嗎？
B: This is he.	B：我就是。
A: You have requested that the level of insurance coverage is 25% above the invoice value. Am I right?	A：您要求訂單保險額的級別高於發票價值 25%。對嗎？
B: Yes, we have had a lot of trouble with damaged goods in the past, so we require that.	B：是的，我們過去遇到過很多次貨物毀損的情況，所以有這樣的要求。
A: I think the amount is a bit excessive. The normal coverage for goods of this type is to insure them for 10% above the invoice value.	A：我認為這個金額有點高。一般這類產品的保險額度僅高於發票總額的 10%。
B: I know that, but I would feel more comfortable with the additional protection.	B：我知道，但是額外的保障會讓我覺得安全些。

A: Will you pay the additional cost if you want to increase the coverage?	A：如果您想要增加保險額，您會支付額外費用嗎？
B: The insurance was supposed to be included in the quotation.	B：保險應該已經都包含在報價裡了。
A: I see.	A：我知道了。
B: I suggest you contact your insurance agent and compare rates.	B：我建議您聯繫保險代理，比較一下價格。
A: Thanks for your advice.	A：謝謝您的建議。

場景問答必會句

> Will you pay the additional cost if you want to increase the coverage?
> 如果您想要增加保險額，您會支付額外費用嗎？

還可以這樣說：

🗨 Would you like to pay the extra cost if I increase the coverage?
如果我增加保險額，您願意承擔額外費用嗎？

🗨 Will you pay the additional cost if we do as your requirement?
如果我們按照您的要求增加保險額，您會支付額外費用嗎？

對方可能這樣回答：

🗨 Yes, I will consider. 是的，我會考慮的。

🗨 But the quotation should include the insurance.
但是報價應該已經包含保險費了。

Scene 96 保險糾紛 Insurance Dispute

場景對話

A: I'm sorry to say that three porcelain teacups is broken.	A：很抱歉告訴您，有 3 個瓷茶杯碎了。
B: This is bad news indeed. Did you make a claim?	B：這確實是壞消息。您申請索賠了嗎？
A: Not yet. Can you tell me the address of inspection and claim agency of PICC?	A：還沒有，您能告訴我中國人民財產保險股份有限公司檢驗和理賠機構的具體地址嗎？

B: Sure, I will send the address to you via email. Do you need any other information?	B： 當然，我稍後會用郵件發給您。您還需要其他信息嗎？
A: Could you tell me the difference between inspection and claim agencies?	A： 您能告訴我檢驗機構和理賠機構的區別嗎？
B: Inspection agencies are responsible for inspecting the loss of your goods and claim agencies are dealing directly with the claim.	B： 檢驗機構負責檢驗貨物的損失，而理賠機構負責直接處理索賠。
A: Thanks. <u>What documents should I provide?</u>	A： 謝謝。<u>我應該提供哪些文件？</u>
B: The insurance policy, the transportation contract, the invoice, pack list, damage certificate and claim inventory, and so on.	B： 保險單、運輸合同、發票、裝箱單、損失證明和索賠清單等。
A: Thank you from the bottom of my heart.	A： 由衷地感謝您。
B: In accordance with the clause of our contract: the seller shall not take any responsibility if any insurance claim concerning the shipping goods happens, but I really want to help you.	B： 根據我們的合同條款，賣方對於與貨物有關的任何保險索賠不負任何責任，但是我真的想幫助您。
A: You are very kind.	A： 您真好。

場景問答必會句

> Did you make a claim?
> 您申請索賠了嗎？

還可以這樣說：

- Have you applied for the claim?
  您申請索賠了嗎？
- Did you ask for compensation?
  您要求賠償了嗎？

> What documents should I provide?
> 我應該提供哪些文件？

還可以這樣說：

💬 What documents are needed?
需要提供哪些文件？

對方可能這樣回答：

💬 Sorry, please inquire the inspection agency.
不好意思，請諮詢檢驗機構。

▌貨物保險 Tips ▌

附加險別

theft, pilferage and non-delivery (TPND)	偷竊、提貨不着險
fresh water rain damage (FWRD)	淡水雨淋險
risk of shortage	短量險
risk of intermixture and contamination	混雜沾污險
risk of leakage	滲漏險
risk of clash and breakage	碰損、破碎險
damage caused by heating and sweating	受熱、受潮險
loss for damage by breakage of packing	包裝破裂險

Unit 8 商業保險

商業保險是指通過訂立保險合同，以盈利為目的的保險形式，為參保者提供人身和財產保障的賠付形式。商業保險分為財產保險、人壽保險和健康保險。

商業保險必會詞

1 insure v. 保險，投保
指參保者與保險公司簽訂合同以減少損失、降低風險的行為。

2 premium n. 保險費
指為投保繳納的費用。

3 premium rate n. 保險費率
保險費率也叫保險率，是應繳納保險費與保險金額的比率。

4 insurance plan 保險計劃
符合投保人需求的保險方案。

5 insurance coverage 保障範圍
保障範圍規定在哪些情況下參保者可獲得保險公司的賠付。

這些小詞你也要會哦：

health insurance 健康保險	car insurance 汽車保險	insurance quotes 保險報價
accident insurance 意外保險	payments *n.* 付款方式	insurance company 保險公司
claim *n.* 索賠	insurance policy 保單	insurance agent 保險經紀人

Scene 97　商保類型 Commercial Insurances

場景對話

A: How can I help you?

B: I'd like to purchase a health insurance.

A：有什麼可以幫您的嗎？

B：我想買一份健康保險。

A: Does your employer provide a health insurance for you?	A：您的雇主有沒有為您購買健康保險？
B: No, He doesn't.	B：不，他不提供。
A: I see. Please fill out this questionnaire first, and then we will figure out a plan that fits your need.	A：我明白了。請先填一下這張問卷，然後我們會規劃出適合您的保單。
B: Okay. Thanks.	B：好的，謝謝。
A: Have you considered purchasing a car insurance? I can offer you a quote if you are interested.	A：您有沒有考慮過上車險？如果您感興趣的話，我可以為您提供一份報價單。
B: I've already bought a car insurance.I think I will start with the health insurance.	B：我已經購買了車險。我想我還是先買一份健康保險吧。

場景問答必會句

> I'd like to purchase a health insurance.
> 我想買一份健康保險。

還可以這樣說：

- I'm thinking about getting a car insurance.
  我想買一份汽車保險。
- I'd like to renew my policy.
  我想續我的保單。

> No, He doesn't.
> 不，他不提供。

還可以這樣說：

- Yes, he does. But I'm seeking for other options.
  是的，他提供（健康保險），但是我想看看其他的選擇。

對方可能這樣問：

- Are you covered by your employer's insurance carrier?
  您的僱主為您購買保險了嗎？

PS

apply for policy 申請保單

Scene 98　保險費率 Premium Rate

場景對話

A: What factors do you think determine the premium rate?

A：您認為有哪些因素會影響保險費率？

B: There are a number of factors that can affect the premium rate. For example, the means of transport, the packing and so on.

B：有幾個因素會影響保險費率。例如，運輸的方式和包裝等。

A: Do the articles to be shipped contribute to the premium rate as well?

A：運送的貨物也會影響保險費率嗎？

B: Yes. Some goods are vulnerable while others are not delicate and not likely to be damaged during the transportation.

B：是的，有些貨物易碎，有一些貨物不易碎，在運輸過程中不易被損壞。

A: Thank you for your information.

A：謝謝您提供的信息。

B: You're welcome.

B：不客氣。

場景問答必會句

> What factors do you think determine the premium rate?
> 您認為有哪些因素會影響保險費率？

還可以這樣說：

💬 What are the factors that affect the premium rate?
影響保險費率的因素有哪些？

💬 What decides the premium rate?
什麼因素決定保險費率？

對方可能這樣回答：

💬 The premium rate varies according to the different regions of the country.
地域不同，保險費率也會發生變化。

> Do the articles to be shipped contribute to the premium rate as well?
> 運送的貨物也會影響保險費率嗎？

還可以這樣說：

💬 How about the type of merchandize to be shipped?
和裝運貨物的種類有關嗎？

對方可能這樣回答：

💬 Yes. It matters.
　　是的，有關係。

💬 No. It doesn't matter.
　　不，沒關係。

💬 Yes. It has to be taken into account.
　　是的，需要考慮。

💬 The type of goods must be considered.
　　必須考慮貨物的種類。

商業保險 Tips

常見商業保險種類

all risks insurance 綜合保險	automobile insurance 汽車保險
aviation insurance 航空保險	earthquake insurance 地震保險
baggage insurance 行李險	exchange risk insurance 外匯風險保險
block insurance 船舶保險	erection insurance 機器安裝保險
building insurance 建築物保險	export insurance 出口保險
bonding insurance 保證保險	capital insurance 資本保險
cattle insurance 家畜保險	commission insurance 佣金保險
forced insurance 強制保險	business liability insurance 營業責任保險
aviation personal accident insurance 航空人身意外保險	air transportation cargo insurance 空運貨物保險
air transport insurance 空運保險	

Unit 9 索賠

索賠是指國際貿易的一方違反合同的規定，直接或間接地給另一方造成損害，受損方向違約方提出損害賠償要求。索賠的依據包括兩個方面：法律依據和事實依據。

索賠必會詞

1 insurance indemnity 保險理賠
保險理賠是指保險人在保險標的發生風險事故後，對被保險人提出的索賠請求進行處理的行為。

2 settlement of claims 理賠
理賠是指違約方受理受損方提出的賠償要求。索賠和理賠是同一個問題的兩個方面。

3 claim letter 索賠書
索賠書是指在經濟活動中，遭受損失的一方為了維護自身的權益，在爭議發生後向違約一方或者向法院提出索賠要求的文書。

4 claims settling agent 理賠代理人
理賠代理人是指代替保險公司從事賠款處理的工作人員。

這些小詞你也要會哦：

settle v. 解決	compensate v. 賠償，補償	withdraw v. 撤銷
claimant n. 索賠人	claims n. 索賠；債權	indemnity n. 賠償
content n. 貨物	conformity n. 一致	liability n. 責任
file / lodge / make / register / raise / bring up a claim 提出索賠		

Scene 99 索賠理由 Claim

 場景對話

A: Mr. Wood, I'd like to talk with you about something that going to be a problem. I'd like, if possible, to see it settled at this meeting.

A：伍德先生，我想和您談談一件比較麻煩的事情。如果可以的話，我想在這次會議上解決。

B: What's going on, Mr. Hanks?	B：什麼事，漢克斯先生？
A: We are sorry to tell you that the goods you sent us are not in conformity with the specifications of the contract, so we are compelled to claim on you.	A：很遺憾地告訴您，貴方運來的貨物與合同不相符。我們不得不向你們提出索賠。
B: Oh, no. You don't mean it, do you?	B：哦，不會吧，真的嗎？
A: As soon as the ship arrived at our port, we had it inspected. A shortage of thirty kilograms was found. From the shipment of two hundred cases of glassware, we find that nearly 20% of wooden cases have been broken, and the contents are badly damaged.	A：貨物一到港口，我們就做了檢查，發現貨物短缺了 30 千克。我們從 200 箱玻璃貨物中抽查了一些，將近 20% 的木箱子已經破裂，裡面的貨物破損嚴重。
B: Could you offer the survey report?	B：貴方能提供檢查報告嗎？
A: Yes, here you are.	A：可以，請過目。
B: It seems that we shall not be held liable for the shortage.	B：我方似乎不應該對短缺負責。
A: Do you want to pass the buck?	A：你們想推卸責任嗎？
B: Of course not. The shipping documents can prove that when the goods are shipped, the number was correct and the goods were in perfect condition. They must have been damaged en route.	B：當然不是。貨運單據表明，貨物在裝運時數量正確，完好無損。所以說，貨物受損一定是在運輸途中發生的。
A: I bet the workers just counted the cases in a careless and absent-minded manner. Otherwise, how could the thirty kilogrames of goods disappeared on the sea?	A：我想工作人員一定是漫不經心地數了數箱子。否則，30 千克的貨物怎麼會從海上消失？
B: Then how much do you want to claim?	B：那你們想要多少賠償呢？
A: We hope that you can replace the damaged goods and grant us a special discount of 5% to compensate for the loss.	A：我們希望你們能更換損壞的貨物，並給 5% 的特殊折扣以補償我方的損失。
B: I'm afraid we can't accept your requirements. Your claim, in my opinion, should be referred to the insurance company, as the mishap occurred after shipment.	B：我們恐怕不能接受你們的要求。我們認為，你們的索賠應提交給保險公司，因為損失發生在裝船之後。

場景問答必會句

Could you offer the survey report?
貴方能提供檢查報告嗎？

還可以這樣說：

💬 Would you like to show us the evidence?
請問您可以給我們看一下證據嗎？

💬 Have you got any reports in written form?
貴方有書面報告嗎？

對方可能這樣回答：

💬 Yes, we have, but we didn't take it with us. We can fax it to you if you want.
是的，我們有檢查報告，但是這次來沒有帶上。如果貴方需要的話，我們可傳真過來。

💬 I'm afraid we can't provide the report now, but the organization that examined the goods for us can issue a report anytime.
我們現在恐怕無法提供報告，但為我們檢查貨物的機構隨時可以出具報告。

Then how much do you want to claim?
你們想要多少賠償呢？

還可以這樣說：

💬 How can we compensate you?
我們該如何賠償貴公司呢？

對方可能這樣回答：

💬 We should be obliged if you would forward us a replacement for the machine as soon as possible.
如果貴方能儘快將調換的機器運送至我方，我方將不勝感激。

💬 You should compensate us by 3%, plus the inspection fee.
貴公司應賠償我們 3% 的損失，商檢費也應該由貴公司承擔。

Scene 100　提出索賠 File a Claim

　場景對話

A: Good morning, Mr. Anderson! Thanks for your coming. I hope we can have all the problems settled this morning.

A：早上好，安德森先生，謝謝您能過來。我希望我們能在今天上午解決所有的問題。

B: I hope so, too, Miss Xia.

B：這也是我所希望的，夏小姐。

A: I'm sorry to tell you that the quality of the goods you shipped last week is much inferior to that of the goods of our last order.

A：很遺憾，貴方上週發運的貨物質量與我方上次所訂的貨物質量相比，要低劣得多。

B: What do you mean by "inferior quality"?	B：你說"低劣"是什麼意思？
A: To our astonishment, about 20% of the goods were moldy and in many cans there were even small brownish bugs crawling in and out. We can't accept them in this state.	A：令我們驚訝的是，大約 20% 的貨物已發霉，甚至在許多罐頭內有褐色小甲蟲爬出爬進。這樣的貨物我們無法接受。
B: How come? I mean, our exports have to pass a rigid inspection before they are shipped. Our Inspection Bureau won't let go anything defective.	B：怎麼會這樣？我的意思是，我們出口的商品必須在裝運前經過一道嚴格的檢查。我們的檢查局不會放過任何瑕疵品。
A: As much as I respect your Inspection Bureau, it's obvious that the cans are no longer suitable for consumption. This is the survey report issued by CCIB.	A：雖然我很尊重你們的檢查局，但是很明顯罐頭已經不能食用了。這是中國商品驗檢局簽發的檢驗報告。
B: That's weird!	B：真奇怪！
A: We have suffered a loss of 20% on the selling price because of the inferior quality of the products you sent to us. We have the right to claim against you for compensation of all losses.	A：由於貴方所運送的貨物質量問題，我們損失了售價金額的 20%。我們有權要求貴方賠償我們的所有損失。
B: What's your requirement?	B：你們有什麼要求？
A: You should take back all the disqualified goods and compensate us for the value of the goods plus all losses sustained due to return of the cargo, such as the freight, storage charges, insurance premium, interest and inspection charges.	A：貴方應該收回不合格產品並向我方做出賠償，也包括因退貨而造成的相關損失，如貨運費、倉儲費、保險費、利息和商檢費等。
B: I think after we make an investigation of the matter, we'll consider the allowance.	B：我想等我們對此事進行調查後，我們會再考慮補償。
A: We hope you will settle this claim as soon as possible.	A：我們希望貴方儘早解決索賠問題。

場景問答必會句

> What do you mean by "inferior quality"?
> 你說"低劣"是什麼意思？

還可以這樣說：

How could our goods be of inferior quality?
我們的貨物怎麼可能質量低劣？

對方可能這樣回答：

💬 There are too many defective items in this shipment.
這批貨裡次品太多了。

💬 The quality of the goods you sent to us last week is too poor to suit the requirements of the market.
貴方上週發運的貨物質量實在太差，根本就無法滿足市場的要求。

PS

defective *a.* 有缺陷的

What's your requirement?
你們有什麼要求？

還可以這樣說：

💬 What do you want as compensation?
貴方想要怎麼賠償？

對方可能這樣回答：

💬 We claim compensation of $1,000 for the inferiority of quality.
我方要求賠償 1000 美元來補償劣質品。

💬 Kindly remit us the amount of claim at an early date.
請儘早將賠償金匯給我方。

Scene
101 索賠談判 Claim Negotiation

 場景對話

A: Mr. Bush, I'd like to discuss the indemnity clause with you.	A：布什先生，我想和您談談賠償條款的問題。
B: OK. We regret to hear that the goods you received didn't meet the quality standard expected.	B：好的，我方很遺憾地獲悉，貴方收到的貨物質量與你們的期望不符。
A: We had the material inspected immediately when the goods arrived, and found that at least fifty cases were damaged, which made up 20% of the total quantity.	A：貨物一到港，我們就進行了檢查，發現至少有 50 個箱子損壞，佔了總數的 20%。
B: Have you found the cause of the damage? Did the damage happen during transit?	B：你們找到導致損壞的原因了嗎？是在運輸過程中造成的嗎？
A: The damage was caused by rough handling when the goods were loaded on board at the dock.	A：貨物是因為裝船時的粗暴搬運而遭到損壞的。

B: As the shipping company is liable for the damage, your claim for compensation should, in our opinion, be referred to them for settlement.	B：鑒於貨運公司應對這次損失負責，我方的意見是，你們應該向他們提出索賠來解決問題。
A: Mr. Bush, on inspection we also found that 30% of the two hundred cases of pears have rotten. We are compelled to claim on you to compensate us for the loss, $10,000, which we have sustained by the disqualified goods.	A：布什先生，經過檢查我們還發現 200 箱梨中有 30% 的梨已經爛掉了。我們必須向貴公司索賠 1 萬美元，其與不合格貨物的價值相等。
B: Do you have any evidence?	B：你們有相關證據嗎？
A: Here's a survey report issued by a well-known public surveyor in London.	A：這是由倫敦的一位著名的公證人簽發的調查報告。
B: Apparently, the goods were in good condition before shipment. We do not accept any claims for compensation for the loss incurred in transit, because you bought the goods F.O.B. Houston and on shipping quality, not on landed quality. Your claim, in our opinion, should be referred to the insurance company.	B：顯然，貨物在裝船前完好無損。因為您買的這批貨是休斯敦港船上交貨價，以裝船質量而不是以到岸質量為準，對任何運輸途中產生的損失的索賠，我們都不予接受。我們認為，你們應該向保險公司索賠。

場景問答必會句

> Have you found the cause of the damage?
> 你們找到導致損壞的原因了嗎？

還可以這樣說：

- Have you discovered what led to the damage?
  你們發現是什麼原因造成了損壞嗎？
- Do you know why the damage happened?
  您知道為什麼會發生損壞嗎？

對方可能這樣回答：

- A thorough examination showed that the leakage was due to improper packing.
  在徹底的商檢之後發現滲漏是由於包裝不當引起的。
- Not yet, but we'll find out the reason as soon as possible.
  還沒有，但我們會儘快找到原因。

Do you have any evidence?
你們有相關證據嗎？

還可以這樣說：
💬 Can you prove your words?
貴方能證明嗎？

對方可能這樣回答：
💬 Of course. We can show you the report anytime if you need.
當然。如果您需要，我們可以隨時出示報告。

💬 These photos can't be too evident.
這些照片很明顯了。

Scene 102 同意索賠 Accept a Claim

場景對話

A: Mr. Reed, have you been informed of the little problem occurred in our cooperation?	A：里德先生，您已經得知我們合作中發生的小問題了嗎？
B: Yes, I got your email last night.	B：是的，我昨晚收到了您的郵件。
A: OK. The inspection reveals that both the quantity and quality of the wheat delivered are not in conformity with those stipulated in the contract, though the packing is all in good condition.	A：好的。檢查顯示貴方發來的小麥數量和質量均與合同規定的不相符，儘管包裝完好。
B: Could you show us the survey report issued by the specialized organization?	B：可以請您出示一下由專門機構開具的調查報告嗎？
A: Sure. Here you are. The goods were inspected by the China Commodity Inspection Bureau.	A：當然。請過目。這些貨物是由中國商品檢驗局進行檢查的。
B: Well, their testimony is absolutely reliable. Mr. Young, We'd like to express our sincere apologies for the poor quality of the products. We accept the claim, but can you tell me how much you want us to compensate you for the loss?	B：他們的檢查報告肯定可靠。楊先生，對貨物的質量問題，我方向貴方表示誠摯的歉意。我方同意理賠，但貴方能否告訴我們，貴方想要我們賠償多少損失？

A: This is a statement of loss and you should indemnify us $25,000.	A：這是損失清單，貴方應賠付我方 2.5 萬美元。
B: We are prepared to make you a reasonable compensation, but not the amount you claimed.	B：我們準備給你們合理的賠償，但並非您要求索賠的金額。
A: What's your opinion?	A：您的意見是什麼？
B: We are not going to carry these damaged goods back. Would you accept to buy these goods at half price? We'd like to use the payment as our compensation fee.	B：受損的貨物我們不打算運回去了，能以半價賣給你們嗎？我們想把這部分費用當作賠償金。
A: Your proposal to settle the claim is satisfactory. We'll take it.	A：貴方關於解決索賠的建議令人滿意，我們願意接受。

場景問答必會句

> Could you show us the survey report issued by the specialized organization?
> 可以請您出示一下由專門機構開具的調查報告嗎？

對方可能這樣回答：

- I'm sorry that we are unable to show it at present.
  很抱歉我們現在無法出示報告。
- OK. Please give us two minutes. We'll get it prepared soon.
  好的，請給我們兩分鐘時間，我們馬上準備好。

> We accept the claim, but can you tell me how much you want us to compensate you for the loss?
> 我方同意理賠，但貴方能否告訴我們，貴方想要我們賠償多少損失？

還可以這樣說：

- We'll compensate you. Could you give us an exact number?
  我們會賠償的，貴方可以報個具體的賠償數目嗎？

對方可能這樣回答：

- We have to ask for compensation of $25,000 to cover the loss.
  我們不得不向貴方索賠 2.5 萬美元以彌補損失。
- We hope you can allow a 30% reduction in price.
  我們希望貴方同意降價 30%。

Scene 103　退貨 Return of Goods

 場景對話

A: Mr. Baker, <u>could you explain why the consignment is not up to the standard stipulated in the contract?</u>	A：貝克先生，您可以解釋一下為什麼這批貨的質量低於合同規定的標準嗎？
B: What do you mean?	B：您的意思是？
A: Look at the photos. The paintwork on the body of the cars that you sent us has become discolored.	A：看看這些照片，您發給我們的汽車上的外漆都褪色了。
B: How could it be?	B：這怎麼可能呢？
A: We have looked into the matter and found it was due to a chemical imbalance in the paint used in spraying the vehicles.	A：我們已經調查了此事，發現是由於噴這批車使用的油漆成分比例不當造成的。
B: Could you show me the survey report?	B：能讓我看看調查報告嗎？
A: Sure. Here it is.	A：當然。給您。
B: We should take the responsibility for that. We'd like to express our sincere apologies for the poor quality of the products.	B：我們應該對此負責。對貨物的質量問題，我方向貴方表示誠摯的歉意。
A: <u>Then could you send perfect goods to replace the defective ones?</u>	A：那貴方能儘快將符合標準的產品運送給我方以替換那些瑕疵品嗎？
B: We will give immediate attention to your request for the claims.	B：我方會立刻處理貴方提出的索賠要求。
A: I'll return the goods to you, postage and packing forward. When do you think we can get the replacements?	A：我會把貨退給你們，郵費和包裝費到付。您估計我們什麼時候才能收到替換的貨物？
B: You should receive them within a week.	B：一週內就能收到。
A: To be honest, we are far from satisfied with this order.	A：老實說，我們對這次訂貨很不滿意。
B: I apologize for the inconvenience and please permit me to point out that this kind of fault rarely occurs in our factory. I promise it'll be the last time for us to make such kind of mistake.	B：給您帶來了不便，我深感歉意。請允許我指出一點，我們的工廠很少出這類問題。我保證這是我們最後一次出現這種問題。

?A 場景問答必會句

> Could you explain why the consignment is not up to the standard stipulated in the contract?
> 您可以解釋一下為什麼這批貨的質量低於合同規定的標準嗎？

還可以這樣說：

💬 How can the goods be that inferior?
這批貨的質量怎麼會如此低劣呢？

對方可能這樣回答：

💬 We'd like to express our sincere apologies for that.
我方向貴方表示誠摯的歉意。

💬 We regret the loss you have suffered and agree to compensate you.
我方對貴方所受的損失深感抱歉，同意向貴方做出賠償。

> Then could you send perfect goods to replace the defective ones?
> 那貴方能儘快將符合標準的產品運送給我方以替換那些瑕疵品嗎？

還可以這樣說：

💬 You're supposed to deliver the goods with high quality to the destination as soon as possible; otherwise, this business will be in vain.
你們得儘快把高品質產品運送到目的地，否則這次交易將會無效。

對方可能這樣回答：

💬 OK. We'll get the goods prepared in the shortest time.
好的，我們將在最短時間內準備好貨物。

💬 That will be a little difficult, because we don't have enough stock.
這有點困難，因為我們庫存不足。

索賠 Tips

For Damage of Goods 貨物破損索賠

Dear Sir,

Our order number is LK-7. The glasses you supplied to our order of July 4th were delivered by the shipping company this morning.The two hundred cartons of goods appeared to be in perfect condition.But when I carefully unpacked them, I found that 30% of them were badly damaged.

We trust you can understand that we are expecting the compensation for our cracked goods.

Yours faithfully,

John Watson

敬啟者：

我們的訂單號是 LK-7。我方於 7 月 4 日從貴方訂購的玻璃杯已於今早由貨運公司送達。裝有貨物的 200 個紙箱完好無損。但當我小心打開時，發現有 30% 的玻璃杯嚴重破損。

相信貴方能理解我方要求對損壞貨物的索償。

約翰·沃森

敬上

仲裁是指當事人根據他們之間訂立的仲裁協議，自願將其爭議提交由非官方身份的仲裁員組成的仲裁庭進行裁判，並受該裁判約束的一種制度。

爭議仲裁必會詞

1 arbitration tribunal 仲裁庭
仲裁庭是指對某一爭議案件進行仲裁審理活動時的組織形式。

2 arbitration committee 仲裁委員會
仲裁委員會是解決平等主體的公民、法人和其他組織之間發生的合同糾紛和其他財產權益糾紛的常設仲裁機構。

3 award *n.* 仲裁裁決
仲裁裁決是指仲裁庭對當事人之間存在爭議的事項做出的裁決。仲裁裁決自做出之日起產生法律效力。

4 ICC 國際商會
國際商會 (The International Chamber of Commerce) 是全球唯一的代表所有企業的權威機構，國際商會下屬的國際仲裁法庭是全球最高的仲裁機構。

這些小詞你也要會哦：

claimant *n.* 申訴方	defendant *n.* 被訴方	specification *n.* 規格
arbitrator *n.* 仲裁員	debtor *n.* 債務人	convention *n.* 公約
usage *n.* 慣例	provision *n.* 條款	counterclaim *n.* 反訴

Scene 104 質量糾紛 Quality Dispute

 場景對話

A: Could you help us straighten out the trouble concerning the bicycles?

A：您能幫我們解決有關自行車產品的問題嗎？

B: OK. Can you give me the facts?

B：當然，您能講講情況嗎？

A: The inspection reveals that the bikes were found rusty when they were unpacked.

A：檢驗表明，開箱時發現自行車已經生鏽。

B: Do you have anything to prove your words?

B：有什麼證據嗎？

A: We have here a copy of the inspection certificate issued by the Commodity Inspection Bureau and a set of photos taken on spot.

A：這是商檢局開具的檢驗證明書影印件和一組現場照片。

B: How many bikes are like this?

B：有多少自行車出現了這種情況？

A: 30% of all the goods have rust stains.

A：30% 的自行車有鏽斑。

B: Our manufacturer has always attached great importance to the quality of their products. Maybe the rust stains are due to the dampness at sea.

B：我們的廠家對他們的產品質量向來很重視，這些鏽斑是有可能在海上受潮造成的。

A: But our experts have the opinion that the rust stains are due to poor workmanship. Please look at the pictures. They surely prove that the derusting of the bikes before plating was not thoroughly done.

A：但是我們的專家認為，鏽斑是由於工藝粗糙所造成的。請看照片，可以肯定，電鍍之前自行車的除鏽工作做得不徹底。

B: Well, it seems that the manufacturer has not lived up to their standard in this case.

B：看來這次廠家沒有達到他們的操作標準。

A: The evidence shows that the manufacturer didn't strictly observe the proceeding requirements as stipulated in our contract.

A：證據表明，廠家沒有嚴格遵照我們合同中規定的加工要求。

B: I'm sorry for that. We will get this matter resolved as soon as possible and hope to compensate you for your loss.

B：我很抱歉。我們將儘快解決該問題，並賠償貴公司的損失。

A: Thank you for sorting out the matter for us.

A：謝謝您為我們解決此事。

場景問答必會句

> Could you help us straighten out the trouble concerning the bicycles?
> 您能幫我們解決有關自行車產品的問題嗎？

還可以這樣說：

📝 Could you help us deal with the problems of the bikes?
你們能幫我們解決有關自行車產品的問題嗎？

對方可能這樣回答：

🖳 Sure. Could you explain the problems in details?
好的，您能詳細講講這些問題嗎？

🖳 Please specify the problems first.
請先詳細說明一下情況。

PS

specify v. 詳細説明

> We have here a copy of the inspection certificate issued by the Commodity Inspection Bureau and a set of photos taken on spot.
> 這是商檢局開具的檢驗證明書影印件和一組現場照片。

還可以這樣說：

🖳 My colleagues have taken some pictures of the goods.
我的同事拍了一些貨物的照片。

🖳 I can ask my colleagues to scan the report and send it to me if you need.
如果你們需要的話，我可以讓我的同事把報告掃描一下，然後發過來。

Scene 105 解決糾紛方式 Way of Resolving Dispute

 場景對話

A: Hello, Mr. Wang. It's our first time to cooperate with a Chinese company, so we need to ask you some questions.	A：您好，王先生。這是我們第一次跟中國的公司合作，所以想向您請教一些問題。
B: That's all right. We'll try our best to help you.	B：好的，我們會盡我們所能來幫助你們。
A: Thank you. As we know, it's inevitable to have some disputes in international business. Could you tell me how to resolve disputes in your country?	A：謝謝。我們都知道，國際貿易中難免會發生糾紛。在貴國通常是怎樣解決這些糾紛的呢？
B: As a matter of fact, most disputes can be settled in a friendly consultation, with a view to developing a long-term relationship.	B：事實上，本着發展長期合作關係的意願，大多數爭議都可以通過友好的協商來解決。
A: Would you seek for the legal means if the consultation can't help resolve the dispute?	A：如果協商解決不了的話，會通過法律途徑來解決嗎？
B: Litigation is of course one way of resolving dispute. But actually we don't use it frequently.	B：訴訟當然是解決糾紛的一種手段。不過實際上我們很少採用這種方式。

A: Then what should we do?	A：那麼我們該怎麼辦呢？
B: In case of any dispute, and no settlement can be reached through friendly negotiations, then we can submit the case to an international arbitration organization for arbitration.	B：如果出現爭議，而且又無法通過友好談判來達成一致意見，那我們就只能將爭議交由國際仲裁機構來仲裁解決。
A: Where should the place for arbitration be?	A：應該在哪裡進行仲裁呢？
B: The customary practice is to hold arbitration in the country of defendant.	B：通常的做法是在被告方的國家進行仲裁。
A: What about the charges of arbitration?	A：仲裁費用由哪方承擔呢？
B: Generally speaking, all the fees for arbitration shall be borne by the losing party unless otherwise awarded by the court.	B：一般來説，所有仲裁費應由敗訴方承擔，除非仲裁庭另有裁決。

場景問答必會句

> Could you tell me how to resolve disputes in your country?
> 在貴國通常是怎樣解決這些糾紛的呢？

還可以這樣說：

🗨 Would you like to share with us some useful methods of settling disputes in your country?
可以跟我們分享一些貴國解決糾紛的方式嗎？

🗨 What do you do when disputes happen between you and your partner?
當你和商業夥伴之間發生糾紛時，您會如何應對呢？

對方可能這樣回答：

🗨 I think negotiation is the best way to solve problems.
我想協商是解決問題的最好方法。

> Would you seek for the legal means if the consultation can't help resolve the dispute?
> 如果協商解決不了的話，會通過法律途徑來解決嗎？

還可以這樣說：

🗨 Will you choose the legal means when the other methods are useless?
其他方法不起作用時，你們會選擇法律途徑嗎？

🗨 Will the legal means be one of your choices in the settlement of disputes?
在解決糾紛的過程中，法律途徑是你們的選擇之一嗎？

對方可能這樣回答：

🗨 Actually we won't use the legal means unless we have to.
實際上除非萬不得已，否則我們不會選擇法律途徑。

💬 In my opinion, maybe you don't agree, legal means is the most effective way to resolve the dispute.

可能您會不贊同，但我認為法律途徑是解決爭端的最有效的方法。

Scene 106 仲裁制度 Arbitration Policy

 場景對話

A: Mr. Chow, <u>do we have to settle the dispute by arbitration?</u>	A：周先生，<u>我們必須通過仲裁來解決分歧嗎？</u>
B: It is not necessary to submit a case to arbitration as long as the two parties can discuss the matter in a friendly way.	B：如果雙方能夠友好協商，就沒有必要申請仲裁。
A: <u>Could you offer me some information about the arbitration system in China?</u>	A：<u>您能提供一些有關中國的仲裁制度的信息嗎？</u>
B: Yes, no problem.	B：好的，我很樂意。
A: Must the arbitration be gone through only in China?	A：仲裁必須在中國進行嗎？
B: No, arbitration can be conducted either in China or in other countries.	B：不，仲裁可以在中國進行，也可以在其他國家進行。
A: Are there any general arbitration institutions in China?	A：中國有常設仲裁機構嗎？
B: Yes, for example, the Foreign Trade Arbitration Commission is just such an institution.	B：有。比如中國國際貿易促進會對外經濟仲裁委員會就是這樣的機構。
A: Does the dispute have to be arbitrated by Chinese arbitration authorities?	A：通過仲裁解決糾紛時，必須由中方的常設仲裁機構受理嗎？
B: It is up to the contract signed by the two parties.	B：這要根據雙方當事人簽訂的協議來決定。
A: What kind of person can be the arbitrators?	A：什麼樣的人能當仲裁員呢？
B: We think that the court consisting of arbitrators from both sides must be fair and able to handle the dispute without bias or partiality.	B：我們認為由雙方指定的仲裁員組成的仲裁庭必須公正，並且能夠不偏不倚地處理爭議。
A: OK. Thank you very much.	A：好的，非常感謝。

場景問答必會句

> Do we have to settle the dispute by arbitration?
> 我們必須通過仲裁來解決分歧嗎？

還可以這樣說：

🖳 Is arbitration the only way to resolve the dispute?
　仲裁是解決分歧的唯一方法嗎？

🖳 We may find a better way to resolve the dispute other than arbitration.
　除了仲裁，我們應該可以找到更好的解決分歧的方法。

對方可能這樣回答：

🖳 Actually it's better not to settle disputes involving arbitration.
　其實最好不要通過仲裁來解決爭議。

🖳 Negotiation is far better than arbitration.
　協商要比仲裁好得多。

> Could you offer me some information about the arbitration system in China?
> 您能提供一些有關中國的仲裁制度的信息嗎？

還可以這樣說：

🖳 Could you tell me something about the arbitration in China, in terms of the policies?
　您能提供一些有關中國的仲裁制度的信息嗎？

對方可能這樣回答：

🖳 Sorry, I know little about that. You can ask Mr. Wang, he's an expert in that field.
　不好意思，我對此也知之甚少。您可以問問王先生，他是那個領域的專家。

🖳 I've got a book for you, which introduces a lot of basic things of the arbitration in China.
　我給您帶來了一本書，這本書裡有很多關於中國的仲裁制度方面的知識。

Scene 107　訴諸仲裁 Resort to Arbitration

 場景對話

A: Good morning, Mr. White! Today I have a problem to clarify with you.	A：早上好，懷特先生，今天我有個問題想要跟您說清楚。
B: What's the problem?	B：什麼問題？

A: Last May we bought five hundred tons of red beans from you. The goods should have reached us last June, but the shipping date has been delayed several times. <u>Have you ever considered about delivering the goods?</u>	A：去年 5 月，我們從貴公司購買了 500 噸紅小豆，貨物應於去年 6 月份運抵我處，但船期一拖再拖。<u>貴公司有考慮過發貨的問題嗎？</u>
B: As far as I know, this shipment has not been delivered.	B：據我所知，這批貨物至今尚未發貨。
A: Then how will you deal with the goods? Now the marked price for red beans has fallen sharply and our buyer has changed his mind. He doesn't want the consignment.	A：那麼你們準備怎麼處理這批貨呢？紅小豆的市場價格急劇下跌，我們的買主改變了主意，他不想要這批貨了。
B: As for the delay, I'd like you to recall first. <u>What have you done about the L/C establishment?</u>	B：關於延期發貨的問題，我希望您先回憶一下。<u>貴方是如何處理信用證的？</u>
A: I remember we just did as what the contract said.	A：我記得我們就是按照合同約定來辦事的。
B: We urged you several times to open the L/C, but you simply ignored us.	B：我們曾多次催促貴公司開證，可貴公司置若罔聞。
A: But we've had the L/C opened at last.	A：但我們最終還是開證了。
B: The L/C you opened has gone far beyond the accepted time. It is now invalid. To effect the delivery is out of the question.	B：貴司開信用證時早已過了約定的開證日期，已經失效了。我們是不可能發貨的。
A: If you are not sincere in handling these problems, we'll have to submit them for arbitration.	A：如果您沒有誠意解決這些問題，那我們只能提請仲裁。
B: If you insist, I've got no other way out.	B：如果你們堅持這麼做，恐怕我也沒有辦法了。

場景問答必會句

> Have you ever considered about delivering the goods?
> 貴公司有考慮過發貨的問題嗎？

還可以這樣說：

💬 Have you taken the delivery into your consideration?
　 貴公司考慮過發貨的問題嗎？

Have you put the delivery on your schedule?
貴公司考慮過發貨的問題嗎？

對方可能這樣回答：

Of course. We're doing our utmost to hasten the shipment.
當然，我們正在盡最大努力加速裝運貨物。

We're sorry for that, and we'll get the goods dispatched with the least possible delay.
很抱歉，我們將儘快發貨。

PS

do one's utmost 盡全力

hasten *v.* 加速；催促

What have you done about the L/C establishment?
貴方是如何處理信用證的？

對方可能這樣回答：

If the L/C is the only payment that you can accept, you should let us know at that time.
如果你們只能接受信用證付款，那你們在當時就應該説清楚。

爭議仲裁 Tips

1. 仲裁機構

1) 中國國際經濟貿易仲裁委員會 (China International Economic and Trade Arbitration Commission)
2) 國際商會仲裁院 (International Chamber of Commerce Court of Arbitration)
3) 解決投資爭議的國際中心 (The International Center for the Settlement of Investment Disputes)
4) 斯德哥爾摩仲裁院 (Arbitration Institute of the Stockholm Chamber of Commerce)
5) 美國仲裁協會 (American Arbitration Association)
6) 香港國際仲裁中心 (Hong Kong International Arbitration Center)
7) 倫敦國際仲裁院 (London Court of International Arbitration)

2. 仲裁術語

仲裁 arbitration	索賠 claim
爭議 disputes	罰金條款 penalty
不可抗力 force majeure	仲裁庭 arbitral tribunal
產地證明書 certificate of origin	檢驗證書 inspection certificate
商品檢驗局 commodity inspection bureau	

Unit 11　收款問題

外貿活動中不可避免會涉及收款和催款問題。處理此類問題時，語氣要誠懇、彬彬有禮，不可輕易表現出懷疑對方。但對於某些屢催不付的客戶，態度則要強硬些。

收款問題必會詞

1. **reminder** *n.* 提醒
   到付款日時，應先以郵件、傳真和電話等形式提醒客戶。

2. **balance** *n.* 餘款
   外貿活動中，一般先付定金 (advanced payment)，催繳的多為餘款。

3. **overdue** *a.* 逾期的
   "逾期的應付款項"可以用 overdue payment 來表示；"逾期的餘款"則為 overdue balance。

4. **settle** *v.* 結算
   "結算帳目"可以用 settle an account 或 clear an account 來表示。

這些小詞你也要會哦：

defer *v.* 使推遲	invoice *n.* 發票	account *n.* 賬戶
remaining *a.* 餘下的	check *n.* 支票	delay *v.* 延期，推遲
deadline *n.* 截止期限	remittance *n.* 匯款	debt *v.* 債務

Scene 108　向客戶催款 Press for a Payment

場景對話

A: Hello, Mr. Jason. How are you?	A：您好，傑森先生，您還好嗎？
B: I'm good. Thank you.	B：我很好，謝謝。

A: I've sent you an email as a reminder of your overdue balance of $5,000, but I did not get any reply.

A：我給您發了郵件，提醒您支付餘下應付的 5000 美元貨款，但未得到回覆。

B: Sorry. I have been on a short vacation.

B：不好意思，我正在休短假。

A: That's all right. I just wanted to confirm that you received my email.

A：沒關係。我就是想確認一下您是否收到了我的郵件。

B: Yes, I did.

B：是的，我收到了。

A: When can we expect you to arrange the payment?

A：你們什麼時候安排付款？

B: Don't worry. I will attend to it tomorrow morning.

B：別擔心，我明天一早就會開始處理。

A: That's great. Your cooperation will be greatly appreciated.

A：很好。萬分感謝您的配合。

場景問答必會句

> I've sent you an email as a reminder of your overdue balance of $5,000, but I did not get any reply.
> 我給您發了郵件，提醒您支付餘下應付的 5000 美元貨款，但未得到回覆。

還可以這樣說：

- You did not respond to our first reminder of your overdue balance of $2,000.
  我們提醒過您支付應付的 2000 美元貨款，但您沒回覆。

PS

reminder *n.* 提醒

- We have not received any response from you to the recent reminder we sent you on May 20th about your overdue account.
  我們 5 月 20 日發了您的逾期帳目的提醒給您，但沒有收到任何回應。

> When can we expect you to arrange the payment?
> 你們什麼時候安排付款？

還可以這樣說：

- We suggest an immediate payment of the amount due.
  我們希望貴方儘快付清餘下貨款。

- We can no longer allow this account to continue to go unpaid.
  我們要求貴公司立即支付此帳目。

對方可能這樣回答：

- We will attend to it the first thing tomorrow. 我們明天一早就會立即處理。

- The person in charge of this has been on a business trip. 此項目的負責人出差了。

Scene 109 確認收到款項 Confirm the Receipt of the Payment

 場景對話

A: Hello. Mr. Jackson. I'm calling to confirm the receipt of your payment.	A：您好！傑克遜先生。我打電話是想告訴您我收到了您的款項。
B: That's good. I'm sorry about the delay.	B：太好了。很抱歉，我們付款遲了。
A: That's all right. You always make your payment promptly.	A：沒關係。你們付款總是很及時。
B: Your products are of good quality that we would attach importance to it.	B：那是因為你們的產品質量很好，我們非常重視。
A: Thank you. We hope we can count on your continued cooperation and support.	A：謝謝。我們希望能夠繼續得到您的支持，繼續與您合作。
B: Sure. Look forward to continuing the wonderful relationship we've had over the last several years.	B：當然。希望我們能夠延續這幾年來良好的合作關係。

場景問答必會句

> I'm calling to confirm the receipt of your payment.
> 我打電話是想告訴您我收到了您的款項。

還可以這樣說：

💬 This is to acknowledge that we have received your advance payment.
茲證明我們收到了您的預付款。

對方可能這樣回答：

💬 When can you arrange the production?
你們什麼時候安排生產？

PS
advance payment 預付款

> Your products are of good quality that we would attach importance to it.
> 那是因為你們的產品質量很好，我們非常重視。

還可以這樣說：

💬 We enjoyed doing business with you.
和你們合作很愉快。

收款問題 Tips

1. 外貿催款技巧

1) 催款要直接：催款最有效的方式就是有話直說，不要繞彎子。
2) 催款要知根知底：在催款前，先弄清造成拖欠的原因——是疏忽，還是對產品不滿；是資金緊張，還是故意拖欠。應針對不同的情況採取不同的催款策略。
3) 不要怕因催款而失去客戶：到期付款是理所當然的事。害怕催款引起客戶不快或失去客戶，只會使客戶得寸進尺，助長這種不良行為。
4) 收款時間至關重要，堅持"定期收款"的原則。時間拖得越久，貨款越難收回。

2. 收款函電小模板

Dear Mr. Johnson,

It has been two months since we delivered your goods. We wondered whether you have received the copy of BL? If so, please kindly help us to arrange the balance payment on the 5th container. It will be greatly appreciated if it can be done by today. We need the money back to run next containers and make sure the shipping date can be kept as per schedule.

We would very much appreciate your prompt processing of the payment on your side.

Yours sincerely,

Jack

Wanyuan Trading Co.

親愛的約翰遜先生：

我們把貨物交付給你們已有 2 個月了，我們想知道您是否收到了提單的副本？收到了的話，請幫我們安排第五集裝箱的餘款支付。如果今天可以安排支付，我們將很感謝。我們需要這筆錢來操作下一個集裝箱，確保按期發貨。

我們將萬分感謝你們立即處理付款事宜。

傑克

萬源外貿公司

敬上

Chapter 5

貿易類型——
貿易形式多種多樣

Unit 1 補償貿易

補償貿易是國際貿易中以產品償付進口設備和技術等費用的貿易方式。採用補償貿易方式，可以引進先進的技術和設備。同時"以進帶出"，利用設備提供方的銷售能力進入國外市場，是利用外資的一種有效途徑。

補償貿易必會詞

❶ compensation trade 補償貿易
指交易的一方引進設備和技術，然後以該設備和技術所生產的產品，分期抵付進口設備和技術的價款及利息。也叫回購（Buy-back）。

❷ direct product compensation 直接產品補償
指雙方在協議中約定，由設備供應方向設備進口方承諾購買一定數量或金額的由該設備直接生產出來的產品。

❸ other product compensation 其他產品補償
指所交易的設備本身並不生產物質產品，或設備所生產的直接產品非對方所需時，可由雙方協商，用回購其他產品來代替。

❹ labor compensation 勞務補償
指雙方根據協議，由對方代為購進所需的技術和設備，貨款由對方墊付。己方按對方要求加工生產產品後，從應收的工費中分期扣還所欠款項。

這些小詞你也要會哦：

negotiation n. 談判，協商	commissioning n. 調試	manufacture v. 製造，加工
installment n. 分期付款	mutual a. 相互的	consult v. 協商，諮詢
entrust v. 委託	equipment n. 設備	authorize v. 授權

Scene 110 補償貿易談判 Compensation Trade Negotiations

 場景對話

A: Good morning, Mr. Smith.　　　　　　　A：早上好，史密斯先生。

B: Good morning, Mr. Brown.	B：早上好，布朗先生。
A: We are quite interested in the performance of your equipment, but it is too expensive. So <u>are there any other ways to discuss it?</u>	A：我們對您的設備性能很感興趣，但是價格太貴了。因此，<u>還有其他商量餘地嗎？</u>
B: Of course. You can buy our equipment through compensation trade.	B：當然有。您可以通過補償貿易的方式購買我們的設備。
A: Thanks. Could you be more specific?	A：謝謝。您能說得具體一些嗎？
B: In principle, we agree with you to pay 10% of the total price in advance, but the payment should be done within fifteen days after signing the contract.	B：原則上，我們同意貴方先預付設備總價的 10%，但必須在簽訂合同後 15 天內支付。
A: No problem. And we'll use the products to pay the balance. Is that OK?	A：沒問題。之後我們用設備生產的產品支付餘款。您覺得可以嗎？
B: We agree, but how long should it take to complete the payment?	B：我們可以接受這種方式，但要多久才能還清貨款呢？
A: We'll complete the payment within three years.	A：我們會在 3 年內還清。
B: OK.	B：沒問題。
A: In addition,<u>you should be responsible for the installation, commissioning of equipment, as well as the buy-back.</u>	A：另外，<u>由你們負責設備的安裝、調試和產品回購。</u>
B: Of course, but the price of the buy-back shall be determined according to the international market price at the time of the shipment.	B：當然，不過回購價格會根據出貨時的國際市場價格而定。

🗣️ 場景問答必會句

> Are there any other ways to discuss it?
> 還有其他商量餘地嗎？

還可以這樣說：

💬 Can we negotiate it in other ways?
　 有其他協商方式嗎？

對方可能這樣回答：

💬 We can do compensation trade with each other.
　 我們可以通過補償貿易的方式來交易。

💬 Compensation trade is a good way.
　 補償貿易是一個不錯的方法。

> You should be responsible for the installation, commissioning of equipment, as well as the buy-back.
> 由你們負責設備的安裝、調試和產品回購。

還可以這樣說：

💬 You should do your part in installation, commissioning and buy-back.
　由你們負責安裝、調試和回購。

補償貿易 Tips

補償貿易函電小模板

Dear Sir or Madam,

　　We have received the letter from your company. Thanks for your attention to the equipment of our company.

　　After discussion, we think this is a new equipment in good condition, though the price is a little high. Therefore, we propose to sell through compensation trade.

　　You can pay 10% of the total price in advance, and then pay the balance by using the products manufactured by the equipment. The terms of payment can also be consulted. In addition, we'll be responsible for the installation and commissioning of the equipment.

　　If you agree to the above-mentioned proposal, please reply as soon as possible.

Sincerely yours,

Mary,

敬啟者：

　　我們已收到貴公司的來信。感謝您對本公司設備的關注。

　　經過討論，我方認為，儘管價格偏高，但此為全新設備，而且狀況良好。因此，我方提議通過補償貿易的方式出售。

　　貴公司可以先預付設備總價的 **10%**，之後用該設備生產的產品支付餘款，支付期限可另行商議。此外，我方還會負責設備的安裝和調試。

　　若貴公司同意上述提議，請儘快給予答覆。

瑪麗

敬上

易貨貿易

易貨貿易是指買賣雙方在換貨的基礎上，把等值的出口貨物和進口貨物直接結合起來的貿易方式，不涉及貨幣收付，也沒有第三方介入。

易貨貿易必會詞

❶ modern barter 現代易貨
現代易貨是基於傳統易貨發展起來的一種全新易貨方式，指政府、企業（或個人）之間不用現金而進行的商品或服務的等價交換。通常涉及電子商務平台和新交易媒介，且交易對象多樣化。

❷ direct barter 直接易貨
直接易貨又稱一般易貨，是最普遍且應用最廣泛的易貨形式。

❸ comprehensive barter 綜合易貨
綜合易貨主要用於兩國之間根據記帳或支付協定而進行的交易。

❹ barter trading platform 易貨交易平台
易貨交易平台指易貨公司為參與易貨的會員企業搭建的虛擬易貨集市，由易貨平台公共界面、易貨管理控制系統和後台三部分構成。

這些小詞你也要會哦：

barter v. 以貨易貨	liquidate v. 清算	transact v. 交易
virtual a. 虛擬的	commodity n. 商品	turnover n. 成交額
compensation n. 補償	multilateral a. 多邊的	profitable a. 可盈利的

Scene 111　易貨貿易談判 Barter Trade Negotiations

場景對話

A: Manager Wang, our company has introduced a new healthy food. Would you be interested?

A：王經理，我們公司新推出了一款健康食品，不知道貴公司是否感興趣？

B: It's pretty good. We would like to buy it, but there's no enough cash.	B：相當不錯，我們很想購買，但公司現在沒有足夠的現金。
A: <u>Do you think the barter trade is available?</u>	A：那您認為可以採用易貨貿易的方式嗎？
B: That would be a good solution, but we haven't used it before.	B：這倒是個辦法，不過我們以前沒用過這種方式。
A: Barter business won't get involved in monetary payment, which can solve your problem of cash shortfall, and it is also helpful for us to open a new sales channel. So it is of mutual benefits for both of us.	A：易貨交易不涉及貨幣支付，可以解決你們現在現金短缺的問題，也有助於我們開闢新的銷售渠道，對我們雙方都有利。
B: You're right. Our company specializes in all kinds of office supplies. <u>Which product would you like to exchange?</u>	B：您說得有道理。我們公司主營各類辦公用品，貴公司想交換哪種產品呢？
A: We would like to give our food in exchange for your water dispenser.	A：我們想用我們的食品換取你們公司的飲水機。
B: No problem, we have a lot of inventory.	B：沒問題，我們有很多庫存。
A: We need to further discuss about the quantity, price, delivery time and location of our exchanging goods.	A：關於互換產品的數量、價格、交貨時間和交貨地點等事項，我們需要另行商議。
B: That should be done.	B：可以。
A: If this transaction is successfully completed, we sincerely hope that our company could make a long-term cooperation with you.	A：如果本次交易成功，我們真誠希望能與貴公司長期合作。
B: We hope so too.	B：我們也希望如此。

場景問答必會句

Do you think the barter trade is available?
那您認為可以採用易貨貿易的方式嗎？

還可以這樣說：

Do you agree to swap with your other equivalent products?
可以用貴公司的其他等值產品交換嗎？

PS

barter trade 易貨貿易

swap with 與……交換，做交易

> Which product do you want to exchange?
> 貴公司想交換哪種產品呢？

還可以這樣說：

🗩 What kind of product does your company need urgently?
貴公司目前急需哪種產品呢？

對方可能這樣回答：

🗩 We need many office supplies, but the specific one for exchanging should be further discussed.
我們需要的辦公用品有很多，具體交換哪一種，還需要進一步商榷。

🗩 What we need now is water dispenser, but assigned supplier has been confirmed.
我們公司目前需要飲水機，但已經有指定的供應商了。

易貨貿易 Tips

易貨貿易函電小模板

Dear Sir,

In the sales promotion fair last week, we were quite interested in your company's promotional foods for the delicacy and reasonable price. And we were informed that the work clothing we are making also meets your requirements. Therefore, we're interested in conducting barter business with you.

If your company agrees to the barter business scheme we've proposed, please give us a definite reply to make further negotiation.

Yours sincerely,

Jack

敬啟者：

在上週促銷會上，貴公司展示的促銷食品味道可口，物美價廉，我們對此很感興趣。經瞭解，得知貴公司對我們生產的工作服亦有需求。因此，本公司有意與貴公司開展易貨交易。

若貴公司同意我方提出的易貨交易方案，請給予明確答覆，以做進一步協商。

傑克

敬上

Unit 3 寄售貿易

寄售貿易指出口商 (寄售人) 先將貨物運到進口國，委託代銷商在當地市場銷售，再將貨款扣除佣金後匯交出口商。

寄售貿易必會詞

1 consignment sale 寄售貿易
寄售的實質是寄售的貨物的所有權仍屬出口商。

2 principal *n.* 委託人
在寄售方式下，委託人就是寄售人或貨主。

3 commission *n.* 佣金
佣金是在商業活動中，具有獨立地位和經營資格的中間人為他人提供服務所得的報酬。

這些小詞你也要會哦：

consignor *n.* 寄售人	dispute *n.* 爭議	negotiation *n.* 協商
exporter *n.* 出口商	overseas *a.* 海外的	guarantee *v.* 保證
deliver *v.* 運送	warehouse *n.* 倉庫	display *v.* 展出

Scene 112 寄售貿易談判 Negotiation on Consignment Sale

 場景對話

A: Shall we move to the next point, the terms of consignment?	A：我們接下來談一下寄售條件怎麼樣？
B: Okay. Let's start with the period of time, shall we?	B：可以。我們首先談一下協議期限好嗎？

A: Good. Usually, the similar contracts are based on twelve months. <u>Why don't we follow the sales and commence on about July 1st, 2015 and continue through July 1st, 2016?</u> There are still more than two months before July 1st. We have enough time to make all necessary preparations.	A：好的。通常同類合同以 12 個月為限，<u>何不從 2015 年 7 月 1 日左右開始銷售，直到 2016 年 7 月 1 日</u>？距 7 月 1 日還有兩個多月時間。我們有足夠的時間做必要的準備工作。
B: I suggest that after starting the operation, we two sides meet around October 15th to decide on acceptable sales for the remainder of the consignment period. I believe it will certainly benefit both of us.	B：我建議開始銷售後我們雙方在 10 月 15 日左右會晤一次，確定一下剩餘的時間可接受的銷售額度。我相信這樣做對雙方都有利。
A: Good idea. You'd guarantee that our products will be displayed and sold in all large malls in Shenyang.	A：好主意。貴方要保證我們的產品屆時在瀋陽的各大購物中心陳列出售。
B: As long as your products arrive here before April 15th, 2015, we'll be able to manage all the sales to your entire satisfaction.	B：只要你們的產品能在 2015 年 4 月 15 日前到達瀋陽，我們保證其銷售情況會令貴方滿意的。
A: The goods will be delivered by train from Beijing where we've rented a warehouse.	A：我們在北京租了倉庫，貨物將由火車從北京發出。
B: OK.	B：好的。

場景問答必會句

Shall we move to the next point, the terms of consignment?
我們接下來談一下寄售條件怎麼樣？

還可以這樣說：

What do you think about the terms of consignment?
您對寄售條件有什麼想法嗎？

對方可能這樣回答：

That's OK.
我沒有異議。

I still have some questions concerning our contract.
在合同方面我還有一些問題。

We can't agree with the alterations and amendments to the terms.
我們無法接受對條款的變動和修改。

We look forward to your reconsideration about the commission.
希望貴方能再考慮一下佣金的問題。

PS

concerning *prep.* 關於
alteration *n.* 改變；變更
amendment *n.* 修改，修正
look forward to 希望

> Why don't we follow the sales and commence on about July 1st, 2015, and continue through July 1st, 2016?
>
> 何不從 2015 年 7 月 1 日左右開始銷售，直到 2016 年 7 月 1 日？

還可以這樣說：

💬 I think we can begin the sales on about July 1st, 2015, and continue through July 1st, 2016. Do you agree?

我覺得我們可以從 2015 年 7 月 1 日左右開始銷售，直到 2016 年 7 月 1 日止。您同意嗎？

對方可能這樣回答：

💬 Good. We agree.

很好，我們同意。

💬 That sounds good, but we have other plans.

聽起來不錯，但是我們有別的想法。

寄售貿易 Tips

寄售貿易常用表達

- We entertain the business on a consignment basis.
  我們願以寄售的方式接受本交易。
- We will send you account sales on a monthly basis.
  我們每月會向您提供售貨清單。
- We have been in this line of business for over ten years and we are confident that we can find a market for your goods.
  我們在此行業有 10 年從業經驗，有信心能為貴公司的產品找出銷路。
- We will try to sell your products at the best price we can obtain.
  我們會以最好的價格銷售貴公司的產品。
- According to our experience, your products will find a ready market in China.
  根據我們的經驗，貴公司的產品會在中國很暢銷。

Unit 4 加工貿易

加工貿易是貿易類型中的一種，通過各種不同的方式，進口原材料或零件，利用本國的生產能力和技術，加工成成品後再出口，從而獲得以外匯為體現形式的附加價值。

加工貿易必會詞

❶ processing trade 加工貿易
加工貿易是指經營企業進口全部或者部分原材料、零部件或包裝物料，經加工或裝配後，將製成品出口的經營活動，包括進料加工、來料加工、裝配業務和協作生產。

❷ accept customers' materials for processing 來料加工
來料加工貿易是指外商提供全部原材料、零部件和包裝物料等，必要時提供設備，由承接方按外商的要求進行加工裝配，成品交由外商銷售，承接方收取加工費。

❸ processing with imported materials 進料加工
進料加工貿易是指企業用外匯在國際市場購買原材料或零部件，按自己的設計圖紙加工裝配成成品再出口銷往國外市場的加工貿易方式。

❹ shipping order 裝貨單
裝貨單是指接受了託運人提出裝運申請的船公司，簽發給託運人的用以命令船長將承運的貨物裝船的單據。其縮寫為 S/O。

✎ 這些小詞你也要會哦：

import n. 進口	commodity n. 商品	current n. 當前的
advantage n. 優勢	freight n. 運費	shipping advice 裝船通知
deferred payment 延期付款	payment on terms 定期付款	

Scene 113　材料和樣式 Material and Style

 場景對話

A: Hello, sir. <u>What do you think of the material?</u>

A：您好，先生，<u>您覺得這種材料怎麼樣？</u>

217

B: Well, it is good for product and also for our cost.	B：嗯，這種材料對產品來說不錯，成本也不高。
A: I'm very happy to hear that. <u>Do you have any suggestions about the style?</u>	A：聽您這麼說我很高興。<u>您對款式有什麼建議嗎？</u>
B: I'm not sure. I just think the style is a little weird.	B：不太確定，只是覺得這個款式有點奇怪。
A: OK. I will let the designer to improve it again.	A：好的，我會讓設計師重新改進。
B: Thank you. When can you show me the sample?	B：謝謝。什麼時候可以給我看樣品？
A: Within one week. I will call you.	A：一週以內。我會給您打電話。
B: If you have any question, please feel free to ask.	B：有什麼問題，請隨時給我打電話。
A: All right.	A：好。

場景問答必會句

> What do you think of the material?
> 您覺得這種材料怎麼樣？

還可以這樣說：
- Is the material good? 這種材料好嗎？

對方可能這樣回答：
- They are really what I want! 這正是我想要的！
- The material is not suitable for the products.
  這種材料不適合用來做這款產品。

be suitable for 適合

> Do you have any suggestions about the style?
> 您對款式有什麼建議嗎？

還可以這樣說：
- What advice do you have? 您有什麼建議嗎？

對方可能這樣回答：
- In my view, the style looks a little odd.
  在我看來，樣式顯得有些奇怪。
- You'd better select another material for this kind of style.
  對於這種款式，您最好選擇另一種材料。

in one's view 在……看來

you'd better do sth. 您最好……

Scene 114 交付條件 Delivery Condition

 場景對話

A: Hi! I'm very glad to tell you that your order is ready for delivery now. <u>Can you make an advance payment as soon as possible?</u> Then, we will deliver your goods on time and do not affect your business.

A：嘿，很高興告訴您，您的訂單現在已經準備好了隨時可以發貨。<u>您能儘快支付預付款嗎？</u>這樣我們就能按時發貨，不影響您的業務。

B: Thank you for informing us. I can do it in three days.

B：謝謝您通知我們。我會在 3 日內付款。

A: That's great. Do you know our account?

A：很好。您知道我們的賬戶嗎？

B: Yes, of course. I will give you the bank slip after I finish the payment.

B：當然知道。完成支付後，我會把銀行水單發給您。

A: You are very thoughtful. Please send to this email address: better@gmail.com.

A：您想得真周到。請發送到我的郵箱：better@gmail.com。

B: Sure. Can you deliver the goods immediately after receiving my bank slip?

B：好的。在您接到銀行水單之後，您能立即發貨嗎？

A: Oh, of course. When do you want to receive the goods?

A：哦，當然。您想要什麼時候收到貨物？

B: About August 28th. Can you make it?

B：8 月 28 日左右。您能趕上嗎？

A: Absolutely! The goods will arrive in your city on August 27th if I receive your bank slip in three days.

A：絕對可以！如果我在 3 日之內收到您的銀行水單，貨物會在 8 月 27 日到達您的城市。

B: I can assure you that payment will be made in three days. After I get the goods I will pay the rest.

B：我保證在 3 日內支付。在收到貨物之後，我會支付剩餘款項。

A: Well, please do not worry. You will get your goods as expected and everything will go well.

A：好，請不要擔心。您會如期收到貨物，一切都會順利。

場景問答必會句

Can you make an advance payment as soon as possible?
您能儘快支付預付款嗎？

還可以這樣說：

💬 Will you do advance payment as early as possible? 您能儘快支付預付款嗎？

對方可能這樣回答：

💬 I will do it on May 15. 我會在 5 月 15 日付款。

💬 Sorry, we do not accept advance payment. 對不起，我們不接受預付。

加工貿易 Tips

加工貿易函電小模板

Dear Sir or Madam,

How are you?

My name is Tanya, and on behalf of the president of ABC Company, I'm sending you this email.

ABC Company is a constantly growing company in China with high technology and good management and has recently been looking for a partner. As you are a leading company in this industry, we'd like to cooperate with you. We would like to supply you with the assembly line, relative technology and the testing instrument. I am wondering if you would be interested in that.

Looking forward to your reply.

Sincerely,

Tanya

Assistant President

敬啟者：

您好！

我叫塔尼婭，謹代表 ABC 公司的總裁給您發郵件。

ABC 公司是一家不斷發展壯大的中國高科技公司，公司管理良好，最近正在尋找合作夥伴。在瞭解貴公司是這個行業的佼佼者之後，我們想和您合作。我們可以為貴公司提供裝配生產線、相關技術和檢驗儀器。不知道您對此是否感興趣。

期待您的回覆。

塔尼婭

總裁助理

敬上

Unit 5 代理

外貿代理指由我國的外貿公司充當國內外供貨部門的代理人，代其簽訂進出口合同，並收取一定的佣金或手續費的做法。

代理必會詞

1 sole / exclusive agent 獨家代理
獨家代理是指在指定地區和一定的期限內，享有代購代銷指定商品的專營權，委託人在該地區內不得再委派第二個代理人。

2 forwarding agent 運輸代理
運輸代理是指根據客戶的指示，為客戶的利益而攬取貨物的人，其本人並非承運人。

3 express agency 明示代理
明示代理指的是被代理人以明確的方式將代理權授予代理人，可以分為口頭形式和書面形式。

4 implied agency 默認代理
默認代理指的是根據被代理人的一定行為，基於某些公認的準則而推定其為代理人。

✎ 這些小詞你也要會哦：

agent n. 代理人	principal n. 委託人	buying agent 購貨代理
selling agent 銷售代理	agency agreement 代理協議	appoint v. 指定
turnover n. 營業額	entrust v. 委託	overseas a. 海外的

Scene 115　申請代理 Apply for Agency

 場景對話

A: Mr. Hand, if you haven't been represented here, <u>would you let us be your agent?</u>

A：漢德先生，如果貴公司在這裡沒有代理的話，<u>能讓我們成為你們的代理商嗎？</u>

B: Frankly speaking, you're not the only one who applies for an agent for us in your country. Would you like to show us your advantages?	B：坦率地講，你們不是唯一向我們申請在貴國做我們代理商的公司，能讓我們瞭解一下你們的優勢嗎？
A: <u>We have twenty years' experience in agency</u> and we believe that we could work up very satisfactory in pushing the sales of your products.	A：我們有 20 年的代理經驗，我們相信在推廣貴公司產品方面能夠讓貴公司滿意。
B: The other companies are also experienced.	B：其他公司也都經驗豐富。
A: We have local knowledge and wide connections, as well as a group of well-trained salesmen.	A：我們熟知本地區市場，有廣泛的社會關係，並且有一支訓練有素的銷售隊伍。
B: Can you analyze the marketing situation of your areas?	B：您能分析一下你們地區的市場形勢嗎？
A: Generally speaking, the market is promising, especially the high-quality oriental products. If you can sign a sole agency agreement with us, it will double your turnover.	A：整體來說，市場情況不錯，尤其是高質量的東方產品。如果貴公司和我們簽訂獨家代理協議，我們能使銷售額翻番。
B: I appreciate your kindness. We think it's necessary to make sure of your competitiveness.	B：感謝你們的好意。但是我們有必要瞭解你們的競爭力。
A: Our firm is among the leading firms of importers and distributors for many years' standing in this area. We believe that our experience in international trade will undoubtedly meet your requirement.	A：我們公司在這個領域有多年的經驗，在進口商和批發商中居領先地位。我們相信我們多年的國際貿易經驗能夠完全符合貴公司的要求。
B: What are the minimum annual sales you can guarantee if we appoint you as our agent?	B：如本公司指定貴公司為代理商，貴公司能保證的最低年銷售額是多少？
A: We guarantee an annual sale of 2,000 cases.	A：我們保證 2000 箱的年銷售量。
B: We'll make our decision and let you know as soon as possible. Thank you for your appreciation of our products.	B：我們會做出決定，並儘快通知你們結果。謝謝你們欣賞我們的產品。

 場景問答必會句

> Would you let us be your agent?
> 能讓我們成為你們的代理商嗎？

還可以這樣說：

💬 We hope that you will point our company as your agent.
我們希望貴公司能指定我們作為貴公司的代理商。

對方可能這樣回答：

💬 We won't consider agency in your market at present.
我們目前不考慮在你們地區設置代理。

💬 We'll leave aside the problem of agency until next week.
我們暫時把代理問題擱置到下週再考慮。

PS leave aside 擱置，不考慮

We have twenty years, experience in agency.
我們有 20 年的代理經驗。

還可以這樣說：

💬 We have sufficient canvassing abilities to be your agent.
我們有充分的調研能力來做貴公司的代理。

💬 We trust that our experience in foreign trade marketing will entitle us to your confidence.
我們堅信我們在國際貿易市場上的經驗能夠取得貴公司的信任。

PS canvass v. 調研

Scene 116 拒絕代理 Decline an Agent

💬 場景對話

A: Mr. Fox, have you received my email?	A：福克斯先生，您收到我的郵件了嗎？
B: Yes, I received it a week ago.	B：是的，我一週前收到了。
A: What's your opinion? <u>Will you consider our proposal to act as your sole agent?</u>	A：您的意見如何？您能考慮我們擔任貴公司獨家代理商的建議嗎？
B: Frankly speaking, I feel that it's not a mature time for you to act as a sole agent for us.	B：老實說，我感覺貴公司做我們獨家代理商的時機還不成熟。
A: Why not?	A：原因何在？
B: As the volume of business conducted by you is not big enough, we won't consider you as our agent.	B：由於貴公司的業務量不夠大，我們不考慮由你們來做代理。

A: Though the order is not grand, it will help you to establish your market channel and expand the influence of your products in the region. Don't you think so?	A：儘管我們的訂貨量不大，但它會幫助你們在這個國家建立市場渠道，並擴大你們的產品在這個區域的影響力。您不這麼認為嗎？
B: Do you have any special promoting methods?	B：你們有什麼特別的促銷方式嗎？
A: I'll submit a detailed proposal to you later.	A：我稍後會提交一份詳細的計劃給您。
B: We shall not consider pointing you as our sole agent until your sales record convinces us.	B：我們現在不考慮指定貴司為我司的獨家代理，除非你們的銷售成績説服了我們。
A: You mean it depends on the sales?	A：您的意思是這取決於我們的銷售額嗎？
B: Yes, we hope you will continue your effort to push the sales of our products.	B：是的，希望貴公司繼續努力推進我司產品的銷售。

場景問答必會句

> Will you consider our proposal to act as your sole agent?
> 您能考慮我們擔任貴公司獨家代理商的建議嗎？

還可以這樣說：

- If you are not already represented here, we should be interested in acting as your sole agent.
  如果貴公司在這裡沒有代理的話，我們有興趣做貴公司的獨家代理商。
- Could you consider about appointing us as your sole agent in this area?
  貴公司可以考慮讓我們擔任貴公司在該地區的獨家代理商嗎？

對方可能這樣回答：

- If we come to terms, we'll appoint you as our sole agent.
  如果達成協議，我們將指定貴公司為我們的獨家代理。
- Your proposal will be gone through careful consideration.
  我們會認真考慮貴公司的建議。

> I'll submit a detailed proposal to you later.
> 我稍後會提交一份詳細的計劃給您。

還可以這樣說：

- We'll make full use of our local knowledge and wide connections.
  我們將充分利用自身的本土化優勢和廣泛的社會關係。

Our well-trained salesmen will prove that we can be a good agent.
我們訓練有素的銷售隊伍將證明，我們能夠勝任代理工作。

Scene 117 代理協商 Discuss with an Agent

  場景對話

A: Mr. Hawk, we are willing to negotiate with you on your proposal to act as our agent.	A：霍克先生，我們想跟您討論一下貴公司擔任我們代理的提議。
B: Thank you for offering us this opportunity.	B：謝謝您給我們這次機會。
A: What's your plan to push our products?	A：你們準備怎樣推廣我們的產品？
B: <u>Well, we'll do a lot of advertising in newspapers and on TV programs.</u> We'll also send our salesmen around to promote the sale of your goods.	B：我們會在報紙上和電視節目裡多登廣告，還會派出銷售員到各處推廣你們的產品。
A: What is the territory to be covered?	A：代理地區包括哪些地方？
B: All of North America.	B：整個北美。
A: What are the minimum annual sales you can guarantee?	A：你們能保證的最低年銷售額是多少？
B: We propose the guaranteed annual amount to be 400,000 dollars for a start.	B：我們建議能保證的年銷售總額一開始先定為 40 萬美元。
A: What rate of commission will you charge?	A：你們收取多少佣金？
B: <u>We usually get a 7% commission of the amount on every deal.</u>	B：<u>我們通常收取每筆交易額 7% 的佣金。</u>
A: That's fine. We look forward to a happy and successful cooperation with you.	A：很合理，我們期待與您愉快合作。

場景問答必會句

> We'll do a lot of advertising in newspapers and on TV programs.
> 我們會在報紙上和電視節目裡多登廣告。

還可以這樣說：

🗨 We've prepared a specific plan. If you're interested, we can discuss about it in tomorrow's meeting.

我們準備了一份詳細的計劃，如果貴方感興趣的話，我們可以在明天的會議上進一步討論。

對方可能這樣問：

🗨 Do you have any plans of promotion?

你們有什麼推廣計劃嗎？

We usually get a 7% commission of the amount on every deal.
我們通常收取每筆交易額 7% 的佣金。

還可以這樣說：

🗨 How about a 7% commission?

7% 的佣金怎麼樣？

🗨 What's your usual practice in giving commission?

你們通常給代理商多少佣金？

Scene 118　任命代理 Appoint an Agent

  場景對話

A: Mr. Sharp, we're willing to negotiate with you on your proposal to be our agent.	A：夏普先生，我們想就任命貴公司擔任我司代理一事進行洽談。
B: OK. That is necessary.	B：好的，這很有必要。
A: Could you tell us your detailed plans for sales promotion? We may proceed with our negotiation about the terms of agency agreement.	A：可以說說貴公司的詳細促銷計劃嗎？以便我們繼續磋商具體的代理條款。
B: I'm sorry for that. We just have some ideas. <u>Could you give us some time for making plans in written form?</u>	B：我很抱歉，我們只有一些初步想法。<u>可以給我們一些時間來整理書面計劃書嗎？</u>
A: We can't give you exclusive agency of the whole European market without having the slightest idea of your possible annual marketing turnover.	A：如果貴公司沒有任何關於市場銷售額的計劃，我們不可能給貴公司整個歐洲市場的獨家代理權。

B: We'll get it prepared before next Monday.	B：我們會在下週一之前把計劃書準備好。
A: OK. We hope you will do your best to push the sales of our products.	A：好，我們希望你們盡最大努力銷售我們的產品。
B: Of course. Do you have any special requirements?	B：當然。你們還有什麼特別要求嗎？
A: Every six months, we'd like to receive a detailed report from you.	A：每 6 個月我們需要收到詳細的報告。
B: What's the report about?	B：關於什麼的報告呢？
A: Your market report should show the current market conditions and users' comments on our products.	A：你們的市場報告應説明市場情況及使用者關於我們產品的想法。
B: OK. We'll pay close attention to the market and consumers' comments.	B：好的，我們會密切關注市場情況和用戶評價。

場景問答必會句

Could you give us some time for making plans in written form?
可以給我們一些時間來整理書面計劃書嗎？

還可以這樣說：

We'll be obliged if you allow us to spend some time in finishing the written plan.
若能給我們點時間來完成書面計劃書，我們將感激不盡。

對方可能這樣回答：

I think you'd better get such kind of documents prepared in advance next time.
我認為貴公司下次最好提前準備好各種文件。

That's OK. We can discuss about the plan tomorrow.
沒問題，我們可以明天討論計劃書。

What's the report about?
關於什麼的報告呢？

還可以這樣說：

What content should be included in the report?
報告應該包括哪些內容？

對方可能這樣回答：

Apart from the current sales conditions, the sales prospects of the item and your program in detail should also be included in the report.
除了目前的銷售情況，該產品的銷售前景和你們的詳細計劃也應寫進報告中。

💬 We need you to analyze the market from all kinds of perspectives in the report.
我們需要貴公司在報告中從各個角度對市場進行分析。

Scene
119 續約代理 Renew an Agent

 場景對話

A: Good morning, Mr. Longman. Nice to see you again.	A：早上好，朗曼先生。很高興再見到您。
B: Nice to see you, too. Mr. Liu, I've received your email about agency. Do you want us to act as your agent for the new products?	B：我也很高興見到您。劉先生，我收到您有關代理的郵件了。貴公司想要我們擔任新產品的代理嗎？
A: That's right. We have done business with each other for four years and we get along well with each other. We are glad to offer you the agency for the sale of our products in your city.	A：沒錯，我們已經合作了 4 年，而且關係一直很好。很高興邀請貴方擔任我們在貴方城市的產品代理。
B: Thank you for the confidence you have for us, but shall we make some points clear before we can give you a definite answer?	B：感謝你們對我們的信任。但是，在給您明確答覆前，我們可以明確一些事情嗎？
A: OK. Go ahead, please.	A：好的。請說。
B: First, we should have to be sure whether any of your new products overlap what we are handling.	B：首先，我們得弄清貴公司新產品中是否有與我們已經代理的產品重複的品種。
A: Oh, I see.	A：哦，我知道了。
B: Second, could we sell the similar products of other companies while acting as your agent?	B：其次，我們在擔任貴公司的代理時可以銷售別的公司的相似產品嗎？
A: I can give you the answer to the second question now. To be our agent, you should not sell similar products from other manufacturers without our prior approval.	A：我現在就可以回答您的第二個問題。作為我們的代理商，如果沒有我們預先許可，貴公司不得銷售其他廠家相似的產品。
B: I think I'm quite clear now after your explanation. Thank you.	B：經您解釋後，我想我已經很清楚了。謝謝。

A: Then I'll arrange another meeting with you when our draft contract is ready.

A：那麼當我方準備好協議草案後，我會安排與您再次會面。

場景問答必會句

> Shall we make some points clear before we can give you a definite answer?
> 在給您明確答覆前，我們可以明確一些事情嗎？

還可以這樣說：

We'd like to make sure of something before we make a decision.
我們想在做決定之前先確認一些事情。

> Second, could we sell the similar products of other companies while acting as your agent?
> 其次，我們在擔任貴公司的代理時可以銷售別的公司的相似產品嗎？

還可以這樣說：

Second, if we accept your proposal, could we act as the agent of other companies in the same field?
其次，如果我們接受貴方的提議，那我們也可以在相同領域擔任其他公司的代理商嗎？

對方可能這樣回答：

If you wish to work for other firms as well, you must obtain our permission first.
如果您要為其他公司服務，首先要征得我們的同意。

I'm afraid you can't. During the validity of the agency agreement, you should not handling any other products of the same line or competitive types.
恐怕不行。在代理協議有效期內，你們不得代理任何其他相同或具有競爭性的產品。

代理 Tips

代理常用英語表達

1. I would like to discuss with you our agency of your cellphone.
   我想跟您討論一下貴公司的手機的代理問題。

2. We would be appreciated if you would consider our application to act as a sole agent for the sale of your products in our country.
   如果貴方能考慮我們的申請使我們成為貴公司產品在我國市場的獨家銷售代理的話，我們會很高興的。

3. We are pleased to offer you an exclusive agency for the sale of our products in your country.
   我們很樂意指定你們成為我方產品在貴國的獨家代理。

4. Thank you for offering us the sales contract for your products and we appreciate the confidence you have placed in us.
   謝謝貴方提出讓我們代理你們的產品，我們很感激你們對我們所表示的信心。

5. As your agent, we'll make greater efforts to push the sales of your products.
   作為你們的代理，我們將更加努力地推銷貴公司的產品。

Unit 6 技術轉讓

技術轉讓又稱技術轉移，指技術在國家、地區或行業之間輸入與輸出的活動。

技術轉讓必會詞

❶ transfer *n.* 轉讓
轉讓就是把自己的東西或合法利益讓給他人，有產權、債權、資產、股權、經營權、著作權和知識產權轉讓等。

❷ proprietary *n.* 所有權
所有權是所有人依法對自己財產所享有的佔有、使用、收益和處分的權利。

❸ patent *n.* 專利
專利指專有的利益和權利。

這些小詞你也要會哦：

market *n.* 市場	right *n.* 權利	achievement *n.* 成果
entity *n.* 實體	design *n.* 設計	trademark *n.* 商標
copyright *n.* 版權	advanced *a.* 先進的	assignment *n.* 轉讓
transferor *n.* 轉讓人	apply *v.* 申請	transferee *n.* 受讓人

Scene 120 轉讓專有技術 Transfer of Know-how

  場景對話

A: I'm interested in your proprietary technology. Would you like to sell it?	A：我對您的專有技術感興趣。您願意出售嗎？
B: Why don't you buy the right to use the patent?	B：您為什麼不購買專利使用權呢？
A: I think buying the proprietary technology is better than buying the right to use the patent.	A：我認為購買專有技術比購買專利使用權好。

B: But it is much more expensive than the right to use the patent, isn't it?

B：但是購買專有技術比購買專利使用權要貴很多，不是嗎？

A: How much will you ask for it?

A：您的要價是多少？

B: Four times the price for patent.

B：專利使用權價格的 4 倍。

A: That is too expensive. The highest price I can accept is triple the price for patent.

A：那太貴了。我能接受的最高價格是 3 倍。

B: Is it possible for you to increase it?

B：您有可能提高一點價格嗎？

A: Sorry, your price is much higher than I expected.

A：對不起，您的價格比我預想的高太多了。

B: Well. We might call the whole deal off because there is hardly any need for further discussion.

B：好吧。那我們也沒有必要再談下去了，交易就到此為止吧。

A: All right.

A：好吧。

場景問答必會句

> Why don't you buy the right to use the patent?
> 您為什麼不購買專利使用權呢？

還可以這樣說：

🗨 I recommend you to buy the right to use the patent.
我建議您購買專利使用權。

🗨 Why not buy the right to use the patent?
為什麼不購買專利使用權呢？

PS

rather than 而不是

對方可能這樣回答：

🗨 I would like to buy the proprietary technology rather than the right to use the patent.
我想要購買專有技術，而不是專利使用權。

🗨 Can you tell me the price of buying the right to use the patent?
您可以告訴我購買專利使用權的價格嗎？

> Is it possible for you to increase it?
> 您有可能提高一點價格嗎？

還可以這樣說：

🗨 Would you like to increase a little?
您願意再加點嗎？

🗨 We will not accept it.
我們不會接受這個價格的。

Scene 121 轉讓專利 Transfer of Patent

 場景對話

A: We'd like to buy your technical license to improve our present products.	A：為改善我們的現有產品，我們想要購買您的技術許可證。
B: Thank you for your interest. Our machine and technology are of advanced world levels.	B：謝謝您對我們的許可證感興趣。我們的機器和技術具有世界級先進水平。
A: That's why we are here. Can you give me more details about rights that the license will grant to us?	A：這就是我們來這兒的原因。您能告訴我們這項許可證會給予我們哪些權利嗎？
B: Sure. This license will grant you rights to use our information and technology of our products.	B：當然，這項許可證會給予你們使用我們產品的信息和技術的權利。
A: Is the core patent included in the license?	A：這項許可證包括核心專利嗎？
B: Yes, it is.	B：是的，包括。
A: Good. And how long will you allow us to use the patent?	A：好的。你們將允許我們使用這項專利多長時間？
B: For ten years. But you have no right to grant any rights to third parties.	B：10 年。但是你們無權將任何權利授予第三方。
A: I see.	A：我明白了。

場景問答必會句

> Can you give me more details about rights that the license will grant to us?
> 您能告訴我們這項許可證會給予我們哪些權利嗎？

還可以這樣說：
💬 Then, what rights can we enjoy? 那麼，我們能享受哪些權利呢？

> How long will you allow us to use the patent?
> 你們將允許我們使用這項專利多長時間？

還可以這樣說：
💬 How long can we use the patent? 我們可以使用這項專利多長時間？

🖲 What is the duration of using the patent for us? 我們使用這項專利的期限是多久？

對方可能這樣回答：

🖲 You can renew as long as you need. 只要您需要，您可以續簽合同。

🖲 How long do you want? 您想要多久？

技術轉讓 Tips

1. 技術轉讓詞匯

patent certificate 專利證書	protection 保護期
standard forms 標準形式	patent right 專利權
duration of patent 專利保護期限	approval 批准
patentee 專利權人	grant 授予
technician 技術員	infringement 侵權
be limited by region 受區域限制	validity 有效性

2. 技術轉讓函電小模板

To whom it may concern,

I have two questions.

Will you consider buying the patent? Do you wish to discuss technical cooperation with us? If the answers to both of the two questions are yes, I would really like to discuss the technology transfer with you. We are looking for a long and steady partner in technical cooperation.

Looking forward to your reply.

Best regards,

Li Gang

敬啟者：

我有兩個問題需要問您。

您考慮購買專利嗎？您願意和我們討論技術合作嗎？如果這兩個問題的答案是肯定的，我將非常高興和您討論技術轉讓的事宜。我們正在尋找長期、穩定的技術合作方。

期待您的回覆。

李剛

敬上

Unit 7 合資合作

由兩個或兩個以上不同國家的投資者共同投資、共同管理和共負盈虧，並按照投資比例分配利潤和股權的投資經營方式就叫合資合作。

合資合作必會詞

1 joint venture 合資企業
合資企業指由兩家公司共同投入資本成立，分別擁有部分股權，並共享收益和風險，共享對該公司的控制權。

2 cooperative enterprise 合作企業
合作企業指在合同中約定投資或者合作條件、收益或者產品的分配方式、風險和虧損的分擔方式、經營管理的方式和合作企業終止時財產的歸屬等事項的企業。

3 after-sales service 售後服務
售後服務指在商品出售以後所提供的各種服務。

4 actual loss 實際損失
實際損失指相對於賬面損失的實際損失。

這些小詞你也要會哦：

share *n.* 股份	account *n.* 賬戶	administration *n.* 經營
acquire *v.* 購得	delegate *v.* 委派	allowance *n.* 津貼
enterprise *n.* 企業	appendix *n.* 附錄	appoint *v.* 任命
branch *n.* 分公司	allocate *v.* 分配	annual *a.* 年度的

Scene 122 尋找項目 Look for Projects

場景對話

A: Hi, my name is Joy and I'm calling you on behalf of the president of International Investment Inc.

A：您好，我叫喬伊，代表國際投資公司的總裁給您打電話。

B: Hi, it's nice to talk to you.	B：您好，很高興和您通話。
A: <u>Are you looking for any new projects to invest in?</u>	A：<u>您在尋找新的投資項目嗎？</u>
B: Yes.	B：是的。
A: Our company has been working on some new projects. Would you be interested in them?	A：我們公司正在做一些新項目。您有興趣嗎？
B: What are they mainly about?	B：這些項目主要做些什麼？
A: Petroleum and gas. We have several projects in South Asia.	A：石油和天然氣。我們在南亞有幾個相關項目。
B: Really? <u>Could I talk to you face to face sometime?</u>	B：真的？<u>我們能約個時間當面談談嗎？</u>
A: Certainly.	A：當然可以。

場景問答必會句

> Are you looking for any new projects to invest in?
> 您在尋找新的投資項目嗎？

還可以這樣說：

🖵 Do you intend to invest a new project?
　 您打算投資一個新項目嗎？

🖵 Would you like to make an investment in some project?
　 您想要投資某個項目嗎？

對方可能這樣回答：

🖵 No, I have no current plan but anything can change.
　 不，我目前沒有計劃，但是任何事情都可能變化。

🖵 Sure thing.
　 當然。

> Could I talk to you face to face sometime?
> 我們能約個時間當面談談嗎？

還可以這樣說：

🖵 I think I should talk to you in person.
　 我覺得我應該和您當面談談。

🖵 May I visit you at your company?
　 我可以到您的公司去拜訪您嗎？

Scene 123 技術引進 Technology Import

 場景對話

A: Shall we briefly discuss the technology transfer now?	A：我們現在來扼要討論一下技術轉讓的問題好嗎？
B: Of course.	B：當然可以。
A: Is your technology appropriate to our need?	A：貴方的技術適合我們的需求嗎？
B: Yes. Our advanced technology enables the products to be more competitive on the international market.	B：是的，我們的先進技術能夠使產品在國際市場上更具競爭力。
A: Great. I hope the technology enables our products to achieve significant economic results.	A：太好了。我希望這項技術能使我們的產品取得可觀的經濟效益。
B: Absolutely. It can also improve the quality of your products.	B：當然。這項技術也有助於提高產品的質量。
A: Would you like to provide us with the necessary technical data?	A：您願意為我們提供必要的技術數據嗎？
B: Yes, I can also offer you some more information if you need.	B：是的，若您需要，我方也可以提供更多的信息。
A: Thanks. For the success of our joint venture, it's extremely important for us to acquire the information concerning the product design and the production processes.	A：謝謝。為了使合資企業取得成功，對我方來說，獲得與產品設計和生產過程相關的信息是極其重要的。
B: I totally agree with you.	B：我完全同意您的說法。

場景問答必會句

> Is your technology appropriate to our need?
> 貴方的技術適合我們的需求嗎？

還可以這樣說：

🖻 Is your technology suitable for our need?
　 您的技術符合我們的需求嗎？

對方可能這樣回答：

💬 Sure. The technology is designed for your projects.
當然。這項技術是專為你們的產品設計的。

💬 Please do not worry about that.
請別擔心那一點。

> Would you like to provide us with the necessary technical data?
> 您願意為我們提供必要的技術數據嗎？

還可以這樣說：

💬 Can you offer the necessary technical data?
您可以提供必要的技術數據嗎？

💬 Please provide us with the necessary technical data.
請為我們提供必要的技術數據。

Scene 124 合資經營條件 Conditions on Joint Participation

 場景對話

A: I propose to sign an agreement for a project producing clothes.	A：我建議簽訂一份合作生產服裝項目的協議。
B: Good idea. <u>Would you please tell me the total investment in the project?</u>	B：好主意。<u>請告訴我這個項目的總投資是多少？</u>
A: Five million US dollars in total because I think it should be a moderately sized joint venture.	A：500 萬美元，因為我覺得這家合資企業應該是中等規模。
B: Then how much would the registered capital be?	B：那麼註冊資金是多少呢？
A: Three million US dollars.	A：300 萬美元。
B: <u>What's the percentage of your contribution?</u>	B：<u>貴方打算出資多少呢？</u>
A: Half of the total investment.	A：總投資金額的一半。
B: Therefore, we will offer the other 50%. Sounds reasonable.	B：所以，我們提供剩下的 50%。聽起來挺合理的。
A: Thank you.	A：謝謝。
B: Pleasant cooperation!	B：合作愉快！

場景問答必會句

> **Would you please tell me the total investment in the project?**
> 請告訴我這個項目的總投資是多少？

還可以這樣說：

▢ Please tell me the total amount you will invest. 請告訴我您將投資的金額。

> **What's the percentage of your contribution?**
> 貴方打算出資多少呢？

還可以這樣說：

▢ How much money would you like to contribute? 您想要出資多少？

對方可能這樣回答：

▢ That depends on how much you can contribute. 這取決於貴方能出資多少。

▢ It is not decided. （我們出資多少這件事）還沒有決定。

合資合作 Tips

合資合作函電小模板

Dear Sir or Madam,

　　We are specialized in trading with the major dealers in China. Now, we'd like to develop the overseas business and find a partner to establish a joint venture. We are writing to you in order to ascertain whether cooperation between us could be established.

　　We look forward to hearing from you soon.

Best regards,

Zhang Qi

敬啟者：

　　我們專業從事與中國各大經銷商的貿易。現在，我們想發展國外市場，尋求一位合作夥伴來成立一家合資公司。給您寫這封郵件是為了確認您是否願意和我們合作。

　　期待您的佳音。

張琪

敬上

Unit 8

投資

投資可分為實物投資和證券投資。實物投資是指以貨幣投入企業，通過生產經營活動取得收益。證券投資是指購買企業發行的股票和公司債券，間接參與企業的利潤分配。

投資必會詞

1 investment *n.* 投資
投資指的是將某種有價值的資產，包括資金、人力和知識產權等投入到某個企業、項目或經濟活動中，以獲取經濟回報的商業行為或過程。

2 real estate 房產
房產是指有牆面和立體結構，能夠遮風避雨，可供人們在其中生活、學習、工作、娛樂、居住或貯藏物資的場所。

3 bond *n.* 債券
債券是一種金融契約，是政府、金融機構或工商企業等直接向社會借債籌措資金時，向投資者發行，同時承諾按一定利率支付利息並按約定條件償還本金的債權債務憑證。

4 fund *n.* 基金
從廣義上説，基金是指為了某種目的而設立的具有一定數量的資金。常見的種類有信託投資基金、公積金、保險基金和退休基金等。

這些小詞你也要會哦：

interest *n.* 利息	index *n.* 指數	broker *n.* 經紀人
option *n.* 期權	capital *n.* 資本	collateral *n.* 抵押品
note *n.* 單據	duration *n.* 期限	earnings *n.* 收益
hedge *n.* 對沖	income *n.* 收入	adviser *n.* 顧問

Scene 125 投資評估 Investment Appraisal

 場景對話

A: Our investment project will be evaluated next month. You are responsible for supporting the evaluation. <u>Do you know how to do it?</u>	A：我們的投資項目下個月就要進行評估了，你負責這次評估的支持工作。知道要怎麼做嗎？
B: Sorry, I'm not sure.	B：抱歉，我不是很確定。
A: You should collect information for the review analysis.	A：你應該為審查分析收集信息。
B: <u>What kind of information should I collect?</u>	B：<u>我應該收集哪些信息呢？</u>
A: Something about the enterprise and project overview, market analysis, financial forecast, etc. in accordance with the requirement of the assessment agency.	A：按照評估機構的要求，收集與企業和項目概況，市場分析和財務預測等有關的一些信息。
B: OK. Is that all?	B：好的。就這些嗎？
A: They may also require additional information. Anyway, you need to provide them with what they ask for. Is that clear?	A：他們還可能要求其他信息。總之你盡力提供他們所需要的材料。清楚了嗎？
B: Yes. I will try my best.	B：清楚了。我會盡全力的。
A: You can come to me if you have any question.	A：有任何問題，歡迎隨時找我。
B: Thank you.	B：謝謝。

場景問答必會句

> Do you know how to do it?
> 知道要怎麼做嗎？

還可以這樣說：
💬 Do you know your work content?
知道你的工作內容嗎？

對方可能這樣回答：

💬 Yes, I have done that before.
是的，我以前做過此類工作。

💬 Yes, I have rich experience about that.
是的，我在這方面的經驗很豐富。

💬 Sorry, I have no experience about that.
抱歉，我沒有這方面的經驗。

What kind of information should I collect?
我應該收集哪些信息呢？

還可以這樣說：

💬 Please tell me the information I should collect.
請告訴我應該收集的信息。

💬 Would you like to tell me the information I should collect?
您願意告訴我應該收集的信息嗎？

對方可能這樣回答：

💬 I don't know exactly. The assessment agency will inform you.
我不是很清楚。評估機構會通知你的。

💬 Just do as required by the assessment agency.
按照評估機構的要求去做就好。

Scene 126　投資風險 Investment Risk

 場景對話

A: I'd like to make some investment but I do not know how to avoid the risk.	A：我想要投資，但是不知道怎樣規避風險。
B: What would you like to invest in?	B：您想要投資什麼？
A: What do you think of stock?	A：您認為股票怎麼樣？
B: Stock is a kind of investment with high risk and high return.	B：股票是一種高風險、高收益的投資。
A: High risk! That's definitely not for me. Do you know any investment with the lowest risk?	A：高風險！那絕對不適合我。您知道哪種投資的風險最小嗎？

B: Any investment has risks. I think diversified investment is good for you. You know, it's better that we don't put all our eggs in one basket.	B：任何投資都有風險。我認為您適合做分散投資。您知道，我們最好不要把所有雞蛋放在同一個籃子裡。
A: So what exactly is diversified investment?	A：分散投資是什麼意思？
B: It means investment in different asset types or different securities at the same time.	B：它是指同時投資不同的資產類型或不同的證券。
A: And what advantage does diversified investment have?	A：分散投資有什麼優勢？
B: Without reducing revenue while it reduces the risk.	B：在不降低收益的同時降低風險。

 場景問答必會句

What would you like to invest in?
您想要投資什麼？

還可以這樣說：

- What are you willing to invest in?
  您想要投資什麼？

對方可能這樣回答：

- I do not know. 我不知道。
- Could you offer me some advice?
  您能給我提一些建議嗎？

Do you know any investment with the lowest risk?
您知道哪種投資的風險最小嗎？

還可以這樣說：

- Which investment has the lowest risk?
  哪種投資的風險最小？
- Is there an investment with the lowest risk?
  有沒有風險最小的投資途徑？

對方可能這樣回答：

- Usually high risks will bring high profits.
  通常，高風險會帶來高收益。
- Sorry, I'm not sure about that.
  對不起，我對這一點不太瞭解。

Scene 127　投資比例 Proportion in Investment

 場景對話

A: How much is the total amount of investment?	A：總投資是多少？
B: The money has to be enough to offer the construction funds, so I think it is about four million US dollars.	B：這筆錢必須足夠提供建設資金，所以我認為應該是大約 400 萬美元。
A: No, we also need money for circulating. I think the figure should be six million US dollars.	A：不，我們也需要流動資金。我認為金額數應該是 600 萬美元。
B: You are right. How much would you be prepared to invest in this venture?	B：您是對的。貴方計劃在這家合資企業投資多少？
A: We lay out 50% of the total investment.	A：我們計劃投資總投資額的 50%。
B: Is there any regulation on the proportion of investment by foreign investors in your country?	B：貴國對外國合營者的投資比例有什麼規定嗎？
A: As far as I know, it should not be less than 20%.	A：據我所知，外國合營者的投資不能少於 20%。
B: I see. How long will the joint venture last?	B：知道了。合營的期限有多長？
A: We can fix the term for five years first.	A：我們可以先定 5 年。
B: Good. The period can be prolonged later if we can run the venture well.	B：好的。如果運營不錯，我們可以延長期限。

 場景問答必會句

> How much is the total amount of investment?
> 總投資是多少？

還可以這樣說：

💬 What is the price of the total amount of investment?
　　總投資是多少？

> Is there any regulation on the proportion of investment by foreign investors in your country?
> 貴國對外國合營者的投資比例有什麼規定嗎？

還可以這樣說：

🗨 Do you have any regulation on proportion of investment by foreign investment in your country?
貴國對外國合營者有投資比例方面的規定嗎？

對方可能這樣回答：

🗨 The regulation is rather flexible and it depends on the circumstances.
規定很靈活，具體情況具體分析。

Scene 128 投資糾紛 Investment Dispute

  場景對話

A: Hi, there is something we need to talk about. Are you available now?	A：您好，有一件事咱們需要談一下。您現在有時間嗎？
B: Yes. What is it?	B：我有空。請問是什麼事？
A: I've paid three million US dollars for the joint venture and that money allows me to have the right to use the warehouse.	A：這家合資企業我出資了 300 萬美元，這筆投資允許我有使用倉庫的權利。
B: Yes, you are right.	B：是的，沒錯。
A: Then why don't you let me put my stuff in the warehouse?	A：為什麼您不允許我將物品放到倉庫裡？
B: You can only put something involving the joint venture into the warehouse.	B：您僅可以將與本合資企業有關的物品放到倉庫裡。
A: But the contract has not stipulated that. Could you make a phone call to your president?	A：但是合同上沒有這樣明確規定。您可以給您的總裁打個電話嗎？
B: Sure.	B：好的。

場景問答必會句

> Why don't you let me put my stuff in the warehouse?
> 為什麼您不允許我將物品放到倉庫裡？

還可以這樣說：

🗨 What is the reason that you do not allow me to put my stuff in the warehouse?
為什麼您不允許我將物品放到倉庫裡？

Why can't I put my stuff in the warehouse?
為什麼我不能將物品放到倉庫裡？

對方可能這樣回答：

Sorry, I do not know about it.
抱歉，我不知道這件事。

I just act according to the rule.
我只是按規矩辦事。

> Could you make a phone call to your president?
> 您可以給您的總裁打個電話嗎？

還可以這樣說：

Could you call your president?
您可以給您的總裁打電話嗎？

I suggest that you call your president.
我建議您給您的總裁打個電話。

對方可能這樣回答：

I have done that before.
我已經打過了。

Sorry, my president has gone to America for business.
對不起，我的總裁出差去美國了。

投資 Tips

投資術語

accrued interest 應得利息	all-ordinaries index 所有普通股指數
ask price 要價	asset-backed securities 資產抵押的證券
book value 賬面價值	capital gain 資本增值
certificate of deposits 存款單	commercial paper 商業票據
contract note 成交單	credit rating 信用評級
net asset value 資產淨值	prospectus 招股書

Unit 9 招標

招標是一種普遍運用的、有組織的市場交易行為，交易標的可以是工程、貨物和服務等，與投標相對。

招標必會詞

1 invitation of tender 招標
招標是指招標人（買方）發出招標公告或投標邀請書，說明招標的工程、貨物或服務的範圍、標段劃分、數量和投標人（賣方）的資格要求等，邀請特定或不特定的投標人（賣方）在規定的時間和地點按照一定的程序進行投標的行為。

2 tenderee n. 招標人
招標人是指在投招標活動中提出招標項目而進行招標的法人或其他組織。

3 contract award 發包
發包是指建設工程合同的訂立過程中，發包人將建設工程的勘察、設計和施工一併交給一家工程總承包單位或者將建設工程勘察、設計和施工的一項或幾項交給一家承包單位完成的行為。

這些小詞你也要會哦：

bidding n. 招標	bidder n. 投標人	invitation n. 邀請
receipt n. 收到	eligible a. 合格的	instruction n. 須知
cancel v. 取消	original a. 原來的	document n. 文件
equal a. 平等的	appraisal n. 評估	decision n. 決定

Scene 129 招標信息 Bidding Information

 場景對話

A: I've heard that you are going to call for tender. What kind of project is it for?

A：我聽說您即將發佈招標通知。這是什麼樣的項目？

B: Yes, we are ready to start the invitation to tender. We'd like to build a new oil project.	B：是的，我們準備開始招標。我們想要創建一個新的石油項目。
A: When and where do you open the tender?	A：何時在哪兒開始招標呢？
B: We plan to open the tender on Sept. 22 in Shanghai.	B：我們計劃 9 月 22 日在上海開始招標。
A: When is the closing date?	A：（投標）什麼時候截止？
B: Oct. 31.	B：10 月 31 日。
A: Could you please tell me something more about the conditions for the tender?	A：能否多告訴我一些招標條件方面的信息？
B: I will send the details to you if you are interested.	B：如果您有興趣，我會把詳細信息發給您。
A: Thank you. I'm sorry to have taken up so much of your time.	A：謝謝。我很抱歉佔用您這麼多的時間。
B: It doesn't matter. We'll be in touch.	B：沒關係。我們保持聯繫。
A: OK.	A：好的。

場景問答必會句

> What kind of project is it for?
> 這是什麼樣的項目？

對方可能這樣回答：
- Yes, but we do not get ready now.
  是的，但是我們現在還沒準備好。
- Sorry, I do not know about it.
  不好意思，我還不知道這件事。

> When and where do you open the tender?
> 何時在哪兒開標呢？

還可以這樣說：
- When and where do you plan to open the tender?
  你們計劃什麼時候在哪裡開標？

對方可能這樣回答：
- I will notice you when I know it.
  我知道後會通知您。
- Sorry, I only know the date.
  抱歉，我只知道日期。

open the tender 開始招標

Scene 130　招標通知 Tender Notice

 場景對話

A: We intend to send the tender notice. <u>Have you carefully considered this tender?</u>	A：我們正預計開始招標。<u>您考慮參加這次招標嗎？</u>
B: Yes, we have carefully considered your suggestion and we are willing to take part in the bid.	B：是的，我們認真考慮了你們的意見，也很願意參加這次招標。
A: Thanks for your participation.	A：感謝您的參與。
B: <u>When will you send the formal tender notice?</u>	B：你們什麼時候發正式的招標通知？
A: Next month.	A：下個月。
B: How many firms will you send the tender notice to?	B：你們會給多少家公司發送招標通知？
A: More than ten.	A：10 家以上吧。
B: Thanks a lot. We will study it carefully.	B：多謝。我們會仔細研究這件事的。
A: You are welcome. We are looking forward to receiving your bid documents.	A：不客氣。期待收到貴公司的標書。

場景問答必會句

> Have you carefully considered this tender?
> 您考慮參加這次招標嗎？

還可以這樣說：
- Will your corporation bid it? 你們公司會投標嗎？
- Do you want to bid it? 您想要投標嗎？

對方可能這樣回答：
- Thanks for calling. We wish to tender for this bid. 謝謝通知。我們準備參加這次投標。

> When will you send the formal tender notice?
> 你們什麼時候發正式的招標通知？

還可以這樣說：
- When can I receive your formal tender notice? 我什麼時候能收到正式的招標通知？

對方可能這樣回答：

💬 We have not decided it yet and will notice you as soon as possible.
我們還沒有決定，將會儘快通知您。

💬 The date is temporarily set on Oct. 30. 日期暫定於 10 月 30 日。

招標 Tips

1. 招標術語

call for bid 招標	bid document 招標文件
bid bond 押標金	subject matter 標的物
form of tender 投標書	bid opening 開標
the successful bidder 中標者	letter of acceptance 中標函
evaluation of tender 評標	tender discussion 議標
withdrawal of bid 撤標	requests of clarification 澄清要求

2. 招標函電小模板

Dear Newton,

How is everything with you?

The following are the project requirements. I hope it will help you.

The bidder shall provide the products according to the requirements of equipment technical specifications, quantity and service proposed in the tender document. It is expected that the bidder show the strength of your company with sophisticated equipment, quality service and preferential price.

Best regards,

Chen Huan

親愛的牛頓：

一切還好嗎？

下面是項目要求。希望能對您有幫助。

招標人應該按照招標文件中提出的設備技術規格、數量和服務要求提供產品。

希望投標人藉助精良的設備、優質的服務和優惠的價格展現自己公司的競爭力。

陳歡

敬上

Unit 10　投標

投標是與招標相對應的概念，它是指投標人應招標人特定或不特定的邀請，按照招標文件的要求，在規定的時間和地點主動向招標人遞交投標文件並以中標為目的的行為。

投標必會詞

❶ letter of guarantee 投標保函
投標保函是指在招投標中招標人為避免投標人撤銷投標文件、中標後無正當理由不與招標人簽訂合同等，要求投標人在提交投標文件時一併提交的一般由銀行出具的書面擔保。

❷ bidder 投標人
投標人是按照招標文件的規定參加投標的自然人、法人或其他社會經濟組織。投標人參加投標，必須具備一定的履行合同的能力和條件，包括相應的人力、物力、財力資質、工作經驗與業績等。

❸ bidding documents 投標書
投標書是指投標單位按照招標書的條件和要求，向招標單位提交的報價並填具標單的文書。

❹ bid-opening 開標
開標是指招標單位在規定的時間、地點內，在投標人出席的情況下，當眾公開投標資料，宣佈投標人的名稱和投標價格的過程。

這些小詞你也要會哦：

tender n. & v. 投標	deadline n. 最後期限	bid n. 標書
receipt n. 收到；收據	guarantee v. 擔保	tender committee 投標委員會
tender document 投標文件	furnish v. 供應，提供	supervise v. 監督，管理

Scene 131　投標擔保 Bid Guarantee

場景對話

A: This is our tender which includes the information about company registration, comprehensive proposal, financial strength, track record of previous projects, cost and pricing, and so on.

A：這是我們公司的投標書，包括我們公司的註冊信息、全面的方案、財務實力、以前項目的記錄、成本和價格信息等。

B: Thank you. The tender panel will evaluate and assess all the submitted tenders.

B：謝謝。招標小組將會評價和評估所有提交的投標書。

A: We would like to receive a debriefing on the tender after the process.

A：我們希望在這之後能得到一份投標的任務報告。

B: Sure, no problem. I'll just follow up the process. When the debriefing is ready, I'll let you know.

B：當然，沒問題。我會跟進整個過程。當任務報告準備好了之後，我會通知您。

A: Should we pay any guaranty bond?

A：我們要交擔保金嗎？

B: Yes, you are supposed to pay it on time.

B：是的，你們應該及時繳納。

A: When is the deadline?

A：截止時間是什麼時候？

B: Actually, it's very urgent. You'd better furnish a tender bond by the end of this week. If you can't hand in your guaranty bond, your tender will not be considered.

B：實際上，時間很緊迫。你們應該在本週末前繳納投標保證金。如果無法繳納保證金，你們的投標將不予考慮。

A: Oh, I see. Thanks a lot for your information.

A：哦，我知道了。非常感謝您提供的信息。

B: You're welcome. Good luck!

B：不客氣，祝您好運！

場景問答必會句

Should we pay any guaranty bond?
我們要交擔保金嗎？

還可以這樣說：

Do we need to pay earnest money?
我們需要交擔保金嗎？

🗨 Do we have to guarantee our participation in the tender?

我們參加投標需要擔保嗎？

對方可能這樣回答：

🗨 Yes, bidders need to pay a cash deposit.

是的，投標人需要繳納保證金。

🗨 Yes, bidders need to hand in a letter of guarantee from a commercial bank.

是的，投標人要繳納由商業銀行出具的保證函。

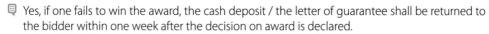

PS within one week 在一週內

🗨 Yes, if one fails to win the award, the cash deposit / the letter of guarantee shall be returned to the bidder within one week after the decision on award is declared.

是的，如果某家公司沒有中標，那麼在開標後的一週內，我們把保證金 / 保證函退給投標人。

Scene 132 投標期限 Bid Deadline

 場景對話

A: Good morning. I'm Wu Qing, a representative of Baima Company. We saw the bidding advertisement from your webpage, and I'm here to enquire something about the bidding.	A：早上好，我是白馬公司的代表武清。我們從網上看到你們的招標廣告，所以我前來詢問一下有關招標的情況。
B: Nice to meet you, Mr. Wu.	B：很高興見到您，武先生。
A: Could you tell me something about the bidding in detail?	A：您能詳細介紹一下有關招標的情況嗎？
B: It's my pleasure. We have invited bids for the construction of a power plant. And we have got more than ten bidders from various countries. Here is a set of bid documents.	B：好的。我們招標建造一家發電廠，目前已有來自不同國家的十幾位投標者參與投標。這份文件裡有關於這個項目的詳細要求。
A: Thanks. By the way, what is the deadline for the receipt of the bids?	A：謝謝。順便問一下，投標的最後期限是什麼時候？
B: The deadline is at 17:00 on July 20, 2015.	B：最後期限是 2015 年 7 月 20 日下午 5 點。
A: Thank you very much for the information.	A：非常感謝您提供的信息。
B: You are welcome.	B：不客氣。

場景問答必會句

> Could you tell me something about the bidding in detail?
> 您能詳細介紹一下有關招標的情況嗎？

還可以這樣說：

💬 May I have a look at the bid documents?
我可以看看招標文件嗎？

對方可能這樣回答：

💬 Of course! I will get you a complete set of tender documents so you can study the requirements.
當然了，我將為您提供全套投標文件，以便您研究（投標）要求。

> What is the deadline for the receipt of the bids?
> 投標的最後期限是什麼時候？

還可以這樣說：

💬 When do you intend to open the tender?
你們打算什麼時候開標？

對方可能這樣回答：

💬 The time period for the bidders to submit their bids (tenders) is set temporarily.
投標人投標的期限是暫定的。

💬 We intend to send the tender notice next month, and the date of the closing of tender is temporarily set on September 10th.
我們公司預計下個月開始招標，暫定 9 月 10 日截止。

投標 Tips

投標英文術語

tendering 投標	pre-qualification period 預審期
bottom price 最低價	tender clarifications 投標說明
tender negotiation 投標談判	bidding conditions 招標條件
bid price 投標報價	bidding / tender book 投標書
letter of award 決標信	closed bidding (sealed bid) 非公開招標
restitution of the guarantee 撤銷保函	win a tender 中標
tender evaluation & award 投標評估及決標	clarification of bidding document 投標文件的澄清
bonding company (surety company) 擔保公司	selective bidding (selective tendering) 選擇性投標

電子商務

電子商務是指採用電子形式開展商務活動，它包括在供應商、客戶、政府及其他參與方之間通過任何電子工具，如 EDI、Web 技術或電子郵件等共享非結構化商務信息，並管理和完成在商務活動、管理活動和消費活動中的各種交易。

電子商務必會詞

① mobile commerce 移動商務
移動商務是指通過移動通信網絡和移動信息終端參與商業經營活動的一種電子商務模式。

② intranet n. 內聯網
內聯網又稱企業內網，是用因特網技術建立的可支持企事業內部業務處理和信息交流的綜合網絡信息系統。

③ extranet n. 外聯網
外聯網是不同單位間為了頻繁交換業務信息，而基於互聯網或其他公網設施構建的單位間專用網絡通道。

這些小詞你也要會哦：

framework *n.* 框架	category *n.* 類別	consortia *n.* 聯盟，公會
promotion *n.* 促銷	e-purchase *n.* 電子採購	exhibit *n.* 展品
mandate *v.* 授權	convergence *v.* 集中	stimulate *v.* 刺激
diverse *a.* 不同的	turbulent *a.* 動盪的	steep *a.* 急劇的

Scene
133 在線交易 Online Transaction

 場景對話

A: OK, we've got the basic information of your products. When can you deliver the goods?

A：好的，我們已經基本瞭解了你們的產品。你們什麼時候能發貨？

B: Delivery will be made ten days after receiving your L/C.	B：收到貴公司信用證後 10 天即可發貨。
A: <u>Could you give us any discount?</u>	A：<u>可以給我們打折嗎？</u>
B: The discount we have offered you is the best we can offer at present.	B：這個折扣是我們目前所能給的最高折扣了。
A: What's the price now?	A：現在的價格是多少？
B: The list price is 130,000 yuan.	B：標價是 13 萬元人民幣。
A: If you can lower the price a little bit, we might take a larger quantity.	A：如果貴公司能降低價格，我們可能會加大訂單數量。
B: Well, we are allowing special terms to customers who place orders before the end of the current month.	B：嗯，對於本月底前訂貨的顧客，我們會給予特殊優惠。
A: What kind of special terms?	A：什麼特殊優惠？
B: We would entitle you to a 10% discount during this month on anything you buy.	B：對於本月購買的任何產品，我們會給予 10% 的折扣。
A: Good. Can you supply from stock?	A：不錯。您能提供現貨嗎？
B: We have sufficient inventory to meet your present needs.	B：我們有足夠的庫存來滿足你們的需求。

?A 場景問答必會句

> When can you deliver the goods?
> 你們什麼時候能發貨？

還可以這樣說：

💬 When will the goods be delivered?
什麼時候能送貨？

對方可能這樣回答：

PS

receipt *n.* 收到

backlog of orders 積壓未交付的訂單

💬 We can deliver the goods within fifteen days upon the receipt of your order.
收到訂單之日起 15 天內交貨。

💬 Well, we've got rather a backlog of orders at the moment. I think it'll take one or two months.
最近我們積壓的訂單非常多，也許要一兩個月才能送貨。

> Could you give us any discount?
> 可以給我們打折嗎？

還可以這樣說：

💬 Is it possible to give us a little more discount?
能否多給我們一些折扣？

對方可能這樣回答：

💬 As you've already had our rock-bottom price, we cannot give you any more discount.
我們提供給你們的報價已經是最低價了，不可能有更多折扣了。

💬 If your order is large enough, we are ready to reduce our prices by 5%.
如果您的訂單足夠大，我們願意降價 5%。

Scene 134 支付方式 Payment

  場景對話

A: Hello. Very nice to see you again!	A：您好，很高興再次見到您！
B: Hello. I'm glad to meet you too!	B：您好，我也很高興再次見到您！
A: Now shall we continue our last conversation? What kind of payment do you prefer?	A：我們能繼續上次的談話嗎？你們想採用怎樣的付款方式？
B: We hope the term of payment is DAP.	B：我們希望用目的地交貨的付款方式。
A: Well, my company always do L/C. DAP may be too risky for us.	A：我們公司一直用信用證付款。目的地交貨付款對我們來說風險太大。
B: But as you know, opening the L/C costs too much, and the procedures are troublesome.	B：您也知道，開立信用證費用很高，手續也很麻煩。
A: Look, it's our first time to cooperate with each other. We have made great concession in the price. And we also hope that we can have a long-term cooperation in the future.	A：您看啊，這是我們之間第一次合作。我們已經在價格上做了很多讓步。我們希望將來能與貴公司有更長遠的合作關係。
B: Of course .We hope so too.	B：當然。我們也希望如此。
A: But we have no precedent. Hmmm, let's see how we can solve this problem.	A：但是我們沒有那樣的先例。嗯，讓我們看看怎麼解決這個問題。
B: How about 30% DAP and 70% L/C?	B：那麼 30% 目的地交貨付款，70% 信用證付款怎麼樣？
A: OK. Deal!	A：很好。就這樣定了！

B: Thank you very much! When shall we sign the contract?

B：非常感謝。那我們什麼時候簽訂合同呢？

A: At any time.

A：隨時可以。

場景問答必會句

> What kind of payment do you prefer?
> 你們想採用怎樣的付款方式？

還可以這樣說：
- Could you tell us your way of payment? 可以跟我們説一下付款方式嗎？

對方可能這樣回答：
- We usually make payment by L/C. 我們一般用信用證付款。
- Payment by L/C is our method of trade in such products.
  用信用證付款是我們在此類產品上採用的交易方式。

> How about 30% DAP and 70% L/C?
> 那麼 30% 目的地交貨付款，70% 用信用證付款怎麼樣？

還可以這樣說：
- I hope you would leave us some leeway in terms of payment.
  我希望您能讓我們在付款條件上保留一些回旋餘地。
- Could you make an exception in our case and accept DAP?
  您能破例接受目的地交貨付款嗎？

對方可能這樣回答：
- We regret to say that we are unable to consider your request for payment under DAP terms.
  很遺憾地告訴您我們不考慮貴公司用目的地交貨付款的請求。
- I'm sorry that we are unable to accept your request.
  很抱歉我們不能接受貴公司的請求。

Scene 135 送貨方式 Delivery

  場景對話

A: We need the products in less than one month in order to get ready for the selling season.

A：為了做好迎接銷售旺季的準備，我們需要在 1 個月之內拿到貨物。

B: OK, we will try our best to satisfy your needs.	B：好的，我們將竭盡所能來滿足您的需要。
A: Then how will you deliver the products?	A：那麼你們將怎樣運送貨物呢？
B: Usually, it is cheaper to have the goods sent by sea, but it takes a longer time. But in your case, it will be far too late to send by sea.	B：通常海運的費用會便宜些，但花費時間較多。鑒於你們的情況，走海運的話就會太遲了。
A: That's true. So are you going to ship them by railway?	A：沒錯。那你們會用鐵路運輸的方式嗎？
B: We don't think it is proper to transport the goods by railway. We would rather have goods carried by road than carried by railway.	B：我們認為此貨物不適合用鐵路運輸。我們寧願用公路運輸，也不會用鐵路運輸。
A: Or by air?	A：或者用空運？
B: Yes, we think so. How about partial shipment? We can ship one fifth of the goods in June and the balance in the beginning of July. What do you think?	B：是的，我們也這麼考慮。分批裝運怎麼樣？我們在 6 月份裝運 1/5 的貨物，餘下的在 7 月初裝運。您覺得如何？
A: That sounds fine to us. We hope that you can do your best to deliver the goods on time.	A：聽起來不錯。希望貴公司盡全力及時發貨。
B: No problem.	B：沒問題。

 場景問答必會句

> Then how will you deliver the products?
> 那麼你們將怎樣運送貨物呢？

還可以這樣說：

💬 Then how will you have the products sent?
　　那麼你們將怎樣運送貨物呢？

對方可能這樣回答：

💬 We usually send it by sea.
　　我們通常走海運。

💬 To move the goods by railway is quicker.
　　鐵路運輸會比較快。

How about partial shipment?
分批裝運怎麼樣？

還可以這樣說：

📧 How about shipment by installments?
分批裝運怎麼樣？

對方可能這樣回答：

📧 Good idea.
好主意。

📧 Your proposal is workable.
您的建議行得通。

📧 No, we hope to effect the shipment once for all.
不，我們希望一次性裝運。

PS once for all 一次性地

電子商務 Tips

電子商務英語常用縮略詞

DNS (Domain Name System)	域名系統
BBS (Bulletin Board System)	電子公告欄
CMC (Common Mail Calls)	共同郵件呼叫
CRM (Customer Relationship Management)	客戶關係管理
CWIS (Campus Wide Information System)	全校園信息系統
DBMS (Data Base Management System)	數據庫管理系統
DES (Data Encryption Standard)	數據加密標準
DDP (Datagram Delivery Protocol)	數據報傳送協議
EDI (Electronic Data Interchange)	電子數據交換
FTP (File Transfer Protocol)	文件傳輸協議
HTTP (Hyper Text Transport Protocol)	超文本傳輸協議

Chapter 6

商品報關——
出入境的必要手續

Unit 1 商品檢驗

商品檢驗是指商檢機構對進出口商品的品質、規格、衛生、數量和裝運條件等進行檢驗和鑒定，並出具證書。這是商品買賣的重要環節和買賣合同的重要內容。

商品檢驗必會詞

1 commodity inspection 商品檢驗
商品檢驗指對進出口商品的品質、規格、重量、數量、包裝、衛生指標、裝運技術和條件等項目實施的檢驗和鑒定。

2 acceptance inspection 接受報檢
接受報檢指對外貿易關係人按照商檢機構的要求報請檢驗。

3 re-inspection *n.* 複驗
複驗指貨物在裝運前由雙方約定的檢驗機構實施檢驗並出具檢驗證書，而在貨物抵達目的港卸貨後由約定的檢驗機構對貨物實施複驗。

4 commodity inspection clause 商檢條款
商檢條款指與進出口貿易商檢有關的合同條款，其中涉及檢驗標準、檢驗機構、檢驗期限、檢驗的時間和地點以及索賠條款等內容。

5 commodity inspection certificate 商檢證書
商檢證書指貨物經檢驗合格後由商檢機構頒發的檢驗證書。

這些小詞你也要會哦：

consignor *n.* 發貨人	consignee *n.* 收貨人	shipping *n.* 貨運，裝運
clause *n.* 條款	claim *n.* 索賠	validity *n.* 有效期
third-party *a.* 第三方的	specification *n.* 規格	packaging *n.* 包裝
load *v.* 裝貨	unload *v.* 卸貨	appraise *v.* 鑒定

Scene 136 商品檢驗及程序 Commodity Inspection & Procedure

 場景對話

A: Hello, Mr. Brown.	A：您好，布朗先生。
B: Hello, Mr. Wang.	B：您好，王先生。
A: Today, we can talk about the issue of commodity inspection.	A：今天，我們來討論一下商品檢驗的問題吧。
B: Hum, of course, this is a very important part of the contract.	B：嗯，當然可以，這是合同裡很重要的一部分。
A: Here's the thing, this batch of ceramic tiles will be submitted for inspection before shipping, and then sent to the destination port. Is that OK?	A：是這樣的，這批瓷磚由我方在裝運前申報檢驗，檢驗合格後再運送到指定港口，也就是目的港。您看可以嗎？
B: That's OK, and who will issue the inspection certificate?	B：可以，那由誰出具檢驗證明呢？
A: The certificate in duplicate will be issued by China Commodity Inspection Bureau (CCIB). The validity period is two years.	A：由中國商檢局出具證明，一式兩份。有效期兩年。
B: But, in order to ensure our mutual benefits, we have right to make re-inspection after the goods arrive at the destination port.	B：不過，為了確保雙方利益，我們有權在貨物抵達目的港後進行複驗。
A: Of course, but the time limit for re-inspection should be established.	A：當然可以，不過得制訂複驗時限。
B: Within thirty days after the arrival of the goods. What do you think?	B：貨物抵達港口後 30 天內。怎麼樣？
A: We agree.	A：同意。
B: We'll accept the goods only if two inspection results are consistent.	B：只要檢驗結果一致，我們就確認收貨。

場景問答必會句

Who will issue the inspection certificate?
由誰出具檢驗證明呢？

還可以這樣說：

🗨 What agency will issue the inspection certificate?
出具檢驗證明的是哪一家機構呢？

對方可能這樣回答：

🗨 The ceramic tiles will be inspected by China Commodity Inspection Bureau (CCIB) through sampling test, and be provided with a certificate.
由中國商檢局對瓷磚進行抽樣檢驗並出具證明。

🗨 The inspection process for export ceramic tiles is more complicated. But if the product doesn't pass the inspection for the first time, we can reapply for inspection to CCIB after the reworking.
出口瓷磚的檢驗流程比較複雜，不過如果第一次檢驗不合格，我們可以在返工後重新向中國商檢局申報檢驗。

> But the time limit for re-inspection should be established.
> 不過得制訂複驗時限。

還可以這樣說：

🗨 You should set the time limit for re-inspection.
您得制訂複驗時限。

對方可能這樣回答：

🗨 Ceramic tiles are fragile. We'll immediately arrange re-inspection after the arrival of goods.
瓷磚屬易碎品，我們會在貨物到港後馬上組織複驗。

🗨 Apart from the time limit for re-inspection, we also need to formulate the claim clause.
除複驗時限外，我們還應該制訂索賠條款。

Scene 137　商檢條款 Commodity Inspection Clause

 場景對話

A: Mr. Miller, should we talk about how to formulate the inspection clause?	A：米勒先生，我們是不是該談談如何制訂檢驗條款了？
B: Yes, Mr. Wang. I hope it will be complete and specific.	B：是的，王先生。我希望條款內容能完整、具體。
A: Definitely. Also we don't want to create unnecessary conflicts.	A：那當然，我們也不希望引起不必要的矛盾。
B: Well, let's talk about the quality first.	B：嗯，讓我們先來談談質量問題吧。
A: OK.	A：好的。

B: I recommend that we ensure the quality of goods through the counter sample. What do you think?	B：我建議通過對等樣品的方式確保貨物的品質，您認為呢？
A: We agree. You need to provide us with sample first, and we'll process it according to your sample.	A：同意。您先為我們提供樣品，然後我們會按照提供的樣品進行加工。
B: That's right. If your sample is approved, then the delivered goods must be identical with the counter sample.	B：好。如果您的樣品通過檢驗，那麼所交的貨物必須與對等樣品相同。
A: We understand. If there's any difference, you have the right to reject the goods.	A：我們明白。如果有任何不符的地方，您有權拒絕收貨。
B: Yes. The counter sample is the only way to ensure the quality.	B：是的，對等樣品是確保品質的唯一依據。
A: We agree.	A：我們同意。
B: Thanks for your understanding.	B：謝謝您的理解。

場景問答必會句

> I recommend that we ensure the quality of goods through the counter sample. What do you think?
> 我建議通過對等樣品的方式確保貨物的品質，您認為呢？

還可以這樣說：

- I think the counter sample is fair and helpful to ensure our mutual benefits. What's your suggestion?
  我認為對等樣品有助於確保我們雙方的利益，是一種相對公平的方法。您的建議呢？

對方可能這樣回答：

- If you are not satisfied with our processed sample, you should provide some advice on how to improve it.
  如果貴方不滿意我們提供的加工樣品，希望貴方能提供修改建議。

PS

counter sample 對等樣品，指賣方根據買方提供的樣品，加工出類似樣品供買方確認，確認後的樣品即對等樣品，或稱"回樣"。這種方式適用於服裝和輕工產品等。

> If your sample is approved, then the delivered goods must be identical with the counter sample.
> 如果您的樣品通過檢驗，那麼所交的貨物必須與對等樣品相同。

還可以這樣說：

💬 Before confirmation, the sample could be altered. But it should be in line with the counter sample on delivery.
在確認前，樣品可能會經過修改，但交貨時必須與對等樣品相符。

PS in line with 符合，與……一致

Scene
138 商檢證明與確認 Inspection Certificate & Confirmation

 💬 場景對話

A: Mr. Wang, we want to confirm something about the inspection with you.	A：王先生，我們想跟您確認一下有關商品檢驗的一些問題。
B: OK, do you have any ideas about it?	B：好的，您有什麼具體的想法？
A: Firstly, according to the clauses of our contract, we require that the goods should be inspected and verified before delivery.	A：首先，根據合同中的條款規定，我們要求貨物必須在裝運之前進行檢驗和鑒定。
B: No problem.	B：沒問題。
A: Secondly, apart from inspecting the quality, quantity and specifications, we demand that your company should provide us with Sanitary / Health Inspection Certificate.	A：此外，除質量、數量和規格檢查外，我們要求貴公司出具衛生健康檢驗證書。
B: We will. But we also demand that the re-inspection should be made as soon as possible after the arrival of the goods, and your company should be responsible for the re-inspection fee.	B：好的。不過我們也要求貨物抵達後貴公司儘快安排複驗，而且複驗費由貴公司承擔。
A: It's reasonable.	A：這很合理。
B: In addition, if the goods have problems due to force majeure, we'll not be responsible for the compensation.	B：另外，如果由於不可抗力導致貨物出現問題，我們不負責賠償。
A: Of course, but your company should inform us timely, and we'll reply as soon as possible.	A：當然，不過貴公司必須及時通知我們，我們會在第一時間給予答覆。

B: OK, we can accept it.	B：好的，可以接受。
A: After the arrival, if we find any problem during the re-inspection, we'll inform you within one week.	A：貨物抵達後，如果我們在複驗中發現問題，會在一週內通知貴公司。
B: That would be fine.	B：好的。

場景問答必會句

> Secondly, apart from inspecting the quality, quantity and specifications, we demand that your company should provide us with Sanitary / Health Inspection Certificate.
> 此外，除質量、數量和規格檢查外，我們要求貴公司出具衛生健康檢驗證書。

還可以這樣說：

In order to ensure the freshness of the goods, it is also necessary to issue the Sanitary / Health Inspection Certificate.
為了確保貨物的新鮮度，出具衛生健康檢驗證書也是很有必要的。

對方可能這樣回答：

That should be done, and we'll deliver the goods in time when the inspection is completed.
這是應該的，並且我們會在檢驗完畢後及時發貨。

Of course, we also don't want to cause a loss to your company because of the inspection.
那是當然，我們也不希望因為商檢問題給貴方造成損失。

> In addition, if the goods have problems due to force majeure, we'll not be responsible for the compensation.
> 另外，如果由於不可抗力導致貨物發生問題，我們不負責賠償。

還可以這樣說：

We'll be responsible for the compensation if it is within the range of our responsibility, except for force majeure.
只要是在我們責任範圍內，我們都會負責賠償，但不可抗力除外。

對方可能這樣回答：

Compensation clauses have been made in our contract. If there are any problems, we'll make a decision after careful analysis.
賠償條款在合同中都有明確規定。如果出現問題，我們會仔細分析後再做決定。

Scene 139　檢驗爭議 Inspection Disputes

場景對話

A: Hello, Mr. Smith. You imported a batch of hardware from our company last month, right?	A：您好，史密斯先生。上個月您從我們這裡進口了一批五金器件，是嗎？
B: Yes, Mr. Wang. Is there any problems?	B：是的，王先生，有什麼問題嗎？
A: I'd like to negotiate the time of delivery with you again. Is that OK?	A：我想再跟您協商一下交貨時間的問題，可以嗎？
B: We've discussed about it, and the clause has been made. Do you have any suggestions?	B：這一點我們已經討論過了，而且已經制訂了條款。您有什麼疑義嗎？
A: Hum, the equipment suddenly failed to work during the processing, and now we are rushing to repair it, so could we delay the delivery?	A：嗯，設備在加工時突然出現故障，目前正在搶修，請問可不可以延遲交貨？
B: How long do you need to delay?	B：您需要延遲多久？
A: About one week.	A：一個星期左右。
B: We have made the clause of delivery delay in our contract. For every week of delay, you have to pay a penalty amounting to 0.5% of the total value of the delayed goods.	B：關於延遲交貨，合同裡也有規定。每延誤一週，就要按延期交貨貨物總額的 0.5% 支付罰金。
A: I know about it, but the equipment failure is just an accident which is out of our control.	A：這一點我也知道，不過設備故障只是個意外，我們也無法控制啊！
B: I think this failure can be avoided. You need to take a good look at our force majeure clause.	B：我認為技術故障是可以避免的，您應該再仔細看一下我們的不可抗力條款。
A: We have to pay the penalty if we cannot deliver on time, right?	A：如果我們不能按時交貨就必須支付罰金，是嗎？
B: That's right.	B：沒錯。

A 場景問答必會句

> **I'd like to negotiate the time of delivery with you again. Is that OK?**
> 我想再跟您協商一下交貨時間的問題，可以嗎？

還可以這樣說：

🗨 As for the time of delivery, could you bend the rules?
關於交貨時間，您是否能通融一下？

對方可能這樣回答：

🗨 The time of delivery is negotiable. Is there any difficulty in your company?
交貨時間可以商量，貴公司是不是遇到了什麼困難？

PS

negotiate with 與……協商，談判

bend the rules 通融；靈活掌握規則

starve for 急需

🗨 We're starving for this batch of hardware. If there are any problems, our production cycle would be affected.
我們急需這批五金器件。如果有問題的話，會影響我們的生產週期。

> **I know about it, but the equipment failure is just an accident which is out of our control.**
> 這一點我也知道，不過設備故障只是個意外，我們也無法控制啊！

對方可能這樣回答：

🗨 Equipment failure doesn't fall within the scope of force majeure. If the delay time is confirmed, your company should perform the contractual obligations.
設備故障不屬不可抗力的範圍。如果交貨時間確實已延遲，貴公司必須履行合同義務。

PS

fall within 屬，在……範圍內

🗨 If you can deliver the goods on time after the equipment has been repaired, you won't need to pay the penalty.
如果在設備搶修後依然能按時交貨，就不必支付罰金。

商品檢驗 Tips

商品檢驗常用詞

port of shipping 貨運港	results of inspection 檢驗結果
port of discharging 卸貨港	visual inspection 外觀檢查
port of destination 目的港	value of goods 貨物價值
Unit price 單價	net weight 淨重
quality latitude 品質機動幅度	settlement of claim 理賠
fundamental breach 根本性違約	

Unit 2 海關檢查

海關檢查是指對出入境貨物、貨幣和運輸工具等進行檢查和徵收關稅的一項國家行政管理活動，旨在保護本國經濟，查禁走私違章案件。

海關檢查必會詞

1 Customs *n.* 海關
海關指國家的出入境監督管理機構，旨在監管出入境貨物、行李等物品，徵收關稅和其他稅費。

2 Customs clearance 海關放行
海關放行指海關接受進出口貨物申報，經查驗和繳納關稅後，由進出口商或代理人提取或發運貨物。

3 green channel 綠色通道
綠色通道即無申報通道，指旅客攜帶無需報關的物品辦理海關手續的通道。

4 red channel 紅色通道
紅色通道即申報通道，指必須經海關檢查和辦理檢驗手續後才可放行的通道。

5 tally *n.* 理貨
理貨指貨主在裝運港和卸貨港接收和交付貨物時委託港口的理貨代理機構完成對貨物的檢驗工作。理貨機構必須出具理貨單證。

這些小詞你也要會哦：

declaration *n.* 申報	arbitration *n.* 仲裁	breach *v.* 違反
entry *n.* 報關手續	broker *n.* 代理人	procedure *n.* 程序
cargo *n.* 貨物	authorize *v.* 批准，認可	pilferage *n.* 偷盜
sanction *n.* 處罰	confiscate *v.* 沒收	bonded *a.* 保稅的

Scene 140 通關手續與協商 Customs Formalities / Consultation

 場景對話

A: Hello, Mr. Wang, I'd like to know something about the cargo clearance.	A：您好，王先生，我想瞭解一下關於通關的問題。
B: Mr. Collins, according to the terms of the contract, we are in charge of this area.	B：柯林斯先生，按照合同規定，這方面由我們負責。
A: I know, but I'd still like to have a general idea about the Customs in your country.	A：我知道，不過我還是想大致瞭解一下你們這裡的通關情況。
B: OK, the export declaration procedure in our country has several parts, including application, inspection, tax payment and final clearance.	B：好的。我們這裡的出口報關流程分為申報、查驗、繳納稅費和放行幾個環節。
A: Self declaration or Customs agent?	A：自理報關還是代理報關？
B: We'll entrust a Customs broker because this job should be done professionally.	B：由於報關工作的專業性很強，我們會委託報關行代為辦理。
A: What kind of documents do you need?	A：具體都需要哪些單據呢？
B: Verification form, commodity inspection form, declaration form, declaration certificate of entrustment, packing list, invoice and contract, etc.	B：核銷單、商檢單、報關單、報關委託書、裝箱單、發票和合同等。
A: How long should it take?	A：報關需要多長時間？
B: It's about one or two working days.	B：大約一兩個工作日。
A: If the time of Customs clearance is delayed, both of us will suffer economic losses.	A：如果清關延誤，我們雙方都會遭受經濟損失。
B: I know.	B：我明白。

場景問答必會句

I'd still like to have a general idea about the Customs in your country.
我還是想大致瞭解一下你們這裡的通關情況。

還可以這樣說：

Could you tell me something about the local Customs procedure?
您能否為我介紹一下當地的通關流程？

對方可能這樣回答：

💬 Our Customs formalities are divided into several parts, and the cargo inspection is the most important part.
通關手續通常分為若干環節，其中商檢是最關鍵的環節。

💬 Speaking of the Customs procedure, apart from application, inspection and release, we also need to pay the fees based on the duty-paid value.
關於通關流程，除申報、驗貨和放行外，還要依據完稅價格繳納關稅。

duty-paid value 完稅價格，指進出口貨物通過海關估價確定的價格，是海關徵收關稅的依據。

> Self-declaration or Customs agent?
> 自理報關還是代理報關？

還可以這樣說：

💬 Both self-declaration and Customs agent have advantages. Which one do you prefer?
自理報關和代理報關各有好處，您喜歡哪一種呢？

對方可能這樣回答：

💬 We are authorized to engage in foreign trade and Customs declaration, so we'll handle the Customs formalities by ourselves.
我們擁有對外貿易經營權和報關權，因此會自行辦理報關手續。

self-declaration 自理報關，指進出口商自行辦理報關業務

Customs agent / broker 代理報關，指由代理人或代理行代為辦理報關業務

Scene 141　海關問詢與檢查 Customs Enquiry / Inspection

🗨️ 場景對話

A: What can I do for you, Sir?	A：先生，有什麼可以幫您的？
B: Could you tell me how to go through the Customs procedures?	B：是的，您能告訴我如何辦理通關手續嗎？
A: What kind of Customs formalities do you need, personal or company?	A：您要辦理哪類通關手續，個人還是企業？
B: I'd like to do the declaration formalities for our exported goods.	B：我想為我們出口的貨物辦理報關手續。
A: Oh, the procedure is a little bit complicated.	A：哦，這個手續有點複雜。
B: Well, what should we do specifically?	B：嗯，具體需要怎麼做呢？

A: First, you need to apply to the export Customs and submit a series of documents twenty-four hours before loading.	A：首先，您要在裝貨的 24 小時前向出境地海關申報並提交一系列單證。
B: what next?	B：然後呢？
A: If your goods don't need to be taxed and inspected, you can go through Customs within one day since declaration.	A：如果您的貨物不需要徵稅和查驗，自申報起一日內就可以辦理通關手續。
B: But what if our goods need to be taxed and inspected?	B：可如果需要徵稅和查驗呢？
A: Then you should appoint an employee to assist the Customs officer to unpack for inspection. If your goods are qualified and taxed, the Customs will stamp on your shipping order to release your goods.	A：那您需要派專員在現場協助海關開箱查驗。經查驗合格並繳納稅款後，海關會在裝貨單上蓋章放行。
B: I see. Thanks a lot.	B：明白了，謝謝。
A: You're welcome.	A：不客氣。

場景問答必會句

> What kind of the Customs formalities do you need, personal or company?
> 您要辦理哪類通關手續，個人還是企業？

還可以這樣說：

- Would you like to handle passenger clearance?
  您是要辦理旅客通關手續嗎？

對方可能這樣回答：

PS

passenger clearance 旅客通關

entry formalities 入境手續

- Yes, I need to go through the formalities at the airport.
  是的，我要在機場辦理通關手續。

- Yes, I'd like to go through entry formalities, but I'm not sure whether these goods need to be taxed or not.
  是的，我要辦理入境手續，但不知道這些物品是否需要繳稅。

> What if our goods need to be taxed and inspected?
> 如果需要徵稅和查驗呢？

還可以這樣說：

- What should we do if our goods are required to be taxed and inspected?
  如果貨物被要求納稅和查驗，我們該怎麼做呢？

對方可能這樣回答：

💬 If your goods are eligible for inspection, the Customs will complete inspection and tax collection within one day after accepting your declaration.
如果您的貨物符合查驗條件，海關會在受理申請後一日內完成查驗和徵稅。

PS

be eligible for 符合……的條件

tax collection 徵稅

Scene
142 應稅物品 Articles to Declare

 場景對話

A: Do you have any articles to declare?	A：請問您有應稅物品嗎？
B: What is the dutiable article?	B：什麼是應稅物品？
A: That means your personal items that exceed the duty-free limits need to pay tax at the Customs.	A：應稅物品就是您入境攜帶的物品超過了海關的免稅限量，因此必須繳納關稅的物品。
B: Hum, I've spent two hundred francs to buy a bottle of perfume in France. Is it a dutiable article?	B：嗯，我在法國花了 200 法郎買了一瓶香水，這屬應稅物品嗎？
A: Anything else?	A：還有其他的嗎？
B: I also bought a bottle of wine.	B：我還買了一瓶紅酒。
A: You don't have to pay taxes on your perfume and wine.	A：您買的香水和紅酒都不用繳稅。
B: Well, thanks a lot.	B：嗯，非常感謝。
A: Besides, do you take along any prohibited goods?	A：另外，您有沒有攜帶違禁品？
B: I have some cheese and fresh fruit.	B：我帶了一些奶酪和新鮮水果。
A: I'm sorry. These things are banned from entry.	A：對不起，這些是禁止攜帶入境的。
B: Oh, I got it.	B：哦，我知道了。

場景問答必會句

> Do you have any articles to declare?
> 請問您有應稅物品嗎？

還可以這樣說：

🖳 Do you have anything dutiable?
您有需要繳納關稅的物品嗎？

對方可能這樣回答：

🖳 Of course, I have. 當然，我有。

🖳 No, I don't. I have already paid.
沒有，我已經繳納關稅了。

> I've spent two hundred francs to buy a bottle of perfume in France. Is it a dutiable article?
> 我在法國花了 200 法郎買了一瓶香水，這屬應稅物品嗎？

還可以這樣說：

🖳 I've bought some personal stuff. Are these duty free?
我買了一些私人用品，可以免稅嗎？

對方可能這樣回答：

🖳 That depends on the total value of goods you've bought.
這取決於您所購物品的總值。

海關檢查 Tips

海關檢查函電小模板

Dear Sir or Madam,

In view of the import-export contract that we have agreed, I would like to take this opportunity to give you a brief introduction about the Customs inspection in our country.

All of the import or export goods in our country can be taken or shipped only after they have been examined and released by the Customs. As for our frozen meat, apart from inspecting the import / export license, we have to submit the Veterinary Inspection Certificate issued by CIQ (Entry-Exit Inspection and Quarantine Bureau). It is the audit basis for the Customs to approve the goods. Moreover, we also need to pay the duties according to the Customs Import and Export Tariff.

For more information about the Customs inspection in our country, please contact us any time.

Yours faithfully,

Jack

敬啟者：

　　鑒於與貴公司的進出口合同已經商定，我想藉此機會為您簡要介紹一下我國海關檢查的相關情況。

　　我國所有進出口貨物都必須經過海關查驗放行後才能提取或裝運。本次出口凍肉，除查驗進出口許可證外，我們還需要提交由出入境檢驗檢疫局出具的獸醫檢驗證書。海關會依據商檢證明核放貨物。此外還應按照《海關進出口稅則》繳納關稅。

　　如果您想瞭解關於我國海關檢查的更多信息，請隨時與我們聯繫。

傑克

謹致

Unit 3 | 商務簽證

商務簽證是指有關人員因為公務或個人原因去目的地國從事短期商務考察或業務洽談時必須持有的商務訪問簽證，在目的地國只能短期停留，並須在簽證規定時間內離開該國。

商務簽證必會詞

1 visa *n.* 簽證
簽證指由國家出入境管理機構簽發的，准許外國公民入境的許可證明。一般簽注在護照或旅行證件上，並說明持有人入境理由和停留時間。

2 Destination Country 目的地國
目的地國指商務簽證申請人出於商務目的而進行實地考察或洽談的國家。

3 Letter of Invitation 邀請函
邀請函指邀請單位出於商務目的向商務簽證申請人發出的邀請函，是申請商務簽證的最基本文件。

4 passport *n.* 護照
護照指由本國簽發的證明該國公民國籍和身份的合法證件。

這些小詞你也要會哦：

investigate *v.* 調查	stay *v.* 逗留	negotiate *v.* 洽談
conference *n.* 會議	eligibility *n.* 資格	security *n.* 安全
issue *v.* 簽發	expiry *n.* 期滿；失效	depart *v.* 出發，啟程

Scene 143　申請簽證 Apply for a Business Visa

場景對話

A: Hello, I'd like to apply for a business visa.	A：您好，我想申請商務簽證。
B: OK, your name and birth date, please?	B：好的，請告訴我您的姓名和出生年月。

A: Li Hong, L-I-H-O-N-G. I was born on May 18th, 1980.	A：李紅，拼音是 L-I-H-O-N-G，出生於 1980 年 5 月 18 日。
B: What's the purpose of your trip to America?	B：您去美國的目的是什麼？
A: We have connections with ABC company in Houston, so I have been invited to attend a conference.	A：我們與休斯敦的 ABC 公司有業務往來，這次他們邀請我去參加一場會議。
B: Have you got a letter of invitation?	B：您收到邀請函了嗎？
A: Yes, I have, and I've also received the itinerary they've made for me.	A：是的，收到了。而且，我還收到了他們為我制訂的行程表。
B: Did ABC company send someone to China before?	B：ABC 公司以前派人來過中國嗎？
A: Their sales manager visited us early this year.	A：今年年初他們的銷售經理來拜訪過我們。
B: When do you intend to go?	B：您打算什麼時候去美國？
A: I'm planning to leave for America at the end of this month.	A：我打算月底出發。
B: OK, we'll issue your business visa as soon as possible.	B：好的，我們會儘快簽發您的簽證。
A: Thank you very much.	A：非常感謝。

場景問答必會句

> I'd like to apply for a business visa.
> 我想申請商務簽證。

還可以這樣說：

💬 I'm going to America to attend a meeting, so I'd like to apply for B-1 visa.
我要去美國參加一場會議，想申請 B-1 簽證。

對方可能這樣回答：

💬 Please let me see your application form.
請讓我看看您的申請表。

> Did ABC company send someone to come to China before?
> ABC 公司以前派人來過中國嗎？

還可以這樣說：

💬 What kind of business do you do with ABC company?
你們與 ABC 公司有哪些商業往來？

Scene 144　簽證條件 Visa Conditions

 場景對話

A: Mr. Wang, our company has developed rapidly in recent years, so I want to set up a branch in the United States.	A：王先生，我們公司這幾年發展得非常好，所以我打算在美國成立一家分公司。
B: That's terrific.	B：那真是太好了。
A: But I heard that the procedure for applying B-1 visa is very complicated.	A：不過，我聽說辦理 B-1 商務簽證的手續比較麻煩。
B: Don't worry about that. Last year, my friend went to America to do the investigation. I was told that applying for L-1 visa is easier for establishing a branch.	B：這個您不用太擔心。去年我朋友去美國考察，他跟我說過如果是成立分公司的話，辦 L-1 簽證會比較方便。
A: What's the difference?	A：這兩種簽證有什麼區別？
B: B-1 visa is generally not allowed to be extended, but L-1 visa can be extended to two or three years each time.	B：B-1 簽證一般不允許延期，而 L-1 簽證每次可以延遲兩三年。
A: Well, you're right. I'll be in America for a long time, so it seems that L-1 visa is more suitable for me. And what kind of materials do I need to hand in?	A：嗯，有道理。我會在美國待很長一段時間，看來還是 L-1 簽證比較適合我。那我需要提交哪些材料呢？
B: They are divided into three parts: materials from your parent company and branch, as well as your personal documents.	B：所需提交材料分三部分：母公司和美國分公司的材料，以及你的個人資料。
A: In addition, what about the dependents visa?	A：另外，那家屬簽證該怎麼辦？
B: Your wife and daughter can apply for L-2 visa.	B：您的太太和女兒可以申請 L-2 簽證。
A: Thank you very much. I'm honored to have a business partner like you.	A：太感謝了，很榮幸有你這樣的商業夥伴。
B: You're welcome.	B：不客氣。

🗨️Ⓐ 場景問答必會句

> **What's the difference?**
> 這兩種簽證有什麼區別？

還可以這樣說：

💬 What are the benefits of applying L-1 visa?
辦理 L-1 簽證有什麼好處呢？

對方可能這樣回答：

PS

duration of each stay 停留期

validity *n.* 有效期

💬 The duration of each stay of B-1 visa has been shortened to one month, but the validity of L-1 visa is one year, and can be extended for up to seven years.
B-1 簽證的停留期已經縮短為一個月，而 L-1 簽證的有效期為一年，並且最長可以延至七年。

💬 B-1 visa is suitable for those making overseas visit in a short time, but L-1 visa is ideal for those who want to set up branch in foreign countries, or top management talents who are transferred to another post in the branch.
B-1 簽證適合短期去海外考察的人，而 L-1 簽證對於在國外成立分公司，或調至分公司任職的高級管理人才非常適用。

> **What about the dependents visa?**
> 那家屬簽證該怎麼辦？

還可以這樣說：

💬 What should I do if I want to take my wife and daughter together to America?
如果我想帶太太和女兒一起去美國該怎麼辦呢？

對方可能這樣回答：

PS

dependents visa 家屬簽證

social security card 社會安全卡
（俗稱工卡）

💬 Your wife and daughter can get L-2 visa. Your daughter is allowed to study in public school, and your wife is also authorized to apply for a social security card to find a job.
您的太太和女兒可以申請 L-2 簽證。您的女兒可以在公立學校讀書，您太太也可以申請工卡找工作。

💬 If the branch is operated normally for more than one year, you and your immediate family members can apply for green card directly.
如果分公司正常運營一年以上，您和您的直系家屬可以直接申請綠卡。

Scene 145 　簽證手續 Visa Procedures

 場景對話

A: Lucy, I'll go to the UK head office to attend an important business conference. Is everything settled now?	A：露西，我要去英國總公司參加一場很重要的商業會議，準備事宜都辦妥了嗎？
B: Except visa. Flight tickets and hotel have been reserved.	B：機票和酒店都預訂好了，現在就差簽證了。
A: Why didn't you get the visa?	A：簽證為什麼還沒辦下來？
B: I'm waiting for parent company to send us a letter of invitation.	B：我正在等總公司給我們發邀請函。
A: What else should we submit?	A：我們還需要提交什麼材料嗎？
B: Our company hasn't sent a formal letter of introduction.	B：咱們公司還沒有出具正式的介紹信。
A: Fortunately, we still have time.	A：不過還好，時間還來得及。
B: Yes, don't worry about it. I'll get all things done.	B：是的，您不用擔心。我會全都辦好的。
A: One more thing, what should I prepare for the interview?	A：還有件事，在面談時需要注意些什麼嗎？
B: I'll prepare some information for you to answer the visa officer's questions.	B：我會幫您準備一些信息，好回答簽證官的問題。
A: Thank you so much.	A：太感謝了。
B: Not at all.	B：不客氣。

場景問答必會句

> Why didn't you get the visa?
> 簽證為什麼還沒辦下來？

還可以這樣說：

💬 When will I get the visa?
　　我什麼時候才能拿到簽證？

可以這樣回答：

🗨 We've got plenty of time, so it doesn't matter if we get the invitation a few days late.

我們的時間很充裕，邀請函晚到幾天也沒有關係。

PS

plenty of 充足的，大量的

🗨 I can apply for your visa immediately after receiving the letter of invitation.

收到邀請函後我就能立即為您申請簽證。

> **What should I prepare for the interview?**
> 在面談時需要注意些什麼嗎？

還可以這樣說：

🗨 What do I need to pay attention to during the interview?

面談時我需要注意些什麼？

可以這樣回答：

🗨 There are FAQS for business visa interview, just answer it honestly.

商務面簽有一些常見問題，您只要如實回答就行了。

PS

FAQ (Frequently Asked Question)
常見問題

🗨 Apart from answering the officer's questions, a letter of invitation will be helpful to apply for your visa.

除回答簽證官的問題外，邀請函也會為您申請簽證提供一定幫助。

商務簽證 Tips

常見簽證種類

tourist visa 旅遊觀光簽證	study visa 學習簽證
journalist visa 記者簽證	diplomatic visa 外交簽證
official visa 公務簽證	immigrant visa 移民簽證
non-immigrant visa 非移民簽證	entry-exit visa 出入境簽證

Unit 4 國際稅收

國際稅收是指兩個或兩個以上的國家政府憑藉其政治權力，對跨國納稅人的跨國所得或財產進行重疊交叉課稅，以及由此所形成的國家之間的稅收分配關係。

國際稅收必會詞

1 tax registration 稅務登記
稅務登記又稱納稅登記，是指稅務機關根據稅法規定，對納稅人的生產、經營活動進行登記管理的一項法定制度，也是納稅人依法履行納稅義務的法定手續。

2 business certificate 經營許可證
經營許可證是指法律規定的某些行業必須經過許可，而由主管部門辦理的許可經營的證明。

3 business tax 營業稅
營業稅是對在中國境內提供應稅勞務、轉讓無形資產或銷售不動產的單位和個人，就其所取得的營業額徵收的一種稅。

4 value added tax 增值稅
增值稅是對銷售貨物或者提供加工、修理修配勞務以及進口貨物的單位和個人就其實現的增值額徵收的稅種。

這些小詞你也要會哦：

tax authority 稅務機關	application form 申請表	prescribed *a.* 規定的
approved *a.* 批准的	penalty *n.* 罰款	surcharge *n.* 追加罰款
tax overdue 滯納金	hearing testimony 聽證	reexamination *n.* 覆議
suit *n.* 訴訟	notice *n./v.* 通知	inspect *v.* 檢查

Scene 146 稅務登記 Tax Registration

 場景對話

A: Hello, my company is a foreign investment enterprise. Would you please tell me how to go through the tax registration?

A：您好，我們是一家外資企業。請問如何辦理稅務登記？

B: In order to register for tax, you must provide the following information: duplicate of business license, articles of association, the Legal Representative's ID and other documents required by the tax office.

B：辦理稅務登記，您必須提供以下信息：營業執照副本、公司章程、法人代表的身份證和稅務部門要求的其他證件。

A: Let me see. Yes, here are all the required documents. And what kind of tax should I pay?

A：我看一下。是的，所有需要的資料都在這裡。我應該繳納哪種稅？

B: Usually, the form of business you operate determines what taxes you must pay. According to your case, you should pay business tax, income tax and value added tax, which means you should register with both the national and local tax offices.

B：通常情況下，您所運作的企業的形式決定了您必須繳納的稅費。根據您的情況，您應該繳納營業稅、所得稅和增值稅，這意味著您應該同時在國家和地方的稅務機關登記。

A: OK. What should I do?

A：好的，我應該怎麼辦呢？

B: Fill in two separate application forms and submit all the required documents.

B：填寫兩張不同的申請表，提交所需資料。

A: How long would it take before we receive the certificate of registration?

A：我們要過多長時間才能收到登記證書呢？

B: In about thirty days after we receive your application. The local tax office will contact you once your application is approved.

B：在我們收到申請的 30 日內。您的申請一通過，當地稅務機關就會聯繫您。

A: Thank you.

A：謝謝！

B: You are welcome.

B：不客氣！

場景問答必會句

Would you please tell me how to go through the tax registration?
請問如何辦理稅務登記？

對方可能這樣回答：

💬 You need go to the national and regional tax authorities respectively according to your conditions.

根據您公司的情況，您需要分別去地稅局和國稅局申請登記。

PS due to=because of 因為，由於

💬 Due to the different kinds of tax, you have to go to the national and regional tax authorities respectively.

由於稅種不同，您需要分別去地稅局和國稅局申請登記。

> How long would it take before we receive the certificate of the registration?
> 我們要過多長時間才能收到登記證書？

還可以這樣說：

💬 How long will it take to finish the registration?

多長時間能夠辦完登記？

對方可能這樣回答：

💬 It is around thirty days since we receive all the documents required.

我們收到所需文件後 30 天左右。

Scene 147　稅務檢查 Tax Examination

 場景對話

A: Last Friday, the tax officers came to our company and inspected our tax affairs. They gave us a notice and claimed unpaid tax with interest plus penalties. But we definitely do not accept their decisions. Can you please tell me what I can do about that?	A：上週五，稅務官員來我們公司，對我們公司的稅務情況進行了檢查。他們給我們下發了通知，要求我們補繳未扣的稅款及利息還有罰款。但是我們完全不同意他們的決定，你能告訴我該怎麼辦嗎？
B: I'm sorry to hear that. Let's see what we can do. Well, you have three options. The first option is asking for hearing testimony, the second is applying for reexamination, and the third is filing lawsuit against the tax agency.	B：很遺憾聽到這個消息。讓我們看看能做些什麼。嗯，你有三種方法，第一種方法是聽證，第二種是申請覆議，第三種是對稅務機構提起訴訟。
A: Can you please explain to me what exactly do these options mean?	A：你能不能向我詳細解釋一下這些方法是什麼意思？

B: Well, hearing testimony is one of your rights. That means when the amount of penalty comes to a certain level, you can claim your right within three days after receiving the notice.	B：聽證是你的一項權利。在處罰金額達到一定程度時，你可以在接到處罰通知的 3 日內申請聽證。
A: OK. What about reexamination?	A：好的，那覆議呢？
B: Reexamination means you can appeal and ask the superior tax authority to reexamine your case.	B：覆議是指你可以提出請求，要求上一級的稅務機關對你的案件進行重新審理。
A: So I guess filing lawsuit against the tax agency is the last step when those two don't work.	A：那麼我想向稅務機構提起訴訟是在其他兩種方法都行不通的情況下，可以採取的最後一種方法。
B: You're right. But filing lawsuit against the tax agency will be too costly. I hope you can make right decision and wisely solve the problem.	B：沒錯。但是向稅務機構提起訴訟成本很高，我希望你能夠做出正確的決定，明智地解決這個問題。

場景問答必會句

> But we definitely do not accept their decisions. Can you please tell me what I can do about that?
> 但是我們完全不同意他們的決定，你能告訴我該怎麼辦嗎？

還可以這樣說：

🗨 I don't think their decisions are reasonable. What should I do?
我覺得他們的決定沒有道理，我該怎麼辦？

對方可能這樣回答：

🗨 I have three suggestions: asking for hearing testimony, applying for reexamination, and bringing suit against the tax authority.
我有三個建議，即聽證、覆議和訴訟。

🗨 You can ask for hearing testimony, apply for reexamination, or bring suit against the tax authority.
你可以申請聽證、覆議或訴訟。

> What about reexamination?
> 那覆議呢？

還可以這樣說：

🗨 What is reexamination?
什麼是覆議？

國際稅收 Tips

國際稅收常用英語詞匯

abuse of tax treaties 濫用稅收協定	active income 主動收入
advance pricing agreement (APA) 預約定價協議	area jurisdiction 地域管轄權
associated enterprise 關聯企業	base company rule 基地公司規定
blocked income 滯留收入	bounded area 保稅區
contribution analysis 貢獻分析	controlling company 控股公司
deemed dividend 認定的紅利	earnings stripping 收益剝離
excess credit position 超額抵扣情況	excess interest expense 超額利息支出

Unit 5 包裝

包裝是指在物流過程中為保護貨物或為便於裝卸、儲運而用容器或材料等物品對貨物進行包封並給予適當標誌，以防止貨物破損或變形。

包裝必會詞

❶ cargo packing 貨物包裝
貨物包裝指為了保護貨物在倉儲、運輸、裝卸和理貨過程中完整無損，採用一定包裝容器和材料等包裝貨物。

❷ packing mark 包裝標誌
包裝標誌指為了便於貨物運輸、裝卸、識別、倉儲和查驗等在貨物外包裝上標明記號，包括文字、圖形和簡要說明。

❸ shipping mark 收發貨標誌
收發貨標誌俗稱"嘜頭"，指供收發貨人識別的標誌，通常由幾何圖形、字母、數字和文字組成。

❹ warning mark 危險貨物標誌
危險貨物標誌指標明危險貨物的特性和類別，提醒人們在裝卸、運輸和保管過程中採取相應防護措施。

這些小詞你也要會哦：

oozing v. 滲出	bundle v. 捆紮	indistinct a. 不清晰的
deform v. 變形	frayed a. 磨損的	tainted a. 腐爛的
frail a. 易損壞的	scratched a. 劃損的	leak v. 洩漏
damp a. 潮濕的	spare a. 備用的	soaked a. 浸濕的

Scene 148 包裝類型 Packaging Type

 場景對話

A: We are ready to pack this batch of export knitwear. Do you have any suggestions?	A：我們正準備對這批出口針織衫進行包裝，您有什麼建議嗎？
B: I don't recommend using plastic bags.	B：我不建議用塑料袋包裝。
A: Why?	A：為什麼？
B: Despite the cost is lower, it is not helpful for environmental protection.	B：儘管塑料袋成本較低，但不環保。
A: It sounds reasonable. Then, what kind of material do you think should be used?	A：有道理。那您認為哪種材料比較合適？
B: I think paper bags are more appropriate.	B：我認為用紙袋比較好。
A: Indeed, paper bags are good for environment, but we also have other solutions.	A：確實，紙袋比較環保，不過我們還有別的解決方案。
B: Go ahead.	B：請講。
A: What about plastic bags for inner packing and carton boxes for outer packing?	A：內包裝用塑料袋，而外包裝用紙箱，怎麼樣？
B: Why?	B：為什麼呢？
A: Because in this way, the carton boxes can be recycled, meanwhile we can reduce the costs.	A：因為這樣做既可以降低成本，紙箱還能回收利用。
B: That's a good idea.	B：好主意。
A: If you don't have any questions, we'll arrange the packaging immediately.	A：如果您沒有別的問題的話，我們馬上安排包裝。
B: OK.	B：好的。

場景問答必會句

> We are ready to pack this batch of export knitwear. Do you have any suggestions?
> 我們正準備對這批出口針織衫進行包裝，您有什麼建議嗎？

還可以這樣說：

📝 Do you have any good advice for the packaging of sweaters?
您對毛衣的包裝有什麼好建議嗎？

對方可能這樣回答：

- Using plastic bags are more cost-effective, but it goes against environment protection.
  用塑料袋在成本上比較划算，但不環保。
- I prefer to use paper bags.
  我更傾向於用紙袋。

PS

knitwear *n.* 針織衫

cost-effective *a.* 划算的，符合成本效益的

go against 不利於

> Then, what kind of material do you think should be used?
> 那您認為哪種材料比較合適？

還可以這樣說：

- What is your favorite material?
  那您最喜歡哪種材料？

對方可能這樣回答：

- Paper bags are more environmentally friendly, but the cost is higher, so I want to find a compromise between them.
  紙袋雖然比較環保，但成本較高，我希望能找到一種折中的辦法。

PS

environmentally friendly 有益環境的

compromise *n.* 折衷辦法

compare with 與 …… 比較

- Compared with plastics bags, paper bags seem to be more environmentally friendly, but they'll largely consume the woods and cause forest degradation, so we need to think about it carefully.
  與塑料袋相比，紙袋看似較為環保，但是在製造過程中會大量消耗木材，造成森林退化，因此需要謹慎考慮。

Scene **149** 檢驗包裝 Packaging Inspection

 場景對話

A: The procedures of packaging inspection are more complex. Could you tell me about it in detail?	A：包裝的檢驗程序比較複雜，您能為我詳細介紹一下嗎？
B: No problem. Packaging inspection mainly includes appearance, specifications, features, logo inspection and so on.	B：沒問題。包裝檢驗的內容主要有外觀、規格、特性和標識等。
A: Can you explain it more specifically?	A：您能解釋得具體一些嗎？

B: It is performed to check whether the carton or wooden cases are clean, dry and without any scratches, whether the shipping mark is clear, and whether the method, quantity, specifications and materials of packaging meet the requirements.	B：主要是看紙箱或木箱內外是否清潔、乾燥，有無劃痕。收發貨標記是否清晰。包裝的方式、數量、規格和材料等是否符合要求。
A: What does the shipping mark mean?	A：什麼叫收發貨標記？
B: It means the logo marked on the packaging of import-export goods.	B：收發貨標記就是在進出口貨物包裝上做的標記。
A: Then what need to be considered during the packing process?	A：那麼在包裝過程中需要注意哪些問題呢？
B: A clear logo and property specification should be marked in the visible place of the packaging for dangerous goods.	B：如果是危險貨物，必須在包裝的醒目位置上注明標記並說明性質。
A: What else should I take into consideration?	A：還有其他需要考慮的問題嗎？
B: You should also try to choose both light and strong materials for packaging.	B：包裝要儘量選用既輕便又結實的材料。
A: In what conditions will the packaging be identified as unqualified?	A：那什麼樣的情況會被認定為包裝不合格？
B: For example, the inner and outer packaging are damaged, deformed, damp and moldy, and so on.	B：比如內外包裝箱破損，箱體變形、潮濕、發霉等。
A: Thank you for telling me this.	A：謝謝您告訴我這些。
B: You're welcome.	B：不用謝。

🗣️Ⓐ 場景問答必會句

The procedures of packaging inspection are more complex. Could you tell me about it in detail?
包裝的檢驗程序比較複雜，您能為我詳細介紹一下嗎？

對方可能這樣回答：

💬 Packaging inspection is mainly divided into transport package checking and consumer package checking, commonly referred to outer package checking and inner package checking.
包裝檢驗主要分為運輸包裝和銷售包裝，也就是通常所說的外包裝和內包裝。

PS

transport package 運輸包裝

consumer package 銷售包裝

Packaging inspection depends on the foreign trade contract and other relevant regulations. It has two forms — sampling and spot inspection.

包裝檢驗取決於外貿合同和其他相關規定，它有兩種形式，即抽檢和當場檢驗。

> Then what need to be considered during the packing process?
> 那麼在包裝過程中需要注意哪些問題呢？

對方可能這樣回答：

The packaging has to meet the sanitary standard.
包裝必須要達到衛生標準。

The packaging process should follow the principle of rationalization.
包裝過程應遵循合理化原則。

PS

sanitary standard 衛生標準

rationalization *n.* 合理化

Scene 150　包裝問題 Packaging Issue

 場景對話

A: Have you started packing?	A：請問你們開始包裝貨物了嗎？
B: Not yet, we just want to talk about it with you.	B：還沒有，正想跟您好好討論一下。
A: What kind of materials are you going to use for outer package?	A：外包裝你們打算用什麼材料？
B: We believe that using carton box is better.	B：我們認為用紙箱比較好。
A: Carton box is nice, but I prefer to use wooden case.	A：紙箱固然好，不過我還是傾向於用木箱。
B: What are the benefits of using wooden cases?	B：用木箱有什麼好處嗎？
A: Wooden case is safer, and can be recycled and reused, so it is environmentally friendly.	A：木箱比較安全，可以反復使用，比較環保。
B: But carton box can also be recycled.	B：可紙箱也可以回收再利用啊。
A: Yes, but the carrying capacity of carton box is too bad, and it is very unsafe to pack these precious crafts.	A：是的，可紙箱的承載力太差，用來裝這批貴重工藝品太不安全了。
B: Ah, you're right.	B：嗯，您說得有道理。
A: Besides, you can also place a layer of waterproof supplies in the bottom of the box in order to avoid damage.	A：另外，建議您在箱底鋪一層防水材料，避免貨物損壞。

| B: Thank you very much for your suggestions. | B：非常感謝您的建議。 |
| A: You're welcome. We're very pleased to work with your company. | A：不客氣。我們很高興能與貴公司合作。 |

場景問答必會句

> Have you started packing?
> 請問你們開始包裝貨物了嗎？

還可以這樣說：

🖥 Is there any progress on the packaging? 包裝有什麼進展嗎？

對方可能這樣回答：

🖥 Yes, we're working on the packaging. If there are any problems, we'll communicate with you immediately.
是的，我們已經開始包裝，有問題的話會與您及時溝通。

🖥 Here is our packaging scheme. Please have a look. 這是我們的包裝方案，請您過目。

> What kind of material are you going to use for outer package?
> 外包裝你們打算用什麼材料？

還可以這樣說：

🖥 There are many ways to pack the goods. Which one do you prefer?
包裝方式有很多種，你們認為哪種比較好？

對方可能這樣回答：

🖥 What we are considering is whether to use carton box or wooden case.
我們正在考慮是用紙箱還是用木箱。

PS
fragile cargo 易碎品

🖥 We believe that it is proper to use wooden case for packing our fragile cargos.
我們認為包裝易碎品還是用木箱比較好。

包裝 Tips

包裝相關術語

paper tape 紙帶	rigid container 固定式集裝箱
crate 板條箱	particular packaging 專用包裝
current packaging 通用包裝	numerical symbols 條形碼
once used packaging 一次性包裝	easy break packaging 易碎包裝
multi-pack 多層包裝	compound material packaging 複合材料包裝

Unit 6

裝運

裝運是指裝載和運輸貨物，涉及裝運時間、裝運港、目的港和裝運單據等問題。海運是最主要的運輸方式，此外還包括鐵路運輸、航空運輸和聯合運輸等。

裝運必會詞

1 time of shipment 裝運時間
裝運時間即裝運期，指賣方根據合同規定將貨物裝上運輸工具或交給承運人的期限，是表明賣方是否履行交貨義務的重要依據。

2 notice of shipment 裝運通知
裝運通知指出口商向進口商發出的關於貨物已於某月某日裝運某船的通知，以便於買方購買保險或準備提貨手續。

3 terms of shipment 裝運條款
裝運條款即裝運條件，指買賣雙方就交貨時間、裝運港和目的港、是否分批裝運或轉運等問題進行協商，並在合同中制訂明確條款，以確保進出口業務順利進行。

4 partial shipment 分批裝運
分批裝運指一批成交的貨物分若干次裝運。

這些小詞你也要會哦：

stipulate v. 規定	compulsory a. 強制性的	document n. 單據
limit v. 限制，約束	vessel n. 船，艦	demurrage n. 滯期費
wharf n. 碼頭	remittance n. 匯款	prepaid a. 預付的

Scene 151 裝運時間 Time of Shipment

 場景對話

A: We are in urgent need of the goods. Could you do something to advance your shipment?

A：現在我們急需這批貨物，請問能不能提前交貨呢？

B: Then when do you need the goods?	B：那您什麼時候需要這批貨物？
A: Is it possible to make it one month earlier?	A：提前 1 個月可以嗎？
B: That's a little bit difficult, I'm afraid.	B：這恐怕有些困難。
A: Why?	A：為什麼？
B: We need time to prepare the goods, so there's no way to ship them in March.	B：我們需要時間來備齊貨物，3 月不可能交貨。
A: What is the earliest time that you can make the shipment?	A：那最快能什麼時候裝運呢？
B: Early April is the best we can do.	B：最快也得 4 月初。
A: It's acceptable, and we'll open the letter of credit ahead of time.	A：那也可以，我們會提前開出信用證。
B: That would be great.	B：那太好了。

 場景問答必會句

We are in urgent need of the goods. Could you do something to advance your shipment?
現在我們急需這批貨物，請問能不能提前交貨呢？

還可以這樣說：

📖 We hope you could complete shipment more promptly. Do you have any way to do that?
我們希望貴公司能提早交貨，您有什麼辦法嗎？

對方可能這樣回答：

💬 We'll manage to advance the delivery, but we cannot give a definite date of shipment.
我們會儘量提前交貨，但我們無法確定明確的裝貨日期。

PS

in urgent need of 急需

definite *a.* 確切的

What is the earliest time that you can make the shipment?
那最快能什麼時候裝運呢？

還可以這樣說：

💬 Could you tell us the earliest time of shipment?
能告訴我們最早的裝運時間嗎？

對方可能這樣回答：

💬 As long as receiving your letter of credit, we'll make shipment immediately.
只要收到你們的信用證，我們就立即裝運。

💬 The shipment will be made no later than early April.
交貨期不會遲於 4 月初。

Scene 152　裝船問題 Shipment Problems

場景對話

A: When can you ship the cargos?	A：貴公司什麼時候能裝運貨物？
B: Within thirty days after receiving the L/C.	B：在收到信用證後 30 天內。
A: Based on the FOB agreement, we'll be responsible for chartering ships, and you need to load cargos on the specified vessels at the port of shipment within the prescribed period.	A：依據雙方對裝運港船上交貨的約定，我們會負責租賃船隻，你們需要在裝運港口和規定期限內將貨物裝上我們指定的船隻。
B: That's right.	B：沒錯。
A: But, we hope to receive the cargos before the New Year. Can you ensure to ship immediately after receiving the L/C?	A：不過我們希望趕在新年之前收貨，你們能確保在收到信用證之後立即裝船嗎？
B: That should be no problem.	B：應該沒有問題。
A: What if you cannot make prompt delivery?	A：如果無法即刻裝船怎麼辦？
B: We'll strive to get the cargos ready before the shipment, and stay constantly in touch with you.	B：我們會爭取在裝船之前把貨物準備好，並且隨時與貴公司保持聯繫。
A: Thank you. We're looking forward to receiving your notice of shipment as soon as possible.	A：謝謝，我們期待能盡早收到你們的裝船通知。
B: In addition, you have to bear all the costs and risks of the cargos when they pass over the ship's rail.	B：另外，貨過船舷後你們必須承擔貨物的全部費用和風險。
A: Absolutely.	A：那是當然。
B: Thanks for your cooperation.	B：謝謝您的合作。

場景問答必會句

> When can you ship the cargos?
> 貴公司什麼時候能裝運貨物？

還可以這樣說：

🗨 When is the time limit for shipping?
裝船期限是什麼時候？

對方可能這樣回答：

🗨 We'll ship the goods by installment.
我們分批裝運貨物。

🗨 We'll plan to deliver the goods two or three weeks in advance.
我們計劃提前兩三週裝船。

PS
installment *n.* 分期，分批
in advance 提前

> But, we hope to receive the cargos before the New Year. Can you ensure to ship immediately after receiving the L/C?
> 不過我們希望趕在新年之前收貨，你們能確保在收到信用證之後立即裝船嗎？

還可以這樣說：

🗨 These goods are very important to us, so we expect that you can effect shipment as early as possible.
這批貨物對我們很重要，因此希望你們能儘早裝船。

PS
effect shipment 裝船，辦理裝運

對方可能這樣回答：

🗨 Sorry, we cannot meet your requirements due to a large number of factory orders, but no later than the time limit specified in the L/C.
很抱歉，由於工廠的訂單量很大，我們無法滿足您的要求，但最晚不會超過信用證規定的時間。

🗨 We'll do the best we can.
我們會盡力而為。

Scene
153 裝運卸貨和交貨 Unloading and Delivery

 場景對話

A: How long do you need to make the delivery?	A：請問貴公司多久能夠交貨？
B: In May or June.	B：5 月份或 6 月份能交貨。
A: Since we have concluded the transaction on DES basis, could you book the shipping space on time?	A：這批貨物是按照目的港船上交貨成交的，你們能準時訂到艙位嗎？
B: Currently, it is difficult to reserve shipping spaces, so we have to wait until June.	B：目前艙位緊張，我們恐怕得等到 6 月份。
A: I see. Then what's your port of discharge?	A：知道了。那卸貨港在哪兒？

B: How about Boston?	B：波士頓如何？
A: Could you change the port of discharge from Boston to New York?	A：能不能把卸貨港從波士頓改為紐約？
B: Yes, the two cities are not far away.	B：可以，這兩座城市離得不遠。
A: In addition, the goods will be paid after you make actual delivery.	A：另外，必須在你們實際交貨之後我們才能付款。
B: No problem, we'll make shipment by chartering ships within the stipulated time, and timely inform you of any changes.	B：沒問題，我們會在規定時間內租船裝運，如有任何變化會及時通知你們。
A: Thank you. You're very considerate.	A：謝謝，您考慮得很周全。
B: My pleasure. We also hope this transaction with your company will go smoothly.	B：這是我們應該做的，我們也希望能與貴公司順利達成交易。

場景問答必會句

> How long do you need to make the delivery?
> 請問貴公司多久能夠交貨？

還可以這樣說：
- What is the shipment time for your company?
  貴公司的裝運日期是什麼時候？

對方可能這樣回答：
- We'll make the delivery in May, but your letter of credit has to arrive here before April 30th.
  我們會在 5 月份交貨，但你們的信用證必須在 4 月 30 日之前開至我處。
- May and June are both optional. It depends on the booking of shipping spaces.
  5 月份或 6 月份都可以，這取決於訂艙的情況。

optional *a.* 可選擇的

> Since we have concluded the transaction on DES basis, could you book the shipping spaces on time?
> 這批貨物是按照目的港船上交貨成交的，你們能準時訂到艙位嗎？

還可以這樣說：
- Is there any problems to book the shipping spaces in May?
  在 5 月份訂艙位有什麼問題嗎？

對方可能這樣回答：
- There should be no problem. 應該沒什麼問題。
- It is not easy to book in May and June. It might be deferred for a month.
  5 月份和 6 月份訂艙都不太容易，可能需要延後 1 個月。

conclude the transaction 達成交易

DES (Delivered Ex Ship) 目的港船上交貨

Scene 154 貨物損失 Goods Loss

 場景對話

A: We found that many parts were damaged when we received the packages.	A：我們在收貨時發現很多配件都損壞了。
B: We're really sorry.	B：真的很抱歉。
A: Have you packed the parts using wooden cases?	A：你們是用木箱包裝的嗎？
B: Of course, we've shipped those parts in strict accordance with your requirement.	B：當然了，我們是嚴格按照你們的要求裝運的。
A: Then why did this happen?	A：那為什麼還會出現這種情況呢？
B: The parts were intact when they were shipped off. It was possibly caused by careless handling.	B：運走的時候都是完好的。可能是裝卸時太小心導致的。
A: How did some parts get damp and rust?	A：那部分配件受潮生鏽是怎麼回事？
B: This is not our responsibility. It was because of the muggy weather.	B：這不是我們的責任，是天氣悶熱導致配件受潮的。
A: Have you taken some damp-proof measures?	A：你們有沒有採取防受潮措施？
B: We've applied engine oil on the parts to avoid rusting.	B：我們在配件上塗了機油，以防止生鏽。
A: Anyhow, the parts were actually damaged, so we want a replacement.	A：不管怎樣，貨物受損是事實，我們要求換貨。
B: How many parts were damaged?	B：有多少配件受損？
A: About 20%.	A：將近 20%。
B: OK, we agree to replace them.	B：好吧，我們同意換貨。

場景問答必會句

> How did some parts get damp and rust?
> 那部分配件受潮生鏽是怎麼回事？

還可以這樣說：

💬 Can you explain why some parts get dampened?
你們能解釋一下部分配件受潮的問題嗎？

對方可能這樣回答：

💬 The ship had been subject to rainstorm which caused some
parts being immersed in the water.
由於輪船遇到暴風雨襲擊，導致部分配件浸水。

💬 It was caused by leaking pipes in the cargo hold.
這是由於艙內水管漏水造成的。

dampen *v.* 使潮濕

immerse *v.* 浸沒

cargo hold 貨艙

Have you taken some damp-proof measures?
你們有沒有採取防受潮措施？

還可以這樣說：

💬 In addition to objective factors, have you taken active
preventive measures?
除客觀因素外，你們有沒有採取主動預防措施？

對方可能這樣回答：

💬 Because of the extreme hot weather, the engine oil
smeared on the parts may have been melted.
由於天氣過於悶熱，可能導致塗在配件上的機油熔
化了。

💬 The wooden cases we've used have moisture-proof function in itself.
我們採用的木箱包裝本身就具備防潮功能。

damp-proof *a.* 防潮的

smear *v.* 塗抹

moisture-proof *a.* 防潮的

裝運 Tips

裝運函電小模板

Dear Sir or Madam,

We have opened the L/C to you at the end of last month, and hoped that you could ship 100,000 shirts within thirty days after receipt of the L/C. Now the time of shipment is approaching, but we haven't received your shipping notice.

These goods are very important to us. Please make sure to make delivery before the end of this month as stipulated in the L/C, otherwise, you should be responsible for all losses that might be caused by the delay of shipment.

We're looking forward to receiving your shipping notice as soon as possible. Thanks for your cooperation.

Yours faithfully,

Julia

敬啟者：

我們已於上月底向貴公司開具信用證，希望貴公司在收到信用證後 30 日內裝運 10 萬件襯衫。現交貨期臨近，我們仍未收到裝運通知。

這批貨物對我們十分重要。請貴公司務必按信用證規定於本月底前發貨，否則因延誤交貨導致的一切損失，均由貴公司承擔。

我們希望能儘快收到貴公司的裝運通知。謝謝合作。

朱莉婭

敬上

Unit 7 出入境

出入境指一國公民經本國政府主管機關批准，持合法證件出入本國國境，或外國人經一國政府批准，持合法證件出入該國國境。

出入境必會詞

① **passport** n. 護照
指由本國簽發的一種證明公民國籍和身份的合法證件，主要分為外交護照、公務護照和普通護照。

② **visa** n. 簽證
指在一國公民所持護照上簽注蓋章，以示批准該持有人出入本國國境或經過國境的一種許可文件，並説明其進入該國的理由和允許停留的時間。

③ **transit visa** 過境簽證
指一國公民在取得前往國家的入境簽證後，搭乘交通工具途徑第三國家的簽證。

④ **immigration clearance** 出入境檢查
指各個國家對出入境旅客實施的嚴格檢查，其中包括邊防檢查、海關檢查、安全檢查和檢疫交驗。

這些小詞你也要會哦：

legitimate a. 合法的	alien n. 外僑	detention n. 拘留，扣押
formality n. 手續	expel v. 驅逐	bearer n. 持證人
residence n. 居留	border n. 邊境	temporary a. 臨時性的
permanent a. 永久性的	departure n. 離境	endorsement n. 簽注

Scene 155 入境諮詢 Inquiry of Entry

 場景對話

A: I intend to go to America for traveling in the next half of the year. Do you know how to go through the entry formalities?	A：我打算下半年去美國旅遊，您知道怎麼辦理入境手續嗎？
B: Have you got a tourist visa?	B：您辦旅遊簽證了嗎？
A: Passport and visa have been done. I'd just like to know about the entry process.	A：護照和簽證都辦好了。我是想諮詢一下入境時的流程。
B: First, you need to fill out I-94 form, that is the entry-exit registration card, and hand it to the immigration officer.	B：首先，您需要填寫 I-94 表格，也就是出入境記錄卡，並把它交給移民官。
A: Should I keep this form?	A：這張表由我保存嗎？
B: Of course, it is very important for foreign tourists. You should return it back when you leave.	B：當然啦，這對外籍遊客非常重要，在離境時是需要交回的。
A: In addition to these, what other materials have to be provided?	A：除了這些，我還需要交什麼資料？
B: You should submit the tax returns. Besides, you also need to answer the immigration officer's questions.	B：您還需要提交報稅單，另外還需要回答移民官的問題。
A: What kind of questions will he ask?	A：移民官會問些什麼問題呢？
B: For example, your purpose for visiting the U.S., duration of stay, place to stay, and the amount of cash being carried with you, etc.	B：例如，來美國的目的、停留時間、住宿地點和隨身攜帶現金金額等。
A: Is there anything else I should do?	A：我還需要注意些什麼？
B: You must provide the return ticket. Otherwise, you might be refused to enter.	B：提交資料時必須提供返程機票，否則很有可能會被拒絕入境。
A: Thanks a lot.	A：太感謝了。
B: That's all right.	B：不用謝。

場景問答必會句

> I intend to go to America for traveling in the next half of the year. Do you know how to go through the entry formalities?
> 我打算下半年去美國旅遊，您知道怎麼辦理入境手續嗎？

還可以這樣說：

🗨 Are the entry procedures complicated when traveling to America?
去美國旅遊時，入境手續很繁瑣嗎？

對方可能這樣回答：

🗨 Not very complicated, just need to fill out the form and submit materials.
不是很複雜，只要填寫表格和提交資料就可以了。

🗨 The procedures are fixed, and you must answer the immigration officer's questions truthfully.
流程都是固定的，您必須如實回答移民官的問題。

entry procedures 入境手續

fill out 填寫

truthfully *ad.* 誠實地

> Is there anything else I should do?
> 我還需要注意些什麼？

對方可能這樣回答：

🗨 You need to provide the immigration officer with traveling schedule if you have.
如果您有旅遊日程表的話，應該交給移民官。

🗨 You must tell the actual amount of cash you're carrying. If it is over ten thousand US dollars or equivalent foreign currency, you need to declare it to the CBP at the time of entry.
您必須如實告知攜帶的現金數額，如果超過 1 萬美元或等值外幣，在入境時必須向海關與邊境保衛局申報。

equivalent *a.* 等值的

CBP (Customs and Border Protection) 美國海關與邊境保衛局

Scene 156　居留諮詢 Inquiry of Residency

 場景對話

A: I've been in England for five years, so am I eligible to apply for permanent residency?	A：我已經在英國待了 5 年，請問我能申請永久居留權嗎？
B: It depends on what kind of visa you've got.	B：這取決於您持有的是哪種簽證。

A: I've got a Tier 1 visa, which is the highly skilled migrant visa.	A：我持有的是 Tier 1 簽證，也就是高技術移民簽證。
B: If so, you need to apply for "probationary citizenship" first.	B：如果是這樣的話，您需要先申請 "見習公民"。
A: What is the time limit for "probationary citizenship"?	A："見習公民" 的最長期限是多久？
B: Five years.	B：5 年。
A: Then what should I do during the "probationary citizenship"?	A：那在 "見習公民" 期間我該怎麼做呢？
B: Your conditions need to meet the basic requirements of being a British citizen. For example, you need to have a stable job and family relations, abidance by law, and pass the "Life in the UK" Test.	B：您必須滿足成為英國公民的基本條件。例如您必須有穩定的工作和家庭關係、遵守法律，此外還必須通過 "生活在英國" 考試。
A: What kind of test is this?	A：這是什麼考試？
B: It is a test that you have to take if you want to become a British citizen or apply for permanent residency, which involves British history, law, culture, politics and other knowledge.	B：這是加入英國國籍或申請永久居留權必須參加的考試，其中涉及英國的歷史、法律、文化、政治和其他知識。
A: How long can I apply for permanent residency after I become a probationary citizen?	A：見習公民期多久後才能申請永久居留權？
B: Three years at least.	B：至少需要 3 年。
A: I see. Thank you for telling me these.	A：原來如此，謝謝您告訴我這些。
B: You're welcome.	B：不用謝。

場景問答必會句

I've been in England for five years, so am I eligible to apply for permanent residency?
我已經在英國待了 5 年，請問我能申請永久居留權嗎？

還可以這樣說：

🗨 What qualifications and conditions need to be met when applying for permanent residency in the UK?
申請在英國的永久居留權需要符合哪些資格和條件？

PS

permanent residency 永久居留權

Tier 1 visa 高技術移民簽證

Tier 2 visa 一般技術移民簽證

對方可能這樣回答：

- If you've got a Tier 1 or Tier 2 visa, you can apply for probationary citizenship after working for five years, and then further apply for permanent residency when you're qualified.

  如果您拿到的是 Tier 1 或 Tier 2 簽證，可以在工作滿 5 年後申請見習公民，符合條件後繼而申請永久居留權。

shelter *v.* 庇護

refugee *n.* 難民

- Apart from Tier 1 and Tier 2 visa, those who temporarily live in the UK due to his or her relatives have got permanent residency or become a British citizen, as well as who need to be sheltered, such as refugees, are also qualified.

  除 Tier 1 和 Tier 2 簽證外，因家屬已獲得永久居留權或成為英國公民而在英國暫居的人士，以及需要庇護的人士，如難民等，也有資格申請。

> Then what should I do during the "probationary citizenship"?
> 那在"見習公民"期間我該怎麼做呢？

還可以這樣說：

- How do I move from probationary citizen to permanent resident?

  我怎樣才能從見習公民變為永久居民？

對方可能這樣回答：

- In addition to satisfying the basic requirements, you need to actively participate in community activities and proactively assimilate into the local society, while providing relevant certificates about the activities, to shorten the time limit for application.

  除符合基本條件外，您需要積極參加社區活動，主動融入當地社會，同時出具相關活動證明，以縮短申請時限。

PS

proactively *ad.* 主動地

assimilate into 融入，同化

- Under the condition of meeting basic requirements, special expertise will also be helpful to your application.

  在符合基本條件的情況下，如果你有特殊專長，對你的申請也很有利。

Scene 157　出境諮詢 Inquiry of Departure

  場景對話

A: I've received an offer from an American University, and I intend to go to study there next month.	A：我已經收到了美國大學的錄取通知書，打算下個月去美國留學。
B: That's so great, and are you all set?	B：真是太好了，那你的東西都準備好了嗎？

A: I-20 form, passport and ticket have been prepared. Do I need any other documents?	A：I-20 表格、護照和機票都準備好了，還需要其他文件嗎？
B: A vaccination certificate is also required.	B：你還需要去開檢疫證明。
A: Oh, I see. Besides, what if the two pieces of checked luggage are too heavy?	A：哦，知道了。還有，我這次託運的兩件行李太重了怎麼辦呢？
B: That won't work then. Each piece of luggage has to be less than thirty-two kilograms.	B：太重肯定是不行的，每件必須限制在 32 千克以內。
A: What about the carry-on luggage?	A：那隨身攜帶的行李呢？
B: There is no limit, but they should not be too heavy.	B：沒有限制，不過也不宜太重。
A: And could you give me some tips about must-haves?	A：關於必備品，您能給我一些建議嗎？
B: You'd better prepare some change before departure. It will be convenient for you to make calls or hail a taxi after landing.	B：離境前最好準備一些零錢，方便你到美國後打電話或打車。
A: Anything else?	A：還有其他的嗎？
B: In order to adapt to the local environment, you should correct your watch to local time after boarding on the plane.	B：為了適應當地環境，你可以在登機後調成美國當地時間。
A: Thanks for your advice.	A：謝謝您的建議。
B: You're welcome. Wish you a good trip and succeed in your study!	B：不客氣，祝你一路平安，學業有成！

場景問答必會句

> I-20 form, passport and ticket have been prepared. Do I need any other documents?
> I-20 表格，護照和機票都準備好了，還需要其他文件嗎？

還可以這樣說：

🗨 Necessary documents are all ready. Is there anything else I should pay particular attention to?
必要的證件都準備好了，還有其他需要特別注意的地方嗎？

PS
I-20 form 美國院校簽發給國際學生以證明其合法學生身份的證明文件

對方可能這樣回答：

💬 You should write down the address and contact number of the person who will pick you up at the airport.
你應該記下接機人的地址和聯絡電話。

💬 You'd better keep copies of important documents.
你最好保留重要證件的副本。

> And could you give me some tips about must-haves?
> 關於必備品，您能給我一些建議嗎？

還可以這樣說：

💬 Before leaving, what else should I do?
臨行前我還需要做什麼其他準備嗎？

PS

must-have *n.* 必備品

traveler's check 旅行支票

for a rainy day 以備不時之需

對方可能這樣回答：

💬 You should note down the number of your traveler's check. You can cancel it immediately if your check get lost.
你應該記下旅行支票的號碼，如果遺失可以馬上注銷。

💬 You'd better carry a thin coat, a bottle of skin cream and other small items for a rainy day. But the capacity of skin cream should not be over 100 ml.
你最好隨身帶一件薄外套、護膚霜等小件物品，以備不時之需，但護膚霜不得超過 100 毫升。

出入境 Tips

出入境相關術語

money exchange 貨幣兌換處	accompanying relative 同行親屬
luggage claim 行李領取處	arrival lobby 入境大廳
transfer correspondence 中轉處	departure lobby 出境大廳
boarding card 登機牌	Customs service area 海關申報處
duty-free items 免稅商品	checked baggage 託運行李

Chapter 7

商貿辦公──
日常這樣辦公

Unit 1 人員招聘

人員招聘在外貿辦公中屬至關重要的環節，它可以為公司選拔人才，提高公司整體水平，推進公司前進。面試又是人員招聘的重要途徑，相關的工作就包括通知面試、面試應聘者、告知面試結果和介紹新近人員等。

人員招聘必會詞

1 resume *n.* 簡歷
簡歷是對個人學歷、經歷、特長、愛好及其他有關情況的簡明扼要的書面介紹。對應聘者來說，簡歷是求職的"敲門磚"。

2 benefits *n.* 福利
福利是員工的間接報酬，一般包括社會保險、帶薪假期和過節禮物等。

3 contract *n.* 合同
合同又稱為契約或協議，是平等的當事人之間設立、變更或終止民事權利義務關係的協議。

✎ 這些小詞你也要會哦：

specialize *v.* 專門從事	raise *n.* 加薪	pension *n.* 津貼
wage *n.* 工資	medical *a.* 醫療的	pension plan 退休金計劃
social security 社會保險	retirement policy 退休制度	labor insurance 勞動保險

Scene 158 通知面試 Notify the Personal Interview

場景對話

A: Is this Ms. Wang?	A：請問是王小姐嗎？
B: Yes, who's calling please?	B：是的。請問您是哪位？
A: This is Ms. Lee. I'm calling to notify you of a personal interview of the assistant's position.	A：我是李小姐，我打電話是想通知您來面試助理這一職位。

B: OK. Thanks. When?	B：好的，謝謝。什麼時候？
A: Next Monday morning.	A：下週一上午。
B: All right, I know. Do I need to bring anything?	B：好的，我知道了。我需要帶些什麼東西嗎？
A: Yes, you need to bring a copy of your resume.	A：是的，您需要帶一份您的簡歷。
B: OK, I will be there with my resume. Thank you.	B：好的，我會帶着簡歷去的。謝謝。

場景問答必會句

> I'm calling to notify you of a personal interview of the assistant's position.
> 我打電話是想通知您來面試助理這一職位。

還可以這樣說：

- We'd like to invite you for a job interview for the position of foreign trade clerk.
  我們想邀請您來面試外貿專員這一職位。
- We've received your resume. We're interested in knowing more about you.
  我們收到了您的簡歷，我們有興趣多瞭解一些您的信息。
- I'd like to set up an interview with you. 我想跟您預約面試。

PS personal interview 面試

> You need to bring a copy of your resume.
> 您需要帶一份您的簡歷。

還可以這樣說：

- I will send the address of our office to you. 我會把辦公室地址發給您。

對方可能這樣問：

- Can I confirm the address of your office? 我想確認一下您公司的地址？

Scene 159 面試開場白 Prologue of Interview

場景對話

A: You are Mr. Green, right? I'm Henry White.	A：格林先生嗎？我是亨利·懷特。
B: Nice to meet you, Mr. White.	B：很高興見到您，懷特先生。

A: Nice to meet you, too. <u>First, tell me a little about yourself, please.</u>	A：很高興見到您。<u>首先，請作一下自我介紹。</u>
B: All right. I graduated from Peking University two years ago. My major was international trade.	B：好的。我兩年前畢業於北京大學。我的專業是國際貿易。
A: According to your resume, you've been working for an import and export company in Shanghai since you graduated. <u>What are your responsibilities there?</u>	A：從您的簡歷我瞭解到，您畢業後一直在上海一家進出口公司工作。<u>您的工作職責是什麼？</u>
B: I'm responsible for exporting cotton to several European countries.	B：我負責向一些歐洲國家出口棉花。
A: So you must have a good command of English.	A：那您的英語一定掌握得很好。
B: Yes. All my clients think my English is good.	B：是的。我所有的客戶都覺得我的英語很好。

 場景問答必會句

> First, tell me a little about yourself, please.
> 首先，請作一下自我介紹。

還可以這樣說：

📭 Can you sell yourself in two minutes? Go for it.
　您能作一個兩分鐘的自我推薦嗎？開始吧。

💬 Can you introduce yourself in English?
　您能用英語做自我介紹嗎？

office secretary 辦公室秘書

對方可能這樣回答：

📭 My name is Lee and I come to apply for the position as an office secretary.
　我叫李，我來應聘辦公室秘書一職。

💬 My name is Philip, and I apply for the position of overseas sales representative.
　我叫菲利普，我來應聘海外銷售代表一職。

> What are your responsibilities there?
> 您的工作職責是什麼？

還可以這樣說：

📭 So what do you actually do at your job?
　您在工作中具體做些什麼？

💬 What's your position?
　您的職位是什麼？

對方可能這樣回答：

💬 I'm a journalist; I work for a newspaper.
我是一名記者，在報社工作。

💬 I'm responsible for exporting glass to several European countries.
我負責向一些歐洲國家出口玻璃。

PS journalist *n.* 記者

Scene **160** 詢問優缺點 Advantages and Disadvantages

 場景對話

A: What would you say is your greatest strength?	A：您認為您最大的優點是什麼？
B: I do know how to deal with customers, that is to say, my interpersonal skills are excellent.	B：我懂得如何與客戶打交道，也就是說，我的人際交往能力很棒。
A: Why do you say that?	A：為什麼這麼說呢？
B: I always take the customers' interest into consideration.	B：我總是替客戶着想。
A: Then what would you say is your most significant disadvantage?	A：那您覺得您最大的劣勢是什麼？
B: My lack of work experience. That's my significant disadvantage. However, I'm a fast learner. I was the Top 3 in my class and I can learn things in a few days which often take other students several weeks. Therefore I believe I can make up for it soon in the future.	B：我缺乏工作經驗。這是我最大的劣勢。不過我學東西學得很快。我是班裡的前三名，往往其他學生需要學習幾個星期的東西我幾天就能學會。因此我認為我可以在將來很快彌補這一不足。
A: I can see that, thanks. We will contact you later.	A：我能看得出來，謝謝。我們稍後再與您聯繫。
B: Thank you.	B：謝謝。

🗨 場景問答必會句

> What would you say is your greatest strength?
> 您認為您最大的優點是什麼？

還可以這樣說：

What are your greatest strength?
您最大的長處是什麼？

對方可能這樣回答：

Patience and caution are my advantages.
我的優點是堅持不懈和謹慎。

My time management skills are excellent and I'm very efficient.
我有很強的時間管理能力，做事情效率很高。

I'm a man of high efficiency.
我是個高效的人。

caution *n.* 謹慎

time management skills
時間管理能力

Then what would you say is your most significant disadvantage?
那您覺得您最大的劣勢是什麼？

還可以這樣說：

What's your greatest weakness?
你最大的缺點是什麼？

對方可能這樣回答：

I get nervous easily in crowds.
我在人前容易緊張。

A quick temper is my weak point.
我的缺點是性子急。

Scene 161　詢問職業目標 Career Objective

 場景對話

A: What's your career objective?	A：您的職業目標是什麼？
B: I hope to lead an energetic and productive sales team.	B：我希望成為一支有活力且高效的銷售隊伍的主管。
A: What do you regard as important when you consider a job?	A：當您看待一份工作的時候主要看重的因素有哪些？
B: I think the most important thing is the nature of the job. One should never do anything he is not interested in. To me, pleasant working conditions with co-operative staff are also important.	B：我認為最重要的是這份工作的本質。一個人不應該做自己不感興趣的事。對我來說，舒適的工作環境和配合良好的員工也很重要。

A: Why are you interested in working in our company?	A：您為何對本公司的工作感興趣？
B: My past experience is closely related to this position. I'm confident I can do the job well.	B：我過去的經驗與這一崗位密切相關。我相信我能做好這份工作。
A: What will you bring to the job?	A：您能為這份工作帶來什麼好處？
B: My business in China, mainly. I know a lot about how the Chinese market works and how business is done here.	B：主要是我在中國的貿易經驗。我很瞭解中國市場的運作情況和如何在中國做生意。

場景問答必會句

> **What's your career objective?**
> **您的職業目標是什麼？**

還可以這樣說：

- What is your plan in the next three or four years?
  您接下來三四年的工作規劃是什麼樣的？
- Tell me about some of your recent goals.
  和我談談您的近期目標吧。

對方可能這樣回答：

- I hope I can become an expert in my field.
  我希望我能成為我所在領域的專家。
- In four years, I would like to see myself as a successful consultant for a world-class firm like you.
  在 4 年後，我希望我能成為一名成功的顧問，為貴公司這樣的世界級公司工作。
- I hope to become a sales manager within a year or two.
  我希望在未來的一兩年內成為一名銷售經理。

> **Why are you interested in working in our company?**
> **您為何對本公司的工作感興趣？**

還可以這樣說：

- Why do you want this job?
  您為什麼想要得到這份工作？
- Could you tell me what made you choose this company?
  能告訴我您為什麼選擇本公司嗎？

對方可能這樣回答：

- This company is a leader in the industry.
  貴公司是行業龍頭。

My major and working experience make me qualified for this position.
我的專業和工作經驗使我能勝任這一職位。

Scene 162 詢問工作經歷 Work Experiences

 場景對話

A: So, what's your major in university?	A：您大學裡學的是什麼專業？
B: Marketing, sir.	B：市場營銷，先生。
A: OK. Have you put what you've learned in school into practice?	A：您有市場營銷方面的工作經驗嗎？
B: Yes, I've ever worked in a food factory for three years.	B：是的，我曾在一家食品廠工作了3年。
A: What have you learned from it?	A：您從這份工作中學到了些什麼？
B: Actually, I'm a lucky dog. What I did in this job was in line with my major. I dealt with the marketing development. And I also did other things, like applying for the relevant licenses, which helped me to gain a general idea about our products.	B：事實上，我很幸運，我的工作和專業息息相關。我負責市場拓展。我也做其他的工作，例如申請相關證書，這幫助我更好地瞭解我們的產品。
A: You did put your energy into your work, and you are a careful and responsible employee. Congratulations, the job is yours.	A：您工作很努力，是個認真負責的好員工。恭喜您，您被錄用了。
B: Thank you very much.	B：非常感謝。

場景問答必會句

> So, what's your major in university?
> 您大學裡學的是什麼專業？

還可以這樣說：

What did you specialize in?
您學的是什麼專業？

Why are you so interested in economics?
您為什麼對經濟學這麼感興趣？

對方可能這樣回答：

💬 I majored in foreign trade.
我主修對外貿易。

💬 I specialized in international finance.
我學的專業是國際金融學。

💬 I majored in computer science because I enjoyed learning about the most advanced technique.
我的專業是電腦，因為我喜歡研究最先進的技術。

> **Have you put what you've learned in school into practice?**
> 您有市場營銷方面的工作經驗嗎？

還可以這樣說：

💬 What have you learned from the jobs you have ever had?
您從之前的工作中學到了些什麼？

💬 Do you have any related experience?
您有任何相關經驗嗎？

💬 Have you ever done this kind of job before?
您以前做過此類工作嗎？

對方可能這樣回答：

💬 I'm experienced in dealing with American clients.
我有很多與美國客戶打交道的經驗。

💬 I have three years experience in staff management.
我有 3 年管理員工的經驗。

staff management 員工管理

💬 Although I have no experience in this field, I'm willing to learn.
雖然在這方面我沒有經驗，但是我願意學習。

💬 I'm familiar with the textile market in China.
我對中國的紡織品市場非常瞭解。

Scene 163 工資談判 About Salary

 場景對話

A: I think your performance is very good. Let's talk about another question.	A：我覺得您的表現很好，我們來討論下一個問題。
B: OK.	B：好的。
A: What salary are you expecting us to pay you?	A：您對薪金的期望是多少？

B: I just graduated from university, so there will be a transition period after I enter the company. So I think the profits I make for the company will be limited at the beginning, thus I don't have any specific requirement about the salary. I hope the salary will be enough to make me economically independent.

B： 我是一名剛畢業的大學生，進入公司需要有一個適應期。所以剛開始時為公司創造的價值有限，因此我對薪水沒有特別要求。我只希望我的薪水能讓我在經濟上獨立。

A: Could you give me a number?

A： 您能給我一個具體數目嗎？

B: I think it is OK to be between 3,000 ~ 3,500 yuan and it is negotiable.

B： 大約 3000 ~ 3500 元，這是可以商量的。

A: OK, we will take it as a reference. We will contact you later.

A： 好的，我們會作為一個參考。我們稍後會聯繫您。

B: OK, thank you.

B： 好的，謝謝您。

場景問答必會句

> What salary are you expecting us to pay you?
> 您對薪金的期望是多少？

還可以這樣說：
- How much do you expect to be paid?
  您的期望薪水是多少？
- What starting salary would you expect?
  您期望的起薪是多少？

對方可能這樣回答：
- I think the appropriate pay would be 4,000 yuan a month.
  我希望的薪水是每月至少 4000 元。

starting salary 起薪

appropriate *a.* 合適的

> Could you give me a number?
> 您能給一個具體數目嗎？

還可以這樣說：
- Would you expect an increase in salary?
  您是否期望漲薪水？
- Do you think you are being paid enough?
  您現在得到的薪水符合您的期望值嗎？

對方可能這樣回答：
- I'm sure you will make me a fair offer.
  我相信您會給我一份公平的薪資。

relate to 與……相關

responsibility *n.* 責任

I think salary is closely related to the responsibilities of the job.
我覺得工資是與工作責任緊密相關的。

Scene 164 福利待遇 Benefit Package

 場景對話

A: May I ask something about the benefits and welfare system in your company?	A：我能瞭解一下你們公司的福利制度嗎？
B: Well, just go ahead. Your starting salary is modest, but the fringe benefits will be considerable.	B：好的，請問吧。您的起薪不會太高，但額外的福利很可觀。
A: Do you have medical insurance?	A：你們有醫療保險嗎？
B: Yes, we do. Medical expenses are covered at 80%.	B：是的，我們有，醫療費報銷 80%。
A: Do employees pay any premium?	A：員工需要支付保金嗎？
B: Yes, 20% of the total premium. The company pays 80%.	B：是的，員工支付保金總額的 20%，公司支付 80%。
A: Do we need to pay social security?	A：我們要交社會保險嗎？
B: Yes. About 7% of your salary.	B：是的，大約是工資的 7%。

場景問答必會句

> Your starting salary is modest, but the fringe benefits will be considerable.
> 您的起薪不會太高，但額外的福利很可觀。

還可以這樣說：

Our benefits are based on seniority.
我們的福利是按工齡發放的。

Our benefits are granted on the basis of your position.
我們的福利是根據職務高低發放的。

Our benefits package includes five insurances and one fund.
我們的福利包括五險一金。

PS

modest *a*. 不太多的；適中的

seniority *n*. 工齡

grant *v*. 准予，授予

> Medical expenses are covered at 80%.
> 醫療費報銷 80%。

對方可能這樣問：

💬 Do you have medical insurance? 你們有醫療保險嗎？

還可以這樣說：

💬 You can enjoy our company's health insurance program. 您能享受本公司的健康保險計劃。

Scene 165　告知面試結果 Interview Result

 場景對話

A: Have you applied for a similar position to any other companies?	A：您是否申請了其他公司的類似職位？
B: Yes. I applied to ABC Company. But if I could choose, I would prefer to work for you. As far as I know your company is a world famous one. And you have successful marketing system, which really interests me and I would really bring my knowledge and interest in marketing.	B：是的。我還申請了 ABC 公司。但是如果我可以選擇的話，我更願意到你們公司上班。據我所知，貴公司是一家世界知名企業。並且你們擁有非常成功的營銷體系，我對這方面十分感興趣，所以我非常願意把我所掌握的知識運用到我感興趣的營銷工作中。
A: Good. Your experience is quite impressive. You get the job.	A：很好。您的相關經驗讓人印象頗深，您被錄用了。
B: Thank you for the offer.	B：謝謝您給我這個機會。
A: Do you have any questions to ask?	A：您有什麼想要問的問題嗎？
B: Yes. When can I sign the contract with your company?	B：有。我何時能與貴公司簽合同？
A: We need to take you on three months probation first, then we can sign a contract with the guarantee of law.	A：我們要先試用您 3 個月，然後簽訂具有法律效力的合同。
B: Got it. Thank you for your time.	B：我明白了。謝謝您抽空面試我。

場景問答必會句

> You get the job.
> 您被錄用了。

還可以這樣說：
- You've been hired. Welcome to our company.
  您被錄用了，歡迎到我們公司來。
- You get the job, so when can you start?
  您被錄用了，您什麼時候能來上班？

對方可能這樣回答：
- It's my honor to be able to work in your firm.
  我很榮幸能夠在你們公司工作。

PS
It's my honor to do sth.
我很榮幸……

> We need to take you on three months probation first, then we can sign a contract with the guarantee of law.
> 我們要先試用您 3 個月，然後簽訂具有法律效力的合同。

還可以這樣說：
- Please read the agreement and sign it.
  請閱讀協議並簽字。

對方可能這樣問：
- May I see the contract first?
  我能先看一下合同嗎？
- When will you sign the contract if I agree to become a member of your organization?
  如果被錄用的話，什麼時候可以和貴公司簽約？
- May I ask how long my probation is?
  我可以問問我的試用期是多長嗎？

PS
probation *n.* 試用期

Scene
166 介紹新進人員 Introduce the New Employees

場景對話

A: Hi. You must be Tom. Nice to meet you. I'm Jack, your new partner.	A：嗨！你一定是湯姆了。很高興見到你，我叫傑克，是你的新搭檔。
B: Nice to meet you too, Jack. <u>Let me show you around.</u>	B：很高興認識你，傑克。<u>我帶你四處看看吧。</u>

A: Thank you.

A：多謝。

B: Don't mention it. I'd like you to meet Mr. Li, our computer engineer.

B：不必客氣。我來向你介紹一下李先生，他是我們的電腦工程師。

A: Glad to meet you, Mr. Li. I'm Jack.

A：很高興見到你，李先生。我叫傑克。

C: Just call me Tony please. Nice to meet you, Jack. Well, which section do you work in?

C：叫我托尼就行了。很高興認識你，傑克。你是哪個部門的？

A: I'm a new guy in Sales Department.

A：我是銷售部的新人。

C: What a pity. We are not in the same department. But I do believe Tom will be a great teacher and partner.

C：真可惜。我們不在同一個部門。不過我相信湯姆會是位好老師、好搭檔。

A: Sure. I'll just start my work today and I have a lot to learn.

A：當然。今天是我工作的第一天，我還有很多需要學習。

B: Take it easy, you can get to know your work step by step. This is your desk.

B：放鬆點，你會一步步瞭解您的工作的。這是你的辦公桌。

A: Oh, thank you.

A：哦，謝謝你。

🗨️ 場景問答必會句

> Let me show you around.
> 我帶你四處看看吧。

還可以這樣說：

💬 Let me show you the lay of the land.
　　我帶你熟悉一下環境。

💬 Come in and meet some of our team.
　　進來和同事們認識一下吧。

💬 I'd like to welcome you to our company.
　　歡迎到我們公司來。

對方可能這樣回答：

💬 It's so nice. Thank you.
　　太貼心了，謝謝你。

💬 I hope I can fit in well.
　　我希望我能儘快融入進來。

PS

show around 帶領……參觀

lay *n*. 位置

> I'd like you to meet Mr. Li, our computer engineer.
> 我來向你介紹一下李先生，他是我們的電腦工程師。

還可以這樣說：

💬 Let me introduce you to our chief editor Mrs. White.
讓我把你介紹給我們的主編懷特女士。

💬 I'm in charge of the Personnel Department, Michael Su.
我是人事部經理，麥克‧蘇。

┃人員招聘 Tips┃

調職申請函電小模板

Dear Mr. Steven:

　　I have been devoting my energy and love to our company, and I really hope I could have long-term development here. As the Marketing Section is the leading department, which is in charge of our main business, I want to have a chance to enter this department to learn more. I promise I will work as hard in the new department as in my current department.

　　I desperately expect your permission.

Sincerely yours,

Tom Smith

尊敬的史蒂文先生：

　　我對公司傾注了極大的精力和感情，我希望在這裡得到長足發展。營銷部是公司的重要部門，負責公司的主要業務。我希望可以有機會進入這個部門學習，我一定會像在現在這個部門一樣努力工作。

　　熱切盼望您的批准！

湯姆‧史密斯

敬上

Unit 2 辦公設備

現代的辦公設備越來越專業化，電話、電腦、打印機、影印機和傳真機等都是外貿商務人士日常工作中不可或缺的"助手"。

辦公設備必會詞

❶ disconnect *v.* 斷開
打電話時，電話會因線路、信號等問題而斷開。出於禮貌，要積極主動重打。

❷ anti-virus software 殺毒軟件
殺毒軟件也稱反病毒軟件或防毒軟件，用於消除病毒、木馬和惡意軟件等。

❸ paper jam 卡紙
卡紙指的是打印機在輸送打印紙的過程中，由於機械裝置的失誤，導致紙張無法正常送出，卡在打印機內部。打印機會因此而停機。

這些小詞你也要會哦：

line *n.* 電話線路	cross *v.* 交叉	mouse *n.* 鼠標
install *v.* 安裝	virus *n.* 病毒	software *n.* 軟件
hardware *n.* 電腦硬件	router *n.* 路由器	service page 打印頁數
bind *v.* 裝訂	ready *a.* 待機的	scan *v.* 掃描

Scene 167 電話 Telephone

場景對話

A: I've just been disconnected from a number. Could you…

A：我剛撥的電話斷了。您能……

B: I'm sorry. Could you speak a little louder? There's a bad connection.

B：很抱歉。您能大點聲嗎？線路不好。

A: The connection is really bad. I've just been disconnected from a number. Is there something wrong with my phone?	A：線路確實很差。我剛撥的電話斷了。是不是我的電話出問題了？
B: There may be a fault on the line.	B：可能是線路出問題了。
A: I see.	A：我明白了。
B: Please tell me your number. I'll call you back as soon as the line is OK.	B：請告訴我您的電話號碼。線路一旦恢復我就馬上給您打電話。
A: My number's 87654321.	A：我的電話號碼是 87654321。
(About ten minutes later.)	（大約 10 分鐘後。）
B: Hello. Is that 87654321?	B：您好。是 87654321 嗎？
A: Yes!	A：是的！
B: The line is OK now. There was a mini fault on it.	B：線路現在正常了。剛才出了點小問題。
A: Thanks for calling me back.	A：謝謝您給我打電話。

場景問答必會句

> The connection is really bad.
> 線路確實很差。

還可以這樣說：
- Are you there, Vanessa? Who is that talking?
  你在聽嗎，瓦妮莎？那是誰在說話？

對方可能這樣回答：
- The noise is disturbing me. I can't hear you clearly.
  有雜音干擾。我聽不清楚你在說什麼。
- I think this line is crossed.
  我想是電話串線了。

PS

connection *n.* 連接

disturb *v.* 打擾

> Is there something wrong with my phone?
> 是不是我的電話出問題了？

還可以這樣說：
- Why won't my call go through?
  為什麼我的電話打不進去？
- My phone has no dial tone.
  我的電話沒有正常提示音。

對方可能這樣回答：

- The telephone doesn't work properly. 電話不好使了。
- Some keys / buttons are sticking. 一些按鍵卡住了。

Scene 168　電腦 Computer

 場景對話

A: Mark. Could you please come and take a look at my computer?	A：馬克，你可以過來幫我看一下我的電腦嗎？
B: Here I am. What's wrong with your computer?	B：我來了。你的電腦怎麼了？
A: I don't know. Just all of a sudden, I found I couldn't get online.	A：不知道。突然間，我發現不能上網了。
B: Let me see. Have you changed anything or touched any key on your computer?	B：讓我看看。你有沒有更改過電腦的設置或按了什麼按鍵？
A: No, I didn't do anything.	A：不，我沒做什麼。
B: All right. It is possible that a loose cable connection could be preventing network access.	B：好吧，有可能是網線鬆了導致不能上網。
A: Oh, yes! The cable is loose. Let me plug it into my computer again.	A：哦，是的！網線鬆了。讓我重新把網線插到電腦上。
B: Here is the Internet now.	B：能上網了。
A: Thank you for helping me out.	A：謝謝你的幫助。
B: That's all right.	B：不客氣。

場景問答必會句

> Could you please come and take a look at my computer?
> 你可以過來幫我看一下我的電腦嗎？

還可以這樣說：

- Would you check our computers?
  幫我們檢修一下電腦好嗎？
- Something has gone wrong with my computer. It always restarts.
  我電腦出了點兒問題，總是自動重啟。

I found I couldn't get online.
我發現不能上網了。

還可以這樣說：

🗨 This computer is running so slowly. 這台電腦運行得很慢。

Scene 169 打印機和影印機 Printer and Photocopier

 場景對話

A: Can you help me with the new printer?	A：你能不能幫我看一下新的打印機？
B: Sure. What is the matter? It worked well yesterday.	B：當然。出什麼問題了？昨天它還能正常工作。
A: But it doesn't work now. This is a new type of laser printer and I still don't know the function of some buttons on the machine.	A：但現在它不工作了。這是一款新型激光打印機，一些按鈕的功能我還不清楚。
B: Let me see. Did you press the "print" button?	B：讓我看看。你按下"打印"按鈕了嗎？
A: Yes, but the computer reads "Please check the connections and try again. "	A：是的，但是電腦顯示"請檢查連接，然後再試一次"。
B: Oh, I see. There is a disconnection between the computer and the printer. Let me have a look. Yes, you forgot to put the plug in the socket of the computer.	B：哦，我明白了。電腦和打印機之間斷開了。讓我看看。是的，你忘了插上電腦插座的插頭。
A: Oh, I forgot it. I'm sorry to have bothered you.	A：哦，我忘了。很抱歉打擾你了。

場景問答必會句

What is the matter?
出什麼問題了？

還可以這樣說：

🗨 Is there anything wrong? 有什麼問題嗎？

🗨 What's the matter with the copier? 影印機怎麼了？

對方可能這樣回答：

💬 The copy machine is out of order.
影印機出故障了。

💬 This copier needs repairing.
這台影印機需要修理。

out of order 發生故障

> Did you press the "print" button?
> 你按下"打印"按鈕了嗎？

還可以這樣說：

💬 Why is the paper getting backed up?
怎麼紙被退出來了？

💬 Why is it easy to get a paper jam?
為什麼總是卡紙呢？

back up 倒退

對方可能這樣回答：

💬 Yes, but it still doesn't work.
是的，但是它仍舊不工作。

Scene 170　傳真機 Fax Machine

 場景對話

A: Kate, could you give me a hand?	A：凱特，能幫我個忙嗎？
B: Sure.	B：當然。
A: I want to send a fax, but I don't know how to use the fax machine.	A：我想發份傳真，但我不知道怎麼用這台傳真機。
B: It's easy. Put the fax in the machine, and dial the number just like you dial on a phone. Press the button "start" after you get through.	B：很簡單。把要傳真的東西放在上面，然後像打電話一樣撥號，接通後按"開始鍵"就可以了。
A: Sounds simple. Let me try.	A：聽起來很簡單，我來試試。
B: Go ahead. You can make it.	B：好的，你會成功的。
A: How can I know if the fax is sent?	A：怎樣才能知道傳真已經發出去了？
B: You can set up the fax machine to print a completion receipt. It will also print an error page if the fax does not go through.	B：你可以設定傳真機打印一張完成回執。如果傳真發送失敗的話，傳真機也會打印一張發送失敗回執。

A 場景問答必會句

I want to send a fax, but I don't know how to use the fax machine.
我想發份傳真，但我不知道怎麼用這台傳真機。

還可以這樣說：
- I found it difficult to use the fax machine. 我不太會用傳真機。
- Do you know how I can fax this? 我怎麼用傳真發送？

對方可能這樣回答：
- I'll show you how to operate it. 我來示範如何操作。
- I can fax this for you. Where to? 我可以幫你把傳真發出去，發到哪兒？

How can I know if the fax is sent?
怎樣才能知道傳真已經發出去了？

還可以這樣說：
- I want to receive the fax. How to give a signal?
  我要收傳真，怎樣給對方信號呢？

對方可能這樣回答：
- You need to do nothing, since our fax machine can receive fax automatically.
  你不用做任何事，因為我們的傳真機可以自動接收傳真。
- Please acknowledge receipt of the fax. 請通知對方已收到傳真。

PS
signal *n.* 信號
automatically *ad.* 自動地
acknowledge *v.* 告知已收到

辦公設備 Tips

電話故障應急

- **中途斷線**

  斷線但是事情沒談完，應由打電話的一方重新撥打，使談話繼續進行。切忌不能因事情差不多談完，就聽之任之。

  再次撥通之後，應先向對方致歉："非常抱歉，剛才電話中途斷線了。"(Sorry, we got disconnected just now.)

- **聲音不清楚**

  如果對方的聲音的確很小，可以說"電話信號不好，您能大聲一點嗎？"(The connection is bad. Please speak a little louder.) 或"很抱歉，能不能請您再說一遍？"(Sorry. Can you repeat that?)

Unit 3　檔案管理

檔案管理亦稱檔案工作，是檔案室直接對檔案實體和檔案信息進行管理並提供使用服務的各項業務工作的總稱。

檔案管理必會詞

① archive *n.* **檔案**
檔案是國家機構、社會組織以及個人從事政治、軍事、經濟、科學、技術、文化和宗教等活動直接形成的具有保存價值的各種文字、圖表和聲像等不同形式的歷史記錄。

② management *n.* **管理**
管理是指在特定的環境條件下，以人為中心，對組織所擁有的資源進行有效的決策、計劃、組織、領導和控制，以便達到既定組織目標的過程。

③ filing *n.* **歸檔**
歸檔指將處理完畢且具有保存價值的事情或文件經系統整理後交檔案室保存備查的過程。

這些小詞你也要會哦：

analysis *n.* 分析	target *n.* 目標	registration *n.* 登記
statistics *n.* 統計	custody *n.* 保管	durability *n.* 耐久性
catalogue *n.* 目錄	index *n.* 索引	conservation *n.* 保護
subject *n.* 主題	classified *a.* 分類的	keyword *n.* 關鍵詞

Scene 171　檔案查詢 File Query

 場景對話

A: Good morning!	A：早上好！
B: Good morning, sir!	B：早上好，先生！

A: Did you look up those files I requested?	A：我要的那些檔案資料都找到了嗎？
B: I'm sorry. I couldn't find any information.	B：對不起。我沒有找到。
A: But I'm completely sure that the information was filed.	A：我確定那份資料已經存檔了。
B: Would you like me to check again under a different heading?	B：讓我在別的標題下再查一下，好嗎？
A: Yes. Would you please clean out all the old files by tomorrow?	A：好的！你能不能在明天之前把所有的舊檔案都清理好？
B: Sure.	B：好的。
A: First of all, find the files I requested right now.	A：首先，馬上找到我要的檔案。
B: Yes, manager.	B：是，經理。

場景問答必會句

> **Did you look up those files I requested?**
> **我要的那些檔案資料都找到了嗎？**

還可以這樣說：
Have you found the files I required?
你找到我要的檔案了嗎？

對方可能這樣回答：
Sorry, I have not done that because I'm very busy now.
抱歉，我還沒有找，因為現在比較忙。

Yes, I found them.
是的，我找到了。

> **Would you like me to check again under a different heading?**
> **讓我在別的標題下再查一下，好嗎？**

還可以這樣說：
Can I check again under a different heading?
我能在別的標題下查一查嗎？

對方可能這樣回答：
No problem.
沒有問題。

OK! I will let Tanya help you.
好的！我會讓塔尼婭幫你。

Scene
172　文件歸檔 Filing

 場景對話

A: Chris, welcome to be a member of us. I need you to rearrange all of these text files and put them in order.

A：克里斯，歡迎你成為我們的一員。我需要你把這些文件全部按順序重新整理好。

B: OK. Wow, look at these files! They almost filled the whole room! I'm not sure where should I start. <u>How am I supposed to organize them?</u>

B：好的。哇，看看這些文件！幾乎堆滿了整個房間！我不確定該如何開始。<u>我應該如何整理這些文件呢？</u>

A: Take it easy. First you can create a basic filing system. Then try to arrange those files in some ordered sequence. For example, if they are labeled with dates, put them in chronological order.

A：放輕鬆些。首先，你可以創建一個基本的歸檔系統。接着試着把那些文件按順序歸檔。例如，如果標有日期，就按時間順序整理。

B: <u>And what about those files that are not labeled with dates?</u>

B：<u>那些沒有標日期的文件怎麼辦呢？</u>

A: See, usually those files are labeled with names. You can put them in alphabetical order by last name.

A：看，通常情況下，這些文件會標有姓名。你可以按姓氏的字母順序排列。

B: Thanks for your help.

B：感謝你的幫助。

A: You are welcome. If you have any questions, please feel free to ask.

A：不客氣。如果你有什麼問題，請儘管問我。

B: That's very kind of you. Thank you so much.

B：你真好，太謝謝你了。

場景問答必會句

> How am I supposed to organize them?
> 我應該如何整理這些文件呢？

還可以這樣說：
💬 What am I supposed to do?
　　我應該怎麼做？

對方可能這樣回答：
💬 Mike is an expert in this area. You can ask him.
　　邁克是這個領域的專家。你可以問問他。

🗨 Sorry, I know just a little bit. 抱歉，我只是略知一二。

> And what about those files that are not labeled with dates?
> 那些沒有標日期的文件怎麼辦呢？

還可以這樣說：

🗨 How to archive this file?
這份文件要怎麼存檔？

🗨 How to deal with this file?
這份文件要怎麼處理？

對方可能這樣回答：

🗨 For the files labeled with names, you should put them in alphabetical order by last name.
對於標有姓名的文件，你應該按姓氏的字母順序排列。

🗨 Sorry, I do not know either.
抱歉，我也不知道。

檔案管理 Tips

檔案管理函電小模板

Dear all,

I'm responsible for all the documents in production department now and I have carefully filed all the documents.

I put all the documents in alphabetical order by last name.

However, please contact me if you can't find the document you want according to alphabetical order.

Best regards,

Mary

大家好：

我現在負責生產部門內的所有文件的歸檔工作，我已將全部文件仔細地整理歸檔。

所有文件按姓氏的字母順序排列。

不管怎麼樣，如果您根據字母的順序無法找到需要的文件，請聯繫我。

瑪麗

敬上

Unit 4 會議籌備

會議籌備包括會議策劃、安排議程、預訂會議室、會議服務和時間地點的安排等，良好的會議籌備有助於會議有條不紊地舉行，提高開會效率。

會議籌備必會詞

1 agenda *n.* 議程
會議議程是為了使會議順利召開所做的內容和程序安排，是會議需要遵循的程序。它包括兩層含義，一是指會議的議事程序，二是指列入會議的各項議題。

2 meeting notice 會議通知
會議通知應包括會議內容、參會人員、會議時間及地點等。會議通知要求言簡意賅、措辭得當、時間及時。

3 meeting services 會議服務
會議服務的內容有很多，包括每次會議開始前檢查燈光、室溫和衛生等，隨時提供必要的會議文件及有關資料等。

這些小詞你也要會哦：

conference room 會議室	foyer *n.* 大廳，休息室	dimension of room 會議室尺寸
setup *n.* 佈局	swirl chair 旋轉椅	dais *n.* 講枱
rostrum *n.* 主席台	labor cost 人工費用	scaled drawing 比例圖

Scene 173 會議策劃 Conference Planning

 場景對話

A: When is the annual global sales and marketing conference this year?	A：今年什麼時候召開全球年度銷售和營銷會議？
B: It's scheduled at the first week of July.	B：安排在 7 月的第一個星期召開。

A: Will it run for the entire week or will it just run through the weekdays?	A：會議將持續一整週還是只在工作日內舉行？
B: Delegates will arrive on Sunday morning. There will be an optional dinner and reception Sunday night. The rest of the conference will take place from Monday to Friday.	B：代表們將於週日上午抵達。週日晚上將舉辦一場晚宴和歡迎儀式，大家可以自由出席。接下來的會議將從週一持續到週五。
A: Where will it take place?	A：在哪裡舉行？
B: We've reserved rooms in the Hillington Hotel in London.	B：我們已經在倫敦的希靈頓酒店預訂了房間。
A: That would be very nice. Will any of the meals be provided?	A：這聽起來不錯。提供餐飲嗎？
B: Lunch will be provided during the weekdays.	B：週一到週五提供午餐。
A: When will the invitations go out to the delegates?	A：什麼時候將邀請函發給代表們？
B: I've written the E-mails, and I will send them right away.	B：我已經寫好了郵件，馬上發出去。

場景問答必會句

> When is the annual global sales and marketing conference this year?
> 今年什麼時候召開全球年度銷售和營銷會議？

還可以這樣說：

🗨 Where are we going to have the meeting? 我們要在哪裡開會？

對方可能這樣回答：

🗨 The meeting will be held in your office. 會議將在你的辦公室裡召開。

🗨 We will arrange the meeting on Tuesday afternoon. 我們將把會議安排在週二下午。

> When will the invitations go out to the delegates?
> 什麼時候將邀請函發給代表們？

還可以這樣說：

🗨 Shall I inform all of the department managers to attend the meeting immediately?
現在要立刻通知各部門經理出席會議嗎？

🗨 Please ensure that those intend to be present are properly informed. 務必確保出席會議的人都通知到。

PS

delegate n. 代表

Scene 174　安排議程 Set the Agenda

 場景對話

A: Excuse me, Mr. Edward. If you've got a minute, I'd like to talk about the agenda of the monthly meeting.

A：打擾了，愛德華先生，如果你有時間，我想和你討論一下月度例會的議程。

B: OK, go ahead.

B：好的，請説。

A: Well, the meeting will be held at two p.m. next Thursday. The items on the agenda include the strategy for the future growth, the marketing strategy and the sales campaign.

A：嗯，會議定於下週四下午兩點舉行。會議的議題包括未來發展戰略、市場營銷戰略和銷售活動。

B: I see. Which one is the first item?

B：我知道了。第一個議題是什麼？

A: The strategy for the future growth. Vice president Lisa will first give us a brief report on the market research we conducted last week, and will analyze the deficiencies of our present strategy.

A：是未來發展戰略。副總裁莉薩將首先就我們上週進行的市場調查做簡短報告，她將分析我們現行戰略的缺陷。

B: OK. How about my speaking time?

B：好的。我的發言被安排在什麼時候？

A: Well, you're scheduled to take the floor at four p.m. to make a conclusion of the meeting.

A：哦，您被安排在下午 4 點發言，對會議做一個總結。

B: OK, I see.

B：好，我知道了。

場景問答必會句

> If you've got a minute, I'd like to talk about the agenda of the monthly meeting.
> 如果你有時間，我想和你討論一下月度例會的議程。

還可以這樣說：

📖 I want to design the agenda once and for all.
我想把會議議程定下來。

📖 Let's just check the conference programme.
讓我們來核對一下會議程序。

對方可能這樣回答：

💬 OK, we can discuss it this afternoon.
好，我們今天下午可以討論一下。

💬 First, we must study out the topic of the meeting.
首先我們必須要擬定會議的議題。

Which one is the first item?
第一個議題是什麼？

還可以這樣說：

💬 We have two items on the agenda tomorrow.
明天我們有兩個議題。

對方可能這樣回答：

💬 Sales strategy is sure to be an item on agenda.
銷售策略必須成為議程上的一項。

💬 Don't talk about too many details about products at this stage.
不要在現階段討論太多產品細節。

Scene 175 日程變動 Change the Agenda

 場景對話

A: Do you have the meeting agenda?	A：你有會議日程表嗎？
B: I think so.	B：我想應該有。
A: We need to make some changes to the agenda and send it out tonight.	A：我們需要對日程做些改動，並在今晚發出去。
B: OK. Let me know what the changes are and I'll revise the agenda.	B：好的。告訴我哪兒需要修改，我來修改日程。
A: All right. The first one is the starting time. It's going to start at nine o'clock instead of half past eight.	A：好的，第一項是會議的開始時間，從 8:30 改為 9 點開始。
B: Fine.	B：好。
A: Also, we'll have to shorten the lunch time to allow for extra thirty minutes on the agenda.	A：另外，我們得縮短午飯時間，在日程表上騰出 30 分鐘的時間。
B: That's not a problem. I'll change the lunch time to 12:15 to 1:30 instead of 12:15 to 1:00.	B：這沒問題。我可以把午飯時間從 12:15 到 1:30 改為 12:15 到 1:00。

A: That's great. Don't forget to tell the caterers.　　A：很好，不要忘了告訴餐飲公司。

B: Don't worry. I'll get it under control.　　B：別擔心，我會安排好一切的。

場景問答必會句

> We need to make some changes to the agenda and send it out tonight.
> 我們需要對日程做些改動，並在今晚發出去。

還可以這樣說：

💭 Is there any chance we can change the date?
我們可以更改日期嗎？

💭 I wonder if we could make it some other time.
我想知道我們是否可以預約別的時間。

💭 This meeting is called off. It will be held tomorrow.
會議取消了，改到明天舉行。

對方可能這樣回答：

💭 What a pity. How about next week? 太可惜了，下週怎麼樣？

💭 That shouldn't be a problem. 沒問題。

> The first one is the starting time. It's going to start at nine o'clock instead of half past eight.
> 第一項是會議的開始時間，從 8:30 改為 9 點開始。

還可以這樣說：

💭 We have to postpone his presentation till the afternoon.
我們不得不將他的演講推遲到下午。

對方可能這樣回答：

💭 I'm not sure that's going to work, actually.
其實我不太確定這是否可行。

Scene **176** 預訂會議室 Book a Meeting Room

場景對話

A: Can I help you?　　A：有什麼能為您效勞的嗎？

B: I'd like to book a meeting room, please.　　B：我想要預訂一間會議室。

A: OK. Can you tell me the date you want?	A：沒問題。您想要哪天的會議室？
B: I'd like to book a meeting room for Oct. 8th, that is next Wednesday.	B：我想要預訂 10 月 8 日的會議室，也就是下星期三。
A: What time next Wednesday?	A：下星期三什麼時候？
B: Let me see. Is that available from three o'clock to five o'clock?	B：讓我想想。下午 3 點到 5 點有空房間嗎？
A: How many people do you need the room for?	A：您需要能容納多少人的房間？
B: There will be twenty people.	B：一共 20 人。
A: OK. There is one you can book.	A：好的，有一間可供預訂的會議室。

場景問答必會句

> **I'd like to book a meeting room, please.**
> 我想要預訂一間會議室。

還可以這樣說：

🗨 I'd like to book the meeting room for next Wednesday.
  我要預訂下星期三的會議室。

🗨 I wonder if you have any meeting rooms available for this Thursday afternoon.
  我想知道星期四下午是否有可使用的會議室。

🗨 Is there a vacant meeting room next Monday?
  下週一有空的會議室嗎？

對方可能這樣回答：

🗨 I need to check the appointment book.
  我需要查一下登記本。

> **There will be twenty people.**
> 一共 20 人。

還可以這樣說：

🗨 I'd like to reserve a meeting room for nine people.
  我想預訂一間能容納 9 個人的會議室。

🗨 Does it have the capacity to hold two hundred people?
  這裡能容納 200 人嗎？

PS

capacity *n.* 容量

Scene 177　會議服務 Meeting Services

 場景對話

A: Is the room all set up for the conference today?
A：今天會議要用的房間都準備好了嗎？

B: Almost.
B：差不多了。

A: Do you have Internet access in the meeting rooms?
A：會議室裡可以上網嗎？

B: Yes, we have Wi-Fi.
B：可以，我們有無線網絡。

A: We also need to confirm the lunch and afternoon break orders from catering.
A：我們還需要向餐飲公司確定一下午餐和下午茶的訂單。

B: That won't be a problem. Anything else?
B：這不會有任何問題的。你還需要我做些什麼？

A: I need you to move the tables to U-form and set up four flip charts in the corners of the room.
A：我需要你去移動一下桌子，把它們擺成 U 形，然後在會議室的角落擺上 4 幅活動掛圖。

B: OK, I see.
B：好的，我知道了。

A: I also need you to set up the interactive whiteboard, the projector and five laptops.
A：我還需要你幫我準備互動白板、投影儀和 5 台手提電腦。

B: OK. What you need will be ready.
B：好的，你需要的都會準備好。

場景問答必會句

> Is the room all set up for the conference today?
> 今天會議要用的房間都準備好了嗎？

還可以這樣說：

- Can you decorate the venue in our company colors?
  你們可以用我們公司的標誌色佈置會場嗎？
- What other services do you provide?
  你們還提供什麼其他服務？

> Do you have Internet access in the meeting rooms?
> 會議室裡可以上網嗎？

還可以這樣說：

🖥 Do you know how to hook the laptop up to the projector?
你知道如何把筆記本電腦和投影儀連接上嗎？

🖥 Are there enough conference tables and chairs?
會議桌椅都夠用嗎？

🖥 Can you provide background music?
你們可以提供背景音樂嗎？

對方可能這樣回答：

🖥 We can provide audio and video services if you require.
如果需要的話，我們可以提供音響和影像服務。

🖥 What genre of music would you like? 你想要哪種音樂類型？

Scene 178 舉辦宴會 Hold a Feast

  場景對話

A: Fancy Foods, Incorporated. This is Jane. How can I help you?	A：美味食物公司。我是簡。請問我能為您做些什麼？
B: Hello, Jane. This is Tom. I'm calling to inquire about your catering services.	B：您好，簡，我是湯姆。我打電話是想詢問關於餐飲服務方面的事情。
A: Yes, what kind of event are you inquiring about?	A：好的，您要諮詢什麼樣的活動？
B: It's about our annual meeting.	B：是我們公司的年會。
A: What date is it?	A：什麼時間？
B: We would like it to take place on October 15th from 4:00 p.m. to midnight. Would you be available then?	B：我們想在 10 月 15 號舉行，下午 4 點到午夜。那個時段你們有空嗎？
A: You're lucky. We are available. How many people?	A：您很幸運。我們有空。晚會有多少人參加？
B: Three hundred people.	B：300 人。
A: OK. What kind of budget are you working with?	A：好的，那您的預算是多少？
B: About $30 per person.	B：大概每人 30 美元。
A: OK, that's great. I'll send you a list of sample menus for you to choose.	A：好的，我會先送一些樣品菜單供您挑選。

🅰 場景問答必會句

> It's about our annual meeting.
> 是我們公司的年會。

還可以這樣說：

💬 It's about our annual staff Christmas party.
　　是我們公司的年度員工聖誕晚會。

> About $30 per person.
> 大概每人 30 美元。

對方可能這樣問：

💬 How many people should we plan for?
　　我們需要準備多少人份的（餐飲）？

PS

approximately *ad.* 大概

還可以這樣說：

💬 Approximately one hundred and fifty people.
　　大概 150 人。

會議籌備 Tips

會議的準備工作

　　在會議召開之前，都必須先考慮開會的原因和目的，即 reasons and purposes of the meeting，然後再着手規劃。規劃的內容包括以下幾方面：

- 會議目的 (purposes of the meeting)：可以分為談判 (negotiate)、規劃 (plan)、解決問題 (solve a problem) 或者做決定 (make a decision) 等。

- 時間和地點 (time and place)：包括開會日期 (date)、地點 (place)、開會時間長度 (duration) 等。

- 與會人員 (attendees)：相關事務包括事先發開會通知 (meeting notice) 和議程 (agenda)，指定誰擔任主席 (chairman)，由誰做會議記錄 (take the minutes)，確定是否有來賓 (guest) 或演講者 (speaker) 等。

- 設備 (facilities and equipment)：除了會場所需設備外，有時還必須考慮是否提供茶點 (refreshments)、餐點 (meal) 以及停車位 (parking space) 等。

Unit 5 商務信函

在外貿活動中，很多事情需要以商務信函的形式來確認，妥善處理商務信函是外貿人士必備技能之一。

商務信函必會詞

1 business line 經營範圍
經營範圍是指國家允許企業生產和經營的商品類別、品種及服務項目，反映企業業務活動的內容和生產經營方向，是企業業務活動範圍的法律界限，體現企業民事權利能力和行為能力的核心內容。

1 specialize in 專營
專營一般是指由政府授權商家獨家經營某些業務，在相關範疇內政府以立法或行政等方法確保沒有競爭者加入，條件就是業者服務及利潤水平由政府管制。

1 turnover n. 營業額
營業額是指企業在生產經營活動中因銷售產品或提供勞務而取得的各項收入。

這些小詞你也要會哦：

reply v. 回覆	irrevocable a. 不可撤銷的	confirm v. 確認
enclose v. 附上	urgent a. 緊急的	due a. 到期的
appreciate v. 感激	liable a. 有責任的	handle v. 經營

Scene 179 查看信件 Check the Letter

 場景對話

A: Hi, are you free now?	A：你好，你現在有時間嗎？
B: Yes. What can I do for you?	B：有，能為您做些什麼嗎？
A: A client sent me an email. Would you like to check the email for me now? It's a little urgent.	A：有位客戶給我發了一封郵件。你能幫我查看一下嗎？有點着急。

B: Of course. I know your email address. Could you tell me your password?	B：當然可以。我知道你的郵箱地址。能告訴我密碼嗎？
A: It is 19907865.	A：密碼是 19907865。
B: Please wait for a moment. Let me check now.	B：請稍等。我查看一下。
A: OK!	A：好的！
B: It is from Jack.	B：這封郵件是傑克發給您的。
A: Yes. <u>Can you tell me the main idea?</u>	A：是的。<u>能告訴我主要內容嗎？</u>
B: He said there is a quality problem and hope you can contact him as soon as possible.	B：他説產品出現了質量問題，希望您儘快聯繫他。
A: Thank you very much.	A：非常感謝。

場景問答必會句

> Would you like to check the email for me now?
> 你能幫我查看一下嗎？

還可以這樣說：
- Please help me check the email now.
  請幫我查看這封郵件。
- Is it possible for you to check the email for me now?
  你現在可以幫我查看一下郵件嗎？

對方可能這樣回答：
- Sorry, I'm away from computer now. 抱歉，我現在沒在電腦旁邊。
- No problem. 沒問題。

> Can you tell me the main idea?
> 能告訴我主要內容嗎？

還可以這樣說：
- I want to know the main idea of this email.
  我想知道這封郵件的主要內容。
- Please summarize the email.
  請概括一下這封郵件的內容。

對方可能這樣回答：
- Sorry. It is written in Chinese but my Chinese is not good.
  抱歉。這封郵件是用中文寫的，但是我的中文很不好。
- Nothing important. Just say Happy National Day.
  沒什麼重要的事情。只是說國慶節快樂。

Scene 180 處理信件 Deal with Mails

 場景對話

A: Where have you been? There is an urgent letter of Goldburg waiting for you to deal with.	A：你到哪裡去了？有一封來自戈德伯格的緊急信件需要你處理。
B: Sorry, I missed a bus and the bus I took got caught in a traffic jam. I'm trying to get there in thirty minutes.	B：對不起，我錯過了公交車。坐上的車又碰上了交通堵塞。我儘量在 30 分鐘內趕到。
A: No, it is late. Our client is waiting over the phone. Do you mind I handle the email for you?	A：不，太晚了。我們的客戶在電話那頭等着呢。你介意我幫你處理這封郵件嗎？
B: You are so kind.	B：你真是太好了。
A: Is there anything I need to pay attention to?	A：有需要注意的事情嗎？
B: No, there isn't. If you have any question, please call me.	B：沒有。如果你有什麼問題，隨時給我打電話。
A: Sure. I will tell you the details when you are here.	A：好的。當你到公司後，我會把詳情告訴你。
B: I will try to get to our office as soon as possible.	B：我會儘快到辦公室的。
A: OK, bye.	A：好的，再見。

場景問答必會句

> Do you mind I handle the email for you?
> 你介意我幫你處理這封郵件嗎？

還可以這樣說：

- Could I see this email? 我可以看這封郵件嗎？
- Please let me check the email so we can answer the client as soon as possible.
  請讓我查看這封郵件，這樣我們就能儘快回覆客戶了。

對方可能這樣回答：

- It is good. 很好。
- I think I'd better take care of it because the client is difficult to deal with.
  我想我還是自己來處理吧，因為這位客戶不好打交道。

> Is there anything I need to pay attention to?
> 有需要注意的事情嗎？

還可以這樣說：
- Are there any issues needed to be aware of?
  是否有需要注意的事情？

對方可能這樣回答：
- Please remember Goldburg enjoy a 5% discount.
  請記住戈德伯格享受 5% 的優惠。
- Nothing special.
  沒有什麼特別要注意的。

商務信函 Tips

商務信函函電小模板

Dear Sir,

We have seen your products in the Expo and are particularly interested in your

portable typewriters, but we require a machine suitable for fairly heavy duty.

Please send us your current illustrated catalogue and a price list.

Best regards,

Zhang Rui

敬啟者：

我們在博覽會上看到你們的產品。對你們的手提打字機非常感興趣，但我們需

要適用於打字量比較大這一情況的機器。

請寄送一份最新的附圖產品目錄和價目表。謝謝。

張睿

敬上

商標註冊

商標註冊是商標使用人取得商標專用權的前提和條件，只有經核准註冊的商標，才受法律保護。

商標註冊必會詞

1 trademark *n.* 商標
商標是商品的生產者或經營者在其生產、製造、加工、揀選或者經銷的商品上或是服務的提供者在其提供的服務上採用的，用於區別商品或服務來源的，由文字、圖形、數字、顏色或上述要素的組合，具有顯著特徵的標誌。

2 registration *n.* 註冊
由主管部門辦理手續，記入籍冊，便於管理查考。

3 assignment *n.* 轉讓
轉讓就是把自己的東西或合法權益讓給他人，可以轉讓的權益有產權、債權、資產、股權、營業、著作權、知識產權、經營權和租賃權等。

4 trademark law 商標法
商標法是確認商標專用權，規定商標註冊、使用、轉讓、保護和管理的法律規範的總稱。

這些小詞你也要會哦：

infringement *n.* 侵權	cancellation *n.* 取消	adjudication *n.* 裁定
disputed *a.* 有爭議的	opposition *n.* 異議	refuse *v.* 拒絕
removal *n.* 注銷（註冊商標）	agency *n.* 代理	change *n.* 變更
enquiry *n.* 查詢	validity *n.* 有效期	defensive *a.* 防禦用的

Scene 181 註冊商標 Registered Trademark

  場景對話

A: What can I do for you?　　A：有什麼可以幫您？

B: I would like to register the trademark for this brand.	B：我想要註冊這個品牌的商標。
A: Does this brand sell well?	A：這個品牌的產品暢銷嗎？
B: Yes, it sells well in this area.	B：是的，這個品牌在這塊區域一直很暢銷。
A: Great.	A：很好。
B: How long do we have to wait before we get the approval after handing in the application?	B：遞交申請後要多久才能收到申請註冊商標的批准書？
A: Sorry, I have no idea.	A：抱歉我不知道。
B: Do you know how long the registered trademark will remain valid?	B：您知道註冊後的商標有效期是多久嗎？
A: That depends on the products you registered.	A：這取決於您註冊的產品。
B: Thank you for your information.	B：謝謝您提供的信息。
A: You are welcome.	A：不客氣。

場景問答必會句

> How long do we have to wait before we get the approval after handing in the application?
> 遞交申請後要多久才能收到申請註冊商標的批准書？

還可以這樣說：

🗨 How long do you need to approve after handing in the application?
　　遞交申請後要多久才能批准？

🗨 When can we get the approval after handing in the application?
　　遞交申請後什麼時候我們才能得到批准書？

對方可能這樣回答：

🗨 About one month. 大約一個月。

🗨 Sorry, I do not know. 抱歉，我不知道。

> Do you know how long the registered trademark will remain valid?
> 您知道註冊後的商標有效期是多久嗎？

還可以這樣說：

🗨 When will the registered trademark expire? 註冊後的商標什麼時候過期？

🗨 I want to know how long the registered trademark will remain valid.
　　我想要知道註冊後的商標有效期是多久？

對方可能這樣回答：

💬 Five years, but you can renew it.
　5 年，但你可以延續商標權。

Scene 182 註冊程序 Registration Procedure

🗨 場景對話

A: Could you tell me the procedure of trademark registration?	A：您能告訴我商標註冊程序嗎？
B: Of course. You should carry out trademark query.	B：當然可以。您應該先進行商標查詢。
A: How long will it take?	A：這需要多長時間？
B: Word mark needs thirty minutes and figurative mark needs twenty-four hours.	B：文字商標需要 30 分鐘，圖形商標需要 24 小時。
A: What comes on next?	A：接下來該做什麼？
B: Application for registration.	B：申請註冊。
A: Would you like to specifically explain it?	A：您願意具體解釋一下嗎？
B: First of all, you need to submit documents. Second, your application will be formally accepted and reviewed. Finally, there comes the reviewing result.	B：首先，您需要提交文件。其次，您的申請會被正式受理和審查。最後，會出來審查結果。
A: What should I do if the review did not pass?	A：如果審查沒有通過，我應該怎麼辦？
B: You can put forward the request for reconsideration within fifteen days.	B：您可以在 15 日之內提出複審請求。

🅰 場景問答必會句

> Could you tell me the procedure of trademark registration?
> 您能告訴我商標註冊程序嗎？

還可以這樣說：

💬 Please tell me the procedure of trademark registration.
　請告訴我商標註冊程序。

對方可能這樣回答：
- 💬 Please ask the person sitting next to the door. 請去諮詢坐在門口的那個人。
- 💬 Sorry, I'm not responsible for this. 對不起，我不負責這類事情。

> What comes on next?
> 接下來該做什麼？

還可以這樣說：
- 💬 And then? 然後呢？
- 💬 What is next? 接下來該做什麼？

對方可能這樣回答：
- 💬 Apply for registering. 申請註冊。
- 💬 The next step is the application for registration. 接下來是申請註冊。

Scene 183　商標轉讓 Trademark Leasing

 場景對話

A: Hi, I have a few questions on trademark to consult.	A：您好，我想諮詢幾個關於商標的問題。
B: OK, go ahead please.	B：好的，請講。
A: My first question is whether we are allowed to transfer the trademark to another company.	A：我的第一個問題是我們是否可以把商標轉讓給另外一家公司。
B: No, you aren't allowed to do that.	B：不，你們不可以那麼做。
A: I see. What can we do if trademark infringement occurs?	A：我知道了。如果發生商標侵權，我們要怎麼辦？
B: Those who are found infringing on your trademark must immediately stop the infringement and compensate for the loss of your company.	B：侵權的人應立即停止侵權行為並賠償貴公司的損失。
A: And how can we protect our rights if an imitation of our brand is found?	A：如果發現有人仿冒我們公司的商標，我們該如何維護我們的權益？
B: The loss of your company must be compensated by them.	B：仿冒者必須賠償你們公司的損失。
A: Thank you for your information.	A：謝謝您提供的信息。
B: Not at all.	B：不用謝。

場景問答必會句

> My first question is whether we are allowed to transfer the trademark to another company.
> 我的第一個問題是我們是否可以把商標轉讓給另外一家公司。

還可以這樣說：
- Can we assign the trademark to another company?
  我們可以把商標轉讓給另外一家公司嗎？

> What can we do if trademark infringement occurs?
> 如果發生商標侵權，我們要怎麼辦？

還可以這樣說：
- What should we do if someone is found infringing on our trademark?
  如果發現有人侵犯我們公司的商標，該怎麼做？

對方可能這樣回答：
- Ask the offender to stop the action at once and require compensation.
  要求侵權者立刻停止侵權行為並要求賠償。

Scene 184　商標形象 Trademark Image

場景對話

A: Shall we get down to business now? I was told that you have some comments to make about the registration of our trademarks.	A：咱們言歸正傳吧？我聽說貴公司對我們的商標註冊有異議。
B: You are applying to register the trademark of "Golden Dragon" for sockets, right?	B：貴公司正在為插座申請 "金龍牌" 這一商標，是嗎？
A: Yes, you are right.	A：對。
B: You may not know that dragon represents an evil omen in our culture.	B：您可能不知道龍在我們的文化中是不祥之物。
A: I'm sorry. What should I do?	A：對不起。我該怎麼辦呢？
B: I think you'd better change the name.	B：我想你最好改變一下名稱。
A: But in that case, the name of our brand is not equivalent in Chinese and in English.	A：但是那樣的話，我們品牌的中英文名稱就不一致了。
B: That's not good.	B：這樣不太好。

A: I will find out a solution though.	A：我會儘快找出解決方案。
B: Good luck!	B：祝您好運！

 場景問答必會句

> Shall we get down to business now?
> 咱們言歸正傳吧？

還可以這樣說：
- Let's get down to business. 我們談正事吧。
- Let's get back to the topic. 讓我們回到正題上來吧。

> You are applying to register the trademark of "Golden Dragon" for sockets, right?
> 貴公司正在為插座申請 "金龍牌" 這一商標，是嗎？

還可以這樣說：
- Is it right that you are applying to register the trademark of "Golden Dragon" for sockets?
  貴公司正在為插座申請 "金龍牌" 這一商標，對嗎？

Scene 185 商標侵權 Trademark Infringement

  場景對話

A: What about this logo I designed for our new line of products?	A：我為新產品設計的這款標誌怎麼樣？
B: It is really nice, but it is almost the same as FAST's logo. Don't you think so?	B：非常好，但是和 FAST 的標誌很像。難道你不這麼認為嗎？
A: No, it's not. The color and the graphic are different.	A：不，不一樣。顏色和圖形是不一樣的。
B: Looking at your logo and FAST's logo side by side, I'd say this is a clear case of trademark infringement.	B：把你的標誌和 FAST 的標誌並排放着看看，我認為這是一個明顯的商標侵權案例。
A: In fact, I purposely made them look a little alike, so customers will associate our products with their brand. So what? That's not a big deal.	A：實際上，我是故意讓它們看起來相似的，這樣客戶就會把我們的產品和它們的品牌聯繫到一起。那又怎樣？這不是什麼大不了的事。

B: If they are too similar, the trademark registry is going to nail us.	B：如果商標太相似，商標註冊局會找我們的麻煩。
A: So what do you want me to do?	A：那你要我怎麼辦？
B: Design it again.	B：重新設計。
A: Oh, no.	A：哦，不。
B: You have no choice.	B：你沒有別的選擇。

場景問答必會句

> What about this logo I designed for our new line of products?
> 我為新產品設計的這款標誌怎麼樣？

還可以這樣說：

What do you think of this logo I designed for our new line of products?
你認為我為新產品設計的這款標誌怎麼樣？

對方可能這樣回答：

Very good! 非常好！

I think you need to redesign it. 我想你需要重新設計。

> Don't you think so?
> 難道你不這麼認為嗎？

還可以這樣說：

Do you agree with me? 你同意我的看法嗎？

對方可能這樣回答：

Yes, you are right. 是的，你是對的。

No, I don't think so. 不，我不這麼認為。

商標註冊 Tips

商標註冊相關術語

trademark office 商標局	word mark 文字商標
figurative mark 圖形商標	associated mark 組合商標
application date of trademark 註冊申請日	trademark registration number 商標註冊號

專利註冊

專利註冊是獲得專利權的必經程序。專利權的獲得，需要由申請人向國家專利機關提出申請，經國家專利機關批准並頒發證書。

專利註冊必會詞

1 patent *n.* 專利
對企業而言，專利是企業的核心競爭力。

2 patent right 專利權
專利權是發明創造或其權利受讓人對特定的發明創造在一定期限內依法享有的獨佔實施權，是知識產權的一種。

3 applicant *n.* 申請人
申請人是指依法享有就某項發明創造向國家專利機關申請專利的自然人或社會組織。

4 patenee *n.* 專利權人
專利權人是專利權的所有人及持有人的統稱。專利權人既可以是單位也可以是個人。

這些小詞你也要會哦：

expired *a.* 過期的	examination *n.* 審查	abandonment *n.* 放棄
fee *n.* 費用	formal *a.* 形式的	abridgment *n.* 文摘
grant *v.* 授予	imitation *n.* 仿造	abuse *n.* 濫用
infringement *n.* 侵權	intellectual *n.* 知識	action *n.* 訴訟
inventor *n.* 發明人	licensor *n.* 許可人	owner *n.* 所有人

Scene
186 專利申請 Patent Application

 場景對話

A: Do you know how to apply a patent?　　　A：您知道怎麼申請專利嗎？

B: Yes, I know something about it. <u>Which classification do you want to apply for?</u>	B：是的，我知道一些。<u>您想申請哪種類型的專利？</u>
A: Patent for invention.	A：發明專利。
B: This kind of patent application is strictly examined, especially the examination of novelty, inventiveness and practicality.	B：這種專利申請審查十分嚴格，特別是新穎性、創造性和實用性的審查。
A: <u>How to get the approval of patent application?</u>	A：怎麼才能獲得專利申請的批准？
B: Usually, the patent applications approved have four characteristics, including exclusiveness, territoriality, term and intangibility.	B：通常來說，受批准的專利申請應具備 4 個特點，包括專用性、地域性、期限性和無形性。
A: What is the rate of patent for invention?	A：發明專利授權率是多少？
B: 40%~50% as of 2014.	B：截至 2014 年是 40%~50%。
A: Thank you very much.	A：非常感謝。
B: You are welcome!	B：不客氣！

場景問答必會句

> Which classification do you want to apply for?
> 您想申請哪種類型的專利？

還可以這樣說：

- Which classification would you like to apply for?
  您想要申請哪種類型的專利？
- Please tell me the classification you want to apply for.
  請告訴我您想申請的專利種類。

對方可能這樣回答：

- I do not know what classification I should apply for.
  我不知道應該申請哪種專利。

> How to get the approval of patent application?
> 怎麼才能獲得專利申請的批准？

還可以這樣說：

- What kind of patent application is supposed to be approved?
  什麼樣的專利申請會得到批准？

對方可能這樣回答：

- I do not know for sure.
  我並不確切知道。
- Satisfy all the requirements.
  滿足所有要求。

Scene
187 申請程序 Application Procedure

 場景對話

A: Would you please help me?	A：您能幫我嗎？
B: Sure, glad to help.	B：當然，很高興幫忙。
A: Do you know how to prepare the application?	A：您知道如何準備專利申請嗎？
B: You need to submit a request, a description and a claim.	B：您需要提交一份申請書、一份說明書和一份要求書。
A: How long I have to wait for the approval?	A：專利的批准要等多長時間？
B: The result will be announced within eighteen months.	B：結果會在 18 個月內公佈。
A: That is too long!	A：這麼長時間啊！
B: The Patent Office needs ninety more days to wait for any possible opposition.	B：專利局還需要 90 天時間看是否有異議。
A: How long will the duration of protection?	A：專利的保護期是多久？
B: Only fifteen years.	B：只有 15 年。

場景問答必會句

> **Do you know how to prepare the application?**
> 您知道如何準備專利申請嗎？

還可以這樣說：

- Please tell me how to prepare the application.
  請告訴我如何準備專利申請。

對方可能這樣回答：

- You chose the right person. 你找對人了。

> How long I have to wait for the approval?
> 專利的批准要等多長時間？

還可以這樣說：

💬 When could I know the result? 我什麼時候才能知道結果？

對方可能這樣回答：

💬 It depends on the classification you apply for.
   這取決於你申請的專利種類。

Scene 188 購買專利 Purchase Patents

  場景對話

A: Are you willing to transfer the patent?	A：你們願意轉讓專利嗎？
B: Yes, we are quite willing to.	B：是的，我們很願意。
A: How would you transfer the patent?	A：你們以什麼方式轉讓專利？
B: As a rule, we transfer our patent in the form of license.	B：一般來說，我們以許可證的形式轉讓專利。
A: All right. But so far as I am concerned, this license only gives one the right to manufacture the equipment, and the necessary technology is not included.	A：好吧。但是據我所知，這種許可證只授予了製造設備的權利，但不包括必要的技術。
B: Don't worry. We will provide all the technical information needed.	B：別擔心。我們會提供所需的所有技術信息。
A: That's good. How long can we use the patent?	A：很好。我們使用專利的期限是多久？
B: Five years.	B：5 年。
A: How much do you charge?	A：你們如何收費？
B: $150,000.	B：15 萬美元。

場景問答必會句

> Are you willing to transfer the patent?
> 你們願意轉讓專利嗎？

還可以這樣說：

💬 Would you like to transfer the patent?
你們願意轉讓專利嗎？

💬 I'd like to buy the patent.
我想要購買專利。

對方可能這樣回答：

💬 Sorry, we do not want to transfer the patent.
抱歉，我們不想轉讓專利。

How long can we use the patent?
我們使用專利的期限是多久？

還可以這樣說：

💬 How long will you allow us to use the patent?
你們允許我們使用專利的期限是多久？

對方可能這樣回答：

💬 I do not know.
我不知道。

💬 Ten years. You can renew it if you would like to.
10 年。如果你願意，可以續約。

專利註冊 Tips

專利註冊常用英語詞匯

abandonment of a patent application 放棄專利申請	abuse of patent 濫用專利權
applicant for patent 專利申請人	author of the invention 發明人
author's certificate 發明人證書	burden of proof 舉證責任
case law 判例法	compulsory license 強制許可證
design patent 外觀設計專利	exclusive license 獨佔性許可證
exclusive license 獨佔性許可證	formal examination 形式審查
indirect infringement 間接侵犯	information in the public domain 公開信息
infringement of a patent 侵犯專利權	infringement of a trade mark 侵犯商標權
intellectual property 知識產權	International Patent Classification 國際專利分類
lapsed patent 已終止的專利	scope of protection 保護範圍

商貿英語溝通王

主編
金利

編輯
吳春暉

美術設計
陳玉菁

排版
辛紅梅

出版者
萬里機構出版有限公司
香港鰂魚涌英皇道1065號東達中心1305室
電話：2564 7511
傳真：2565 5539
電郵：info@wanlibk.com
網址：http://www.wanlibk.com
　　　http://www.facebook.com/wanlibk

發行者
香港聯合書刊物流有限公司
香港新界大埔汀麗路 36 號
中華商務印刷大廈 3 字樓
電話：2150 2100
傳真：2407 3062
電郵：info@suplogistics.com.hk

承印者
中華商務彩色印刷有限公司
香港新界大埔汀麗路 36 號

出版日期
二零一八年四月第一次印刷

本書原名《終極外貿英語話題王》，本中文繁體字版本經由
原出版者華東理工大學出版社授權在香港、澳門及台灣地區
發行。